THE
GRAND
DESIGN

THE
GRAND
DESIGN

A Novel

John Dos Passos

Copyright © 1949 by John Dos Passos

Cover design by Kat JK Lee

ISBN: 978-1-5040-1548-6

Distributed in 2015 by Open Road Distribution
345 Hudson Street
New York, NY 10014
www.openroadmedia.com

for the memory of
Katharine Dos Passos

CONTENTS

THE
GRAND
DESIGN

PART I

QUIET PORTICO

QUIET PORTICO

1

M arch fourth dawned dark that year. The smudged sky hung
low over streets of budding trees and lawns and colon-
nades that echoed Rome, Attic pediments, forensic domes, porticos
built proudly and long ago to frame the tall new men of the republic.
We stood in throngs along the Avenue waiting.

We stood all morning on old newspapers to keep the cold of the
pavement out of our feet, waiting to see the discredited President
whose term had expired ride by in a silk hat beside the President
newly elected. We sat in jerrybuilt stands thumping our feet on
the boards to keep warm. We stood on chairs and teetered on step-
ladders in empty lots.

We dreaded the rain to come, but there was only the raw gusty wind
that tugged at the red white and blue bunting and heckled the flags

and snatched the newspapers out from under our feet and
drove the torn grimy sheets out across asphalt lanes police and
guardsmen cleared:

sheets that told
of panic at the locked doors of banks,
of stalled factories

and foreclosures and sheriff's sales and dispossess notices and outofwork gangs threatening state legislatures and bitter throngs round courthouses
and wheat and corn burned in the stove.

Between the Capitol and the Library of Congress we sat close-packed and shivering in windswept stands watching with anxious eyes the halfmast flags flap and tug at their poles above the watchers on the roofs of the office buildings
and the frockcoated throng of official persons crowding out from under the dome
and the smooth broadshouldered figure confident and tall of the President newly elected who strode out on the arm of his son erect almost jaunty in his legbraces (in spite of paralysis) onto the rostrum above the goldspread eagle holding thunderbolts
to lay his hand on the Bible.

His voice after a moment's hoarseness was confident and full, carefully turned to the microphones, the patroon voice, the head-master's admonishing voice, the bedside doctor's voice that spoke to each man and to all of us:

. . . a leadership of frankness and vigor and support of the people themselves which is essential to victory . . . leadership in these critical days . . .

(At the wheatfarmer's home on the plains the sheriff has driven up to go through with the sale. All around grayfaced men in overalls are scrambling out of splattered jalopies. We form a line silent with tight mouths in front of the farmhouse's rickety stoop. Five of us have guns. A cow lows from the barn. Fowls scatter cackling. The auctioneer has borrowed a table from the farmer's wife. Her face peers out a white blur in the kitchen window. We keep our mouths tight. The auctioneer's face is pale as milk. Nervously he raps on the table with his hammer. We listen silent to the lawyer's jargon. His voice is husky and he stumbles over words. There's a click as a shell slides into place in a rifle. 'Four cents,' a neighbor

says. His voice is sharp and dry. No sound. The sheriff shuffles with his feet. 'Four cents.' No word. We let the auctioneer hurry through his rigmarole. His hammer drops weakly on the table. 'Sold for four cents.'

'All right neighbor, here's your farm back.')

The voice resounded in our ears, the pervasive confident voice:
. . . social values more noble than mere monetary profit . . .

(All morning we sit fiddling at our desks in the broker's office. No business. The ticker idles. Card indexes are pulled open along the wall, ledgers piled over all the desks. In the senior partner's sanctum the accountants are at work. Every few minutes a curlyheaded man in his shirtsleeves with a pencil on his ear comes in to check over a column of figures on the adding machine. The senior partner walks out of his sanctum and breathes hard when he looks down at the paper strip full of figures. Stealthily he goes out the door into the washroom. He pulls a new revolver out of his trousers' pocket, bites down on the bright muzzle with closed eyes, and squeezes the trigger.)

. . . the falsity of material wealth . . . the abandonment of the false belief that public office and high political position are to be valued only by the standards of pride of place and personal profit . . . a conduct in banking and business which too often has given to a sacred trust the likeness of callow and selfish wrongdoing . . .
The voice was confident, exultant. There was a smile on his lips. He talked with shoulders thrown back. We squinted to try clearly to see his face. We strained our ears to listen.

(Not Hiring reads the hastily scrawled card set in the window of the little green shack marked PERSONNEL at the gate of the great plant but the men still stand in line. We stand with limp empty hands staring with appraising eyes at the tall lit windows, black stacks and railroad tracks and slagpiles beyond, listening to the light throb and hiss of steam and the machinery's clank. Our hands slack at our knees we stand in line because we dread. We dread to go home.

We dread to meet the women's eyes. We dread the kids' smeary faces when they cry: 'Daddy's home, we'll eat now.')

This was where we cheered:
. . . I shall ask the Congress for broad executive power . . .
This was where we broke out and cheered:
. . . as great as the power that would be given to me if we were in fact invaded by a foreign foe . . .

We clapped cold hands together. We clapped and hoarsely cheered and the new President sharply tossed his chin and looked down in our faces and smiled.

DANIEL BOONE COUNTRY

A S MILLARD O. CARROLL SIGNED HIS NAME to the last of the letters on the desk in front of him, he caught himself starting an elaborate final flourish. He stopped halfway and screwed the top on his fountain pen. That ham actor inside his head was striking attitudes again. He laid the last batch with the others in the wire basket and yawning leaned back in the swivelchair with his hands in his pockets and his feet thrust out under the desk. The plainfaced clock on the opposite wall said thirteen minutes to five. He straightened up in his chair and pushed the oldfashioned pushbell.

Right away his secretary was there standing where she always stood. He looked up at her long upper lip and netted hair, caught the familiar pursed look about the mouth. 'All right, Louise,' he said.

'That makes our record perfect, Mr. Carroll.'

'How do you mean?'

'We've cleaned up our desk every day this year by ten minutes of five,' she said in her melancholy singsong.

'Business slack,' he answered in a tone he knew would check her. She gave him a reproachful look and retreated with the wire basket through the groundglass door.

He got slowly to his feet and stood looking through the broad window that wasn't any too clean out across the six tracks of the main line of the Kansas and Texas that gleamed in the afternoon light. On the other side were the scaling frame houses scattered among willows where his employees lived. From under him and all around came the hissing and clanking noises of the plant. His ears were beginning to pick out the individual familiar machines when he heard the 4.56, the whistle's hoot, the crossing bell, the rumbled bump of wheels over rails. The red slanting sunlight flashed in sharpedged dazzle on the windows of the coaches. He was still staring out at the train when Louise came back, her lips set for humming, with a sheaf of yellow slips for the filing cabinet in her hand. She let out a surprised squawk. 'Oh Mr. Carroll excuse me. I thought you'd gone.'

A southbound freight joined with the passenger train to drown out their voices. He waved his lightgray stetson at her and strode out of the office. The slambanging of the freight drowned out all the noises of the plant as he ducked through a lane of finished boxes wired up for shipment. He hurried. At a door he met old Slim, his stained felt hat on the back of his head, his jaw and adamsapple sharply thrust out under a twisted nose with a grease smudge on it. Slim opened his mouth to speak. Millard grinned and waved his hat and brushed past. Behind him the heaving and breathing of the plant rose above the clatter of the trains. Ed Gaskin stood on the steps of the shipping room. His face was all creased up with something he wanted to say but Millard sped past towards the parking lot yanking his hat down on his head as he went. He'd reached the Buick and fitted in his key and had his toes on the starter before the five o'clock whistle blew up behind him.

Immediately he was out the gate. Driving he forgot himself completely. His motor hummed with a little easy ticking of valves, the gearshift was a pleasure. Familiar streets were unrolling on either side: the broad avenue in from the plant, full of traffic, crowded between filling stations and automobile agencies; the dusty redbrick stores on Main, the courthouse and the yellowbrick hotel and the marble façade of the bank and then the dusty shingled porches of the lodginghouse belt and the new residences with lawns and trees and the parkway between willows out past the golf club.

He was so sunk in the habitualness of it he wasn't conscious of himself or of what he was doing until he stepped out of the car on the gravel walk beside the white stucco house where he lived and found himself face to face with his wife. Lucile had her garden hat tied on with a lavender scarf. She looked tired. She had a flowerpot in one hand and a trowel in the other. He drew her to him breathing her sweet usual fragrance, kissed her hard and lingeringly on the mouth.

'Lou,' he said still holding her shoulders, 'how am I ever going to tell 'em?'

'What on earth?'

'That I'm pulling out . . . that we're going to . . . you know.'

Her eyes looked at him teasing blue.

'Oz you've decided?'

He nodded.

She laughed. 'It's just as well because I've rented a house.'

'What on earth?'

'Eloise called up and said she'd found us the most wonderful little house in Georgetown so I said go ahead and make a deposit.' She turned in a quick birdlike way she had, set the pot and trowel down on the brick step and shot in through the side door. He stood staring after her with his mouth open. Then he burst out laughing too and followed her into the house.

'But how did you know we were going? I just made up my mind this morning.'

She stopped in the hall, looked in his face for a second still laughing and ran off upstairs. He stepped into the little washroom to wash his hands and face. While he was brushing his hair he stared into his face in the oval mirror: gray eyes under straight dark brows, broad white forehead; limp lightbrown hair thinning maybe, but it still covered his skull. He grinned at himself in a moment of furious boyish happiness. The ham actor inside him had gone. Now he felt all one. Lou has that effect on me he thought.

He ran upstairs after her. She had slipped out of her dress and stood in her slip at the basin in their bathroom washing herself with little dabs of a facecloth. He kissed her bare shoulder.

'Lou have we anybody coming to dinner?'

She shook her head.

'Suppose we go talk to the old man. Do you think he'll be cut up about it?'

'He probably knows all about it already.'

'How do you suppose Eloise knew?'

'She's a great friend of Josephine Watson. The eminent Mr. Walker Watson probably talks in his sleep.'

Back in the car everything seemed to fall into place in his mind. He drove towards town again past the golf club and sped along Prairie Avenue with its big new white houses that were half of them left unfinished when the development company went broke.

'I called Dad and said we'd stay to supper,' Lucile was explaining. 'He said Annie was getting restless about our never staying any more.'

'He'll be lonesome, first the boys now you,' said Millard thoughtfully.

'He won't let on.'

Lucile's father was sitting in the usual place on the porch behind the bigleaved vine, an old man with white hair in a white suit. His face had a caved look, the pale skin hung in a white fold over each side of his jaws. The eyes were sunken but there was still a trace of Lucile's blue in them as they fastened unsmiling on Millard's. Millard felt suddenly like a schoolboy brought up before the principal for flunking a course.

'So you're runnin' out on us,' the old man's voice creaked. 'You have your motives I suppose. You're doin' a foolish thing son an' you'll live to regret it. Well you're both young enough to come back and pick up your lives again. I shan't be here to see it . . . Son, I don't want you to think I don't appreciate what you've done down here because I do, more than you children realize I think. It don't seem as long ago to me as it does to you since you came down here a skinny wreck of a boy just out of the army all wrists and ankles.'

Millard burst out laughing. 'I must have been a sight.'

'But Dad he'd just had rheumatic fever.'

'I sized him up for a comer the first time I laid eyes on him Lucile. You wouldn't give him houseroom until I got him plumped up an' makin' himself a livin' . . . Do you realize you're givin' up a million an' a half dollar concern?'

'Dad I'm not giving it up. I'm taking a leave of absence.'

'How much salary did you take out last year?'

'Fifteen thousand dollars.'

'An' you earned every cent of it an' that was in a depression year . . . An' how much are those humbug politicians in Washington offerin' you?'

'It'll be around eight thousand . . .' Millard felt himself blushing. 'But that's not the point. We owe something to the country . . . I didn't get to go overseas in the war, went and got sick like a damn fool . . .' The clock in the hall started chiming. The old man got shakily to his feet. 'Dad I've got a kind of bug in my head . . . Lucile says it's all right . . . That I might be able to help out,' Millard's voice trailed off uncertainly.

Joel Honeycutt with his white head thrust out before him in a butting attitude was heading for the screened front door. 'Supper's on the table,' he was muttering. He went in first and let the screen door slap sharply to behind him.

'Dad,' said Lucile running after him, 'I bet Annie's made popovers.'

Driving home after the old man had gone to bed they suddenly started talking like conspirators. 'What do you think?' Millard whispered.

'After we've been in Washington six months Dad'll be saying it was his idea all along,' Lucile said.

'Dolphy'll run the plant just as well as I do, if not better.'

'He won't think up anything new but he won't take any rubber nickels.'

'Anyway the old man's all set with Annie, the boys'll be at boarding school. If this isn't the time to make a break I don't know what is . . .'

The car hissed over the pavement through the warm air of the fall night that smelled of ripe grass and sunscorched leaves.

'Oz when you were courting me,' Lucile said suddenly, 'you used to say you'd take me away and show me all the capitals of Europe.'

'It's taken me fifteen years to get around to it . . . Well we're starting with the capital of America.' She didn't answer. 'We don't have anything to lose,' he said as he turned into their drive and let the car slide gently through the doorway of the garage. He turned off the ignition and they sat side by side looking straight ahead of them.

Lucile was humming thoughtfully. 'Oz I just thought. You'll have to get a job for Louise Aldershot.'

'At least I thought I'd be able to get away from that ugly mug.'

'Oz that's mean of you. She's so devoted.'

'But Lou I can't take my secretary everywhere I go. I thought I'd find me a darkhaired beauty familiar with the lobbies of Washington.'

'You'll take Louise Aldershot.'

'Why?'

'Because you'll need somebody you can trust. She's a wonderful secretary . . . and if you don't she's going to cry and you're going to promise her anything.'

'I'm not such a softie as all that.'

'Yes you are.'

'How do you know? You don't ever cry.'

'I don't have to.'

He switched off the light and they both got out of the car. As they left the garage each of them closed one of the doors the way they always did. The house looked quiet and neat and dimlit. From the livingroom radio came the voice:

'My friends . . .'

'Oh we forgot . . . I left it on.' whispered Lucile. 'It's the President's speech . . .' She grabbed his hand and they sat hand in hand on the low bench in front of the fireplace listening:

. . . *'In the execution of the powers conferred on it by Congress the Administration needs and will tirelessly seek the best ability that the country affords. Public service offers better rewards in the opportunity for service than ever before in our history—not great salaries but enough to live on . . .'*

'That's pat,' said Millard.

Lucile shushed him as if they were in church.

. . . 'In the building of that service there are coming to us men and women with ability and courage from every part of the Union. The days of the seeking of mere party advantage through the misuse of public power are coming to a close. We are increasingly demanding and getting devotion to the public service on the part of every member of the Administration . . .'

When the speech was over and the radio began to return to its everyday blather, they got to their feet.

'It's as if he'd been talking straight at us,' said Millard in a shaky voice after he'd switched it off. Lucile was yawning. As they climbed the stairs up to bed they passed the open door of the boys' room. A smell of sweaty athletic clothes and neatsfoot oil came from it. 'It's lonesome when they're out of the house,' muttered Millard.

'Joel's going to call up long distance in the morning.'

'I hope they get some fishing . . . Say I hope your Dad listened to that fireside speech.'

'He wouldn't listen to the President, not for a million dollars in gold,' said Lucile.

The late fall day they started North the familiar road out of town looked terribly ordinary. There had been so many things to attend to in closing up the house that it was afternoon before they drove out the gate. Millard's head ached and his eyes felt sunken in castiron sockets from too many parties saying goodby to friends and too much late work at the office turning over the plant. He knew every signpost and filling station along the straight black highway to the Red River bridge. He waited as he always did for the banked curve that gave the last view of the old town's silvery watertank before it slid out of sight behind a hill which today was violet black from recent plowing. Often he'd felt that home again lift at the first sight of the watertank when he drove in from a business trip east.

He slowed the car and gave a quick glance at Lucile. She sat bolt upright on the seat beside him fast asleep. On the back seat on a blanket among the suitcases the Kerry Blue slept with his nose against his tail. 'Oh God,' Millard groaned. 'We won't get far tonight.'

After they crossed the Red River bridge everything looked different. The road was full of holes. In the fields the corn was stacked in rows of shocks golden in the late sunlight. The oldtime zigzag rail fences were overgrown with honeysuckle. Here and there an unpainted cabin stood up shaggily among overgrown hedgerows against the hazy blue fuzz of distant hills. Millard drove slower and slower. The road wound along the clay bank of the river. Now and then across a weedgrown field past the white flash of a sycamore he caught a glimpse of the muddy swirling current swollen by fall rain. Millard had driven over this road hundreds of times but this afternoon everything looked faraway and terrific the way things used to look when he'd hiked through a stretch of new country as a boy.

Above an open gate that led into a teetering frame farmhouse unpainted and mouldy hung a sign FISHFRY. Under it somebody had tacked a piece of beaverboard scrawled over with the words Fresh Catfish Today. Before he knew what he was doing he turned in and brought the car to a sudden stop in front of the sagging stoop. The jolt woke Lucile. She looked up at him inquiringly. My, he thought, she looked young and pretty, sitting blinking in her gray tailored suit in the new blouse with a white frill down the front she had bought for the trip.

'Aren't we hungry?' he heard himself asking. 'We haven't eaten since breakfast.'

'Of course we're hungry. I was too excited to eat.'

The dog was jumping back and forth over the suitcases wagging his stump of a tail.

'Quiet there Kerry I wasn't talking to you.'

A grayhaired individual gaunt as a string bean in faded bluejeans shambled out onto the stoop and shaded his eyes with his hand to get a look at them.

'Got any catfish?' asked Millard.

'I reckon I could fry you up some catfish. Ain't nothin' else,' the old man drawled.

'Coffee?'

'I've got some coffee in the thermos,' Lucile cried excitedly. 'Where could we eat it?'

The old man pointed to a table with a splotched oilcloth on it under the ruin of what had once been a summerhouse.

'Won't that dawg chase the fowls?' he asked doubtfully.

Lou reached back and snapped the leash on Kerry's collar and they climbed out of the car. The old man had sagged back into the house.

While she rummaged for the thermos Millard walked Kerry down the baked clay path to a landing where three halfswamped skiffs were tied. There was some trouble among a bunch of bluejays that kept darting and shrieking in and out of the yellow sycamores overhead. A kingfisher chuckled as he skimmed across the muddy water. Millard ran back up the hill.

'Why don't we just stay here and set lines for catfish and go coon-hunting?' he shouted out of breath.

There was the blue flash in her eyes. 'Do you know what's happened? We thought we were travelling to Washington but actually we're on a trip.'

'Lou I've got that Indian summer feeling.'

Lucile had cleaned off the oilcloth with a wet paper napkin. They sat there drinking their coffee in the velvety late sunlight looking down into the gulch full of tin cans and old bedsprings eaten with rust and so overgrown with honeysuckle that they seemed part of the landscape until the old man came out holding up with shaky hands a platter piled high with goldenbrown catfish fried in cornmeal.

'Catsup?' he asked.

'No we'll eat it like this . . . My it's good,' Lucile answered already munching.

'Honeymooners?' he asked.

'No.' They laughed and looked in each other's faces and started to blush like schoolchildren. 'Not at our age.'

'Act like it,' he said in a flat accusing tone as he let his gaunt frame sag back into the darkness of the house.

'I could sit here forever,' said Lucile after they had sat a long time eating and looking at each other and not saying anything.

A gust of northwind brushed a sudden chill into the air. She shivered and went to the car to get her fur jacket. He got to his feet and stretched his stiff legs.

'We've got all that gravel road to navigate across the Ozarks,' he said. 'We'd better mooch along.'

Soon the highway left the river and headed up through dense bare thickets into the hills full of lengthening shadows. At a signpost that read Hot Springs Millard turned off over a broad loosely gravelled road. Small stones rattled under the mudguards. The fields were becoming irregularly shaped and cramped between vinegrown hedgerows. Occasionally they passed a cabin open in the middle with a stone chimney at the end from which blue smoke streaked out in the chill wind giving them a taste of fat pine and coaloil lamps as they passed.

'It seems so far away,' said Millard between clenched teeth. 'It all seems a hundred years ago . . . God I love this continent.'

'Makes me think of Indians,' said Lucile.

The sun set yellow and red behind the low purple hills. As soon as it was dusk they found they had a glistening halfmoon riding along ahead of them. They were driving through woodland with only here and there the flicker of an oil lamp or a red swathe of firelight glowing through the open door of a cabin. Then they would smell the huddled smell of coaloil and bacongrease and sometimes the rankness of a penned pig. Occasionally they got a whiff of honeysuckle still in bloom. As they skirted the mistblurred shore of some sort of lake or pond they felt the car lurch in the loose gravel.

'Might have known it,' groaned Millard. 'A flat.'

He twisted the car to the side of the road and got out and pulled off his coat. He had to pull a lot of bags out of the boot to find his jack. He'd forgotten his flashlight.

'I was all ready to enjoy changing a wheel it's so long since I've done it.' He stuck his head in the car grinning a little grimly. 'But I found the jack was busted.'

Her laugh made him feel good again. 'I'm having such a nice time I don't care,' she said. 'I'll let Kerry stretch his legs.'

There was a light high up the hillside above them. As Millard started up the soft clay trail dogs began to bark. Kerry answered from the road beneath. Lucile was hustling him back into the car. At the level of his head an old woman in a pokebonnet was standing in the door of a cabin. The firelight behind her outlined the bulk of her skirts tied in tight at the waist. When she turned her head he saw that she had a pipe in her mouth.

'Hush now, hush now,' she was saying to the hound dogs. They slunk away round the corner of the cabin. Millard hauled himself up on the porch and gave Lucile a hand to come after and asked panting if anybody could fix a flat. For some time the old woman didn't answer. 'You folks just set a while,' she finally drawled in a calm judicial tone. 'Louey'll fix it.'

It was only after Lucile and Millard had sat down formally on the porch on the old woman's stiff ladderback chairs, visiting, as she called it, that Lucile was able to get it out of her that Louey was a colored man and that he just might be at the soft drink parlor two miles up the road.

Millard set out to walk it through the piney night. The wind had gone down with the moon. A few last katydids were sawing in the trees. The pebbles kept getting in his shoes. After what seemed more like five miles than two he saw a little flicker of light ahead. A sallow man in soiled white shirtsleeves was about to close the shutters on a small bare room stacked to the ceiling with old soft drink cases. Millard asked if there was a man named Louey around.

'Louey,' called the sallow man without turning his head.

'I'm looking for somebody to fix a flat,' Millard explained.

'Louey,' the sallow man called again without moving or raising his voice.

'Yassir,' someone answered from behind the cabin.

A pleasantmannered young colored man came out with a bottle of pop in his hand. Sure he'd help the man out, he said. His manner was brisk and efficient. He motioned Millard into the front seat of a rattletrap pickup, and they drove off. The sallow man who was closing the shutters remained with his elbows in the windowsill and one hand on each shutter, looking after them.

Louey changed the wheel in a jiffy. 'Now I patch that tube for you or you all kin take a chance and drive eighteen miles into Hot Springs,' he said.

Millard was getting sleepy. He decided to take a chance. He thanked Louey with a dollar and toiled yawning back up the hill to the cabin.

'So you-all's goin' to Washington to jine the government,' said the old woman severely as soon as she caught sight of him. 'Us folks don't have no truck with no government. I hoped you all was newly wed an' goin' sightseein'. I declare I love sightseein.'

'It was like talking to Dan'l Boone's mommer,' said Lucile taking Kerry's head on her lap as they settled back into the car. Millard was driving cautiously through the lane of tall red bare boles of pines their headlights picked out on either side of the road.

'Funny,' said Millard laughing, 'I feel as if we were seeing it the way he saw it.'

'My,' said Lucile, 'I'm glad we were born in this country.'

At Hot Springs everything was dark. There were no rooms at the hotel. They finally found themselves routing out a dishevelled boy in a tourist court who showed them into a sleazy cabin lit by one dim electric bulb as red as an inflamed eye. They tumbled into the rattling iron bed and fell instantly to sleep.

The next day was cloudless. They ate a big breakfast at the hotel and crossed the Mississippi and drove on across Tennessee. In the swamps the other side of Memphis they stopped along the road for a meal of froglegs and beer. 'I declare I love sightseein,' they kept shouting one to another. Everything they saw made them laugh. When they came to a sign announcing the Hermitage they drove off the highway without a moment's hesitation and walked through the awkward old white mansion that had an air of backwoods pomp trying to remember what they'd learned in school about Andrew Jackson. Further across the state they turned into a stockfarm to look at some Tennessee walking horses. Very late and starved for a steak they headed into Bristol.

Next morning Millard was up at six. 'Has it occurred to you that we may be dawdling because we're worried about what we'll find when we get there?' he asked Lucile severely. She didn't answer because she was brushing her teeth. Then all she'd say was, 'I declare I love sightseein.'

Millard drove fast down the Valley of Virginia under a sky full of puffy white clouds. The houses were brick now with here and there a touch of Palladian elegance in a pediment or a white-columned porch. The doors were full of leaves fresh fallen from the big trees clustered round each house. Here and there a late rose still showed on a scraggly old rosebush. The cattle looked sleek on the hilly pastures. The roadside stands were stacked up with apples. Where they stopped for lunch they bought a bushel basket of winesaps that filled the car with their fragrance. Driving through the pretty little redbrick towns Lucile would beg to stop at antique shops or to look at old buildings but Millard would say roughly, 'We got to make Washington tonight,' and push on. At last she settled for Mount Vernon but it was dark long before they reached Alexandria and the traffic swept them through the eighteenth century redbrick town and across the bridge into Washington. The broad avenues were bordered with trees where patches of autumn leaves still flickered faded yellow under the streetlights. The broad pavements were quiet. There were few people on the leafstrewn sidewalks.

'Washington looks lovely,' said Lucile.

At the hotel the bellboys didn't seem surprised at the dog. Millard and Lucile had hardly been tumbled with their bags into their room, stifling with steam heat after the winey chill outdoors, when the phone rang.

Lucile answered it. It was Eloise Dilling. My she was glad they'd gotten in, she shrieked in her shrill little Louisville voice that jangled the receiver, because they were all invited to dinner at the Gulicks' in Georgetown. No, nobody ever dressed at the Gulicks'. No they absolutely must come because Walker Watson would be there and she knew they'd love the Gulicks. No they didn't need to hurry; the Gulicks never sat down to dinner till eight or eight-thirty. No they mustn't drive. They'd never find it. Just jump into a taxi and come on over. Taxis were the cheapest thing in Washington. Their new house was just down the street from the Gulicks. Eloise had the key. She'd take them to see it after dinner. At last Lucile said all right they would come over as soon as they could.

Just as she put the receiver down Millard came out of the bathroom in his undershirt rubbing the back of his neck with a towel. He was tired from the fast driving. His eyes were bloodshot. 'What's the trouble now?' he asked grimly.

'It was Eloise all of a twitter. She wants us to come over to dinner not at her house but near there with some people named Gulick.'

'Mike Gulick . . . I've heard of him . . . quite a figure in this man's town.'

'Walker Watson's going to be there.'

'Gosh, I'd rather eat a sandwich and go to bed . . . but I guess we'd better go . . .' All of a sudden he grinned and gave her shoulders a squeeze. 'Well Lou, here we go. Over the falls in a barrel.'

Quiet Portico

2

*W*e appointed these men
    we voted in trade associations, garages, union locals,
chambers of commerce.

For some we paid their fares to Washington, some paid their
own way. They arrived by air and by train and on buses. Some
drove their own cars. Some represented everybody, some represented
nobody, themselves maybe.

They spoke for us. They were professionals: lawyers, laborleaders,
sociologists, economics professors fresh from the classroom,
analysts, publicists, officers of foundations and learned societies,
merchandisers, brokers, experts in this and in that, big names to set
up on the letterheads of committees.

They were packed into bureaus and offices, two at a desk, four
and five at a table in conference rooms; some worked on folding
chairs and cardtables in corridors. When the offices closed they
hurriedly ate and went home and sat smoking in their shirt-
sleeves in hotel rooms

    checking programs, industrial pricelists, fair trade practices,
standards of wages and working conditions, poring redeyed over

dogeared acts of Congress in the dense tiny print of the Government
Printing Office, scanning codes that covered

    abrasives, advertising, aeronautics, agricultural implements,
aluminum, artificial flowers, asphalt, automobiles, baking, banking,
barbers, beauticians, bias tape, billiards, boilers, books, brooms,
building, candy, canning, cement, chocolate, cigarettes, copper,
cotton, corsets, dogfood, drugs, fireworks, fish, flour, forestry, fur,

    gloves, gold, handkerchiefs, hats, ice, knitgoods, laundries, lead,
leather, linen, lumber, matches, mercury, oil,

    optical goods, poultry, pretzels, railroads, rayon, rubber, shipping,
shoes, soap, stationery, steel, tailoring, taxicabs, toys, valves, velvet,
wine, women and woolengoods;

    the codes,

    a manyfaceted mirror where we saw for the first time ourselves:
millionheaded multitude of multifarious needs linked into
chains of businesses, trades, skills, occupations, trusts, cooperatives,
combines,

    to make up the shape of the nation.

    Lobbies interlocked; petitions, appeals, telegrams crisscrossed;
pressure groups hired halls; telephones tangled in straining contest.
When the parallelogram of forces stalled

    somebody took it to the White House desk, where smiling the
President leaned back in his chair, drew on the cigarette in its long
holder, tossed his chin and decided

    to appoint a new administrator, arbitrator, coordinator, to impro-
vise a commission, to implement an agency, to draft a directive

    or to request new powers from Congress.

BLUE EAGLE

'**G**EORGETOWN'S CUTE,' cried Lucile as the taxi drew up in front of a white door under a leaded fanlight in a narrow brick street of many trees huddled between small houses with green shutters. The street smelled of autumn leaves and coalsmoke and frosty gardens and dinners cooking. After Millard had paid the driver they stood hesitating a moment on the brick walk before Millard raised his hand to the knocker.

There was no answer for some time and then the door was opened instead of by the housemaid they were expecting by a stout woman in black sequins with her shiny black hair cut in a straight bang across her forehead. She looked searchingly in their faces out of nearsighted shoebutton eyes. Then a sparkle came into the eyes and the rouged thickish lips parted showing pretty little pearly teeth. 'It's the Millard Carrolls,' she shouted. 'We've talked about nothing else all evening just like the first act before the hero comes in . . . My, my, I know somebody who's going to be happy . . . Come right on in and you'll have to forgive the lack of service because the maid walked out on me. That's the third this month.' She ushered them down a white panelled hall past a tall man with sandy gray hair plastered close to a big stony skull who was folded up like a jackknife in a niche under the stairs with his mouth to the telephone. 'That's Mike and of course I'm Marice . . . Walter's had him on the phone for the last half hour. You know how the Judge talks on the phone.'

As they moved past Millard couldn't help hearing Mike Gulick saying, 'Yes indeed, we're having them to dinner this evening . . . well of course I can't say . . . Yes sir I certainly will. Yes they just came into town today . . .' It gave Millard a curious half uneasy half elated feeling to recognize that the man at the other end of the line must be talking about him.

'Anybody want to go to the boys' room? It's the door to the left . . . You take off your coat in the study Millard Carroll and I'll take your wife upstairs . . . Eloise!' she called into the door of the room in back from which swirled out clattering voices and a whiff of rum cocktails and cigarettesmoke.

They heard that familiar shriek and Eloise Dilling, her invalid's face glowing pale under her red hair came stumping out on her lame leg. She hugged them both. 'Oh you darlings. My, I thought you'd never get here.' She clucked around them like an excited hen. 'George,' she called back into the big room in her birdlike shriek.

George Dilling a tall too youthful-looking sallow man with a certain pomp in his manner appeared in the doorway. There was something unsupple about his big frame in his new peppergray suit tailored very tight at the waist. He tossed a curl of black hair glossy as a blackbird's wing off his white forehead and smiled brilliantly. 'George, you introduce Millard to the folks . . . Marice and I will take Lucile upstairs. We can all gossip and powder our noses.'

Millard never had liked George Dilling. He was one of those men the women seemed crazy about; Millard never could find anything to say to him. They shook hands stiffly under the eyes of their wives and stood together by the door.

'Walker Watson's been detained by the President,' Dilling said in a deep undertone. 'He'll probably join us after dinner . . . You go ahead and we'll make the rounds.'

It was a big room lit only by the light of blazing logs in the fireplace. With their backs to the french-windows men and women were grouped on the davenport and in armchairs attentively facing a big lanky man with a red face and a thick red beak like a turtle's who stood in the fireplace with his legs spread and his big hands open to the heat behind his back. 'The farmer,' he was in the middle of saying, 'wants parity . . . a sensible corn and hog relationship . . .'

George Dilling had started on his introductions. At first glance Millard had seen faces that had grown familiar on the front pages of newspapers. J. D. McConnell was sunk in a deep chair with his face in the shadow and a white hand shading his eyes, in the attitude of a man listening to music. His bushy hair was tipped with white above the ears. On the arm of his chair sat a pale blonde girl looking down at him with an attentive listening look. She was introduced as Mrs. Jean Darwin. 'Millard you certainly know Mack McConnell,' added George in his prompter's voice.

'Yes I had the pleasure in Dallas once.' Millard found himself looking into a pair of dark blue eyes with no recognition in them and shaking a limp hand that immediately dropped back into its place where the pleated shirt front bulged out of the black Tuxedo vest.

'Excuse me,' J. D. McConnell said as his eyes turned to meet an understanding glance from Jean Darwin, 'but I'm trapped.'

'Mrs. Rafaelson, Mr. Carroll . . . Mrs. Kubik, Mr. Carroll.' George Dilling's voice had a peevish squeak in it as if he resented his wife's having put this chore on him. Two motherly darkhaired women interrupted some whispered talk about babies to smile brightly at Millard.

'Bruce, this is Millard Carroll from Texarkola. He's come up to help Walker out in agriculture . . . Millard, this is Bruce Slater . . . Bruce and I fight every day nearly but we're respected opponents. Say it ain't so, Bruce.'

Bruce Slater rose from the couch slowly unfolding his long legs and bent his solemn gaze from under heavy brows on Millard's face.

'Mr. Carroll,' he said slowly, 'you may not know much about me but we know a great deal about you and we like every bit of it.'

'It's that passion for anonymity,' said Dilling waspishly, smiling his sour smile for the first time.

Mike Gulick had been standing behind them agitating a cocktail shaker wrapped in a napkin as he looked about the room with his absentminded grin. 'George, you're the perfect greeter.' He spoke with a slight stutter. 'Thank you. You must excuse me, Mr. Carroll, I was impaled on that telephone . . . Now let's see . . . whom don't you know?'

With the shaker held like a football in the crook of his elbow, he put his other arm familiarly round Millard's shoulders. 'You've met Mack, now meet Mick . . . You know Mick and Mack the wheelhorses of the Administration. That is the cant of the columnists . . . Well this is Mick Goldfarb . . . Mick Goldfarb the hardestworking man in Washington . . .' Millard shook hands with a small blackjowled man with thick glasses who snapped 'How do you do?' without looking up or moving off his stiff chair. The next man had a wide smiling beefy face and oldfashioned gold pincenez on the bridge of a sharply hooked nose . . . 'And this is Milt Rafaelson the only man in Washington who never gets mad.'

Mr. Rafaelson got smiling to his feet and extended a pudgy hand. 'Mr. Carroll it's an honor and a pleasure,' he said.

'. . . And now my good friend . . .' Mike Gulick let his voice rise to a barker's roar . . . 'leaving the best to the last, if we can get him to stop talking long enough . . . Beaver Falls I want you to meet Texarkola . . . Nat's the real farmer from the grass roots . . . Nat Kubik meet Millard Carroll.'

Nat Kubik looked from one face to another with his warm cornbelt smile. 'I'm very glad to . . . Shake brother.'

'Nat have a cocktail.'

'I don't need cocktails. All I need for stimulant is my own native indignation at the way you folks carry on in this town. Mick and Mack here, they're always talking about the field as if God in his infinite mercy had created two kinds of people . . . wise guys in government offices and a lot of birdbrains in the field . . . Well I work in the field. The field is where the corn an' hogs come from.'

'Mick Mack and Mike,' interrupted Gulick with a silly giggle. 'Too many Celts this evening. We're in for it boys . . . Well we're not going to wait for Walker. He's the worst man in Washington to ask to dinner,' he said pouring Millard out a cocktail. 'I don't know when that man eats.'

Millard had heard Lucile's laugh outside the hall door behind him. Marice Gulick came in pushing Lucile and Eloise before her and started another minuet of introductions.

Meanwhile Jean Darwin and Mack McConnell had changed places in the easy chair and he had begun, swinging his legs from his perch on the arm, to talk in his even lawyer's voice. Granting that everything Nat said was true, he explained meticulously, we mustn't forget that we came to Washington to meet an emergency. The wise guys of business and industry and those hornyhanded sons of toil like Nat who had bankaccounts in six digits represented as they were by the Republican Party of the unlamented retired incumbent of the White House had proved themselves unable to cope with the depression that had brought the country to stagnation. Government had been forced to step in to restore confidence. Most of the men here present had been engaged in private enterprise at the time and had no more idea of coming to Washington to work in government than the man in the moon. From purely patriotic motives they had given up lucrative careers to risk their future, their good name, everything that made life worth living for a man, to the hazards of public office. To most of them this act entailed a yearly loss of many thousands of dollars. Under modern technology the industrial system, call it the capitalist system if you would, had reached a state where it could not operate without planning from the upper levels. There were too many bottlenecks between production and distribution where robber barons could build their castles and levy tribute on the public. The question before the nation was whether the planning should be done by these robber barons or by government in the interest of the people.

As McConnell spoke the flutelike note of selfsatisfaction in his voice gave Millard a qualm but he forgot it because he agreed so heartily with what the man was saying. The ladies had gone on twittering among themselves for a while. Even they gradually lapsed into listening silence.

The Hundred Days, Mack McConnell went on, had been a time of rapid improvisation to meet the needs of the moment. The Administration had accomplished part of its purpose in shoring up the tottering price structure. Certain men of ill will were refusing to cooperate and probably the time had come for national planning to take a new form. There were problems that would have to be met directly. Labor must have unchallenged the right to organize. Perhaps the day had come for government assistance to small business and to the familysized farm. The demand for a new deal all around for the underprivileged was heard with more and more insistence on every hand. The present Administration had rolled up its sleeves and pitched in to build a more equable society for the American people . . .

For some minutes Marice Gulick had been stirring uneasily round the edges of the room whispering that dinner was on the table and the roast beef getting cold. As attention started to flag McConnell got to his feet and walked over to Nat Kubik who had slumped into a chair and stood over him talking into his face as if he were a jury. 'And this is where you come in, Nat, you and your farmer capitalist friends . . . Out in Nebraska you people still think that you have a chance of unseating the New Deal Administration and bringing back the good old days of privilege and poverty, of scarcity in the midst of plenty. I want you to go back and tell your friends not to waste their money on the Republican Party . . . The voters of this country are going to roll up a mandate for democracy that will stagger you. A man like you,—because I know that you have the real interests of the people of this country at heart—had much better put his influence and his contributions into the Democratic primaries to make sure that we get the best representation possible for the party of liberalism and progress than interest himself in the stale windbags of discredited reaction.'

Nat Kubik slapped his knee as he got slowly to his feet.

'Well I declare Mack you're a smooth talker . . . to make the worse appear the better cause. I'd like to have you talking out through the granges all through the state just to see how you'd answer the questions our boys would ask you. They'd learn something and they'd teach you something I'd bet . . . When'll you come? I'll introduce you to every dirt farmer in the state.'

They were filing with the rest into the diningroom. 'I don't object to your principles,' Nat shouted after McConnell who had dodged out of the way smiling and stood behind Marice's chair. 'What worries me is the way you idealists work it out in detail . . . Half the time you get the opposite results.' His voice trailed off as he took his place beside

Mike Gulick. 'Marice,' he leaned out over his plate to get her attention from the other end of the table, 'we're talking too much and letting this good dinner get cold.'

Mick Goldfarb spoke up from where he sat at Marice's left. His voice was hoarse and he had a way of clipping off his sentences with a little rasp at the end:

'Mr. Kubik the Administration is not going to neglect you farmers. First we must even up the balance. We have to build from the bottom, raise up the industrial worker and the slumdweller so that he can buy more of your good milk and eggs.'

Marice had served the roast. Mike Gulick went round the table pouring the red wine himself. Millard sat quiet eating the rare roast-beef and browned potatoes and horseradish with appetite as he watched Lucile's pretty bantering way of talking to George Dilling who sat beside her. First thing we'll have to do is make a trip to New York to buy her some clothes, she's the prettiest woman here, he thought happily. Having failed to get anything out of Mrs. Darwin on his left but a clear profile and a cold white cheek because she was so intent on what Mick and Mack were saying as they talked to Marice, he fell to chatting with friendly Mrs. Rafaelson about boys and boys' schools.

Meanwhile George Dilling across the table had started to drawl out that every tearjerker in this town would talk till the cows came home about the woes of the industrial worker in the North but very few would listen to what could be told about our rural slums. There was a lilt to his slow voice that gradually penetrated and silenced the other conversations until even Mick and Mack were listening to him. 'What I want folks to remember is the submerged tenth of the American population that lives in rural slums. Of course those I know best are in the South and West but you find them the country over. I was a Methodist minister's son. You know what a circuitrider's life is. I was born and raised in those rural slums. The kids I played baseball with had hookworm and pellegra from not getting the proper food and care. If my blessed mother hadn't worn her fingers to the bone I probably would have been a hookworm case myself. Unless we can bring a new deal to the farm laborer, the migratory worker, the poor Negro sharecropper, the Mexican wetbacks and their families that drift up from the Rio Grande Valley picking fruit and spreading out in summer from the Panhandle of Texas over the Middle West harvesting crops and working in rural canneries and in the Colorado beetfields, always at the mercy of the local labor boss and the agricultural magnates and the sheriff and his deputies . . . Unless you can raise these people up to a position of dignity and selfrespect with some security as to wages and hours your new deal is a mockery and a tinkling cymbal . . .'

The appreciative silence round the table was broken by Milt Rafaelson. 'We've raised their wages and limited their hours you must admit that,' he said in a cheerful offhand tone. 'I was just going over the revised cannery code this morning . . . It might be better but it might be worse.'

George Dilling smiled his vain sour smile. The women were all watching his face. 'It's all very well Milt,' he said, 'to put it down on paper, but you can't get me to say Amen until I see it being enforced . . . I'd like to invite a few of you government workers to spend a day with me out with the lettuce pickers in Imperial Valley. Then you'd see how much directives get enforced. You would find out what our boasted democracy is worth.'

When Dilling stopped talking and settled down to eat the baked apple with meringue on it that everybody else had long ago finished, Marice got up and herded the women off to the other room. The men threw themselves back in their chairs while Mike passed cigars and set out brandy glasses. A big colored woman brought in afterdinner coffeecups on a heavy wrought silver tray.

'Until we have agencies . . . laws with teeth in them that will protect the Negro from peonage and assure the migratory worker's civil rights we will not have true democracy in this country . . .' After he had refused the brandy and drunk off his cup of coffee Dilling was starting to talk again but various side conversations had already sprung up.

'Of course George of course,' Mike Gulick droned soothingly from the head of the table.

Rafaelson had asked Bruce Slater a question. 'Well . . . to be sure . . . the President . . .' With his lugubrious birddog look he mumbled a slow reply.

Goldfarb interrupted him: 'It's been on the President's desk for three months,' he rasped savagely. 'What can you do?'

The conversation got to revolving about first names. Henry and Harry and Harold and Jim, and Millard, not always quite sure whom they applied to, began to feel how new he was to this town. It was a relief when Mike got to his feet and said, 'Let's go and see what the girls are talking about.'

The men got up stretching their legs and puffing on their cigars. As Millard came back from the toilet he caught sight of Mick and Mack and Mrs. Darwin huddled together silently in the hall in their wraps. They were waiting for a cab. They had the impatient air of people going on to some party that they felt would be more interesting and more important than the one they were leaving. 'Damn that cab, we'll be late,' Millard heard McConnell say in a peevish voice.

When Millard walked into the livingroom he found Walker Watson sitting on the davenport in front of the fire with Lucile on one side and Eloise on the other. There were dark bags under his eyes. His long sallow face was gray and tired but it hadn't lost its bashful boyish look. His long hollowchested body was still slender. He sat there sipping a cup of tea and nibbling with his yellow horse teeth on a piece of wholewheat toast held between long tobaccostained fingers.

Millard strode forward with his hand outstretched: 'Well, if it isn't the new boss?' he said.

Eloise deferentially took Walker Watson's teacup and the plate of toast he held on his knees so that he could get to his feet to shake hands.

'Millard we made it,' he said wearily as his tremulous skinny frame slumped back into the cushions of the davenport. 'I'm very very happy.'

He let out a sigh. He took back the cup of tea and started sipping it again with little busy sips. He hadn't changed a bit, his hair was as badly cut as ever, his baggy gray business suit had the same look as if he'd slept in it. Millard drew up a stool and sat down in front of him.

'You men wouldn't get over your swinish stories at the dinnertable so we thought we would just keep him to ourselves,' said Eloise throwing back her head with one of her shrieks.

'Walker how's your health?' Millard asked in a low voice.

'The less said about it the better,' he answered quickly. For a second the corners of his mouth drew down into a look of pain.

As it often happened with Walker Watson Millard suddenly found himself without anything to say. Walker's brow had wrinkled thoughtfully as if he were searching for a remark. The silence between them began to stretch like a rubber band. It was a relief when Bruce Slater appeared pushing Milt Rafaelson forward by the elbow to introduce him.

After Mike Gulick had brought in another big silver tray stacked with highball glasses Millard found himself sucking on his drink in one of the french-windows looking out at the dark boxtrees in the garden. Bruce Slater stood silent beside him for some time.

'Millard,' he said, 'I know you were cleared back home before you received your appointment but Jim's been riding me lately . . . says we're filling the town up with Republicans . . . so I just wanted to ask a couple of questions . . . I have to clear you with Jim.'

'Go ahead,' said Millard a little more aggressively than he intended. 'I haven't any secrets.'

Bruce's face looked more mournful than ever. He studied the boxtrees in the garden and the bottom of his glass and then the boxtrees again. 'How do you stand with Jerry?' he finally asked.

Millard thought a moment.

'Not too well,' he said. 'Jerry and I have known each other for years . . . We've often disagreed on details. He probably thinks I'm a radical as I've always been a progressive in these questions . . . my old man was a Bull Mooser and I started out as a rooter for LaFollette back home. Of course down there I've always voted Democratic.'

'Damn little else you could do,' said Bruce with a look almost of amusement on his face.

'There may be a certain amount of reluctance on account of what I've been telling you . . . After all what good would I be to the New Deal if I'd been a deserving Democrat all my life? . . . Between Jerry and me . . . we've never been friends . . . he's a very much richer man than I . . . but there may be a certain mutual respect, better say tolerance.'

Under his heavy brows the lids dropped a little over Bruce Slater's eyes. 'How about Steve?'

'That's something else again . . . Nothing doing.'

'Can Jerry get you past Steve?'

'Of course Jerry can buy and sell Steve any day. He can do anything he wants to down there . . . Say I thought I'd been cleared down there long ago.'

'It's up to us to get him to want to . . . Walker can't do it but I know somebody who can.'

'Who's that?' Millard asked.

Bruce didn't answer, only looked wiser and mournfuller than ever. Something in his expression made Millard wish he hadn't asked the question.

When Millard turned away from the window again he found that Walker Watson was standing behind them.

'Millard,' he said stifling a yawn, 'I've got to go to bed. Suppose I drop you and Lucile at your hotel.'

They settled into the cushions of the long black Lincoln with Lucile between them. The elderly colored chauffeur looked back enquiringly. Walker Watson sat as if deep in thought hunched into the collar of his big overcoat. 'Oh of course,' he said with a start. 'What's your hotel?'

'The Tarleton,' said Lucile.

They drove across the city in silence. Millard had given up trying to think of things to say.

'Marice is sweet.' Walker after a while began to talk in a musing tone. 'But where was her little friend Jean? You know the blonde girl Jeany Darwin . . .'

'She was there for dinner,' said Lucile.

'I bet that old gadabout Mack McConnell smuggled her but of the way before I got there. That boy burns the candle at both ends, always in his office bright and early too. My stomach wouldn't stand for it.'

'How's Josephine?' asked Lucile, rather pointedly Millard thought.

'She's not well. She's not a bit well . . . She'd love to see you . . . I know she'll love to see you both when she gets back. She's been at White Sulphur all fall.'

The car turned off the street and stopped under the glass awning of the hotel. As they got out Millard began to look enquiringly in Walker's face. Nothing had been settled, nothing said.

'Oh of course.' Walker all at once came to life. 'Millard you come down to the Department at twelve sharp tomorrow. We'll lunch in my office. Ask for Miss Jones and she'll bring you right in. I'll have my desk cleared and we can shut ourselves up for a couple of hours and straighten things out . . . Then in the afternoon you can meet the gang and start getting into harness . . . Do you know I feel kinder mean getting you into it . . . The number of times you're going to wish you were back home.' His interest seemed to have flagged again. A stifled yawn broke out and distorted the last words. 'Well good night.' The car drove briskly off.

Going up in the elevator Lucile said, 'Let's take Kerry for a little walk. I'm too excited to go to bed.'

'We ought to have left that damn dog home,' said Millard. 'I hope he hasn't howled and gotten us put out of the hotel.'

The night had turned cold. They shivered and buttoned themselves up in their coats as they walked Kerry down the broad empty sidewalk towards Lafayette Square.

Marice was a funny girl, Lucile was saying. She had told all about her psychoanalysis and how it cured her of adultery and communism and how she'd had a new baby and couldn't think of anything any more but her husband and his career. A scream. Lucile giggled a little. 'But I wouldn't go around telling everybody all about my operation the first time I met them, now would I?'

'What did you think of Walker Watson seeing him again?'

'Walker's sweet,' said Lucile vaguely.

'He strikes you as a man who has a tough time in life . . . nothing comes easy . . . I think he's great. Yes,' Millard repeated, 'I think he's a great man.'

'It was a wonderful evening.' Lucile yawned. 'Marice may talk silly but she certainly knows how to entertain.'

The square smelled frostily of box. They stood looking up at the statue of Andrew Jackson taking off his hat as he sat his rollicking steed. 'That's Old Hickory himself,' Millard said. 'Remember the Homestead? Gosh. I wish I wasn't such an ignorant bastard.'

Lucile's hand tightened round his arm. Towed by the dog that yanked and tugged on the leash to sniff round benches and bushes they followed the winding paths. As they circled the statue again they found themselves facing the White House across Pennsylvania Avenue. The lofty north porch was white and dim between the spreading skeletons of the big trees. Lucile hung on Millard's arm with both hands and snuggled her chin into his shoulder as they stood staring at the White House without speaking. Then they walked fast round the War Department with its obsolete tiers of small columns and then back across in front of the White House and round the sunken gray Greek temple of the Treasury.

'Tired?' Millard asked suddenly.

She nodded. They circled through the square past Andrew Jackson for a third time.

'Looks like a merry-go-round horse,' said Lucile. She yawned desperately. 'Oz I'm dead,' she whispered.

'Poor lil' girl,' he whispered back and kissed the corner of her mouth. As they started up the path towards the hotel he looked long over his shoulder at the stately modest quiet north porch of the White House. He was thinking of the man in the wheelchair talking into the microphone and his friendly, helpful, so wise, so understanding voice with patience explaining . . . the President. He drew a deep breath. 'Lou,' he said. 'I think I've come to the right place.'

She hugged his arm all the way back to the hotel.

QUIET PORTICO

3

*A*fter the whistle we gather in our workclothes outside the
gate in the boardedup showroom
where an automobile accessories dealer went broke and folded
at the time of the crash.

An old scarfaced organizer and a young boy fresh from college
in a red necktie are straightening sets of bangedup folding seats they
borrowed from some lodge or other. Nobody's swept the floor.

The guys stand bashful against the wall, uneasy, shuffling their
feet. We didn't have time to wash up after the grime and fatigue of
the shift, we don't know where to put down our lunchboxes, we pull
our workgloves on and off. No one wants to sit in the front row.

'Men,' bawls the oldtime organizer. 'We're a-goin' to have a union
in this plant . . . We're a-goin' to have a 'merican standard of livin'
an' better . . . de prevailin' wage rates an' better . . . ain't a-goin' to be
no more speedup . . . no more fines for smokin' in washrooms.'

Half the guys cheer and thump the floor with their feet. Men
stretch their legs out easy, light cigarettes. He's all right, that oldtimer.

Meanwhile the collegeboy hands out mimeographed slips.

'Recreation . . . educational advantages . . . training for better jobs . . . insurance,' he whispers. 'This is one international union that is out to service you workers.'

'We're a-goin' to stand up on our hindlegs an' be 'merican citizens or else we'll close down dis damn plan an' keep it closed till hell freezes over . . . We got a government in Washington dat's backin' us up . . . It's God's livin' trutt as I stand here before you this evenin' an' I hope I may die if every woid I say ain't de trutt . . . De man in de White House is back of us . . . an' he's in dere sluggin'.'

The Movement

'Washington direct no change miss,' drawled the bus conductor as he punched her long green ticket. The voice out of a fishmouth in the middle of a round face purred in her ears. She liked him he seemed so concerned to keep the door shut against the cold gloaming. At first she enjoyed the warmth. She was so cold she felt brittle like an iced skeleton inside her worn broadcloth coat. Her hand in the glove her fingers were coming out of hurt from lugging the suitcase. There was still a seat left by a window.

She let herself drop into it. She let herself sink into the warm breathedout air, into the cosiness of crowded strangers. It was the right bus. She had a seat. Tomorrow she'd wake up away, away from the apartment, away from the office, away from everybody who knew about her and Joe, away from the need of him. She was worn out. Even before the bus started she fell asleep. The breathedout air was a hot flush of velvet about her . . . There was the whirring in her ears, the smell of ether. Dr. Granich's white vealy face with dead eyes and sarcastic lips saying: 'Just a little hemorrhage, nothing serious, you have no further cause for uneasiness, my dear young lady,' and she was in a panic running in the whirling roaring ether smell down a long white hospital corridor and the nurse at the desk . . . a nurse in white at every desk . . . she couldn't run no matter how much she wanted to her legs were melting away with the hemorrhage and the nurse at the desk had a round fishmouth. 'If you feel you must have an abortion.' It was Joe Yerkes dressed like a trained nurse with a crooning southern accent saying, 'Of course if you feel you must have an abortion there's not much use in our gettin' married is there?' 'That's not what I mean, that's not what I mean,' she was trying to explain but no words came. 'And besides I don't quite know how I could explain it to Greta.' That was Joe's cold voice. Nobody but Joe could have said that. It was Dr. Granich's sarcastic lips. 'Not marriage hemorrhage is much more sensible,' he was saying and she was trying to explain no no that wasn't what she meant, love but her lips were dry, love she was trying to explain, but her tongue was dry, love but her throat strangled the nightmare shriek.

She was sitting up in her seat in the dim glow from the floorlights looking into the grinning foxface reeking of peanuts of the man on the seat beside her. His leg was pressed against hers. His eyes glinted as they sought for hers.

'Please,' she said, and pulled her leg away and hunched up in the other direction.

'Cuty you were dreamin',' he said, 'an' so was I . . . dreamin' of a white Christmas.'

He was young but he had one of those voices that made everything he said sound like an indecent proposal. She felt herself beginning to tremble. Every nerve was twisted up taut and trembling. The air in the bus was stifling with the indecency of strangers' bodies. She felt the smell of the exhaust fumes would choke her. She sank her nails into the palms of her hands to keep from going off into a fit of shrieks. Gradually she caught hold of herself. 'No I'm not going to go to pieces,' she whispered to herself.

'Whazzat sis?' came his brash voice. His breath was on her neck.

'I'm sorry.' She heard her voice hiss. 'I'm not feeling well. If you speak to me I'll call the conductor.'

'Aw have a heart,' he said sulkily and subsided into his own seat.

The bus had stopped. She could hear the rustling of the bag and the crunch of his teeth on the peanuts and the wet sound of the saliva in his mouth as he ate them. She had a sudden feeling of nausea. 'Oh God I don't want to throw up,' she prayed. It began to pass. She sat still in the seat with her legs cold and rigid and her eyes closed.

She was wide awake now. Inside of the feverish stifled misery of her head her mind turned back deftly picture after picture to the happy years, Ann Arbor and the smell of apples in the woodshed back of the kitchen in Père's house in the fall, Père's thin face and the blond beard she'd seen grow gray and the way he tapped his pincenez against his nose when he walked up and down on the red and blue carpet of the study dictating. It was in highschool after Mother died that she'd learned shorthand. She remembered the hospital smell again. She and Père were sitting together in a little crowded office at a yellow desk and Père was making a great effort to talk about the economics of the Gladstone era to young Dr. Smart who'd been a Rhodes scholar. Mother looked so plump and rosy under the white sheet pulled up to her chin and smiled her confident sweet smile at them as they rolled her past the door and the nurse tucked a last golden curl under the cloth that bound up her head. That was the last . . . Then there was Dr. Jennings' face taut and his hand tapping Père on the shoulder and the doctor and Père whispering frantic in the hall and the next time she saw her Mother was dead.

After she got over the terrible aching emptiness in the house she'd felt a kind of triumph, she was thinking looking back on it from now, to be able to do the housekeeping and even while she was majoring in history at the university to be smart enough to help Père with his research and to take his dictation in the evenings.

Conceited I guess. For years appleblossom time, summer trips to Europe to visit libraries and English scholars and Germany, walking trips in Bavaria and skiing on the hills back of the town they were always together, falls when the woodshed was full of apples; she'd thought of nothing but Père and his work and the housekeeping and the tickets and keeping the checkbook and the research. There'd been the boys and girls but it had always been as Père's daughter, Dr. Washburn's clever daughter Georgia who helps him with his research . . . Conceited, that was it.

Ann Arbor and the smell of apples . . . The big brass bowl that Professor Pritchell had sent Père from the Far East was always full of apples when they had the faculty tea. That fall she had her first party dress, a kind of strawcolored silk that matched her hair. Professor Yaeger who had continental ways had said she looked like a young Brunhilde, a very young Brunhilde, with a golden fillet in her hair as she sat behind poor Mother's Georgian silver tea service that had come down from great-grandfather Fredericks. Entertaining, she was thinking looking back on it from now, hadn't been much in their line, and mostly she'd just dressed sensibly the way she did now, because of the cost. All Père's money went for books and for trips abroad for research. But that afternoon people came early and stayed late and she was quite giddy with the clink and the chatter and the sweet looks of the young instructors and the couple of graduate students who were asked. 'Georgia you were the belle of the ball,' Père said after they'd all gone, standing with his back to the open fireplace, teetering on the balls of his feet with his hands clasped tight behind him the way he did.

Then there'd been a scratching on the back door and there was Joe Yerkes, the ugly duckling she used to call him to Père, pale and bashful and angry, come to help her wash the dishes. He was the underfed son of a truck farmer whom everybody knew because he was a socialist and used to talk about Debs while he peddled vegetables around town out of a brokendown stationwagon. Père had taken an interest in Joe in his freshman year because he was a brilliant student and full of what Père called 'generous adolescent anger.' Although Joe lived at home he had to earn enough to pay his tuition and to help the old man out a little, so gradually he'd gotten to be the choreboy about the Washburns' house and when the research got so heavy on Père's monumental three volume work on Economic Tendencies in the Victorian Era, he was so helpful about looking up references that Père had asked him to board with them. That was how he became a member of the family. That was in junior year, she explained to herself. It was as if somebody else were talking.

She and Père had a stormy time with him because he had gone to Detroit the summer before to work at Ford's and came back calling himself a revolutionary Marxist. Père still believed in the principles of British Liberalism in the nineteenth century . . . Poor Père I guess he was behind the times . . .

She didn't want to think about all this, she didn't want to think about anything, and particularly she didn't want to think about Joe. She wanted to go to sleep again but as she sat stiffly in the rumbling bus she felt more and more wide awake. Beside her the fresh young man had finished his peanuts and gone to sleep. The air was stifling. She was aching and bruised from the pain of the last weeks. It was all unrolling to spite her in a kind of made up narrative in her head. It was as if somebody were reading it to her out of a book . . . Père had spoken so cruelly about Joe the night they'd eaten dinner in the Rathskeller under the City Hall in Vienna after seeing all the wonderful Renaissance drawings. She couldn't remember how they got on the topic, maybe the bottle of cold Rhine wine had gone to Père's head a little because he never drank anything. 'Joe's been wonderful to us and we've been wonderful to him and I'm fond of the boy as a kind of son, better say a stepson, but I don't want you ever to marry him, Georgia' . . . She had been so happy all the gentle European summer day, they'd had a wonderful day of pictures and musty buildings and trying to use the German phrasebook and now she was dining in style tête à tête with Père and eating gooseliver and sipping Rhine wine out of a beautiful green Bohemian glass with a spiral stem and she was looking forward to a wonderful Viennese pastry for dessert when suddenly it was all spoiled and she felt naked and betrayed . . . 'I don't want you ever to marry him, Georgia.' The bitterness in her voice when she answered had surprised her. Joe was absolutely selfless she had insisted, he was merging himself too much with all humanity, he was going to ruin his career by his unselfish devotion to the cause of the working class. Like Debs he was determined to rise with the working class and not from them. The strained spiteful tone of her voice that long ago day still jangled in her ears.

Père had looked surprised. He cocked one eyebrow like he sometimes did in class. 'Though I admire his intelligence I very much fear that Joe is going to grow up a cruel and selfseeking man.' Père's voice had suddenly become weak and creaky. It trailed off into his paradoxical bearded smile that affected her unpleasantly for the first time in her life. She burst out crying and rushed from the table and ran with streaming eyes under the twilight trees of the Ring to the hotel with all the shabby strollers looking curiously after her. Père followed her up to her room soon after very much upset. He never spoke of Joe to her again.

But Joe had been immensely useful to Père his senior year. He'd come back that fall broad and tanned after a month working in the wheatfields. He seemed a different boy humorous and tolerant and kidding about the comrats and singing Wobbly songs he'd picked up from an oldtimer he'd palled around with. Even his digestion seemed better and he stopped taking sodamints after meals and worrying about his health. He was immensely useful to Père correcting proofs and attending to all the permissions for the use of quotations in *Economic Tendencies* while Georgia was busy with the index . . . What a job I had with that index . . .

The day they all went skiing back up over the hills ranked with appletrees twisted under their outline of snow on the way home they kept checking themselves to marvel at the rainbow colors of the sunset light through the branches. Joe's face had a ruddy flush. All at once as they stood there looking down into Ann Arbor through the snowy apple boughs Joe blurted out that if he could still do chores for them next year he'd stay in school and take his master's degree and do a thesis on something connected with the economics of mass production and Père said tapping him on the shoulder with his ski stick, 'Joseph, instead of a knight of labor we'll make a knight of learning out of you yet, a very much more useful type of knight to worker and employer alike to my way of thinking. In all these matters we need more light and less heat.'

She turned her head with a start. Père's voice sounded so clear in her ears it was almost as if he were sitting beside her. There was only the dim joggled huddle of the would be sheik and the ranked seats and occasionally the lights of a passing car blooming on the frosted windows.

Of course she'd gone to dances with other boys sometimes and even prospective beaux mostly young instructors older than herself had come to call but they'd all seemed damp and boring beside Père. She used to talk to them about economics and history all they wanted but she got uneasy and restless when other topics came up, so the narrator inside her head was explaining, she never had time, Père's schedule was so tight and half the time they didn't have any maid because Père wouldn't eat their cooking so there were the meals to get.

There had been nobody but Joe when Père got his bad cold that turned into pneumonia and Dr. Smart had suddenly announced there was nothing to it but to get him to the hospital and into an oxygen tent pronto. It was Joe who had come sidling in with his necktie all askew and that angry look on his face when she was pacing up and down the marble floor of the hospital lobby. He'd started to argue bitterly that to a Marxist personality was an illusion. Again the hospital smell, the ether smell of anguish and Père's poor gray beard propped against the pillow and the heartbreaking rasp of his breathing. When he died it was Joe who attended to everything while she sat huddled for fear somebody would speak to her in Père's old overcoat on a rocker in the woodshed looking with hot dry eyes out the cracked window at the swelling buds of the first spring thaw. It was Joe who packed up Père's books and put the furniture in storage and carried on the correspondence with the publishers about a new edition of *Economic Tendencies*, so that the night after they'd both graduated cum laude in spite of everything when he came up to her in the drugstore with that angry gray look in his eyes she was ready to do anything he said.

He had brought them each a chocolate soda from the counter and they ate them silently and hurriedly without looking at each other and then went out and walked through back streets where they wouldn't meet anybody they knew while Joe talked and talked.

'But Joe I'm not in love with you,' she remembered herself saying again and again.

It didn't matter he'd insisted love wasn't anything but a physical attraction animals felt in the rutting season, love was a disease of the personality and he didn't believe in the personality. He believed in the masses. They meant more to each other than that, they could be companions and comrades. He needed her help as a comrade. He wasn't coming back to school in the fall now, to hell with the master's degree, he could never make it without Dr. Washburn's help and he didn't want to be a college professor he was a worker by birth, son of a peasant.

'But Joe,' she remembered how she'd gotten the giggles over that. 'I wouldn't call your father a peasant. He's a charming and intelligent man. He's just one of those people who doesn't make a financial success.'

She'd laughed until the tears ran down her cheeks and Joe had been so mad he wouldn't speak for five whole minutes. Then he'd turned to give her one of his angry glares and said believe you me he was through with school and he was through with family. After this his school was the working class of the world and his family was the automobile workers. He was going to Detroit and get him a job and help organize the automobile workers. She heard herself whispering weakly that all right she would come but he mustn't expect anything from her but friendship.

When they went off to Detroit together, the faculty wives raised a terrible cackle but they were both very aloof and superior about anything like that in those days. Joe had gone to work on the assembly line and they'd taken an apartment in Dearborn and she'd wangled herself a job surprisingly easily as research secretary for Andrew Dove who wrote editorials for the *Advertizer* and had a sort of mail order business on the side doing editorials for smalltown papers all over the country. She remembered how she'd felt rather cheap working at that kind of a job but it was fun and Mr. Dove was an easygoing kind of man who let her do most of the work while he stayed up all night drinking and playing poker. He told her she was his dream secretary and raised her to fifty dollars a week and only laughed when she tried to talk to him about socialism and trade unions. That fifty was what supported them when Joe got fired for union activity and blacklisted so that he couldn't get another job in the whole area.

They'd been living together for six months and everybody took it for granted they were married. After he lost his job Joe got more morose and sullen every day and full of notions of persecution. He said he was being shadowed by Harry Bennett's service men. She hadn't believed him at first but he'd turned out to be right. They must have found out about their not being married because the landlady they rented the apartment from suddenly gave them notice to leave that very day. It was a Saturday and they couldn't find any place over the weekend but a hotel. They registered as Mr. and Mrs. Yerkes and when they found they could only get a room with a double bed she suddenly caved in that night and let Joe get into bed with her. The poor boy was so sweet and gentle and affectionate that she decided perhaps she'd loved him all along. After that night she sometimes wished they'd get married just in case but Joe was very careful with his contraceptives and never said anything about it.

The bus was bumping slowly through lighted streets. As it ground round a corner the lights went on. People started to stir. The young man in the next seat, puffeyed and kiddishlooking now after his sleep, groped sullenly for his bag without looking at her. The conductor's voice droned out the name of a town she didn't catch and something about a thirty minutes' layover. As she struggled to her feet she noticed the couple in the seat ahead. Before she knew what she was doing she found herself looking down curiously at them. They were both small and blond and young and terribly asleep. He had his arm around her and his hand cupped over her breast. Her head was on his shoulder and her hands were clasped over the crotch of his trousers. For an instant Georgia found herself smiling down indulgently at them like at two babies in a crib. Then the thought came to her that before this thing with Joe her eyes would have bounded off them. She compressed her lips and put on a frigid look in case somebody had seen her and tugging her coat after her stumbled off the bus.

The cold night air hit her a stinging blow in the face. The haloed lights burned her eyes. She stumbled through the swinging doors into the smelly waitingroom. The ladies' room was a mess, full of dishevelled women trying to dab powder on their faces in front of a grimed mirror. The floor was ankledeep in greasy kleenex. Georgia got the notion they were staring at her. The women's eyes seemed to be reading her thoughts. She went back to sit on a bench in the gritty waitingroom. Better have the men stare at her. They wouldn't know what she was thinking, she told herself grimly.

She was shivering. She felt naked and chilled sitting on the bench in the gritty waitingroom, away from the blanketing warmth in the crowded bus. If only she could stop thinking about things that were over and done with. She bought a package of cigarettes and tried to smoke one walking up and down in the cold outside on the platform but it only made her feel weak and sick. The driver had gone away leaving the door closed so that she had to tap on it for some time until one of the passengers, a grouchy-looking elderly man in a green silk muffler, opened it for her from the inside. She felt she'd drop if she couldn't get back into her seat. The little blond couple had gone. It was chilly in the bus. The seat beside hers was empty. Snuggling back into the rented pillow she missed the foxyfaced young man. She could have handled him all right. It would have been fun hearing his line. Kidding him back she'd have been too busy to think of Joe. Now he was gone and Joe was gone.

She was remembering Joe in his undershirt shaving, the muscled look his arms had when they were a little sunburned, Joe shaving and holding forth about how lucky they were to be alive at this moment when capitalism was collapsing and a new workers' order was taking its place. Roosevelt's New Deal, priming the pump, relief, was only a social-fascist whiting of the sepulchre of depression but it was the great opportunity to build a labor movement.

What she'd let happen between them had wrought a great change in Joe. He'd lost his bashfulness, that kiddish peeve that used to make her so mad at him. Suddenly he'd grown up. There was authority in his voice and manner. Even his clothes seemed to fit him better. She'd been quite scared of him the time she went to see him at the office after he'd gone to work to organize for the union, there he was sitting in his shirtsleeves behind the uncluttered varnished desk taking phone calls and giving orders to the office girl Greta Greenberg whom he introduced as a true idealist because although she was the daughter of a rich cloak and suit manufacturer she had given up everything for the movement.

When the unions joined up into one organization Joe got an office to himself and was put in charge of research with Greta for his assistant. Months went by, but looking back it seemed right away that that night came, the night they went out to the Chinese restaurant to talk it over. Georgia didn't want it that way but Joe insisted it was the comradely thing to do. Greta had on a tangerinecolored suit and a ruffled black blouse and looked very handsome with her arched eyebrows and her big black eyes and her short ruffled black hair. She wore jade earrings and kept saying briskly, 'Now we must all try to be ad-ult.' Joe looked plump and prosperous in his new tweeds. Georgia had never noticed before how big his ears were.

Georgia could still feel that dim and shabby feeling she'd felt sitting beside them. She said yes to everything. She tried to eat the chop suey but its thin greasiness choked her. 'I don't know what I'm doing in Detroit anyway,' she kept saying weakly. She was fighting off a rising nausea. As she sat there in the dark bus rumbling through blackness again she could taste the chop suey and felt again the struggle to keep from throwing up.

When she broke down and cried they'd both been very kind and sad and Joe had paid the bill and they'd gone out into the street full of flashing lightsigns leaving the meal uneaten. Sitting there with her temples throbbing and her head crammed into the musty hired pillow she could still hear her weak voice saying, 'I don't know what I'm doing in Detroit.'

Then he'd come to see her to bring her Dr. Granich's address and had tried to make love to her 'as a comrade's farewell,' he said and the band had snapped in her head and she had said every wounding thing she could think of to him and he'd gotten to his feet and told her very slowly and sadly and solemnly that she had no right to upset him in the middle of an organizing campaign when he needed all his strength to give to the movement and that sex was only a flower picked by the wayside and that he was sorry she hadn't been able to restrain her bourgeois possessive feelings and she'd grabbed him by the arm and pushed him dumbly out of the door. He'd given her a scared look. He was glad enough to have it over with. It was over. And then there was the smell of ether and Dr. Granich's white vealy face with dead eyes and sarcastic lips saying, 'Only a little hemorrhage,' and she lay back sick and helpless as her mind reeled it off again, going over it and over it until she fell asleep.

When she woke up the bus was at the depot in Washington. Ruddy autumn sunlight played on her cheek through the grimed window.

A colored porter held her bag while she went into a booth to call the girl her friend had told her to call who might have a room in her apartment. She found the number. The number answered instantly. A cheerful voice answered, 'Of course. Josie wrote us all about you. We're crazy to meet you. We've got room come right on up jump in a cab and come on out before we all have to go to the office.' Sitting up in the cab driving out through the sunny streets of oldfashioned houses so full of trees that still had scraps of autumn foliage on them she felt like herself for the first time since Père died. She knew she was going to like Washington.

QUIET PORTICO

4

We came driving three on a seat out from town, in from all over the state, from all over the adjoining states, in coupés and town cars and jalopies, sitting on planks in pickups and trucks, packed into buses; there were mule carts and spring wagons. The traffic jammed into long lines through the autumn countryside.

In the city we stood along the curbs and thronged the intersections along twentyfive miles of streets and craned our necks in the harsh roar of the motorcycles of escorting police to see the smiling man flash by in his closed limousine.

Schoolchildren waited in ranks that covered a city block and recited the oath of allegiance in unison and waved American flags and sang America while the President unveiled a tablet dedicating a housing project.

In the stadium we'd been waiting a long time. Tedium of pop-bottles, peanuts, hot dogs, chewing gum. When at last the group of official persons appeared filing onto the platform and the massed bands in uniform blared Hail to the Chief,

bright brasses shining in the sun,

we rose and jumped and stamped our feet and shouted.

He stood in the rostrum adjusting his glasses. The smile. The uptilted chin. The solemn-friendly voice.

'You and I,' *the warm voice purred* . . . 'You and I,' *the kind voice repeated* . . . 'But recovery'—*the insinuating voice coaxed*—'means something more . . . you and I . . .'

The People's Mandate

PAUL GRAVES AWOKE BEFORE DAY. He wasn't cold but he wasn't quite warm enough. He lay there stifflegged under the thin cotton blanket looking out at the unfamiliar darkness of the furnished room. A gray shaft of light from the streetlamp outside the open window picked out a curve in the scrollwork at the foot of the iron bed. He missed his wife's drowsy warmth and the early morning racket of the children. With a yawn and a shiver he sat up and thrust his long legs, every hair on them bristling with cold, out into the draft. All he had on was an undershirt. Cursing the laundry that hadn't sent his pyjamas back he trotted across the floor in his bare feet. He pulled the window down and turned on the heat. As the steam thumped in the radiator he stood under the single electric bulb that dangled drearily from the ceiling and looked around the unfamiliar room. 'Chort,' he whispered and went to the washbasin and fell to shaving his bony black jowls. He bathed and dressed in a hurry. Better go out and get some breakfast.

He already had his hat and coat on when the notion came to him that he might not have any other time to write to Peggy today.

Peggy darling,

[he scrawled] I still don't know whether I'm hired or fired. This lonely little waiting period in Washington is one of the most maddening periods in my life. I cuss myself daily for getting myself into this situation. How's Chapel Hill? I miss you hellishly particularly in the morning when the kids begin to make life hideous for us. The old farmer can't get over his early rising. I'm writing this sometime before day I'm not sure of the time because my watch has stopped and I shan't know what time it is until I go out to buy the papers. The election sure did go our way. If I don't get my Washington job I can settle down to make some money. I think I can still get in on that deal out west and we'll all get stinking rich. Love. Paul.

He put the note into a stamped envelope, wrote the address on it, shoved it in his pocket and strode down the creaking stairs and out into the street.

It was a raw misty morning. The frayed clouds overhead were beginning to kindle from the sunrise. The streets had the dark empty look of an overexposed photograph. On Connecticut Avenue a lighted trolleycar moved jerkily through the gloaming.

Paul walked on downtown with long quick strides looking for an open lunchroom. When the streetlights went out the misty air shone very blue among the dry leaves on the trees. At last he found a lighted drugstore where a smell of fresh coffee from the glass percolator was creeping through the stale air breathedout by last night's crowds. A colored boy with a cigarette behind his ear was swabbing the floor. A white boy in a sweater and earmuffs followed Paul in with a bundle of newspapers on his shoulder.

WINS ELECTION BET; STRICKEN, read one headline. Abraham Penny-packer, 65, of 1566 D Street, S.E., a veteran of the Spanish-American War and prominent in Masonic circles . . . Paul gave a grunt. That was how he'd voted but he hadn't bet. He didn't feel as good about the election as he had expected. He ran his eye down the columns while he drank a cup of coffee and munched on a soggy doughnut. His interest had flagged by the time he reached the bottom of the front page and he left the paper on the counter when he finished his coffee. He gave the pale druggist who looked redeyed from being up too early one of his searching black stares as he paid his check and asked him if the clock over the soda fountain told the right time. 'Western Union Time,' said the druggist and Paul meticulously set the minute hand of his watch to twentysix minutes to eight.

When he stepped out on the pavement again it was daylight. There were cars on the street, loaded trucks. The driver of an empty taxicab slowed down for him. No, Paul told himself, no use wasting the money, besides he was going to walk and get his lungs full of oxygen before he settled down in the office for the day.

Nobody seemed to be stirring at the White House as he walked past. A flock of grackles bound south had crowded into the big trees round the north porch. As Paul crossed Pennsylvania Avenue he heard their racket above the noise of the traffic and wondered if it were spoiling the President's morning sleep, imagining him lying propped with pillows in a big poster bed sleeping late with that victorious smile on his face and a sweet sense of vindication after the moil of the campaign. The White House looked as peaceful as some forgotten old plantation mansion deep in the South.

The sun shone in streaks on the worn gray fluting of the Treasury columns. Crossing the lower part of Pennsylvania Avenue Paul could see the warm burst of horizontal sunlight through the clouds gilding half the dome of the Capitol at the far end. So as not to get to the office too soon he walked across the lawn and up the grassy knoll to the base of the Monument. He had a mind to climb the stairs to the top but the door wasn't open yet. Better wait for the kids to do that anyway. He stood a second looking up the sunny side of the shaft into the autumnal blue sky where melted ranks of faintly saffron clouds. A northwest wind was coming up driving dust and old papers before it in cold gusts. A great place the nation's capital, Paul was telling himself, he couldn't wait to get Peggy and the children up.

With some of the reluctance he used to feel as a school kid days he was afraid he'd find a demerit waiting for him and had to force his legs step by step to take him to school, he crossed the lawns to the Department and walked into the marble vestibule of the old building. The other man waiting for the elevator turned out to be Millard Carroll. Paul found himself shaking hands with him rather formally. There was a grin on his oval face.

'Well they reelected the Boss,' he said.

'And how?' Paul laughed his heehaw laugh: 'That means I'm two grand in the hole.'

'You don't mean you bet on . . . on the reactionaries?' gasped Millard as the elevator started up.

The elderly elevator man was grinning under his white mustache. 'Eleven million plurality. Tuesday was a great day gentlemen,' he was saying as he let them out.

'No,' drawled Paul, 'but I guess it means I'll get my job confirmed. A concern out west went and offered me two grand more than Uncle Sam's paying.' Paul felt himself grinning too, catching at last the contagion of victory.

'Paul come into my office,' said Millard sharply in a serious tone. They walked down the broad corridor with its mahogany doors. The building smelt of soap and mops from the early cleaning. 'I like to get into this place early and get my work started before they start unreeling the red tape and calling you on the phone over every little silly thing,' Millard explained as he put his key in the lock. 'Paul,' he went on, 'I'm embarrassed by all this delay. I've been in this man's town two years and still I haven't learned that you can't do things like you can in ordinary business.' He closed the door of his office behind them.

'Hell man, I know people have to be cleared through the politicos. What's worrying 'em? Me being fresh from Moscow?'

Millard nodded.

'But can't somebody explain that the Soviet Union is where I learned about the virtues of capitalism . . . That's why I'm giving up that extra two grand I was bragging about,' said Paul. He felt himself reddening. 'God never did intend for me to get rich anyway,' he added.

Millard smiled. 'What I want to ask you is this,' he said seriously. 'Once we get started on this project don't walk out on me until we've given it a good try. I want you to stick until we put this project across. Then maybe we'll all go home. After all the Boss has only got four more years.'

'Millard I'm the kind of damn fool' . . . started Paul.

'Check,' said Millard. 'Don't say it . . . Let's see you haven't met Walker yet,' he went on thoughtfully drumming with his short fingers on the corner of his desk.

Paul shook his head.

'Could you have some kind of an outline ready for him tomorrow afternoon?'

Paul let his breath out in a whistle and got to his feet. 'If I could get a really intelligent secretary who could look up the figures for me I might be able to fudge up something . . .'

Millard followed Paul towards the door. 'I'll try to get some people I know to put the heat on. Now's the time when we know we've got the nation behind us,' he was saying.

'You know the way it is,' Paul explained. 'This way I don't know whether to rent a house or bring the family up or what . . .'

'Sure I know,' said Millard. 'Thank you Paul.'

Paul walked back to his office in the back end of the building where they had left out the marble and mahogany and where the corridors were narrower and the partitions ground glass and pine. He pulled off his coat and necktie and loosened his cuffs. His desk didn't have a typewriter in it so he started writing longhand on a sheet of foolscap.

The aim of this project is to save the familysized farm in America, he wrote. Then he stared at the ceiling for a long time. *We have to start with the admission that the main trend is the other way, towards the highly mechani* . . . No. He struck that out . . . *industralized farm often speculatively financed and operated like a big business. But* . . . he underlined the but . . . *there is no reason why we should not use the small unit mechanization that is made possible by complete rural electrification to create an opposite trend: to bolster and make practical the now dying family farm economy.*

Reasons why:

1. The subsistence farm if its debt is kept within reasonable limits is the greatest bulwark against the ups and downs between boom and depression of the market economy. It does not respond to the same laws as finance economy because your basic food and shelter are there . . . However much economic sophists may try to give them a money value their value to the nation should be classified differently . . . He struck out the last phrase with a groan and ran his knotty fingers through his dense black hair. 'I'll have to clear that up,' he said aloud.

The buzzer on his desk had been rasping for some time. Cursing, he picked up his phone. 'Mr. Graves, this is Miss Aldershot, Mr Carroll's secretary,' a woman's voice twanged. 'It's about your secretary . . . I think I've got the right person for you. She's not on the Department's payroll yet but she's going to be.'

'Tell her to come right over.'

'I thought possibly she might come in after lunch.'

'The sooner the better. I'm not going out to lunch,' he said and slapped the receiver down and went back to his writing.

What we want to create, he wrote, *is an agency that will specialize (outside of the regular services of the Department to all farmers) in*

1. elimination of tenancy and sharecropping, or setting up of a system by which the tenant and the cropper can get to live on his own familysized farm which he owns where he has his own garden, milchcows, pigs, poultry etc. which he and his family can work outside of the time he puts in on cash crops.

2. advice on procurement of laborsaving devices through electrification that will make it possible for him and his children to do the work of the farm and to assure themselves a rising rather than a falling standard of living.

3. education: indirect, to make sure that they'll want to do it; and direct, in soil conservation, improved farming methods, etc. through Four H clubs and existing organizations.

4. financing: government assistance in purchase of farms by families that otherwise would go off the land. If they want to work part time in industry let them but let them keep their subsistence farm as their home and as the place to raise their children . . .

He worked on. The untidily scrawled sheets rose into a heap on his desk. Now and then he got up and strode round the small room, occasionally tugging at his bristly hair. On a bulletin board on the wall behind him he had tacked several sheets of paper and now and then added to his sketch of an organization chart. Towards noon the buzzer rasped again. It was Miss Aldershot once more.

'Mr. Graves here's Mr. Carroll.'

'Paul this is Millard.' Millard's voice had a warming friendly burr in it over the phone. 'Are you doing anything after five?'

'I was planning to stay right here till I got this licked.'

'Stay after five . . . unheard of . . .' Millard was laughing.

'In Moscow I used to work round the clock and the Russkis thought it was great . . . They don't leave their offices till three or four in the morning.'

'The less we hear about Moscow the better. But you can't work this afternoon, Paul. I want to take you to meet a friend of ours and then home with Lou and me for dinner. We can go on talking. I want to get all primed up on this agency.'

'Millard, what you say goes, but honest I don't like to lay off when I'm in the middle of something.'

'Today it's necessary Paul,' said Millard with a trace of authority. 'All right I'll pick you up at five-thirty.' When he'd hung up Paul strode up and down the narrow office while he gave himself the satisfaction of cursing out loud a little. There was a knock on the groundglass door. 'Come in,' he shouted savagely.

A buxom blonde young woman in pearl gray was standing in the doorway looking at him out of big pale eyes. She was tall but she seemed to be shrinking under his irritated glare. 'Mr. Graves,' she said haltingly, 'I would have phoned but the receptionist swore you weren't in.' She almost smiled as she went on in a low pretty voice, 'In fact she wouldn't admit you existed at all.'

'You're Miss Washburn,' he answered after a glance into her face and dropped down into his chair. He started pencilling notes on a pad and went on talking without looking up.

'I want some figures . . . I suppose you know your way round this place . . . I don't . . . Farm tenancy . . . any significant figures . . . every ten years back to 1836 or thereabouts. Relation of farm population to industrial population during the same century. Never mind if you can't get them for the particular decades I mention.'

'I understand, Mr. Graves, you want the trend,' she said soothingly.

'Good,' he said without looking up. 'There are two items I'd like by four o'clock at the latest . . . If you have to go over to the Library of Congress let me know how much your carfare is.'

She slipped out as silently as she'd come.

Frowning he started reading through what he had written. Then he tore up a couple of sheets and started writing again.

It seemed hardly any time at all before Miss Washburn was standing timidly in front of his desk with two neatly typed sheets in her hand. He looked at his watch. Four o'clock sharp. He ran through the figures hurriedly. 'Isn't there anything better than that?' he asked. She looked as if she were going to burst out crying. 'Oh well it may do for the time being . . . Say I'm hungry. I haven't eaten all day. Where can I get a bowl of soup?'

'The cafeteria's closed at this hour.'

He threw back his head and laughed. 'Come ahead let's go out and see what we can find,' he said.

She lowered her eyes. 'Thanks. I had my lunch. Suppose I get hold of a typewriter and type your notes up for you while you're out.'

'You won't be able to read my writing.'

'I'll try.'

'Well if anybody calls I'll be back in fifteen minutes.' He stopped in the doorway and half turned around and knitted up his black brows again in a frown. 'Now when you've finished that I'll be wanting everything you can find, and please keep track of your references, on familysized farms in relation to finance, mortgages, bankruptcies, loans, sales, booms in farm real estate . . . during the same hundred years. It'll be a major job in research.'

She blushed. 'I'll try, Mr. Graves, but it's a big order.' Paul was already striding down the corridor towards the stairway.

He'd left his hat and coat in the office. Outside the wind had blown up colder. Thoughtfully breathing on his fingers to warm them he zigzagged through a region of dusty little brick houses sunk in seedy yards behind the pinnacled brick anachronism of the Smithsonian. The thing about value is you can't use the same standard all through the picture, he was thinking. Economic relativity. Farm economics could be measured by the same scale of values as business economics. At last he spied a drugstore that had a flyblown sign *Sandwiches* in the window beside the fountain. When he settled down on the stool after giving his order he pulled a pad out of his pocket and started to make notes on it. After absentmindedly stuffing two sandwiches into his mouth and washing them down with a glass of milk he set off with his long fast stride towards the Department.

He'd hardly settled at his desk when there was that damned Miss Aldershot on the phone again explaining that Mr. Carroll was leaving his office a little earlier than he expected. It was only the presence of Miss Washburn quietly typing at a little table across the room that kept Paul from blowing up. When he found Millard Carroll placidly pulling on his overcoat over his blue checked muffler in his outer office he couldn't help blurting out that if he was going to get anything accomplished he'd have to get him a place where he could work undisturbed.

Millard patted him soothingly on the back and laughed. It was the Washington tempo, he explained as they went down in the elevator, he'd tried to buck it at first but he hadn't gotten to first base. 'And now Paul,' he said with his mischievous smile as they roamed through the ranks of cars in the parking lot looking for his Buick. 'I'm going to take you to a teaparty. Here we are, hop in . . . I'll get in the other side.'

'Have a heart,' groaned Paul.

Millard sat laughing behind the wheel as he threaded his way through the traffic into the parkway round the rivershore to Georgetown. 'I've got to go and pick up my wife,' he explained. 'You don't have to drink tea. The Judge will give you a highball.'

'I don't drink when I'm in the middle of a piece of work,' said Paul sourly.

'There won't be anybody except us and the Oppenheims. The Judge has asked to meet you. We have to rely very largely on his help in getting this whole project past the Boss's desk.'

'I thought the President was for it.'

'The Boss is a very busy man . . . things get forgotten . . . You'd be surprised at the things that get forgotten.'

Paul didn't answer. He began to get over his sulk when Lucile Carroll climbed into the back of the car. Her fresh face smiled out of the big collar of her gray fur coat with a rosy outdoors look, Paul thought. He liked her cheerful bantering cowcountry way of talking.

When Millard drew up before the plain oldfashioned brick house with lace curtains in the tall narrow windows, Paul couldn't help feeling that sunk feeling in the pit of his stomach he used to have in college on the way to an examination. A colored maid opened the door into a narrow hall and ushered them through olivegreen portières into a plain sittingroom where a whitehaired woman in plain black silk was sitting behind a Dresden china teaset.

'The Judge is delayed in his study. He'll be down directly,' she said in a matter of fact New England voice. 'Meanwhile let's have a nice cup of hot tea . . . Unless you gentlemen would rather have a highball.'

Paul brushed off the suggestion absentmindedly. He was trying to hold a couple of sentences in his head that explained the farm project clearly and concisely. When Millard and Lucile admitted that they would prefer highballs Mrs. Oppenheim called 'Michael.'

'Coming Mother,' a boy's voice answered from behind the curtains. A moment later a palefaced precocious-looking boy of about thirteen with bright black eyes and sharply arched nostrils over full lips and a musician's shock of curly black hair sidled in selfconsciously and stood behind his mother's chair giving each guest's face a sharp bold appraising glance.

'This is my son Michael,' Mrs. Oppenheim explained. 'Michael do the honors of the Scotch . . . You know where it is. Your father can't come down for a few minutes yet.'

The boy nodded with sulkily pouted lips and in a moment came back through the curtains with a tray on which were a siphon of soda and a pinched bottle of Haig and Haig and ice and glasses. Meanwhile the colored maid was passing hot scones and Lucile and Mrs. Oppenheim were talking about schools. The Carrolls had two boys about Michael's age. Yes, Paul admitted he had three, only younger, the youngest was born in Berlin when he was in the Soviet Union. Then he had a girl too.

Why had they had to go to Berlin, Mrs. Oppenheim asked a little sharply.

'The hospitals are better there,' said Paul.

'I suppose you are sick of people saying tell us all about it. I can't ever hear enough about the Soviet Union. Maybe it's that I think that if I can hear enough I can make up my mind.'

'Well I can't say that I've made mine up,' said Paul, sticking his long legs out in front of him. Immediately he drew them back and sat on the round upholstered stool with his knees drawn up and his teacup resting on them. One thing I do say is "Let's not have it here."'

'I'd so like to know what you mean by that,' said Mrs. Oppenheim.

'Well let's see if I can explain . . .' Paul had begun drawling out his words to give himself time to think when he noticed that nobody was looking at him any more. The Carrolls had risen to their feet. Judge Oppenheim had come into the room slipping through the olivegreen curtains the way his son had. The first thing Paul noticed was that he had the same build as his son. He was no taller and very little broader. He had the same arched nostrils over full lips, the same curly hair, only the Judge's hair was steely gray, and, instead of the pettish spoiled child look on the boy's face, there was a mild, enquiring, almost confiding expression in the mature square lines of the father's face. The teacup rattled and the tea spilled into the saucer as Paul rose to his feet with a jerk. When he was introduced the Judge held his hand a little longer than most people did and seemed to be scrutinizing him in an appraising way as a man would scrutinize a rare coin he'd just acquired.

'Judge, I brought you my wild man,' said Millard.

Paul got his hand loose from the Justice's small hand. The Judge's eyes were surrounded like a parrot's by thousands of tiny wrinkles. Their profound smiling scrutiny began to give Paul the fidgets.

'Mr. Graves,' the Judge was saying in a tone of boyish enthusiasm, 'I've heard a great deal about your work and plans and I can hardly wait to hear more. Although I can hardly call myself an agricultural expert, I hope I can at least listen intelligently. My life has been far from bucolic. It has been passed in libraries and classrooms and in lawyers' offices and in court. It's only through Nell,' he smiled gallantly towards his wife as if he were taking off an invisible hat to her, 'who is an enthusiastic flower gardener, that I have any relation at all to the world of growing things . . . No thank you dear I'm going to take a few drops of whiskey today . . .' He waved away a cup of tea. 'I'm reaching the age where the cold wind tires me. How right the Aztecs were to forbid drunkenness to the young and encourage it in the old. Whiskey is the milk of the aged. I must say that I like to see a young man refuse a drink.'

'Thank God,' said Millard, 'I don't fall into that category any more.'

'You feel you've aged since you came to Washington?' asked the Judge with the wry smile of a man who felt to his marrow the pains of other men.

'There are days when I feel I've put on twenty years.'

'You ought to see the white hairs I find in his hairbrush,' said Lucile.

'Mr. Graves was just going to tell us about the Soviet Union,' said Mrs. Oppenheim. Russia was the last thing Paul wanted to talk about. He was afraid he would forget some important point when the time came to explain the agency project. He began to drawl about the steppes and the climate and the dreariness of the North European plain. He had the uncomfortable feeling that he wasn't making himself clear. He was searching for a way of switching the conversation to family size farms in America.

'Perhaps,' the Judge interrupted somewhat severely, 'if we had more of their devotion to the public interest and were less blinded by the selfseeking incidental to the profit system by which we were all conditioned from the cradle we should be able better to understand their problems.'

'I wonder if selfseeking with them doesn't just take a different form,' said Mrs. Oppenheim. 'Oh, I hope it doesn't,' she sighed.

'Well Millard what's the good word?' said the Judge suddenly leaning forward in his chair with a sharp foxterrier expression on his face.

'Tough sleddin',' said Millard humbly.

'What particularly rough spots do you find in your slide?' the Judge's tone was playful. '. . . To carry on the metaphor.'

'The Farm Bureau lobby for one, Judge Oppenheim . . . The big boys make so much noise that Congress never hears about the other seventyfive percent of the farming people and I'm sometimes afraid the President doesn't either.'

'Have you seen Bruce recently? I gathered a somewhat different impression from him yesterday. Bruce is very openminded on the subject and he has direct access not only to those quarters but to the gray eminence,' the Judge pulled his full lips into a thin acid smile, 'who or shall I say which? heads the Democratic National Committee . . . Of course you have Walker.'

'There are times,' said Millard, 'when I doubt if anybody has Walker.'

'There are times,' said Judge Oppenheim with a sudden sting in his voice, 'when doubt is selfindulgence.' He paused and bent on Paul his possessive smile of a schoolmaster giving advice to a prizewinning pupil. 'How often since I've come to Washington have I felt that little rise of the nausea of despair like the beginning of seasickness. But I have always understood in time that the only way to shake it off was to keep your eyes fixed on the great aims.'

Paul thought the moment had come for him to make his speech but when Judge Oppenheim finished he looked into the eyes of each of his listeners in turn as if trying to gauge the effect of his words and then, like the turning off of a light, all interest went out of his face and left it with a sagging look of fatigue. Paul had his mouth open to begin when he noticed that nobody seemed to expect him to say anything. Mrs. Oppenheim and Mrs. Carroll kept up a conversational jogtrot for a moment, but they soon ran down. In the first pause Millard got to his feet.

Back in the car nobody said anything. Later, waiting for the light to change at the end of the Georgetown bridge, Millard suddenly turned to Paul and asked 'Well?'

'He's certainly a man of some brains,' Paul drawled.

'Why Paul,' Millard roared. 'He's a wonderful human being. He's the greatest man in this town. It's not so much what he does as what he is. Like he says he really does keep his eye on the great aims.' The car cruised slowly along a quiet brick street of russet trees and dooryards and garden walls.

'Oz,' said Mrs. Carroll from the back seat, 'do you think it was very nice of you to make that crack about Walker?'

'Lou I'm as fond of Walker as anybody but he has to be needled. I can talk to him till the cows come home but the Judge can needle him . . . I bet he's got him on the phone right now.'

He turned a corner and drove up to the curb in front of a green door in a brick wall.

'Come on in Paul,' he said. 'It's small but we call it home.'

He opened the green door with a key and let them into a narrow red tiled passage between stucco walls covered with a gnarled netting of vines.

'You ought to see it when the boys are here,' said Mrs. Carroll. 'The poor little house simply bulges. My they hate it. Where we come from we're used to plenty of space.'

The house door opened right into a livingroom with a graywhite rug and chairs and settees upholstered in cream set round an open fire. 'Can I mix you a drink?' asked Millard.

Paul shook his head. 'Thanks. I've got too much on my mind tonight.'

'Let me have your hat and coat,' said Mrs. Carroll.

Paul looked himself up and down absentmindedly till they all burst out laughing.

'He hasn't got a hat and coat,' said Millard.

Paul blushed red and muttered that he must have left them at the office, he didn't wear them very often to tell the truth. They settled down around the fire. Millard fussed with the logs. Paul refused a cigarette.

'We'd intended to have the Walker Watsons to dinner with you tonight,' said Mrs. Carroll sitting down to chat, 'but Mrs. Watson's in the hospital again. It's too bad. I'm afraid she's a very sick girl. She's one of the sweetest people in the world. When is your wife coming up to Washington, Mr. Graves?'

'We still make our home in Chapel Hill. When you have children in school you can't move around very freely. If this thing works out and if we can find a house I'll probably move the whole outfit up in the spring.'

'Paul,' said Millard with conviction, 'the last "if" was wiped out this afternoon.'

Paul didn't answer. He was staring glumly into the fire with his elbows on his knees. 'Frankly Millard, I'm in a daze,' he said after a long silence.

'You don't need to be,' went on Millard in his genial deep reassuring voice. 'I've been in this town long enough to know when the machinery's oiled right . . . This time it is. Want to wash up?'

When Paul came back from the bathroom he found the doors open into a small diningroom in back and candles lit and Millard standing at the head of the table carving a leg of lamb.

'Do you remember,' Millard started where he'd left off, 'those advertisements of twenty mule team borax? They always used to intrigue me when I was a boy. Well the Boss has a job very much like that every time he starts a new agency in this town. The mules all want to follow the nosebag of their private careers or this notion or that and he's got to get them to hauling together as a team. That's why he's got to have fellows like Bruce.'

The phone had been ringing for some time in another room. The maid leaned over Millard's shoulder and whispered in his ear. He excused himself and went out of the room.

'Poor Oz,' said Mrs. Carroll. 'They never let him eat in peace. You know before we came to Washington I thought if you were in the government and you decided to do something you could just give an order and you got it done.' She shook her head comically.

Millard strode back into the room with his broad confident smile. 'That was Mike . . . you know, Mike Gulick. He wants us to come around after dinner. He's got Ed James there, you know the Washington Heresay column, and Ed says he got it from Bruce that the President is going to launch the project for our agency at his first press conference. That means Congress is ready for the bill setting up the agency. This immense plurality is going to speed everything up, so the scene is all set for Secretary Watson to take a bow. It'll turn out to have been his idea all along.'

'Oz you seem to have it in for Walker today,' said Mrs. Carroll.

'Walker's a great man. I'm devoted to him but sometimes he takes so darn long to make up his mind and once it's made up it doesn't always stay made up. If Walker hadn't happened to have lunch with the governor of our home state about the time Paul hit Washington, this whole business would have been a going concern by now and we would have saved months of time.'

'Not to mention the gray hairs,' said Paul.

'The opposition comes mostly from the South. They think our operations are going to raise farm laborers' wages and they are damn right they will. They damn well ought to be raised. Our boys down there haven't had the sense to figure out the proposition that raising farm wages is going to make the South more prosperous instead of less prosperous, landowners, commission merchants, the whole damn pack of them . . . Now we'll have to make up for lost time. To my way of thinking time is of the essence, we have four years to carry out what experiments we can induce the Boss to underwrite. He's got the people behind him but he'll underwrite only what he thinks is politically practical. That's how he gets things done . . . But in these four years we have the chance, in my opinion, of finding the formula that will keep our American system going for another century. All these miseries that are being inflicted on the unhappy peoples of Europe won't have a chance to spread around the world if we have real deepseated prosperity and growth in this country . . .'

Paul started to say something but Millard hurried on, smiling into his face in the friendly way he had. 'Anyway I'm as bad as Judge Oppenheim. Here I got you out to have you prime me on the details of the project and what I'm doing is delivering a Fourth of July oration . . . We agree about all these things anyway . . . that's why we're here.'

'Every time he goes to Capitol Hill Oz gets more eloquent. It's catching,' said Mrs. Carroll.

Paul folded his napkin and set it beside the dessert plate off which he'd just eaten the last of a piece of pie.

'No sir,' he said. 'It's been good medicine. I was getting discouraged. Now I feel so much better I'm going down to the office and get up my organization chart for tomorrow afternoon.'

'You're sure you won't go over to the Gulicks'? Marice'll scratch our eyes if we don't produce you,' said Mrs. Carroll.

Millard drank down the last of his coffee. 'Just wait a moment while I take a shot in the dark,' he said getting to his feet. 'Let me see if I can raise Walker and make sure he's kept a couple of free hours tomorrow afternoon.'

'I'm sure you would like the Gulicks,' insisted Mrs. Carroll. 'It's the only house in Washington where people ever let themselves go . . . Ed James calls it the house of monologues.'

'Some other time I'd love to,' said Paul.

The room was very quiet. The fire crackled. Mrs. Carroll was sweet and pretty but Paul was wondering what on earth he could talk to her about. At last Millard came back with a triumphant smile on his face.

'All right Paul you can call up the wife and tell her to come on up and rent a home. Walker's rarin' to go. The Judge is dining at the White House tonight and I guess he got the Boss to tell Bruce to call Walker before dinner to ask him what in thunder he was waiting for. Walker says he's hot for it. He was bawling me out for holding things up. He wants the whole business on the President's desk by the first of the week. He'll be free at two P.M.'

Paul was already on his feet. 'Goodnight Millard . . . Goodnight ma'am, thanks for the nice meal,' he said and hurried out into the sharp wintry air of the streets. He blundered undecidedly around the blocks of narrow brick oldtime houses for a while until he found himself walking downhill towards a brightlighted thoroughfare that turned out to be Pennsylvania Avenue. He hopped a streetcar that carried him past the familiar shapes of the State Department, the White House and the Treasury. Then walking fast and ramming his hands in his pockets to keep warm he followed a cross street between great government offices down to the Mall and headed for the dimly lit building of the Department.

The night elevator man looked at him with amazement. The corridors were empty. Only his office was lit. A sound of typing came from it. When he opened the door he first gave a swift glance at his desk to see if anything had been disturbed and then he looked at the girl at the little table in the corner. There was something steady and competent about the way she carried her shoulders, the way she sat up straight on her chair.

'Miss Washburn you are a sight for sore eyes,' he said.

She looked up at him with her shy halfsmile, but she didn't stop typing.

'Now after hanging around this man's town for three months nearly going crazy doing nothing they tell me the thing's got to be on the President's desk by the end of the week,' Paul said without looking at her. 'I'm glad you don't mind working nights.' He picked up the telephone and snapped the switch on and off. 'There must be some way to get an outside line on this damn thing. Maybe you can do it.'

She got up and walked quietly over and sat down to the phone. 'I've got it, Mr. Graves, what number do you want?'

'I want to call Chapel Hill . . . N.C.. . . . party to party . . . Mrs. Paul Graves . . . reverse the charges . . . The operator'll find her.'

'Here you are Mr. Graves,' said Miss Washburn after a while. 'The operator asks is it a personal call.'

'Of course it's a personal call,' shouted Paul snatching the receiver. 'It's my wife . . . Peggy, darling, how are you honey? Well I wrote you a discouraged note this morning . . . I was all ready to throw the whole business up. I would still if it weren't for Millard. He turns out to be a wonderful man to work for. He and his wife are both dandies. If he attends to the politics . . . no I mean the heaving and hauling inside the Administration . . . I may be able to get somewhere with the technical side of the thing. It would be funny if I turned out to be an administrator instead of a humdrum little old scientist. Anyway it's worth making a stab at. Millard says we've got only four years to work for our country. After that I can go back to the lab. How soon could you get up here and start looking for a house? Living in Washington will be a great experience for the kids . . . Chort who has whooping cough . . . Oliver? Oh well it's not dangerous but that means they'll all get it . . . Was it Georgy or Pauline had it? Oh hell I'll have to come down and spend Sunday if I can. Now Peggy, don't worry . . . I'll try to fly down Saturday afternoon. It's just a nuisance . . . Goodnight darling.'

He put down the receiver and found himself looking across the room into Miss Washburn's pale blue eyes.

'Don't that beat the Dutch? My littlest boy's got the whooping cough. Every mother's son of 'em'll get it . . . Well if we work for two hours we can still get home before midnight. I want to be down here bright and early in the morning . . . Can you take some dictation?' Already she had her pad and pencil out and was looking up at him expectantly. He started to walk with swinging strides back and forth across the tiny office.

QUIET PORTICO

5

*T*o make America over from Portland, Oregon, to Brownsville
on the Rio Grande, from the southwest deserts to the forests of
spruce and fireweed and fir round the lakes the glaciers left,
  in cities and suburbs and county courthouses,
  we stand in line, we sit at deal tables to fill out forms, we answer
the questions of socialworkers, we tell our tales, spell out our histo-
ries
  for government jobs:
  bricklayers, cabinetmakers, carpenters, cabbies, journalists, jan-
itors, farmers, egyptologists, bookmakers, mesmerists, musicians,
poets, pediatricians, furnacemen, oilers, lathe operators, chiro-
podists, cooks
  there's a job for everybody
  (if you can't do anything else you can take the applications of
the others)
  to make America over.

  In a shack on a hill where they have cleared the queasy trees (a
fire hazard) we sit in our shirtsleeves and con over the plat. Fingers

*point. Here's the site of the new dam. There the unfinished threelane
highway curves down the mountain they had to freeze to hold the
sliding shale to the dam already completed where into their places
above the turbines in the new powerplant,—*

*tall, white, as a cathedral spacious, silent and reverberant with
dread,—*

*the electrical workers with careful derricks part by part gently
with held breath lower*

the generators.

*Here: concrete, white, smoothwalled, fitted with washing-
machines, electric stoves, refrigerators, deathray lamps to kill flies,
landscaped, graded*

are the houses for workers in office and mill;

schools properly oriented for the seasons,

a kindergarten in a sunpocket.

*That shelterbelt of trees should be moved threeeighths of an inch
to the north northwest. This upland stretch unsuitable for contour-
plowing can be the golfcourse. Here the athletic fields with bleachers
cut in the rock. Down by the stream the recreation building*

and the workshop for hobbies.

FORECASTS

BY THE TIME HERBERT SPOTSWOOD STUMBLED aboard the
train his wind was gone. The weight of the two bulky parcels was
pulling his arms out of their sockets. No porter was on hand. To get the
heavy satchel and the recording machine round the curve of the corridor into the parlorcar he had to push one in front of him and hold
the other behind. The recording machine hacked at his shins while the
satchel bumped the calves of his legs. A fool to try to carry them. In
another second he would have missed the train. It was the first time
in ten years he had travelled in a parlorcar. The familiar stuffy plush
and varnish smell made him think of when Ada and I were on our
honeymoon . . . No it was much later; Glenn was two and so cheerful
about wetting the upper berth: 'Daddy it wetted me,' and nineyearold
Tyler's little brown angry face screwed up in repudiation, didn't care to
be associated with such people, as he trotted off to find a seat in the
day coach and Ada's hazel eyes had been so round and she'd made her
sweet mouth into an o. Women were wonderful about things like that,
Jeannette laughing her sly foreign laugh as she cleaned up the dog mess
on the zebra rug . . . As the train began to move fast he slumped against
the door of the drawingroom. The door began to swing open. For a

moment he fought for his balance. The car sped through an area of sun-light into the dark of the tunnel. Trying to get his balance he was leaning into the drawingroom as the door swung wide. There was someone in there. 'Sorry' he said. The sweat was running in his eyes. He was puffing. 'Sorry,' he said again. A roundfaced baldheaded man was looking up at him over a table full of typed sheets. Charley Nice, but the face was old. The face bounced like a ball up off the typewritten sheets. He saw the clerical collar, the chubby hands. 'Aren't you Charley Nice?' he puffed.

'Jehosophat. It's Herb.'

Two hands reached out and took his bags and drew him into the compartment. He dropped into the opposite seat and sat there wiping the steam off his eyeglasses.

'Charley,' he panted when he caught his breath, 'at first sight I took you for your father the professor.'

'I'm old enough to be my grandfather,' said Charley Nice boister-ously. 'As the Irishman put it.'

'Herb I thought you were in Geneva.'

'Charley I understand you're a bishop.'

'Something of the sort,' Charley said, with pursed lips collecting the typewritten sheets back into his briefcase. 'These can wait . . . I have to deliver a memorial sermon out at the Cathedral. It'll be hot as Hades in Washington . . . but tell me about yourself, about Geneva.'

. . . Geneva, the shine of wet slate on mansards, the morning smell of French bread, the light gray stone streets in the rain, the starched officials of various nationalities at green baize tables and the honking taxis and the happy road through green hedgerows out to the Villa Fleuri and the little smells of Jeannette's house, brass polish on the stairs, and the buttery faint oniony sorrel soup smell from the kitchen and the smell of furniture wax from the hardrubbed carvings on the Louis Treize chairs and armoire in the drawingroom; chocolate, and always the little crisp tarts with cream, and the lacy sachet musty smell of her bedroom and lipstick and Egyptian cigarettes and cambric che-mises, and her.

He felt something he didn't quite want to show in the viveur's smile he was smiling. 'Geneva,' he was saying dreamily. 'I hardly know where to begin. I thought you were your father.'

'Our birthdays are only a week apart if I remember right.' Charley was a little sharp. 'We're sixty years old the pair of us.'

'I can't realize it.' Herb rubbed his hands together. The fingers still stung from the weight of the bags. He let his eyes half close and leaned back comfortably against the upholstery. 'My life has been a series of beginnings,' he said. 'And now everything has to start up again. I have resigned my position at Geneva. The League means nothing any more. We have to write off another failure. I've been in New York three most exhausting months. Every day at my lawyer's. Negotiations over a contract . . . But tell me about yourself.'

He leaned forward smiling. He ought to ask about the children and what was Charley's wife's name? How could he forget it? A blank hardened across that corner of his mind.

'Edith is as well as could be expected. Andy's at Annapolis, oddly enough and little Edie just got married.'

'My, my,' said Herb vaguely while he searched for their faces in the recesses of his memory. Inside him pleasure was bubbling up . . . What luck; Charley, a chat about old times with Charley Nice . . . 'My, my, Charley, the hours we used to sit on the edge of a creaky cot up in that attic room arguing grace against works . . . I'm on my way to Washington. Where are you bound?'

'On my way to officiate at a little memorial service,' Charley was repeating unctuously. Herb had forgotten to listen. He was remembering Charley's pale moon face above Ada's open grave, nose sharp and red and running from the lash of sleet and the red clay clods knocking on her casket.

'Well I lived on at Geneva,' he began briskly. 'It was a delightful life. A strange thing for a man of fifty, I felt I had never lived before; the lake, the interest of the international events, the ease and comfort . . . My life you know had not been very happy since my dear Ada's death . . . The companionship of charming people . . . I'll tell you about them someday.'

'I heard about the boy.'

Herb felt a little stinging in the eyes. 'Charley,' his voice was mellow, 'it brings so much back to see you. I was just remembering what a pillar of strength you were at my dear wife's funeral. Glenn died but he died in a good cause. I can't tell myself the boy was mistaken . . . What wonderful luck,' his words echoed his thoughts, 'to run into you on the train like this. All these weeks in New York I've felt painfully solitary. It seemed lonely to be home. In Geneva I had become accustomed to companionship . . . I've been very busy. Never worked so hard in my life. Of course everybody has been very nice, very flattering. I've just signed a contract to broadcast over the radio.'

The train was standing in a station. They were looking out at the crowded legs on the platform.

'Newark?' asked Charley gently. 'Express to West Philadelphia,' a conductor's voice called as if in answer from the corridor. As the train began to move again they smiled easily at each other.

Charley's hand pudgy and white in its black sleeve was pressing the button for the bell.

'Shall we . . . er . . . heed the admonition of the Apostle Paul and take a little stimulant for our stomach's sake?' he was saying hesitantly. They both laughed. 'You never used to be much of a drinker Herb,' he went on with more confidence, 'but maybe you've changed with the times as I have. There are problems in the life of a bishop my dear Herb that I find are best solved with bourbon.' His face took on a sly cherubic look that seemed irresistibly comical to Herb. The bishop's look he thought indulgently. He laughed again. 'A little drink to old times, why not?' . . . Delightful, five hours to drink and chat with good old Charley . . . 'I've always feared and hated drink,' he added. 'You know the curse it was in my father's life. But in Geneva I did fall a little into the European style.'

The train soared out of the station into the sun. They sat silently smiling as they looked out at the hot sunlight sloshing over parked automobiles along blocks of frame buildings. The colored porter returned with glasses full of brightly clinking ice that turned amber as quickly smiling he poured in the whiskey out of tiny individual bottles. The sweet pungence of the bourbon was in their noses. How perfectly delightful . . . The train was speeding smoothly across the Jersey meadows glaucous under the yellow August haze.

'It is very interesting that you've taken up radio,' Charley began in a leisurely tone. 'I've played with the idea myself.'

'It's odd you haven't heard me during the last month . . . Saturday at four-fifteen. That was sort of a trial.'

Charley rolled up his eyes. 'I'm so busy Herb. I never listen . . . Sometimes to a concert on a rainy Sunday afternoon.'

'Now I'm going to get a better spot, fifteen minutes of comment on the European news, the threat of war, the Hitlerite insanity. It's not so easy as it sounds. I've had to give myself a regular course in elocution. Of course ever since our seminary days I've been interested, as you have, in how best to use my voice. But speaking on the air the problems are rather different. It's not a question of being heard in a hall, you are talking to each man individually. Proper delivery has been the secret of the President's magic. I've studied him from disks. To be effective in radio there must be something a little special. The enunciation is the trademark. I talk into this recording machine and it spouts my words back at me so that I can hear how they sound. Then I do it again just like a schoolgirl practicing her scales until I've perfected it. There are programs I've repeated thirty times before I was satisfied.'

'How very interesting. So you are really going into it professionally.'

'Since I signed this new contract I think I can say very definitely . . . Charley I had to leave Geneva and come home. I had to try to make the American people aware of the terrible things that are preparing in Europe.'

'Will the Germans fight over Danzig?'

'They'll fight when they're ready. This reign of terror, this crazy anti-Semitism is already spreading through Europe like a plague. Glenn understood it and he gave his life to stop the spread of that plague.' He had to blink fast to get the tears out of his eyes.

'Tough, tough, it must have been tough on you old man . . .' Charley's kind face was pursed up with sympathy.

'He was no communist. He died a soldier in the cause of decency, of Christian civilization . . . The least I can do is to give what few years I may have left to carrying on the good work. The American people have got to be awakened. It was a wrench I can tell you to leave Geneva.'

. . . Geneva, the Villa Fleuri, Jeannette's oldfashioned long gloves and parasol that windless afternoon he took her rowing on the lake when he'd felt a mere hobbledehoy again in his shirtsleeves with the sun on his arms and the slender dreamy sails slipping through the turquoise murk on the horizon and she'd pulled off a glove to dabble a hand in the water like a girl, and he'd said they looked like a couple in those illustrated songs that had come with the first movies. He was still a boy when he was with Jeannette . . .

'A bird can't fly on one wing,' Charley Nice was saying. He rang the bell again.

'It's all very close to me,' Herb went on, 'on account of my friendship with a very charming person . . . The Baroness von Hildesheim was the daughter of a rather prominent French Jewish family. She was brought up a Catholic, fashionable convents and that sort of thing, and in due time was married off to a young Bavarian nobleman. The baron went off to Montecarlo and ran through his family fortune and hers in short order. They were separated for reasons I shan't go into and she has lived for years in Geneva supporting herself as an employee of the Secretariat of the League of Nations. She has a large Catholic and Jewish connection of relatives spreading all over France and Germany. For the last five years she has brought me almost daily firsthand reports of this madness that is creeping inexorably over Europe. National Socialism is not a normal political movement. It is a contagious disease. Under its sway normally decent people perform acts of bestial brutality.'

There was an incredulous look on Charley Nice's face as he picked up his fresh full glass of whiskey and water to keep it from spilling from the shaking of the train. Boring him, Herb thought, but he couldn't stop talking. He took a hasty gulp.

'I gave up my position and returned to this country three months ago. I had thought of a lecture tour and started to make the necessary arrangements—lectures in churches, to women's clubs and civic organizations, you know the sort of thing—when someone suggested that I could reach more people over the radio. I bought this machine although it was very expensive. You know I've always been quite modest in my expenditures. Well one of the great broadcasting corporations granted me an audition and I must say they have been most flattering. Another concern wanted to sign me up so as a result my lawyer has arranged for a substantial contract. Now I am on my way to make Washington my headquarters. I've always felt that Washington was more my home than any other city in America.'

'You'll find it extraordinarily crowded, even in summer. With each successive term there seem to be more deserving New Dealers,' said Charley drily. 'I hope you have a reservation.'

'Our representatives have secured a suite for me at the Boardman Park.'

'Then you are in clover.'

There was a pause. They both looked out of the window at the big trees slowly spinning in the green unfolding countryside. An almost visible bar of restraint was growing up between them.

'Then you think there will be a war,' said Charley shakily. 'It's almost too dreadful to contemplate.'

'There must be a war. This cancer can only be cut out with the knife.'

'But you were always such a pacifist.'

'I am still. I made more sacrifices for that cause than most, but ten years at Geneva have taught me that there are worse things than war, things we never imagined in the old idealistic days at Columbia.'

'At that time I disagreed with you, Herb. I was revolted by the *Lusitania*, the sinkings on the high seas, by the German atrocities in Belgium. I was in a very emotional state but it has been borne in upon me since that perhaps you were right. As a cure for German aggression war turned out to be worse than the disease. I have felt that the results of Versailles proved you right. It is my hope that the method of quarantining the aggressor will prove effective. I have come to believe simply and with all my heart that in the end Christ's way is the only way.'

'Can you apply Christian principles to a gorilla?' Herb felt his lip give a tiny scornful twist as he spoke. There was something bland about Charley's face since he'd become a Bishop that he didn't remember in the old days. 'If there is a murderer at large on the streets,' he was talking too loud but he had to be heard above the rattle of the train, 'you have to call the police and have him apprehended before he shoots somebody else, apprehended or shot.' He brought his fist down on the little table between them.

'I suppose it seems odd,' began Charley Nice with a certain stiffening into what must be his pulpit manner, 'in these days of unbelief to hear a churchman speak of Christianity . . .'

Herb interrupted: 'If we had applied the principles of Christianity to Europe after the last war something might have been saved, but we thought only of our own comfort, our own profits, and we let the level of civilization sink and sink until now we have National Socialism, the persecution of men of good will like you and me with every sort of humiliation, imprisonment, physical torture. The fate of Ossietski, the hideous anachronism of the move against the Jews, the crucifixion of a race . . . It's absurd to speak of a Jewish race. The Jews represent at most a slightly divergent religious and cultural group having the same racial background as the rest of Europe. Can you condone these things?' Herb surprised himself by the rasp of hatred in his voice.

'My dear Herbert I am not condoning anything. I am merely suggesting that the experience of the last war—as you yourself have so brilliantly written in articles of yours I have seen and read with some admiration—that the experience of the last war has proved that war is not the best way of combating this kind of aggression.' The bishop's voice had become cold and crisp.

'There can be no peace while this horror is at large in the world.'

Herb sat up straight on the edge of his seat glaring into the bishop's smug face.

'Good and evil have always had to struggle for mastery,' the bishop intoned. 'All I am saying is that I do not believe in doing evil that good may come of it.'

'To fight a fire you sometimes have to dynamite buildings.'

'We tried that method last time.'

'There can be no compromise between civilization and barbarism.'

'Let's try a little Christianity.'

They were spitting their words in each other's faces. The train came to a stop with a jolt: 'West Philadelphia out this way please,' chanted the porter.

Herb looked at his watch. Three hours more to go. He glanced from the round face of his watch into the fatty curves of the bishop's round face . . . Three hours! How on earth am I going to stand him for three hours? he was thinking.

As the train gathered speed Herb got to his feet and stood on tiptoe to open his suitcase on the rack. He took out a manila envelope full of typed sheets.

'If you'll excuse me Charley,' he said, 'I've got to get ahead with my notes.'

'Yes yes,' said the bishop in an embarrassed kind of way. 'I'll polish up the sermon a bit.'

Herb took off his distance glasses and put on his reading glasses and proceeded to try to forget Charley Nice's presence.

When the train was nearing Washington the porter came to brush them up and to take away their bags. After the porter had gone they sat staring out at the green Maryland landscape swollen with late summer now and then looking at each other in a guilty sort of way. Neither of them seemed able to find anything to say. At last Charley Nice launched into a description of his daughter's marriage to a wealthy young man named Sawyer Vandam who he was very much afraid wasn't much of a match.

As they stepped out of the aircondition pullman into the steamy heat of a Washington August Herb's head was spinning in a whirl of memories . . . Ada and the boys and all their bags being pulled off the train by those two laughing black porters into the blistering sun of the platform at the old Seventh Street Depot, and the four trunks and fifteen packages and the two little boys being stuffed into a musty herdic that took them to the oldfashioned boarding house on Thomas Circle where they had lived when they were first married and Ada in her leg of mutton sleeves humming 'Maryland my Maryland' as she unpacked, running so happily around the room because coming back from the Middle West felt like coming home . . .

'We'll take a cab,' Charley Nice was saying, 'and I'll drop you off at the Boardman Park. I go right past there on my way out.'

Herb insisted on carrying his own bags so Charley Nice felt he ought to carry his too and sweated dreadfully from the unaccustomed exertion. They were both dripping by the time they reached the taxistand. When the cab started they leaned back panting with halfclosed eyes in the slight freshness the wind made in their faces. Driving out Massachusetts Avenue past angular redbrick houses under great trees full of sap and greenness simmering in the heat, Herb was breathing in the old accustomed Washington smell of scorched leaves and asphalt and tramped grass and wilted summer clothes. He felt almost as if he were going to drive up to the door of the old apartment, walk up the one flight and find Ada in her long teagown with parted lips smiling her tired smile waiting for him at the head of the stairs.

When the cab finally stopped at the hotel Herb could not help a feeling of relief. He and Charley shook hands as if they had just met casually on the train. Herb was registering at the hotel desk before he remembered that they hadn't made any arrangements to meet again. Charley Nice, my best friend through all these years, he thought with a pang of surprise. But the young man with the slickedback hair behind the desk was beginning a little speech as he read the signature on the card. 'Herbert Spotswood . . . It's indeed a pleasure Mr. Spotswood . . . Several of us have been following your program . . . a pleasure and an honor.' Herb's head made a slight bow in acknowledgement. His chest puffed out ever so little. Broadly smiling he followed the bellboy across the soft hotel carpet to the elevator.

QUIET PORTICO

6

*U*nion? *Mister you're askin' if we like the union. Lemme tellyer we started the union in a secret meetin' in an old fallendown barn in the east end of town. The strike was broken. It was the old sellout. Half the good guys were in jail. The guys in jail they held a convention the same time we did till the turnkeys went after 'em with the firehose. When the convention adjourned we come down the hill and there was two delegates of the old sellout crowd pointin' the finger at us for the Coal an' Iron Police.*

'Red? Mister, my mammy used to say I had red injun blood but mostly I'm red because I got so blame mad at the scabs an' the low-down way the Company treated us. Why should I be for the Stars and Stripes? It's never given no protection to me an' mine. I seen the troupers ride down women an' children carryin' lil' American flags every one of 'em. I seen them bloody troupers shoot into a picketline led by an old man with the Stars an' Stripes an' a gold fringe on it like Gettysburg.

'Preacher says we're followin' the red flag of Rooshia but I told him I'd foller the Devil's flag into Hell if he'd give us decent livin' an' decent workin'. Only time we're citizens in this man's country

is when some joker comes suckin' around to be elected sheriff or governor or president or sumpen. They'll promise the moon itself but all the time they got their mind on the mealticket.

'Piecards, delegates, organizers, they ain' much different from the politicians. I ain' got much use for the bigmouths an' the blatherskites, but Mister that doan mean I'll take pity on a scab. If they don't wanna strike lettem stay home. Brass knuckles an' base-ball bats is the medicine for scabs. The workin' man's got to stick together. The international workin' class, tell me that's where I swear my oath of allegiance.

'I'm willin' to take a chance on it, Mister. A workin' man's got to be a citizen of someplace, even if it's Hell itself.'

CLASS WAR

A T THE FOOT OF THE HILL just across from the big distillery a few miles outside of Baltimore a tire blew out. Joe Yerkes yanked at the wheel and pulled the battered fourdoor sedan to a shuddering stop on the side of the road. He jumped out of the car his narrow face pale with anger and stood staring down at the left rear wheel.

'Damn Fascist rubber companies . . . Their tires are no good,' he muttered. 'It would happen just when we were two hours late . . . Winthrop,' he called to his passenger, 'come out here and undo the spare tire while I try to get the jack to work.'

As he spoke he thrust his head into the rear of the car which was stacked to the ceiling with white squares of cardboard with slogans printed on them. All Aid for Spanish Democracy and Save the Defenders of Madrid and one that started Southern Share Croppers . . . had fallen down against the windows. Among them were crisscrossed bundles of the sticks they were to be carried on. After a great deal of rummaging under the seats Joe dragged out a jack and a canvas bag of tools. The cars in an endless stream of traffic swished as they sped past, treads hissing on the rough macadam.

'Here you are Winthrop,' he said waving the lug wrench invitingly.

The young man who was still sprawled in the front seat looked at it without interest. He was a drowsylooking young man with red hair and buck teeth and a very small turnedup nose. 'I was asleep,' he said yawning. He pulled himself together and let himself very gradually down from the car. He took gingerly hold of the lug wrench. 'W-w-what's this?' he asked.

'That's to take the lugs off the spare tire. It's in the back. Unscrew them. We'll save time,' Joe shouted above the screaming of the gears of a truck climbing the hill, pronouncing his words with exasperated care as if he were trying to make himself understood by a foreigner.

'Baltimore's a hell of a reactionary-looking town,' said Winthrop meditatively fumbling with one of the bolts that held the tire.

'We're supposed to be at the League Against War and Fascism at eleven,' shouted Joe kneeling beside him in the dirt and trying to get the jack plumb under the rear axle. 'They are supposed to picket the White House at noon so as to get the noon hour crowds. I'm supposed to have you there in time to get arrested for the afternoon papers.'

When a great truck loaded with shiny new cars rumbled past, Joe looked up at them with an appraising eye. Winthrop left the wrench on the nut he'd been fumbling with and leant over to make himself heard better:

'I'm pretty sick of being mother's son, do you know it?' he said. 'I just want to be one of the masses.'

'Well I suppose it's not your fault if you've got a name that will make the headlines,' said Joe soothingly. 'Cops Beat Son of Noted Writer. At three-fifteen this afternoon Winthrop Strang son of the noted magazine writer and wealthy socialite Anna Winthrop Strang was severely beaten by the brutal cossacks of the Washington police force . . .'

'You don't th-th-think they'd do that do you Comrade Yerkes?' Winthrop asked in a worried stutter.

'I'm no comrade I'm just a laborskate,' said Joe savagely pumping on the rod of the jack. 'Say for chrissake get a stone,' he panted. 'This damn jack is shaky.' He straightened up to get a kink out of his back.

'What?'

'A stone to block the front wheel,' shouted Joe as a green truck whizzed past him uncomfortably close. He went off shuffling with his feet among the dusty weeds at the road's edge. Two bricks were all he could find. He came back and placed them carefully in front and back of the opposite front wheel.

'Mother'll be awful mad,' Winthrop was saying in a childish tone when Joe went back to the rear of the car to take the spare. Winthrop hadn't been able to get the lugs loose. Joe snatched the wrench out of his hand and did it himself.

'Why? Isn't she a good radical? Isn't she against war and fascism?'

'Sure but she's such friends with you know who.'

'Who? I don't know a damn thing about Washington. I've never been there in my life.'

'The hostess of where we are going to picket . . .' said Winthrop with a sly smile. 'The First Lady.'

Joe carefully pulled the wheel off the axle and gave it a push towards Winthrop. 'Here hold that.' He adjusted the spare wheel and got the lugs back on. 'Hand me the wrench,' he added breathless.

'What?'

'The lugwrench for chrissake, the thing you have in your hand.'

When he had the lugs nearly tight, Joe got to his feet brushing the dust and gravel from his knees. 'Now I can breathe easier. I was sure she'd fall off that damn jack.' Suddenly he turned his hard gray eyes on Winthrop's face. 'Isn't she a Social Fascist just like her husband?'

'Mother says she's a real progressive.'

'A real progressive would have helped the Spanish workers,' said Joe absently. He was groping round the floor of the car for a rag to wipe his hands on. He didn't find any. The sweat was running down his face but his hands were too dirty to put in his pocket after his handkerchief.

'Winthrop reach in my pocket for my handkerchief,' he cried in desperation, 'and wipe my face off . . . You didn't get your hands dirty, not you . . . That's something you can do.'

'You sure changed that tire in short order Comrade Yerkes,' said Winthrop as he meticulously followed instructions. 'That comes from your experience as an automobile worker.' His voice had a tone of girlish admiration that made Joe want to push his face in. A motorcycle with the cutout off roared in his ears.

'For chrissake can the comrade,' he shouted snatching the hand-kerchief and peevishly wiping his hands on it. 'I've got work to do organizing the automobile workers on a national basis.'

Winthrop gave him an adoring look. 'Of course I understand,' he said. 'I'll call you Joe if you don't mind.'

Joe was tightening the lugs on the extra wheel on which the ruined tire still hung limp. 'Won't be much turnin value on that tire,' he was muttering. A series of big beertrucks whizzed past and drowned out his voice.

'I don't mind anything,' he shouted at Winthrop when he could make himself heard, 'except wasting my time. I ought never have given you a lift or your damn cards. Suppose some cop took a fancy to pull me for something. Believe you me it would look silly for an organizer for the C.I.O. to be carting all this mess.'

'It's all the same great cause,' answered Winthrop in a singsong tone. The wind from a Greyhound bus almost knocked them down.

'That's the trouble with these damn comrades, help 'em in one thing and they expect you to go the whole hog,' Joe grumbled as they climbed back into the car. 'We are all out for the same thing in the end,' Winthrop whined. Joe was reaching for his watch. 'Quarter of eleven. We can make it yet,' he said.

'The triumph of the international working class,' said Winthrop as if reciting a lesson. 'The only hope for a boy like me,' he added putting his hand annoyingly on Joe's sleeve, 'with a mother like my mother is to lose himself in the international working class.'

Joe put one foot on the starter and another on the clutch pedal and turned the car out into a gap in the stream of traffic. 'You said it Winthrop,' said Joe.

Cars and trucks, two lanes one way and two lanes the other way, wound in a ribbon of noise over green hills scarred with filling stations, used car lots, ranks of tourist cottages, billboards. Once inside the city limits the traffic scattered. It seemed quieter driving smoothly along a broad avenue lined with trees. The houses behind their little door-yards had a modest selfeffacing look. Joe Yerkes carefully observed the speedlimit.

'Well it's the nation's capital,' he said. He couldn't keep the feeling of awe that had come over him out of his voice. This is the first time I was ever here. Winthrop you got to help me find the address. I'm going a little slow, no use getting a ticket on the last lap of the journey.'

'The citadel of reaction,' said Winthrop.

'The Administration sure has given us the green light to organize the workers,' said Joe thoughtfully.

'Mother says that's all politics. She says the President . . .'

'Organize first and ask questions afterwards,' interrupted Joe, 'but I guess we'd better not forget that he's the biggest Social Fascist of the lot.'

'Mother says Washington has the most reactionary population in the United States. Look at their attitude towards the Negro.'

Joe slammed on his brakes to stop for the red light at the entrance of a traffic circle.

'That cop had a mean face . . . a lyncher's face,' he whispered out of the side of his mouth.

Slowly they swung round a small park with green lawns where fat robins hopped in and out of the shade of magnolia trees in bloom.

'Are you sure you know the way, Winthrop?' asked Joe a little breathless as they came out behind a trolley car to find themselves bearing down on the Capitol. Winthrop nodded his head sadly. He was wishing the drive wouldn't come to an end so soon.

'Believe you me I don't want to get picked up by a traffic cop, not in this town,' said Joe.

The great spreadout buildings with the mounting stone steps and the façades and the dome bulging up from clustered columns into the sunny sky had a deserted look. There were few cars parked in the wide plaza in front. Joe turned off the trolley tracks into the broad empty pavements, driving very slowly. 'Of course Congress isn't in session,' he said ruminatively. 'Boy there'll come a day when under those domes, up those steps will throng the representatives of the workers.'

'Gee you ought to put that in a speech sometime,' said Winthrop kindling.

'I have.'

'You don't suppose they'll beat us bad do you?' said Winthrop stuttering. 'I've been on p-p-plenty p-p-picketlines but I've never gotten b-b-beaten up.'

'They won't kill you,' said Joe, 'not quite. What's that white building over there?'

'That's the Union Station.'

'Now which way do we go?'

'I was just w-w-wondering.' Winthrop was stuttering worse than ever.

'When I see a guy looks like a working stiff I'll ask him,' said Joe grimly.

'They are all fascist-minded bureaucrats in this town,' said Winthrop.

'A bureaucrat's nothing but a white collar worker . . . a worker can't be a fascist. Where the hell did you go to school?' asked Joe.

'Mother kept sending me to different schools, but I kept being fired out of them,' Winthrop answered brightly.

Joe drew up to the curb in the skimpy park opposite the domed white station and asked an elderly Negro. The Negro answered vaguely to turn to the left and keep on going.

'They're on our side,' said Winthrop. 'They know what capitalist oppression means.'

All too soon Joe drove him up to the door of a brokendown dwelling house on a shabby brick street. Winthrop noticed with some relief that Negroes lived in the other houses on the block.

'Shake a leg now,' said Joe. 'I can't park here all day.'

Winthrop jumped out of the car and ran up the iron steps into a dusty hallway. On the peeling front door somebody had pasted a strip that read League of Youth. It made Winthrop feel better to read it.

Inside a number of young men and women were standing around waiting. He went up to a slender youth whose skin was a light cocoa color who wore hornrim spectacles and a creamy summer suit that looked freshly pressed. 'Comrade help me bring in the stuff,' he asked pleadingly.

'Sorry comrade I'm busy waiting for a long distance call,' said the cocoacolored young man in a fluty voice. 'I represent the Negro press.'

Winthrop hurried on through into the crowded empty room

beyond. The first thing he saw was Dr. Sparling typing at a bare kitchen table in the middle of a crowd of youngish people of all sorts who were chattering and talking and reading the *Daily Worker*. There was a studiouslooking Chinese, a couple of Negro intellectuals, some stocky little dark men that might be Porto Ricans, a group of Jewish girls with glasses who looked like college students. Dr. Sparling tossing her mop of gray hair off her big square face looked up at him out of cold eyes.

'Winthrop we thought you'd yellowed out on us,' she said severely, her fingers still rattling on the keys.

'We had a f-f-flat,' he stuttered. 'Can't some comrade help me get in the slogans. They are all in the car.'

A pleasantfaced husky young man in rolledup blue shirtsleeves with a compass tattooed on his forearm hurried out with him. A maritime worker, thought Winthrop, proud to be rubbing shoulders with him as they walked side by side down the steps to the car.

'Well there's still time,' said Dr. Sparling briskly, jumping to her feet when they came back staggering under armsful of placards, 'if the camera men'll wait. We've got the *Daily Worker* boy right here but we need the capitalist press.'

The young man with the compass tattooed on his forearm was bringing in another load. A skinny longhaired boy with glasses took a hammer out of the pocket of his overalls and started tacking the cards on the sticks in a businesslike way. Dr. Sparling stood looking down at them sourly smoking a cigarette.

'They were supposed to read No Recognition of Franco the Butcher,' she said looking accusingly into Winthrop's face.

'We stopped at Thirteenth Street and loaded them up. We just took what they gave us.'

'These must date back to the Scottsboro boys.'

'Maybe they gave us the wrong ones.' Winthrop started to stutter again.

'Quiet please friends.' Dr. Sparling tossed the hair off her face, lifted one hand and raised her voice suddenly. 'You all know we are picketing the White House. Mr. Strang will lead the picketline. Pennsylvania Avenue is at the end of this street. We turn to the right and then we have only three short blocks to go before reaching the State Department. We give the State Department a good boo as we pass for the bunch of fascist butchers they are and then we go right on past the White House and start our chant: American workers will not allow . . . the recognition of Franco . . . the butcher of Spain. We shout that over and over again as we walk slowly past the White House and then in front of the Treasury if the cops have let us get that far, we turn and retrace our steps. It's absolutely essential that we walk past the White House on the same side of the street. This is Comrade . . . I mean Mr. Strang.'

Winthrop felt himself blushing at the applause that followed his name. Every eye was on his face.

'This is a protest of the youth of America and not of any particular class or of any political party . . . We mustn't forget that if we talk to reporters,' Dr. Sparling went on in a schoolteacherly tone. 'All right let's go.'

Their handclaps were still ringing in his ears as he set off with the stick of his placard held firmly in his hand. Dr. Sparling still smoking walked nonchalantly beside him. The noon sun was hot on his bare head. The broad sidewalk of the Avenue was packed with the noontime crowds. 'All right stare dumb monkeys,' he heard Dr. Sparling mutter through the cigarette clenched in her teeth. He threw out his chest and walked looking straight before him trying to turn that set look on his face into a smile of disdain . . . Wear a sheer mask of proletarian will, he told himself.

He hated the faces. Damn fascists. He hated the faces that bobbed staring, questioning, leering towards him over the sunny pavement. Damn fascists. The taximan and the other guy who looked like a dick, leaning derisive against the yellow cab. A thickset little man with glasses who clapped approvingly. The cudchewing girls trooping bareheaded out of the drugstore. The towheaded boy looked like a worker. Winthrop was ready to smile but the big mouth opened in a coarse yawp. It wasn't at him they were laughing. It wasn't for laughing at him that he hated them, it was for laughing at the slaughtered brownfaced young workers of Spain, at the beaten Negro boys of the South. 'There'll come a day . . .' Comrade Yerkes' words reechoed in his head . . . 'there'll come a day when up those steps will throng the representatives of the workers.'

He'd reached the corner opposite the State Department. The stubby columns piled on stubby columns had an arid look under the hot summer sun. He glanced out of the corner of his eye to see if Comrade Sparling were still there. She must have dropped behind. He was alone leading the picketline. That boo. As he crossed the street he tried to put all his hatred into that boo.

He could already see the columns of the north porch of the White House cool white and quiet in the shadow beyond the empty lawn shaded by glistening bigleaved trees when he found himself face to face with a police lieutenant.

The eagle shone silver on the police lieutenant's cap. He was a goodlooking young man with a tan. He had a pleasant blueeyed smile. He was smiling right into Winthrop's face. He was saying in a pleasant tone: 'All right boys. Not this side of the street.' As he spoke he pointed politely with his whole arm towards the green trees of Lafayette Square. The traffic on the avenue had stopped for a light. Before Winthrop knew what he was doing he was crossing the street. The boo died on his lips. He could hear the excited chatter of the other pickets behind him. As he crossed the street he started the chant: American workers will not allow . . . On the other pavement more smiling cops beckoned him on. The picketters were winding among the flowerbeds of Lafayette Square like a group of sightseers admiring the cannas, the neatly cut lush grass, the magnolias in bloom. Cops and camera men were marshalling them to be photographed in front of the bronze statue of Andrew Jackson sitting his rollicking horse.

'Good work Winthrop,' one of the college girls was saying in a tone of relief. 'What could be better? If the capitalist press will carry our message. What could be better?' A seriouslooking reporter was already noting down what she said on a pad. The slim cocoacolored young man in the cream suit Winthrop had noticed at the office of the League of Youth had hold of his lapel, and was looking in his face with big gold eyes. 'Now Mr. Strang,' he whispered, 'tell me about yourself for the Negro press.'

PART II

THE SHIP OF STATE

... And when the weeds begin to grow
It's like a garden full of snow
And when the snow begins to fall
It's like a bird upon the wall
And when the bird away does fly
It's like an eagle in the sky ...

THE SHIP OF STATE

1

*W*e read the newspapers. We listened to the radio. On commuters' trains our eyes followed the close columns of print. At breakfast we set down our coffeecups to listen
to voices
     in the know
       at the front
         at headquarters
who had it from the very highest authority
that the old bad world from which our fathers fled . . .

London Bridge is falling down . . . falling down
(We were weak in geography. In school none of the kids paid attention to geography. The teacher yawned over a few steel-engravings of rivers and hills, a delta and towns long ago in a scuffed book that had lost its cover; we couldn't keep our eyes on the maps on the wall or the boundaries of countries
or the hard names of foreign places.
We were weak in history: 1066, 1492; waxwork groups in fancy dress, the headsman with his axe, a suit of armor, a king and a

queen and a knave off a deck of cards, revolutionaries storming a palace, a list of gentlemen in powdered wigs who affixed their names to a document . . . We hadn't any use for history. History was over. History was what our fathers came over steerage to get away from. Americans we stood in drab today and turned our faces west.)

London Bridge . . .
But now we read the papers . . . is falling down. The scareheadlines sold plenty papers. Scotland's burning. We listened to the news commentators over the radio. The advertizers got hep to the spots where the hot news was. War orders primed assembly lines. Rearmament made jobs, better prices for the farmer. Politicians began to take credit for prosperity . . . Every year we celebrated Armistice Day.

In the headlines in the voices of correspondents broadcasting from the spot—they scolded at us as if it were all our fault—off the presses, out of the airwaves came the old dread, again,
man's hatred for man;
again the clangor of tanks through city streets, shellfire, grenades, the dread in the bumble of bombing planes massed in formation; again the harsh voice shouting the word of command, the crack of the rifles of the firing squad, and the whimper of frightened children, and the hunched shuffle of sorefooted multitudes
filling the roads and the country lanes and the bypaths across mountains.
The old bad world
is falling down
from which our fathers fled (sedulously we celebrated Armistice Day, put flags in the cemeteries). In ruin History stands
a roadblock armed with machineguns, flamethrowers; the footpaths are mined. Geography's a concentration camp where in barbedwire pens the sick survivors starve.
When we turn on the radio the air is full of scolding voices cursing America
because we tried to build a refuge
on a new continent
in peace.

Our Own House in Order

MILLARD SAT IN THE WARM TUB listening to the sunset note of a robin that drifted in through the open bathroom window with the smell of cut grass from the backyards. He leaned his head back against the edge of the tub with his eyes closed. For a second he tried not to think of anything. He pulled himself gradually out of the water, dried himself, put on clean shorts, and enjoying the freshness of the air against his body walked slowly into the bedroom. Lucile sat at her dressing table fixing her hair and humming.

'My things are pleasant this evening,' Millard drawled as he groped in the closet for his white shirt. 'We're usually in such a rush.'

'Oz . . . in three more weeks the boys'll be home and we'll all be together,' Lucile said dreamily.

'Lou you're homesick.'

'The weather's too good,' droned Lucile . . . 'Makes me think of the wild flowers across all that big empty country.'

'I've enjoyed Washington today.'

'But I want to go home to God's country in the spring.' Lucile got to her feet with a jerk and came towards him looking him in his face with that pert blueeyed look he loved so. 'Well maybe this is our last year,' she said briskly. 'What's the latest on the third term?'

'I kind of hope he won't run. I'd like to see him do like Andrew Jackson,' Millard said as he tied his necktie before the glass.

They were at the foot of the stairs ready to start out. 'No Kerry no you can't come,' they were telling the dog who was jumping up and down in front of the door into the little yard that led to the street. The phone rang. Lucile gave her head a shake and answered it.

'It's the Judge;' she shaped the words exaggeratedly with her lips. As Millard walked across the room he felt something he didn't like in the obsequious way he approached the phone as if it were Judge Oppenheim himself.

'How are you sir?' he asked hoarsely.

'Well thank you,' came the cricket-dry voice that flowed on with feminine fluency. 'I hope you and Lucile are well. Millard I'm afraid there's bad news coming from Europe, but that's not what I called you about. I've been wondering if Mike Gulick wouldn't be useful to you in the Department as a sort of liaison man for your project with Congress and the White House and with other departments. I understand he's getting less and less happy about his present associations. He's a man of independent means anyway and I happen to know that he's very popular with a certain great lady. He and Bruce Slater are old friends. I think they went to college together. I've been watching him since he first came to Washington very much the parlor radical. He's broadened out. He proved himself a good soldier in some of the struggles for justice and civil liberties in the old days, but he was bohemian, he was scholastic, he smelled of the Brevoort. Now he's steadying down. Both he and Marice, who is a very important part of the combination, have grown in stature in the last years. They've put away the childish things of Greenwich Village.'

'Of course Judge,' Millard found himself explaining, 'I think the world of Mike. In fact we're on our way for dinner there right now.'

'Well I just wanted to drop a seed,' the Judge went on with a little dry laugh. 'Of course we may have trouble with our political friends. He's not a deserving Democrat, though I think actually he can claim membership in the for Roosevelt before Chicago club and if I remember rightly he performed some useful services at the 1932 convention. He has a liberal political background. His labor record is very good. In fact I understand that Madam Secretary has her eye on him for her department. It's the merest seed. You and Walker and Mike might find yourselves alone for a moment. Well I won't hold you. I'm dining out myself.'

'Good night, Judge.'

Kerry sat mournfully looking after them with his head on one side as they went out the door.

'Well that's one more thing I've got to take up with Walker,' said Millard knitting his brows as he felt in his pocket to make sure he had the latch key. The sense of freedom he'd had while he was dressing had gone.

'How does he know?' asked Lucile shaking her head. 'How does he always know?'

When they stepped out of the little brick alley strewn with fallen wisteriablossoms that led from their house Millard felt on his legs through the thin trousers the heat of the maytime sun still radiating from the brick pavement. The Gulicks lived on the next block. It gave Millard a pleasant smalltown feeling to be able to stroll around there bareheaded. He liked going to the Gulicks', he was thinking, he was always sure of good drinks and a good meal and good talk. 'I hope Walker really comes this time,' he said aloud. 'I've got some bones to pick with him. He isn't a man you can get anything out of at the office.'

'You and Walker . . .' began Lucile, but they had already arrived.

The Gulicks' front door stood open. They'd hardly set foot on the brick step before they began to hear Marice's voice rattling on the telephone . . . 'But you really must come,' she was insisting in her quick wheedling tone. 'Don't dress don't try to get here on time, don't do anything inconvenient, but do come. There's an old friend of yours here already and Walker Watson is coming specially to meet you . . . and you know you did say you would . . . You wouldn't want to see Mike and I lynched by a large party of friends for not producing you, now would you? . . . Strung up on a lamppost by the infuriated mob . . . Well I won't insist. You just see how you are feeling after your broadcast.'

'Why what's the matter Marice? Guests getting independent?' asked Millard laughing as he pumped her hand.

The peevish look went off her face. She showed her pearly teeth between thickly rouged lips. 'How sweet of you to come early . . . It's exasperating . . . His secretary said he'd come and now the old buzzard says he can't. Too exhausted after his broadcast. I told him not to come till eight but he was stuffy about it. He was mad because I got him on the phone says he gives strict orders not to be disturbed when he's getting ready to broadcast.'

'Who's that?' asked Lucile with a giggle.

'Herb Spotswood, the whispering commentator,' said Marice making a face.

'We hear him too often as it is,' said Millard. 'Not that I don't agree with a good deal that he says.'

'He has to come tonight,' a precise thin woman's voice interrupted sharply. Jean Darwin had emerged suddenly from the living room and stood in the shadow under the stairs tall and blonde with a fluffy silver fox neckpiece round her shoulders. 'I'll get a cab and go over and get him after his broadcast. He'll come,' she repeated in metallic tones. Millard and Lucile both said good evening but they couldn't tell from her pale expressionless face whether she had noticed them or not. She brushed past and out of the house.

Marice put an arm around each of their shoulders and pushed them gently before her into the livingroom whispering in their ears with her resonant whisper, 'Mack has brought his latest complication . . . Maybe that's why Jean's in such a pet . . . Lou don't let me forget. I've got more things to tell you . . . scandal . . . my dear scandal . . .'

'Won't you let me in on it?' Millard grumbled.

'Millard there are some things a man should only learn from his wife.'

Everybody was sitting on the terrace in the shallow garden shaded by ailanthus trees round a marble table that had a bowl of swamp magnolias on it. Their sweetness was heavy in the stagnant air saturated with the smell of sappy leaves and of women's perfume and coiling cigarette-smoke. People hung balanced in the late afternoon stillness like fish in an aquarium. Mike Gulick had just tossed back his stony bald head. Ed

James plump and redfaced in a white linen suit sat drowsily smiling, and Mack McConnell was charging the jury with uplifted finger while a slender dark girl in a handsome white satin evening dress kept her big brown eyes fixed on his face. There was poor Eloise Dilling but no George and Paul Graves' nice rawboned wife Peggy. Millard and Lucile sat down on either side of Peggy Graves on the castiron bench. It was evidently a relief to her to find them there. 'Don't seem right for me to be here without Paul,' she whispered to Lucile.

'I know. It's all my fault,' said Millard with a fatherly smile. 'I had to pack him off to Chattanooga.'

Marice was leaning over the back of the bench. 'It's a regular hen party,' she was saying down their backs. 'Usually we have too many men but tonight . . .'

'Isn't this something new, Marice?' asked Lucile as a Japanese-looking butler with a small sour apologetic face swam past carrying high a tray of mint juleps in silver goblets beaded with cold.

'Mike gave me those on our wedding anniversary. Who would have thought we'd ever have stuck it out twenty years?' She shook her fringy black bang with a laugh.

'No I mean that character,' Lucile said.

'Don't be alarmed, Taki's a Korean and he works part time for the FBI,' Marice answered in her noisy whisper. She heard someone in the hall and ran off.

Meanwhile Millard was trying to listen to a polite but persistent argument between Ed James and Mack McConnell on the wages and hours bill. Ed insisted that the Administration was paying too high a price for the farm block's support. Mack said that no price was too high for the accomplishment of one of the main aims of the New Deal.

'Don't ride us too hard on that, Ed,' Millard spoke up. 'We've got to get fifty million for farm tenant loans.'

'Compromise, the balancing of one set of interests against another. That's the oil that makes democracy work,' intoned Mack.

'It's a mighty high grade of oil in this case,' drawled Ed James in his lazy teasing Louisiana voice. 'Two hundred and twelve millions for farm parity, eightyfive millions for surplus crop disposal, fifty millions for farm tenant loans . . .'

'Chicken feed,' sniffed Mack. 'Government finance is only book-keeping.'

'The last figure's an investment. You'll get back more than you put in,' insisted Millard seriously.

'We are establishing the working man as a first class citizen of this republic,' said Mack, 'and at the same time we are proving to the farmer that it's not at his expense that we are doing it.'

'More rabbits out of the hat,' Ed said giggling.

'That's what hats are for,' said Mack with a puckish look on his smooth actor's face. He brushed his hands together with a magician's gesture.

'Ed, aren't we getting away from the point,' said Millard when they had stopped laughing. 'In 1929 nine hundred thousand farms in this richest country in the world had an annual income of less than four hundred dollars and a million, seven hundred thousand farms had a gross income of less than six hundred dollars, and half of that went for costs, that means an average income per farm family of twentyfive dollars a month . . . One third of the farm families of the nation were slum families then and after seven years of the New Deal they still are . . . I don't say that we've found the cure or that surplus crop disposal or tenant loans or resettlement are anything but palliatives, but I do insist that instead of doing too much we aren't doing enough.'

Nobody answered.

To give himself time to think up more recent statistics Millard buried his face in the mint that sprouted out of his julep. For an instant the voices round him dimmed. Try as he would he couldn't call to mind the 1939 figures. Suddenly he was tired. Whole areas of his brain seemed numb. He wasn't having as good a time this evening as he'd expected, if he could only sometimes be free of the strain and effort of trying to push this thing. Way back in his head he was already trying to itemize the points he had to make with Walker if he could catch him alone for a second after dinner.

He looked up and there Walker was standing in the french-window looking out into the garden through the screen doors with that puzzled lonely stare his face so often wore. The sallow skin hung haggard off his long bony cheeks. There were dark patches under his eyes. He looked sick and miserable. Millard caught sight of the band of black on the sleeve of the baggy gray suit and remembered with a twinge that this was the first time he'd seen him since Josephine's death. On either side of Walker stood Marice and Mike. Their faces were big with news.

Iron chairs scraped on the flagstones as people got to their feet. Walker Watson's twisted hurt smile swept across the group like the beam from a lighthouse. When it lit on his face Millard felt himself trying to put something that would help the man to bear this load of grief into his own smile. The narrow garden all at once seemed crowded like a massmeeting. Mike and Marice moved round the edges of the group whispering in people's ears with the manner of ushers at a funeral: 'Chamberlain is about to resign.'

Everybody talked at once and then was silent. In the sudden lull Mike Gulick who had been standing with his heels raised by the rim of the tiny pool under a niche with a bronze dolphin in it in the middle of the garden wall, cleared his throat and spoke to nobody in particular.

'Walker was telling us in the hall . . . Hitler's Norway drive was a gigantic feint to catch the British off balance. It has succeeded. He has launched a cowardly and unexpected attack on Belgium and Holland. At this moment the German bombers are destroying Rotterdam block by block.'

At the same time the small black figure of the butler appeared at another of the french-windows. He bowed with expressionless face and said, 'Madam is served.'

'Come on children let's sit down,' said Marice in a matter of fact voice, as she turned to drive her guests back into the house like a flock of chickens at roosting time. 'We need a little hot soup to buck us up.'

Millard felt his fingers grow cold and the chill creep up his spine. A warm hand seized his for a second and dropped it. It was Lucile standing beside him. Without looking at him she was already off talking in a low serious voice to Ed James. The columnist's face had taken on an alert professional look, something calculating and sly had come into it. Millard followed them with Peggy Graves. 'Paul was saying this was going to happen,' Peggy was muttering in a dazed kind of way. 'How do you suppose he knew?'

'It surely is a surprise to me,' said Millard in firm frank tones. 'It shows I ought to put in some time boning up on foreign affairs.'

While they were still thronging in confusion round the table in the diningroom waiting for Marice to find them their places, Jean Darwin, her face long and pale and expressionless above the platinum fuzz of the silver fox neckpiece, moved into the room. In her wake came a small man with a knotty triangular countenance under round spectacles. His grizzled reddish hair was cut in a brush and he wore a clipped grizzled mustache. Under the point of his chin was a dotted bow tie round a wing collar. As Mike eagerly introduced Herb Spotswood he bowed to each person with a resentful I told you so look. He stood firmly with his small hands grasping the top of his chair and said in the tone of a schoolmaster addressing a recalcitrant sixth form:

'We allowed them to bomb Madrid. Now it's Rotterdam . . . Next it will be London and Paris, and then what is going to keep them from doing the same to New York and Washington?'

Meanwhile Mike had induced Jean Darwin to part with her fur and carried it out into the hall. She sat down slowly and immediately began intently to listen. Her arched eyebrows gave her face an expression of intense concentration.

'There are technical problems,' Walker Watson was saying wearily as if he had heard this all too often before. 'Their bombers haven't the range yet . . . At least that seems to be the opinion of the experts. We still have a few years' breathing space to put our own house in order.'

'That's talking,' blurted out Millard louder than he expected. 'Let's put our own house in order first.'

'They will never give us the time,' said Herb Spotswood severely. 'The world cannot subsist half slave and half free.'

People were already settling down to the meal. The chicken casserole as usual was delicious but Millard was too preoccupied to notice what he was eating. Miss Powers the willowy darkhaired girl from one of the New York fashion magazines who had come with Mack McConnell was keeping up a confidential chatter in his ear.

'Mr. Carroll I'm so excited . . . To think that I should be meeting the man in all Washington I was craziest to meet,' she was saying tossing her head in the direction of Walker Watson who sat at the other end of the table listening to Marice with his head on one side, occasionally opening his mouth wide to drop a piece of bread in it.

Millard was inattentive. Miss Powers tried another gambit. 'Do you know there's an interesting thing about Washington? It's the only place I've ever been where food was important socially. The Washington hostess doesn't care how she dresses but if she doesn't set a good table she can't get anybody to come.'

'I hadn't thought of it,' said Millard in an absentminded tone. As he hurriedly cleaned up his plate he was trying to figure out what this news would mean to the agency. Peggy Graves sat silently smiling beside him. He turned and gave her a quick look trying to think of something to say. Peggy and Paul now, he thought, they were his kind of folks.

'We're in for a tough time,' he said, just to say something.

'Paul's been saying that for years,' her voice twanged in answer. 'He used to say life in Moscow was a preview of the world to come . . . Isn't it too bad he's not here tonight?'

It was a relief when dinner was over and people started spreading themselves around in the livingroom and out into the blue twilight of the little garden. Millard stood in a corner with his after dinner coffeecup in his hand trying not to get involved in talk for fear that he'd lost the moment to corner Walker Watson. The scraps of conversation round him were hurried and discontinuous. 'Hitler . . . Mein Kampf . . . That ends the phony war . . .' kept cropping up like a refrain. From where he stood he could watch through the open door the hall fill with people leaving and new people arriving. Highballs appeared. Looking for a place to set his coffeecup down he found himself face to face with Ed James and, of all the unexpected things, with Jerry Evans.

Jerry looked bigger and more redfaced and richer than ever in his soft blue shirt and well fitting white flannel suit. Tonight he seemed to be a little tight. He jumped to his feet and grabbed Millard's hand in his big fist and looked into his face with his old insolent glare. 'Why Millard you old horsethief I'm right glad to see you,' he shouted. 'When I heard you'd walked out on an honest to God successful business an' joined the prunes an' prisms up here you could have knocked me over with a feather.'

This time there was something genial about his bluster. It seemed to Millard that he was genuinely glad to see him.

'Jerry,' he asked. 'Isn't this a little off your beat?'

'Ask Ed. He's responsible. I had to track him down an' now he's got me right in the parlor with the pinks . . . But look I've got a question I want to ask you righteousness boys. Now Millard don't get me wrong I know you ain't up here for the light wines an' beers . . . By the way any time you want to sell out your interest in Honeycutt and Carroll you know where to come . . . I know you came up here at a sacrifice because you believed in Mr. Big in the White House an' in the things he's trying to do to this Godforsaken country . . . The trouble with bein' a dogooder is you find yourself in some strange company . . . Times I've shelled out for some humanitarian purpose I've found I was doin' more harm than good mor'n once right to the people I was tryin' to help . . . The case I want to put to you and Ed is this. It's about these poor damned oil men. I don't know if you've been followin' it. It's up to Ed to do a scorcher on it in my opinion. At the President's request they did their best to cooperate, agreein' to prices an' workin' conditions for the industry, an' then some bastard in the Department of Justice slaps an indictment on 'em—a criminal indictment under the antitrust laws mind you—not a civil suit, an' convicts 'em of combination to set prices. They were fined but they might have gone to jail. I'd have been as guilty as they were if I hadn't had a couple of Philadelphia lawyers who smelt a rat from the beginning. All these boys were guilty of was tryin' to cooperate with the Blue Buzzard. Now is that fair 'n' square, I ask you men?'

'Jerry,' said Millard slowly. 'I'm not competent to judge. I haven't followed the case.'

'If you were still down in Texarkola I bet you'd be competent to judge. That's what I mean about the dangers of dogoodin'. First thing you know you are contributin' to a frameup on some innocent men. Ed's goin' to do a scorcher. You tell 'em, Ed.'

'Jerry if my own investigation bears out what you're saying I certainly will.'

'I'm goin' to hold you to that.'

'Now I want to ask you a question Jerry,' said Ed James. He cleared his throat: 'Just supposing the Skipper didn't care for a third term or thought the tradition was too tough for him what would people down your way say to the young fellow who's holding forth on the terrace right now?'

Jerry didn't answer. The three of them stood looking through the fly screens in the french-window out into the dark garden. Past a couple of shadowy heads they could see by the light of a candle flickering on the table beside him Walker Watson's gaunt face. The lids had dropped half over the eyes in an expression of weariness. He was listening to what someone they couldn't see was saying.

Jerry let out a whistle and slapped Ed James on the back. 'What a big black cat you've just let out of the bag.'

'Well Jerry that's my business and profession,' said Ed with a pleased smile.

'What do you say to that Millard?'

'Too deep for me,' said Millard laughing as he moved away but he couldn't help feeling his heart beat faster at the notion ... Walker President would mean top ranking for the agency. There would have to be a new secretary. Who better than ... You shut up, Millard said to the ham actor inside his head.

He was pushing his way out through the screen doors into the garden. Walker sat leaning way back in a wicker deck chair talking up into dark sky. Jean Darwin sat on a round leather stool beside him with her head bent in a listening daffodil droop while on the other side Miss Powers was curled on a pillow on the flagstones with her big eyes tilted up into his face. Mack and Mike Gulick sat with a spellbound expression on their faces on the iron bench while Herb Spotswood with his arms on the table nervously puffed on a cigar. By the time Millard got into earshot Walker had paused to pour the rest of a bottle of cocacola into his glass.

'Rotterdam ... Rotterdam ... And while we sit here what the last war left of Europe's civilization is smashed in blood and flame,' Spotswood whispered shrilly. Nobody looked up when Millard dragged a heavy iron chair into the circle and sat down.

'I don't suppose anything that happens can shake the ideas a feller was brought up in,' Walker started talking again in a slow groping voice as if reaching back into his memory to continue an argument with himself. 'You see I was brought up, and I guess you folks were, in this notion of moral progress.' One hand held the cocacola glass. He propped his chin with the other and talked down into his sleeve in a deprecating kind of way. 'My poor mother brought me up in the notion that you could make the world better by behaving right yourself. She kinda thought of goodness as catching, and I suppose badness too. Dad and Mother were both great for Sunday school and foreign missions. They sure did believe that hard work was the way to teach the young idea how to sprout. Dad had a farm . . . the cold spring mornings I've gone out barefoot to do the chores . . . Along with the farm Dad kept a little grocery store at the four corners. The trouble was he never could get himself to refuse credit to anybody who was a godly man and a good churchmember, but for some reason the righteous didn't flourish out our way like the ungodly did so when Dad died while I was still kneehigh to a grasshopper Mother had to sell out. If it hadn't been that she had me to raise and educate I think she would have gone out as a missionary to China. She always kind of hankered after the heathen. She'd always taught school to help out Dad and in her spare time when she had any she acted as a volunteer welfare worker. I don't know how but she got herself a position at Hull House under that great and good woman Jane Addams. So from the rural slums of Nebraska I was switched to the urban slums of Chicago. I don't think for one moment in her life my dear Mother had a doubt that with good will and selfsacrifice that jungle could be cleaned up and turned into sweetness and psalmsinging. But even my poor mother had to admit that it would take some time for goodness to triumph in the Chicago public schools so to keep me from growing up a little gangster she shipped me back out to Uncle Harry in Nebraska. Uncle Harry had the business brains of the family. He had discovered at an early date that a man could make a better living by writing about farming than by actually walking behind the plow. He had a strong dose of the family religion so his little paper doled out about half oldtime religion and half uptodate agriculture. When he first started I used to drive the papers to be mailed every Thursday in a spring wagon, then when I got out of school and Uncle Harry found I had a little of the gift of gab he

used to send me around to farm organizations granges and cooperatives and the like to make little speeches at their meetings to get people
to subscribe to the paper . . . I don't know what started me on this.' He
leaned back in the chair and yawned.

'Oh do go on,' said Jean Darwin in a choked voice.

'Wonderful,' exclaimed Mike Gulick deep down in his chest.

'Lincolnesque,' sighed Miss Powers.

Walker Watson brought his glass up under his nose and stared
down into it thoughtfully without touching his lips to it.

'We certainly weren't all saints out in Nebraska,' he went on, 'but
Chicago in those days was something different . . . Chicago was
more of a battlefield than a city . . . Now this is what I'm trying to
explain . . . Whenever the tragedy and wickedness of life—something
like this horrible bombing of a town full of defenseless women and
children—when this kind of wickedness starts to get me by the throat
I remember my poor little mother, just a not very well educated rural
schoolteacher from Nebraska who'd been poor as a church mouse all
her life, starting out down Halstead Street with a resolute look on her
face to go to some slum dwelling out back of the stockyards maybe
and wrestle with the poverty and crime and debauchery of the tough-
est city in the world. It never fazed her for a moment and we can't let
it faze us.'

When he stopped talking people began getting up silently like after
a church service. Walker Watson bent his long legs, set his feet on the
floor and hauled himself section by section to his feet. Millard's throat
was dry.

Mike Gulick rushed forward his face beaming and grabbed Walker's hands and shook them violently. Millard took a step towards them.
Walker was looking in his face in a puzzled sort of way as if trying
to recall something. 'Say Millard there's something we need to thrash
out. Don't let's get away without . . .'

At that moment Marice her black eyes popping under her bang
burst out through the screen door from the livingroom. 'Walker,' she
called, 'I'm sorry to interrupt, but you're wanted on the phone . . . It's
the White House.'

THE SHIP OF STATE

2

*W*here we sat on the front porch in the dry air sweetened by the last blossoms in the groves of orange and grapefruit we could hear the bees humming in the beanfield. The crop would be good. Just this morning the commission merchant drove up and offered a price for the whole forty acres. He'd send his gang in to pick 'em. Dad was figuring on the back of an envelope the price of plowing and preparing the land and fertilizer and labor and seed 'Yep I'll take it,' he said. 'At the price these Mexicans ask I wouldn't break even if I picked 'em myself. Not a bad profit at that, twenty percent, amortizing the cost of the land and the crop loan and the mortgage. Times are looking up.'

The same minute we all remembered
     that inside the envelope was a letter from the uncle who'd stayed in the old country. When the Russians took their half of the country he'd lost the farm—he had ten hectares so they said he was a landowner, he could read and write English so they said he was a spy—and the Germans had arrested Aunt Olga because they said her people were Jewish and he didn't know where they had taken her
     and he'd escaped in a motorboat across the Baltic
     and he was sick and heartbroken and old, without money
     and wanted our help to get to America.

In the Field

AT THE TOP OF THE HILL Paul put his foot on the brake. The station wagon stopped with a jerk slewing around a little in the gravel and Georgy shouted, 'Yay there's the farm.' Paulino joined in and Bettina and little Oliver shrilly took up the cry.

'Now troupers,' said Paul in an oratorical voice, 'we must get ready for the bad news.'

'I beg the cow's dead,' said Paulino.

'Or the pig's sick,' shouted Georgy.

'Or the house has burned down,' screeched Bettina in a tone of triumph.

'That shows how much sense you've got. You can see the house,' said Paulino disgustedly.

Paul wasn't listening. He was looking down at the nineteen acres of rolling clay so red you could see its color through the misted green of the pasture and the fluffy green of the willowtrees down by the run. The red ran in streaks through the field of blond winter wheat, which, now that it was beginsing to ripen, didn't look so good as Paul had hoped it would, and glared off the furrows of the contourplowed hillside where his corn was planted. The corn was up in curving ranks of fragile feathery tufts bright as little green flames against the red. In the lower corner of the pasture the fence was down. The shingled shed by the barn where he kept the tractor seemed to be sagging.

'Oh well we'd better go and face the music,' Paul groaned and let his clutch slip in and brought the car gently down the hill and across the rattling plank bridge to a stop between the great shaggy locusts in front of the stoop. 'Always expect the worst,' he said, 'and you'll never be disappointed.'

'What a crêpehanger,' said Peggy. 'Why, things look wonderful.'

The kids were already out of the station wagon and had shot off in all directions. Paul and Peggy loaded themselves with bags and packages of groceries. As they stumbled up onto the stoop one step creaked.

'I must see if I can't find some lumber for a new step,' Paul muttered apologetically. 'I wonder where Wills and Sally are.'

'It's Saturday. They've gone to town,' Peggy said.

'They mighta waited. They knew we were coming.'

'You know how they are about Saturday afternoon.'

The front door was open. In the cool hall Paul breathed in deep the familiar farmhouse smell of mouldy plaster and coaloil lamps. A triangular piece had fallen from the ceiling and lay at the foot of the pine stairway.

'We've got to get this dump replastered,' he sighed as he set down the heavy suitcases. 'Anyway the old place is still standing . . . Say those kids ought to help bring in the stuff . . . Paulino . . . Bettina,' he bellowed from the stoop. 'Come and help bring in the things.' They came straggling in brighteyed and breathless.

'Daddy the dam we built is still there,' they shouted.

'Mummy there' two little lambs,' shrieked Oliver galloping round the corner of the house.

'Well I might have expected it,' Georgy announced grumpily. 'Wills plowed up the ballfield.'

'We'll lay out a diamond in front of the house,' Paulino said in his steady practical tone.

Paul and Peggy were in the kitchen. There was fuel in the tank of the oil stove and a fire had been laid in the old range. 'Look,' said Peggy. 'Sally didn't forget us after all.'

Getting supper kept them busy until dusk and then while Peggy and Bettina did the dishes Paul and the boys walked all over the farm in the afterglow. While they were looking over the cornfield Wills appeared from the direction of the tenant house. He was a tall mulatto with high flushed cheeks.

'Well Mr. Paul hit's about time,' he said glumly. 'I near lost my mind gettin' the different kinds in the right rows.'

'You wait till you shuck out the ears. You'll think we're all crazy. But if we can raise some certified seed we can get eight dollars for it at least.'

'I sure would like to see some foldin' money, Mr. Paul,' said Wills.

'Wills I've leaned over backwards to give you the breaks,' Paul said looking him hard in the face. Wills looked down at the ground and made no answer.

That night after the kids had been induced to go to bed Paul in his undershirt strode barefooted through the halffurnished rooms of the big house. The white plaster was cracked and peeling and webs and spider eggs choked up the corners. An occasional stain on the ceiling indicated a leak in the roof. A streak of light came from the boys' room. He pushed open the door to find Georgy reading in his cot by the light of a candle. Paulino in the cot opposite was fast asleep, his face lean and brown like Paul's own face pillowed in a bare arm.

'Lights out Georgy,' Paul said in his sharp tone of authority. Georgy frowned, squinted hurriedly at the page as if trying to gulp it all in one look and blew out the candle.

Across the hall moonlight streamed in over Bettina's little bed. My how she'd carried on about Oliver being put in her room for the night, and now there was an angel's smile on her little face abandoned to sleep in a swirl of golden curls. Through the open window heavy sweetness came in from the swampy thickets down by the run. A mockingbird was singing his head off.

Paul tiptoed back into their room where Peggy was combing her hair in front of the pocked mirror of the old walnut bureau. 'Peggy listen,' he said. She turned her face up towards him with her comb in her hand. Magnolia blooms shone bright white in the moonlight amid the dense black foliage of the tree outside the window.

'It's too sweet,' she looked up at him and spoke out of the middle of a yawn. In contrast with her dark hair and eyes the skin of her cheeks and shoulders looked milky in the yellow lamplight.

Paul slipped out of his trousers and underclothes and into a suit of pyjamas and let himself drop on the bed. He lay outside the covers looking at the white moonlit window and the yellow lamplight in the mirror and Peggy's slow movements as she combed her hair.

'My it's been a struggle.' He lay talking up at the ceiling. 'Seems like I'd been struggling with this damn house ever since I was Oliver's age. When I was Paulino's age I don't think a day passed that I didn't worry about the mortgage. Then when I was in school . . .'

'When I first knew you all you could think about was the mortgage,' Peggy drawled smiling sleepily into the mirror. 'I used to feel terrible because first I thought I'd never have a beau and then when I did get one all he'd talk about was his dad's mortgage.'

'I don't suppose a country doctor had any right to have a farm anyway . . . It was kind of a relief when Mother let it go after Dad's death and moved up to Raleigh.'

'But when there was a chance to foreclose and get it back you were hot on the trigger and so was I,' said Peggy. 'Lord I'm tired.' She got heavily to her feet.

Paul sat bolt upright on the bed. 'And still we haven't got the place on its feet. You wouldn't think it now but when Dad was a young man and able to give some time to it Hawks Nest was a mighty good farm. All we got back is the rump. All that good pasture land along the creek was released. That's what I need now to grow my seed corn. Peggy I was a damn fool sticking my head into this Washington mess.'

'If we'd moved west we'd be further away than ever.'

'Gosh I'm too tired to sleep.' Paul closed his eyes and let his head drop back on the pillow.

'Listen. It's so lovely,' whispered Peggy.

The mockingbird sang and sang in the locust tree. Outside the window the blossoms shone in the dark magnolia.

'Wills feels he isn't getting anywhere . . . I don't much blame him except that if he owned the place without us to finance it he'd be worse off yet. That's what he doesn't know,' said Paul as he got up to blow out the lamp. 'Say Peggy, do you think we ought to tell him to get in under Farm Economy and get himself a loan to buy a farm? Gosh I hadn't thought of that . . . absentee landlords is one of the things we are fighting.'

'Paul it's bedtime . . . the children will be up at the break of day.'

Peggy kissed him softly and climbed into bed beside him.

'We got to hold on somehow . . . At least it's a place to put the kids out to grass summers.' He began to talk again lying on his back but Peggy wasn't listening. She was breathing softly and regularly. She was asleep. With his arm crooked over his head to keep the moonlight out of his eyes he turned towards her until his lips touched her warm smooth shoulder and all at once he dropped off himself.

In the morning the sun was already hot when they woke. The kids were outside shouting and scampering. Right away they were all in a bustle. There was the fire to start in the range, and wood to chop and the kids to police so that each one had his own chores. Then there was the search for a plank out in the barn that would fit the stoop and cleaning the rust off the saw and little Oliver's excitement over the small armored woodlice that scuttled to cover out of the rotten wood of the old step that had to be torn out. Then there was the long inconclusive talk with Sally and Wills about the fall plowing, and suddenly Peggy had dinner on the table.

It was already late and they had to start for Raleigh with their mouths full of roastbeef to catch the plane, leaving Sally sour and silent and greenfaced to putter in the kitchen and to keep an eye on the kids. They were all too busy and excited about work on the dam that was going to make a swimming pool down in the run to notice Paul's leaving. After all the clamor it was a relief when he and Peggy were alone in the station wagon out in the road.

'Better write to Washington,' he was saying. 'I'll be back from Alabama before you can get out a letter . . . Well as usual here I go off minding everybody's business but my own. Maybe we ought to be plain old dirt farmers.'

'I'd just as soon, at least I think I would,' said Peggy. 'But how would we educate the children?'

When they reached the airport they found that the plane was three quarters of an hour late. Sitting in the front seat of the station wagon waiting they went over the routine of the chores. Bettina was to feed the chickens, George was to do the milking. Paulino was to help Wills with carpenter work on the barn and the fences. Oliver was to feed the pigs. They talked about the garden that hadn't been put in and Wills' little patch of tobacco that he set so much store by. Then they ran out of topics and began to fidget. Already Paul's mind was running ahead to his conferences with the local men of the agency down in Alabama and Peggy was beginning to worry about what the children were up to. Before the plane came she started home and left him to read the Sunday paper in the quiet little airy waitingroom at the airport.

His eye had hardly run wearily down a half column of European warnews before his mind was back in his plans for the agency. The blueprint was unrolling in his head. It was the floorplan of an airy foursquare farmhouse, two bedrooms, bathroom, livingroom, kitchen with a good enamelled sink and an electric stove and a washing machine and a cement walk leading out back to the barn and garage and implement shed and a simple dairy for cooling milk; a paved road flanked by the power line and telephone led to the rural center, where the cooperative dairy was and maybe a small cheese plant and refrigerated lockers and the rural school and a couple of stores and a church, and became a four lane highway to the town where there would be factories and warehouses and merchandizing centers and motion picture theatres and highschools and meeting halls. This was his America. If you could get the rural economy functioning well enough to reverse the trend and suck the people back out of the obsolete gangrenous cities . . . Americans had never learned to build decent cities because they didn't need them, maybe. As the blueprints unrolled in his mind it was as if he skimmed in an imaginary plane over a model countryside contourplowed reforested resettled. God there was so much land in this country. There was room for us all to live spaced out, to reach a balance between largescale organization and individual human stature . . . Stature.

The muffled voice from the loudspeaker squalling out his plane departure roused him with a start. Stepping up the light rubber treads of the steps and past the stewardess' smile into the plane was like stepping again into a different world. He let himself sink into the comfortable seat with his briefcase on his knees and closed his eyes. His hands were sore from the unaccustomed physical work. He could feel under his toes the red dust that had seeped into his shoes and through his socks. It was the way he used to feel as a boy when he put on his store clothes after a season at the farm to go back to school. He still felt himself that boy with his life before him but now his boys, Paul and Georgy, were the age he used to be, sprouting up so fast with no thought but of themselves, getting between him and Peggy, getting between him and his old picture of himself, going through it all now on their own. He wanted those kids to grow up men of stature. With an almost physical effort of the will he closed up that book and buried himself in a report from the regional branch of the agency he was going to visit in Montgomery. The plane levelled off. The motors droned drowsily.

He couldn't keep his mind on the smudgy mimeographed paragraphs of the report. The plane he was riding in was merging with the imaginary plane in his head. Looking down on the hazy ruddy contour map below with its roads and hills and watercourses and the vague crosshatching of the towns, he kept telling himself that it was the basic structure of people's lives that counted, the houses they lived in, the way they made their living. It was their daily control over their destinies that counted. The oldtime American farmer had lived a hard life fighting weather and prices but he was the master of his destiny. It was that feeling of being master of your destiny that was frittered away in largescale organizations, in city life, in industrial plants and labor unions. If you could make a man a little more independent at the source of his livelihood he would be able to make over all these organizations into organs for selfgovernment instead of organs for slavery. That was what he meant by stature, that was what he must explain to the people in the agency. America must mean stature for its citizens. It was only if those kids grew up to some extent master of their destiny that they could grow up free men.

When he tightened his seatbelt for the landing it was late and the afternoon had grown sultry. As the plane circled he got glimpses of the windings of a broad mudcolored river and of a pinkish checkerboard of streets and green blobs of trees cooking in a dense haze of heat. When the door was opened the close air poured in. Immediately he began to sweat. A row of thunderheads towered round the horizon. There was an agency car drawn up among the taxicabs and from it tumbled the large redfaced figure of Gibbs Dupee.

'Gibbs, you shouldn't have given up your Sunday afternoon to come out and meet me,' Paul said. 'I wasn't counting on you till tomorrow.'

'Didn't have a thing in the world to do,' drawled Gibbs as he heartily shook Paul's hand.

The downtown streets had a bakedout abandoned look in the sultry summer Sunday afternoon. The elevator wasn't running so they stumped up two flights to the office.

'I thought we could have a quiet chat,' panted Gibbs out of breath. 'Tomorrow it'll be all conferences an' that kind of crap an' I shan't be able to get in a word edgewise.'

Paul started to answer. 'Hush.' Gibbs raised a finger and pointed dramatically to the groundglass door they were walking past. *The Farmer's Friend* was engraved on the glass in oldfashioned fancy letters. Gibbs stopped in his tracks and his red face took on an intent listening look.

From some inner office came the rasp of an old man's voice ... 'First thing you know they're goin' to organize farm labor ... they're goin' to make us pay every damn nigger fifty cents an hour at the same time as they take any possible profit out of our hides with confiscatory taxes an' raise the price of farm products so that a man'll have to be a millionaire to buy himself a beefsteak.'

His face screwed up with disgust Gibbs beckoned Paul to follow and tiptoed with exaggerated stealth down to the end of the hall. There he opened the agency door with a key and closed it silently after them. With an expression of conspiracy in his face he looked around at the maps and charts hung on the green walls of the waitingroom and suddenly he started to shout: 'It never fails. There he sits night an' day, Sundays and holidays ... Monday to Saturday ... The man is tireless. He used to represent the cotton interests,' he spluttered. 'Now he represents the cattle breeders. Night an' day there pours from that office defamation, propaganda, reactionary slander in an endless stream. He ought to be in jail.'

'But Gibbs,' said Paul grinning, 'didn't you work for that crowd in the old days?'

'That was before I saw the light,' said Gibbs seriously. '. . . Here let's get some air in here.' He threw up a window. 'We're in for a period of muggy weather, thunderstorm weather, never fails when the farmer is tryin' to get his small grain thrashed out. Ever smoke a cigar?'

Paul shook his head.

'Well I will although the doctor has given me a serious warnin' to cut 'em out. I need somethin' to sooth my nerves. I get palpitations of the heart every time I hear that old buzzard givin' tongue from the rooftops . . . He never stops . . . Tireless.'

Paul pulled off his coat and tie and dropped into a chair.

'But Gibbs think of the high blood pressure those boys get every time we settle one of their prospective tenants on his own farm.' Paul threw back his head and let out his long hehaw laugh. 'I got a farm myself. I'll be sore as a boil when my tenant moves on . . . He'll probably be one of our clients . . . Gibbs,' he added seriously, 'I want to find a way of explaining to people down here what we're trying to do . . . show 'em the blueprint. Maybe you can help me.'

Gibbs had sat down at his desk and begun to talk in a whisper leaning forward towards Paul. 'Now Paul here's what I wanted to talk to you about before we had the whole gang on our necks.' Gibbs had gone off on his own tack, Paul told himself, better let him get it off his chest. Gibbs was pointing theatrically to the map of the state on the wall. 'Now if you will remember you sent an order through when this thing was first set up to make a careful selection of prospects in one district: of family history, recommendations, previous experience, etc., an' in another to take everybody who applied who wasn't an alcoholic or who didn't have a criminal record.'

Paul sat up in his chair. 'This is an experiment, no use carrying out an experiment without controls,' he said gruffly.

'Experimentin' with the taxpayer's money that's what old vinegar puss down the hall will call it,' said Gibbs.

'No more useful way to spend the taxpayer's money if he only knew it,' said Paul.

'Well, here's what happened.' Gibbs pulled two typewritten sheets out of the top drawer of his desk with a sweep and handed them to Paul. 'Now this first report from district 'a' . . .' He jumped to his feet and went to the map on the wall like a lecturer and shook a thick forefinger at a group of counties in the northeastern corner of the state . . . 'gives us seventyeight point five percent of successes: families who our local supervisors report to be doin' well, an' report 'b' from this section over here of under approximately similar conditions, number of families, proportion of nigra and white, literacy, etc., gives us seventynine percent where there is no selection of any kind. We just took anybody who applied. Now what the hell does that mean? Are our methods faulty? Are we pickin' 'em wrong or have we hit some damn kind of democratic least common denominator in the farmin' population?'

Paul stared hard at the two sheets of figures and percentages. 'That's very interesting indeed,' he said slowly.

'What worries me is, if that boy down the hall gets hold of these figures, he can make monkeys out of us. I've been keepin' these reports under lock and key until I got instructions. In my opinion they are dynamite.'

'I'll have to study them,' said Paul.

Gibbs got to his feet. Once more his eyes travelled carefully round the green walls as if looking for hidden listeners. 'Paul,' he said, 'there's another thing I want to ask you. Please don't take it amiss but just for my own information I'd like to know if there's anythin' in this Walker Watson boom.'

'What boom?' asked Paul blankly.

'Presidential boom,' whispered Gibbs.

'Gibbs,' said Paul getting to his feet without answering the question, 'I'll have to take this stuff over to the hotel and study it tonight.' He yawned. 'Give me all the background you can . . . Here put it all in an envelope.'

As they walked down the illswept hall they heard again the croaking hayseed voice. '. . . Whom God loveth he chasteneth. The good

Lord I devoutly believe loves the farmers of the United States an' he has set the New Deal on our necks to try us an' to chasten us.' As they passed the office of *The Farmer's Friend* a small blackbrowed man in a dusty widebrimmed black felt hat stuck his head out of the door like a chipmunk peeking out from a hollow log, scowled at them and pulled it back. On the way down the stairs Gibbs gestured over his shoulder with his thumb. 'See him?' he whispered glumly. 'That's what he is tireless.' Paul burst out laughing.

Outside the street was dark from a coming thunderstorm.

'Now Paul,' said Gibbs as they climbed into his car, 'if you have the time Mrs. Dupee would only be too honored to have you come out to the house for supper.'

'Thanks, Gibbs, thanks. You better drive me to the hotel. I always maintain that the best place in the world to think is alone in a hotel room . . . Do you suppose you could come by for me at six A.M? I want to drive around to see some of our clients before we go back to the office for that conference at noon.'

Gibbs screwed up his big loosehung face. 'What man has done man can do,' he said as he drove up under the awning of the hotel. The rain had begun to fall by the bucketful.

In spite of the thundershowers that had kept on all night it was hot again next day at noon for the luncheon conference. When Paul glanced in the door on his way to the washroom the low ceiling of the basement coffee shop seemed to press down on the huddled faces of young men, and schoolteachery women in wash dresses, and middle-aged men in their shirtsleeves. While Paul washed his face, dabbling cold water on it with his long fingers, he tried to think how he could say something that would link their daily office routine and their paper work and their humdrum preoccupations with the blueprint he held in his head. The people he'd seen during the long morning, the things they'd said kept getting in the way of the phrases he was trying to form.

There had been the superintendent of the cooperative dairy a tall obsequious man with a red adamsapple sticking out of his long wattled neck and a plug of tobacco lumping out his cheek and the feckless way he stood over two young towheaded fellows in overalls who were sweating over the cream separator trying to take it down to remove a broken part. Before Paul knew what he was doing he'd snatched the wrenches out of their hands and was taking down the machine himself. The sweat had run in his eyes and ears, he had greased up his shirt, and he had felt silly when he had finished up the job and triumphantly extracted the oily little scrap of frayed brass, standing there wiping his hands on a piece of waste.

'Tell me the Secretary's headin' into the presidential nomination,' was all the superintendent had found to say.

'First I've heard of it,' Paul had answered and turned his black stare on him. Probably made an enemy there.

Then there was the skinny gray elderly couple who had kept up a feeble querulous peeping like a pair of young turkey poults, scared of the Lectricity, worried about the pump in the cooling shed that they'd had fixed for seven dollars and sixtytwo cents but they were afeared it would break down again. They'd never lived with Lectricity before they said, they were sure it was dangerous in thundershowers . . . was it true it caused cancer? They pulled the main switch every time it looked like rain, safer they reckoned . . . 'If he wa'nt so reckless like,' the old woman had said pointing at her husband, 'we never woulda taken the step.'

Gibbs had asked for their milk receipts and proved to them with pad and paper that they were making better money even after interest and amortization were paid off than they ever had in their lives before but still they kept complaining in those peeping voices with their scrawny necks stuck out that suppose they got sick, suppose the cows got sick and died, suppose the shed was struck by lightnin' . . .

There was the ruddy young man in a torn shirt heavily sweated under the armpits who had come storming out of his house barefoot and said he couldn't ask them in because the wife was poorly and the baby had whooping cough but he wanted them to know here and now that he needed more cattle. Was there any way of gettin' the U-nited States Government to loan him the money to buy fifty head?

There was the bent old black woman in a white turban with rheumy eyes with blue whites who opened up the closet full of clean jars of fruits and vegetables all put up according to government specifications in the manner of a nun showing off a sacristy. A tiny brown girl in a pink dress had followed them everywhere with the whites showing all the way round her eyes. 'Don't you like 'em better than the old way, aunty?' Gibbs had asked. 'No sir . . . Yes sir,' she'd stuttered. 'We ain't eat none of 'em yet, they're too purty.'

Paul felt the sense of frustration tightening about him like a shirt too tight at the neck. He stood a long time wiping his hands on the towel. When Gibbs stuck his red face in the door and beckoned to him with an important air, Paul felt he had to do something. He fished an envelope out of his pocket and jotted down words on it: . . . 'The deep freezer and the preserving kettle and the electric cooler are the things that are going to make civilized life possible in the back country . . . Add to that a well-run cooperative to market the crops and a sensible system of rural banking run in the public interest' . . . he wrote and walked in with his long stride to take his place at the speaker's table against the wall.

Luncheon dragged on tediously. Paul was too busy trying to think what he was going to say himself to taste his food or to listen to the reports of the local district supervisors. He told the story of fixing the cream separator on himself as an example of how a man who was administering something ought not to behave, but it didn't come out right. It sounded boastful and selfimportant. They didn't know how to take it. His job and theirs he insisted, trying to make himself clear, was to try to keep in the minds of everybody working for the agency, the feeling that it was part of a great blueprint for the American future. He was pleased with the phrase himself but he had the feeling he hadn't said it loud enough. There were coughs. People were moving their feet and making a clinking noise with their coffeespoons. He told them about the old couple who were scared Lectricity might cause cancer and got a laugh out of them. 'Lord, I'm no speaker,' he whispered to Gibbs as he sat down.

The only question was from a young man at the next table who leaned over confidentially and asked in a loud whisper if it was true that Mr. Watson might get the presidential nomination. If it was it would mean a lot to the agency.

'I'll let Mr. Dupee answer that one,' Paul answered morosely. 'He knows more about it than I do.'

It was a relief to be out on the road again alone with Gibbs driving at a smooth clip towards the northeastern part of the state. The green rolling country hugely dappled with contourplowed cornfields slid by on either side of the black highway. There were big oaks and whitetrunked sycamores in the valleys.

'We have left the northern edge of the Black Belt,' Gibbs was saying. 'You will notice that our detractors notwithstandin' this is not submarginal land. This is corn and cotton country. My great grandfather moved into this country from Charleston with a drove of cattle an' a wagon train not much more than a hundred years ago with his slaves an' his blooded horses an' his barrels of French crockery an' the ladies ridin' pillion in pokebonnets for fear of sunburn. I've got more than a spectator's interest in seein' this country come back, Paul.'

'Do you still own any of it?' Paul asked.

Gibbs shook his head. 'The Northern troops paid us the compliment of burnin' the old home plantation an' the First National Bank absorbed the remains when I took a tumble in cotton in '29 . . .'

Paul sat thinking for a while. That's what he'd wanted to tell the folks at that conference, he began to explain slowly. The early settlers, his folks and Gibbs' folks, had had some sort of a plan in their mind, a notion of how a free man ought to live on the earth. Now we'd lost that plan for America, lost it in the press of business. The New Deal was out to recapture that plan, an effort in that direction, better say, the beginning of an effort.

'I'll tell you boy, the New Deal's been the salvation of the South,' Gibbs answered emphatically. 'Upon my soul and body it has.'

Paul didn't say anything more. He wasn't making clear what he meant. He let himself slump back in the seat, looking out at the red earth and the rail fences. This was the kind of country he liked, back country. Crows walked sedately among the corn. Buzzards circled overhead on ragged wings. On the harrowed hills teetered bare unpainted shacks without dooryards, back country cabins.

As they passed one gray sunbleached ramshackle cabin two very pretty girls, one blonde and one brunette, stylishly dressed, fresh and clean as if they were coming out of a beauty parlor, ducked out from under the cranky porch all the shingles had peeled away from and came trotting in their highheeled shoes down the dusty red path towards the highway. Most likely on their way to the bus stop, Paul thought looking back at them. He felt he knew them. He felt he knew every room in that house, the old quilts on the castiron beds, the close smell of coaloil lamps, the privy, the rickety well or the spring down in the hollow, the flyeaten mules in the pasture, the old plows and harrows rusting under the shed, the mouldy bits of harness hanging in the barn, the sickly women, the tobacco-chewing old men. He knew their lives. Back country lives. They were his people. He came from the same mixture of black Scots-Irish borderers and broadfaced blond Saxon stock. They were frontier people, pioneers stranded a hundred years ago in the scrubby hills. And now they were streaming away into the cities or into migratory labor camps, factory fodder, millhands, a faceless race. God I wish I had the gift of gab, Paul thought. He glanced at Gibbs and wondered what he was thinking.

Gibbs was driving fast. He too seemed a little sunk by the conference. He didn't say anything, but every time they drove past a piece of contour plowing he gave Paul a light nudge with his elbow.

Paul sat silent looking out at the brilliant green of early summer under the sky full of white clouds and the red hills enfolding and revealing and swallowing up again the great dark trees along the streams as the car sped past. It was late afternoon before they shot over the crown of a grassy hill into a scarred shallow valley the color of bleached bones, laced with railroad tracks and smudged with smoke from the chimneys of industrial plants.

'Here we are at last,' said Gibbs. 'Bob Green'll be bitin' his nails. He's a nervous sort of cuss.'

They wound through quarries, crossed railroad tracks, dove down a broad rutted road black with coaldust between long glassed-in sheds of steel mills and came out on a battered main street of sleazy stores with false fronts of sooty red and yellow brick. Gibbs drew up in front of a small hotel built of concrete blocks moulded to represent stone. Flies buzzed against the unwashed window of the lobby. In a collapsed leather chair under a withering palm sat a lighthaired young man with hard blue eyes behind nose glasses. He got to his feet and came to meet them.

'Bob it wasn't our fault,' shouted Gibbs. 'Honest to God it wasn't . . . Bob meet the brains. I always knew there was brains in Washington behind this business an' after what he had to say to us poor benighted provincials at the little informal conference we held down at Montgomery, I knew where some of them are . . . This boy studied to be a Baptist minister, Paul, but we mustn't let that worry us. They tried to make a hardshelled Baptist out of him but he turned out a liberal instead . . . a hardshelled liberal.'

The young man's grip was fanatical. 'I have a two hour program mapped out,' he said. 'Do you think you can take it?'

'Let's go,' said Paul.

'We'd better go in my car,' said the Reverend Green grimly. 'The roads won't be what you gentlemen are used to.'

Gibbs locked up his Buick and they followed the Reverend Green across the street to his battered Ford coupé. He hadn't given up the ministry, he explained in a low voice with downcast eyes as he put his foot on the starter, but it had occurred to him that before he could honestly preach the kingdom of God in heaven he should try to bring a little bit of it to pass on earth. In his opinion that was what the great Christian in the White House had set out to do . . . 'And I tell you gentlemen quite frankly that I'm for him . . . Now before I take you to see what has been accomplished in these three counties since the Government established its resettlement program, I want you to see how some people are still living in the richest Christian nation on earth in the year of our Lord nineteen hundred and forty.'

The three of them were squeezed into the narrow seat. As they drove out of the town and past the industrial noman's land beyond and up a winding clay road through scrub country of cutover pine where a few skinny cattle grazed, Paul suddenly found himself talking:

'I'm not taking this trip to tell you fellers things,' he started hesitantly. 'I'm out trying to find fellers who'll tell me things . . . I agree with you Mr. Green, that the Administration in Washington is trying to establish something in this country. Whether you call it the kingdom of God or American democracy doesn't matter so long as we all mean the same thing.'

'Without God we can only go in one direction.' The Reverend

Green stopped the car abruptly at a turn in the road. 'To heathen-
ism and hell,' he said. 'Now if you don't mind taking a little walk into
that clearing yonder . . .' They followed him through the cornstubble
and weeds of an abandoned cornfield. On the porch of a little cabin
a woman in a dirty print dress sat rocking. Before they'd even had a
chance to pass the time of day, the Reverend Green was pointing out
the sores round her mouth. He made her open her mouth to show
her bleeding gums. She was toothless. 'Pellagra,' he said, pointing his
finger at her. Paul found himself standing first on one foot and then
on the other from embarrassment. As they walked back to the car he
asked why the poor woman hadn't been taken to a hospital. She lived
on the border between two counties and neither one of them wanted
to take her case on, answered the Reverend Green. 'All right,' said Paul
quietly. 'The bus fare to Birmingham can't be more than a couple of
dollars. Here's five . . . You see she goes there . . . But Mr. Green,' he
added as they squeezed back into the small coupé. 'We mustn't forget
that every social system has its casualties. The aim of resettlement is
to give people like that the means of making a living so they won't get
to be relief cases.'

A little further along the road they found an old Negro hoeing in a
patch of sweet potatoes. 'Howdy Reverend, howdy gentlemen,' he said
cheerfully. He had a wooden leg and explained proudly how he'd cut it
himself out of a locust sapling.

'A truck ran over him when he was walking back from town with
his week's groceries on his back,' intoned the Reverend Green. Further out, in the midst of forsaken fields grown up in persimmon and
sumach they went to a shack where the Reverend Green showed them
a stout man who lay in a mess of filthy bedding his eyes glassy with
fever while a hollowfaced woman in patched rags hovered over him. A
half a dozen scabby children tagged after her. In a mournful singsing
she told the story of how he had been hurt in the tubing plant and a
company lawyer had induced him to sign a quitclaim for a hundred
dollars compensation and the wound in his leg had festered and was
getting worse and now they didn't know what in the world they were
going to do.

'None of these people came to grief through their own fault,' the

Reverend Green said bitterly as they drove away. 'They are all good churchgoing people.'

'But they are relief cases,' Paul insisted. 'They aren't our problem. You don't have to show me the misery there is in the world. I know something about it . . . Maybe that's why I'm in this kind of work.'

'In these counties . . .' The Reverend Green stalled the motor when he slammed on the brakes at the turn back into the highway as if to give emphasis to his words, 'relief is in the hands of the politicians and the politicians are mostly landlords who save it for their own tenants.'

'Can't you do anything about it?'

'The New Deal hasn't made so much impression on the solid South as you might think.' The Reverend Green gave him a tightlipped glare.

It was beginning to get dark. Paul was suggesting in a conciliatory tone that maybe they'd better visit some projects before night fell. 'You know what the buildings look like . . . It's the Christian souls that dwell in them that count,' said the Reverend Green. They were passing a brilliantly lit barn. 'Isn't that Hodgins' place?' asked Gibbs Dupee.

'It is,' said the Reverend Green.

'Suppose we turn in there to see if old Hodgins won't give us a glass of buttermilk. This is dry work,' Gibbs said.

They drove into the pool of light that flooded into the blue gloaming from the cavernous cowbarn. Inside Paul could see rows of stalls and the backs of flickering tails of cattle. A grayhaired man in spectacles came out peering into the dusk from the clean recently washed concrete alley between. He wore blue overalls and rubber boots.

'Hullo Ed . . . Mr. Graves meet Mr. Hodgins,' shouted Gibbs. 'Ed we're inspectin' our little resettlement project an' we thought we'd look in to see what the malefactors of great wealth were up to.'

'You've come to the wrong place Gibbs,' Hodgins said quietly. Then he turned genially to Paul. 'Mr. Dupee here, he can't forgive me because I'm doin' the same thing he's doin', only what I do don't cost the taxpayer a cent. In fact I make money and pay taxes on it. That's treason to the New Dealers. Talk about resettlement. Well I've resettled four tenants on the ruins of an old family plantation. I sell 'em the farms and buy their milk from 'em. I got a boy come over from Georgia, can't even read and write, in five years he's bought his place and a herd of pretty fair milkin' cows and now he has twentyfive hundred dollars in the bank and I've made a profit on him right along. Of course I wouldn't be expandin' my business if it weren't that the wars and rumors of wars were buildin' up employment in the valley so that folks have money to buy more milk than they did.' As he talked he led the way into a big white airconditioned dairy building back of the barn. A young man in blue overalls brought them out icecold buttermilk in paper cups. 'No,' Hodgins went on. 'I want to see your project succeed. There's an element in this country that can't help themselves. If the government can manage to show them the way to get on their own feet I'm all for it . . . after all milk is milk and that's what we need to raise healthy kids the wide world over.'

'Suppose our cooperative undercuts your prices?' asked the Reverend Green in his sharp voice.

Hodgins laughed quietly. 'You try,' he said. 'Why, if you gave it away, I'll still have a better product and a market for it.'

'Why?' asked Paul.

'Because everybody's business is nobody's business,' said Hodgins dryly.

It was pitch dark before they reached the resettlement project. Only one of the dwellings was complete. When they knocked at the back door a young woman timidly squinting past a lamp held out in front of her opened it half way. She was barefoot and her hair hung down in spikes over her face. Two tiny children hung onto her skirts. 'Oh it's you Reverend,' she said in a tone of relief and started to pour out a whining story about how the power had failed and the cows had gotten out through the electric fence and how they didn't have any lights or water and how her husband had been all day looking for the cows and how she was frightened most to death for fear somethin' had happened to him.

'The fine southern Bourbons of our local light and power company have not been any too cooperative,' the Reverend Green explained tartly over his shoulder.

She said she'd like to ask them in but everything was all of a tumble. Down home they'd never had any trouble like this, she repeated several times, looking reproachfully into the men's faces. From behind her came the wail of a very young baby. She wouldn't let them go until they'd promised to drive her husband back if they met him on the road.

Next the Reverend Green wanted Paul to inspect the foundations of the unfinished dairy with a flashlight but Paul said he knew those dairies by heart from the blueprints and Gibbs added that he'd have to hit the road if he was to get home by midnight. As they drove back to the town Paul talked figures and costs. 'When I was little I used to hear my dad preachin' in the pulpit against the sons of Belial,' the Reverend Green said as he brought the car to a stop with a jerk in front of a dimly lit hotel. 'Now I know what he meant . . . He meant contractors with a government contract.'

They laughed as they pulled themselves out of the cramping seat. For a wonder the coffeeshop was still open. A fagged waitress was waiting on a lone customer, impatiently watching every mouthful he ate with eyes halfclosed with sleep. He turned out to be a man Gibbs knew named Joe Wilks so they sat down at the table with him. Gibbs swallowed a bowl of soup and then left in a hurry for the long drive home. The Reverend Green wouldn't eat anything. His wife would have his supper on the table, he said. But before he took his leave he wondered if Mr. Graves would answer one question. Mysteriously he beckoned Paul into the corner of the diningroom.

He understood, he whispered in Paul's ear, that there was some chance of Secretary Watson getting the presidential nomination. Was he a good man, a Christian churchgoing man? He had heard rumors, probably spread by Republicans, that he frequented racetracks and light women. Paul burst into his braying laugh. 'Mr. Green,' he shouted, 'politics is something I don't know anything about and I don't intend to know anything about . . . Mr. Green goodnight.'

The Reverend Green gave him a reproachful look and said he'd call for him to take him to the airport in the morning.

Paul was still laughing when he sat down at the table again to try to induce the impatient waitress to bring him a little more supper. Joe Wilks saw him laughing and started to laugh too. He was a cheerful sort of man and he and Paul hit it off right away. He had a red head and a lobsided face and an expansive manner. He was a labor organizer, he explained. Immediately he launched on the story of his life. For fifteen or twenty years they'd had a local here in the mills, half a hundred frightened guys expecting to be fired every time they held a meeting and now the boys were pouring in by the thousands. 'It's manna from heaven,' he said. 'In the old days I'd sneak into town like a peddler an' like as not the Klan would get wind of me an' ride in their robes down Main Street so's I'd have to take a powder pronto an' now I drive a Pontiac an' they cash my checks at the bank an' the night clerk at the hotel says, 'How about a small suite Mr. Wilks?' an' the ladies from the Community Chest put a flower in my lapel an' ask for a contribution . . . It's manna from heaven.' He let out a Scotch comedian's hoot.

'Well I'm a Newdealer myself,' started Paul, 'but sometimes I wonder if we are getting as much accomplished as we should.'

'Accomplished? Listen . . .' started Joe Wilks.

The waitress had relented enough to bring Paul a small steak paperthin and fried to a crisp. He stuck his feet way out under the table and ate slowly with his head thrown back drowsily listening, now and then letting out one of his long heehaw laughs, which seemed to be just what Joe Wilks needed to keep him talking.

'When I was a youngster I worked as checker on a mine tipple up above Birmingham an' I tell you I was God's angry man. Union was strong medicine those days. My boys ud pour out their water— that meant they weren't goin' to work no more that day—if the superintendent so much as pulled a hair out of his nose . . . It was a crime. We had the superintendent sick in bed with worry half the time. An' then the mineowners they hired 'em a little group of uglies to beat up our boys. It was murder an' mayhem every Saturday night. Last time I got out of the hospital I gave it up an' took to songwritin' an' then I did a stint of publishin' a newspaper an' a turn in vaudeville. You northerners don't know it but we got radicals in these hills that date back to Andy Jackson.'

'I'm not a northerner, I'm a tarheel,' said Paul.

Joe Wilks let his voice boom:

'An' then the Great White Father spoke an' said, "Let there be unions," an' there was unions an' a good payin' job for anythin' that looked like an organizer. I tell you, Mr. Graves, it's manna from heaven.'

Suddenly it seemed the funniest thing in the world. They both shouted with laughter.

'If you gentlemen don't mind continuin' your conversation in the lobby,' the waitress broke in tartly, 'I've got to close this place up and go home.'

'Sorry Annie, sorry,' said Joe Wilks giving her a wink.

When he got to his feet Paul found he was groggy with fatigue. 'Well Mr. Wilks look me up when you come to Washington,' he said still laughing. 'Put it there,' shouted Joe Wilks.

Upstairs in the creaky iron bed that seemed to carry in its sag the imprint of thousands of previous occupants Paul stretched out uneasy for fear of bedbugs and lay giggling quietly to himself. All day he'd had a feeling of struggling uphill through deep sand and now as his muscles relaxed and drowsiness began to steal over him he could hear Joe Wilks' infectious titter and his comedian's voice saying, 'I tell you Mr. Graves it's manna from heaven.' He went off to sleep.

By the middle of the next afternoon he was back in his office at the Department. He'd hardly gotten his coat off before Miss Stevens his secretary was standing in front of his desk with a sheaf of yellow sheets in one hand and a stack of letters in the other. On her cool smooth little face like a porcelain doll's was the expression of concealed reproach she always wore when he'd been away on a field trip. It was five before he had a chance to call Miss Washburn. He asked her to step around. Immediately she was standing in the doorway looking down at him out of her bluegray eyes with her aching halfsmile. Paul got to his feet.

'Sit down,' he said gently. 'Well how's Miss Facts and Figures?'

'I'm fine. Was it a trying trip?'

'Confusing. As usual I brought home a conundrum.' He dug savagely in his briefcase for Gibbs Dupee's figures.

She looked at them with almost playful intentness.

'That's worrying 'em down where I've just been. Now in all the record piled up in this man's town there must be something I can compare those results with.'

'I better get busy,' she said.

As she was leaving he heard his voice saying softly, 'Say Facts and Figures.' She turned back. 'What are you doing this evening?'

'I guess I'll be working on this.' She gave the typewritten sheets a little shake.

'Do you suppose you could take an hour off to stroll around in the heat and listen to my ravings? There are times I've got to talk. Every time you talk to anybody about anything in this man's town it gets to be a conspiracy. I like to talk about things and forget it.'

'It's a lonesome town for a girl,' she said quietly. 'We might go to the concert in that park out Sixteenth Street.'

'Great. Let's leave here at seven.'

She nodded. 'Nobody in the office can make out your hours,' she said.

'They think I'm crazy?'

'They think we're both crazy.' She went away spinning her fingers around at the level of her ears. The gesture seemed very comical to Paul.

The minute they were out of the door walking across the too green grass of the Mall in the stagnant afternoon heat, he started to talk. What was worrying him in this business, he explained scowling, was that there seemed to be something incommensurable between what went on in the agency office—the policy level—and what went on in the field. We had in government today, at least that was his guess, the most wellintentioned crowd of people since the very early days of Washington and Jefferson. A man like Millard Carroll had sacrificed a business and a very sizable income. There were hundreds like him. He couldn't make out Walker Watson but behind that latter day Lincoln stuff there seemed to smoulder something that was not entirely selfinterest. Anyway grant 'em all a hundred percent patriotism from the gentleman in the White House down and the best possible plan of operations that could be braintrusted out and you would still have this gap between the plans at the policy level and the poor devil in the field being moved around by forces too big for him to understand. In a business, no matter how huge, Standard Oil say, the problem was simple. The aim was to make money. You could tell, at least a good accountant could tell, what every smallest branch was doing. But the aim of government enterprise was presumably to secure the wellbeing of the population. That wasn't so easy. Did she think reform ought to start at the bottom instead of the top? He didn't wait for her to answer. 'I know those poor whites like my own kin,' he said. 'They are my kind of people. I feel humiliated for them. For some reason it humiliates people to be helped by a government agency. These damn dogooders are always sticking their fingers in people's sores. Sometimes I think they enjoy it . . . I went down there to explain to the men in the field what we're planning up here and I came back confused and humiliated . . . Are we going at this thing the wrong way?'

'That's what my father would have said.' Her voice was low and almost apologetic.

'Who was your father, Facts and Figures?'

'He was a college professor . . . He was a belated nineteenthcentury liberal of the Manchester school.'

'That's why you're so hellishly welleducated.'

'He kind of brought me up to help with his research.'

'I wish my dad had had time to train me for a scientist . . . I had to train myself and it's not easy. The only thing I learned from him was early rising. Then I got in with a bunch of reds and had to go to Russia to see how it was working and came back all ready to fall for the New Deal. Anything seemed an advance over Stalin's methods for producing fewer and better Russians. But now I wonder if I oughtn't to give up attending to other people's business and go back to plain old lab work like I enjoy.'

'The boy . . .' She stumbled over the word. He turned and saw that her face was flaming red. 'A boy I grew up with,' she went on pronouncing the words carefully, 'who also helped Dad with his research when we were in school became a labor organizer and a Communist . . . he pretty near carried me along with him.'

'I'm glad he didn't,' said Paul. 'You stick to your education. No solutions are as simple as that.'

He noticed that she had turned very pale.

'Have you had anything to eat, Facts and Figures?' he asked in a tone of concern. 'Let's see, where are we?'

They stood on a corner waiting for the light. They were at Fourteenth and K on a broad sidewalk full of limp slowly moving people in summer clothes. Paul had been talking so hard he hadn't noticed that he'd been dragging her along at his usual racing pace. The exhaust from the cars made the stagnant air stifling. He'd sweated through his shirt and the coat of his seersucker suit.

'Oh for an airconditioned lunchroom,' he said. 'I hope you won't mind if we just sit up at a counter and eat a bowl of soup . . . I got the habit of economizing when I was working my way through school and it's very fortunate because now I have four children to raise and educate on a Washington salary and I damn well have to.' Suddenly he laughed. 'The only place I ever felt rich was in the Soviet Union . . . the contradictions of socialism.'

'My you've got a funny laugh,' she said.

'Peggy, that's my wife, she says it sounds like the braying of a jackass.'

'Why not that little place over there?'

'Can't be any worse than the others,' he said.

Their combined check was a dollar ten.

'What started me on this train of thought,' Paul said as they left the greasy heat of the lunchroom for the cooler air of the street, 'was meeting a dairyman down near one of our resettlement projects who said he was doing the same thing we were doing, selling grazing land to tenants only he was making money on it.'

'But resettlement is selfliquidating, isn't it?' She looked up in his face with a smile. She seemed steadier on her feet now that she'd had something to eat.

'Facts and Figures, that's only a word.'

It turned out to be a long drag out Sixteenth Street before they came to Meridian Park. Several times he offered to take a taxi but she refused. He could feel a stream of sweat pouring down the hollow of his back. She seemed to be getting tottery again and he had to put his hand under her elbow to help her up the long flight of stone steps up to the park. From the top they caught a breeze. The place was jammed. Every chair seemed taken. In the dimness faces were crowded like flowers in a bed on both sides of the oblong pond that gave back a reflected glimmer from the lights in the orchestra shell. The orchestra was playing something by Sibelius. The long gruff strains seemed exciting in the hot densely crowded night. He couldn't find her a chair but he managed to find her a scrap of balustrade to sit on. She was so tired he had to give her a boost to get her up there. For a second he felt her damp woman's body limp in his arms. He suddenly thought of Peggy as a warm flush spread through his blood. He stood a little away from her waiting for the breeze to cool his wet clothes. Oughtn't to be doing this, never again, he told himself.

'So the family's at Chapel Hill,' she said in a dead formal voice when the music stopped.

'I put 'em out to grass down on the farm,' he answered. His voice too sounded false in his ears. She must be thinking the same things he was thinking. He began to wish it were time to take her home. They went on talking constrainedly like strangers making conversation. When her bare arm crossed the back of his hand as she slid down from her perch he pulled his hand away as if her flesh had burned him. In the middle of the next number he said abruptly, 'Let's get out of here before the crowd' and led her down the steps to Sixteenth Street again. Hurriedly he helped her into a cab and slammed the door on her with a gruff 'Good night.'

THE SHIP OF STATE

3

L *unch hour we stood by the watercooler battin' the breeze.
That's how the argument started. This egg he was a troublemaker, he didn't speak English good. Said he was a seaman on some
Swede ship. He was a seaman all right 'cause he had a foreign girl's
name tattooed on his arm an' a wreath of flowers under it. Jumped
ship at Hoboken 'cause he wanted to be a 'Merican citizen . . . a fat
chance he had, a illegal entrant.*

*'Well the shopsteward he says that Russia is the workers' father-
land and this guy burns up an' says does the shopsteward savvy
Katorga. He says his dad and his brothers are all in Katorga if they
ain't dead yet. He comes from some damn little country I doan know
the name of it I guess an' he says they came to his village an' put a
cordon of troops round every house an' they told the folks they'd have
to pack up because they was agoin' to move the population into holy
Russia an' nobody wanted to go but they didn't have no guns an'
there wasn't nobody to help 'em because Hitler had made this here
pact with Stalin an' they told the men to pack separate because they
were goin' to have a sanitary inspection. They just let 'em take one
little satchel an' they had to leave the cows in the barn an' the crops*

in the field an' all their dough if they had any an' so they herded 'em up like sheep to the railroad station but when they found the men bein' put on separate trains from the women an' children, there rose an awful kiyi but they said that was the rules an' a guy gives this egg the word that where the men was goin' was Katorga an' in the rumpus an' shootin' an' the women 'n children yellin' bloody murder he gives 'em the slip an' gets into the woods an' away.

'An' that's when the shopsteward he steps up an' says this egg's a no good Nazi an' he says he ain't no Nazi an' the shopsteward he slugs him one an' goes after the foreman an' gets him fired right then an' there an' they're goin' to turn him in for illegal entry an' I guess he'll go back where he came from all right an' a good riddance, a troublemaker, but what I wanted to ask, 'cep' just then the whistle blowed an' I didn't get no satisfaction, was where the hell's Katorga.'

The Yanks Are Not Coming

C OMING?' Louise Aldershot's dry voice crackled in Georgia's ears. Georgia smiled up from her desk at the long yellow face under the little pieshaped straw hat outlined against the ground glass door. It was the hick look she liked Georgia thought to herself. 'Well I don't see why I shouldn't . . . Suppose we walk?' she said softly.

'Horses walk,' said Louise with a little quick grin that showed her long teeth.

'Just this once,' said Georgia in a pleading tone. She reached for her gloves and handbag.

Crowded into the elevator Georgia was busy pushing little smiles out onto her face and trying to look civil and gay. It wasn't that she didn't like them she wanted to tell them but she couldn't feel easy with so many people at once. She felt choked as the crowded elevator dropped. After they had poured out of the elevator the other office-workers stood irresolute for a moment in the marble hall. Men lit cigarettes. Girls craned into their handbags to get a final peek at their street makeup. Georgia walked straight out. It was a relief to break away and to stretch her legs out of doors in the steamy afternoon. She set off at a fast pace across the grass. She had to stop to let Louise catch up with her. The grass was dry but there was a pleasant smell of wet gardens in the air from rain somewhere nearby.

'Have a heart,' said Louise. 'I'm no Marathon runner.'

Georgia let her feet drag and strolled beside Louise across the Hall. Louise's face had taken on a vague expression of worry. 'He's having a tough row to hoe . . .' From something about the way Louise emphasized the pronoun Georgia knew right away she meant Mr. Carroll. *He* always meant Millard Carroll. 'When a man gets to want to be President it makes it hard for the rest of us.'

'There ought to be some better way of running the public business,' Georgia said.

Louise's heels clicked significantly as they came out on a cement walk.

'Politics is awful,' she drawled, 'but Walker Watson is a wonderful man just the same.'

'I suppose he's afraid of the southern Bourbons,' Georgia said. 'They don't want us to set their sharecroppers up as selfrespecting farmers who own their own farms. They want to go on exploiting them.' Georgia was talking mechanically. These were all things she had said before. Paul, she was thinking, Paul's the only one who's working for the sharecroppers, who truly understands them, who feels they are his people.

Louise nodded and nodded.

'What's Mr. Carroll going to do?' asked Georgia.

'*He'd* do a wonderful job if they only let him,' Louise said and closed her thin mouth tight and wouldn't say any more.

Paul, Georgia went on thinking . . . She hadn't intended to think of him at all but once she let herself speak his name out loud inside her head thoughts of Paul began to flow through her blood in a warm river. It was something forlorn and spare and backwoods she liked about him most, something he and the sharecroppers had in common. Paul's name was so loud inside her head she felt herself blushing. She was afraid Louise would read Paul's name on her face. She started to chatter about the little brown suit she'd seen at Woodward and Lothrop's that she wished she could buy. Too expensive till she'd saved some money. Then of course it would be gone. What an awful place Washington was to shop.

As they turned the corner of the Treasury towards Lafayette Square they found themselves in a crowd. Through the throng and the packed traffic they could see that some sort of scrimmage was in progress on the opposite pavement. Behind the stiff blue caps of a row of capital police picketers' placards tilted above tossing heads. THE YANKS ARE NOT COMING, they read.

'Radicals,' sniffed Louise scornfully.

'They are demonstrating against war.' Something about the ring of the old angry protesting tone in her own voice made Georgia remember Detroit with a wince of pain. 'I think they are right,' she whispered.

'I don't like those dictators,' said Louise.

The police had cut off the sidewalk in front of the White House. Louise and Georgia were caught on the corner at the edge of a group waiting to cross the street. They stood on the curb looking over at the opposite sidewalk. The picketers were being pushed back. There was a certain amount of shoving but the police weren't using their clubs.

'It's a shame,' muttered Georgia beginning to feel trapped and flustered.

In a short time the picketers melted away and people could cross the street again between two lines of policemen. The policemen's faces were red and some of them were sweating but on the whole they had a sheepish friendly look. After all it's not their fault Georgia was telling herself. Louise had tight hold of her arm. 'I declare,' she was exclaiming, with an unexpected schoolgirl twitter, 'that's what I like about Washington. You can really see things happening.'

Georgia burst out laughing. 'Only if you don't take the bus,' she said and gave Louise's hand on her arm a little squeeze.

The first face Georgia saw in the rank of faces held back along the opposite pavement was Greta Greenberg's. Greta looked small and chic and brown under a little hat with red flowers on it. 'Cossacks,' she was shouting. Georgia tried to brush by without recognizing her but Greta opened her mouth wide again. 'Why Georgia I didn't mean you.' She burst out laughing. A big policeman with a face like a meatchopper was lunging her way. Immediately Greta grabbed the two girls' arms and burrowed in between them. 'Here lemme walk between you.'

Before Georgia knew what had happened they were all three of them walking fast in step past the old Belasco Theatre.

'Don't ask me how Joe is,' Greta was whispering up into Georgia's ear. 'That's over. What a heel.'

Georgia found herself coolly introducing Greta to Louise.

Greta started to giggle. 'I don't suppose I ought to say that of a good liberal, ought I?'

At the corner of H Street she left them. 'You girls saved my life. I've got to write this story for the *Daily Worker* . . . I'm in newspaper work now.'

'Who's she?' asked Louise after they had turned up Connecticut Avenue. 'I declare she's real cute.'

'I used to think she was the girl I hated most in the world, but I guess hate doesn't stay by you any more than love.' Georgia felt herself blushing. What a silly pretentious thing to say, she was thinking before the words were out of her mouth.

'My brothers used to say Jewish girls were pretty but they took an awful risk . . . Wasn't that mean? Well maybe they're right,' Louise went on without a pause. 'The British are trying to get us into their war again.' Suddenly she shook her head until the flat straw hat teetered on her skimpy hair. 'I don't like those dictators . . . and Georgia,' she added in the same breath, 'I'm not goin' to walk another step . . . Not another step. Don't your dawgs hurt?'

They had walked as far up Connecticut Avenue as the corner of M. Georgia waited there for the bus without a murmur. Seeing Greta had taken the stiffening out of her knees. She climbed in obediently after Louise. Paul, she kept repeating his name to herself in a childish monotone as she swayed in the huddle of men and women behind the driver.

The heavy portal of the apartment house and the soiled marble lobby and the shabby look of the old man at the dim switchboard and the smell of oil from the elevator and of gritty mops drying somewhere gave Georgia the squeeze in the pit of her stomach she always felt when she came home.

'Well I declare,' cried Louise as she paused in the doorway of 7d to pull her key out of the lock. 'What on earth's going on?'

The narrow livingroom was littered with dresses and underwear and stockings. From the open door of the bathroom came a sound of tumbling water and a smell of bathsalts and a great deal of steam. Their roommates Elsie and Phyllis were flitting back and forth in their slips like children playing puss in the corner.

Elsie stopped combing her rinsed blond hair long enough to let out a breathless shout: 'We're going to the Dixie Ball.'

'I haven't got anything to wear,' wailed Phyllis and slammed the bathroom door after her.

'It's too hot for dancing,' said Louise making her sour mouth. 'Georgia,' she added reproachfully, 'you walked my dawgs off.'

Georgia felt a little contrite smile flicker round her mouth. 'You rest your hands and feet and I'll get supper,' she said.

With her handbag still under her arm she hurried into the kitchenette. For a moment she stood staring up at the shelves cluttered with canned goods, jars with labels, torn breakfast food boxes, trying to think what Louise would like. She snatched at a can of mushroom soup. She wrinkled up her nose at the stale smell that came from it as she poured it into the double boiler. How Père would have stormed. 'Slop,' he'd have said, she remembered almost laughing as she bustled around with her handbag still under her arm because she couldn't find any place to set it down. In her head those pictures were coming into focus and dropping out of sight like in an oldfashioned stereopticon: the big old kitchen at Ann Arbor with its worn yellow oilcloth and all Mother's cookbooks on a little shelf back of the coal range and the cut crystal bowl on its lace mat in the middle of the mahogany table in the diningroom and the flat silver fitted into compartments in the sideboard and Père, his little boy smile breaking through his beard, sitting at the head of the table waiting to carve a capon. Now instead of Père's she was seeing Paul's face tilted over his desk, his sharp eager black look when he scanned a report. Paul never knew what he was eating, she'd bet his wife was a slattern . . . Georgia suddenly found her eyes full of tears. 'Oh, it's so sordid living cramped up with a lot of women,' she whimpered aloud in a tiny crybaby voice.

With big crimpers in her hair and wearing her prim blue wrapper Louise was standing in the door behind her. 'Well they've gone . . . What a relief,' she was saying. 'The place is a sight. But what's gotten into you Georgia? There you go muttering over the stove like an old nigra mammy." Georgia gave her head a shake and forced a smile. 'Supper'll be ready in a jiff,' she said in a false cheerful tone.

There wasn't any cream left in the icebox so she poured evaporated milk into the soup. She cut up a head of iceberg lettuce for salad . . . My, Père used to hate iceberg lettuce . . . She popped some baker's rolls into the oven and started to fix the tray with a paper lace doily. 'Do you want a glass of milk?' she called out over her shoulder.

When Georgia brought out the tray Louise was sitting at the table under the stainedglass lamp doing the crossword puzzle in the back of the *Star*. 'I know you're only young once but I don't like those girls running around with every Tom Dick and Harry,' Louise said without looking up. 'That's one thing I like about you Georgia you don't run around.'

Georgia felt she was going to cry again and went into the bathroom to wash her face. She took her time hanging up the girls' things and cleaned the spilled facepowder off the glass shelf over the washbasin with some tissue. Then she darted into her bedroom to comb her pale hair back from her forehead. Her eyes were quite red and puffy.

'I feel awful,' she muttered.

'The soup's scrumptious Georgia,' Louise said, talking with her mouth full of crackers, when Georgia sat down opposite her. 'You've certainly got a hand with the seasoning. Sometimes I wish you and me could get a nice quiet place to ourselves.'

'But I like having the girls. They are really sweet,' said Georgia.

'Georgia you're not eating anything.'

'Sometimes my stomach kinda squeezes up . . . I'll eat in a minute.'

A smell of burning bread spread out from the kitchenette. 'Heavens, the rolls!' cried Georgia running to the stove. They weren't too far gone. She scraped off the burned tops and split them and put some butter on them and brought them out. The smell of burning stuck to her fingers.

'That's what comes of trying to do too many things at once,' said Louise bleakly. 'No wonder you're flustered with the girls running around here like crazy and leaving the place all of a litter.'

After they'd washed the few dishes and put them away Georgia saw

Louise making for the top drawer of her bureau. Right away she knew what was going to happen. Louise was going to get out the cards and suggest they play Canfield. 'You wouldn't want to go out to a movie now Louise would you?' she timidly asked.

'And stand in line for two hours . . . After all that walking I haven't got the strength.'

'You play solitaire . . . I've got some notes to go over I brought back from the office.'

'Don't you ever do anything but work?'

Georgia smiled and shook her head. She brought a yellow folder out of her handbag. Immediately the room became excruciatingly quiet. Louise would puff out her cheeks and let the breath out slowly through pursed lips whenever she turned up the right card. Through the open windows with a gust of the warm night soured by the smell of exhausts came the sound of cars hissing over the pavement, occasionally a horn or the rattle of a truck. Georgia was pretending to be absorbed in her work but as her eyes followed the lines of smeary mimeographed words the sense kept slipping out of her head . . . Paul, she was thinking, Paul.

The telephone rang. She flew to the little table by the door. It wasn't Paul. The voice was so familiar though it confused her. 'Who, who?' she kept asking.

It was Joe Yerkes' voice that burred cajolingly at the other end of the line. 'No don't come here.' Her heart beat fast. She couldn't listen to what he was saying. 'All right,' she heard herself answer in a rasping tone. 'I'll come but I'm afraid I'm not very good company. Where? K and Seventeenth? Be there in half an hour.'

Louise looked up from her cards. 'Isn't it much too late?' she asked absentmindedly.

'I'll just run out for a minute. I wanted a breath of air anyway. I've got such a headache . . . It's an old friend of my father's, somebody I went to school with . . . He wants some advice.' Her tongue was chattering along in spite of herself.

'Better take a wrap,' said Louise. 'These Washington nights are treacherous.' As Georgia reached for the doorknob she settled back contentedly to her cards.

Joe was stouter but he didn't look very different. He had on a pros-perouslooking doublebreasted suit but his ears still stuck out from his head.

'George have you eaten?' he asked hurriedly as he headed her into the restaurant. Most of the customers had already left. Tired-looking waiters were clearing ravaged tables. The air was thick with a smell of food and drink and stale cigarettesmoke.

'Isn't this rather expensive?' asked Georgia.

It seemed funny to be called George. Nobody called her that now. Paul called her Old Facts and Figures, the thought seemed to give her armor all over.

'What the hell? I've got an expense account,' Joe was saying in his old defiant way. 'Let's have a good dinner, George.'

'I've had my supper,' she said . . . This is all very long ago she was telling herself comfortingly. 'I'll just take a cup of coffee.'

'Won't you have a drink?'

She shook her head.

'How did you know where to find me?'

Joe smiled his narrow smile. 'I have my operatives,' he said.

'But what on earth do you want to see me for?'

'Don't be like that George. It seemed too silly us both being in Washington and never seeing each other. You're my oldest friend in the world. No conventional bourgeois notions can change that, now can they? Why wouldn't I come to you when I'm in trouble?'

'Give me a cigarette,' said Georgia weakly.

'We've got too many things in common. You haven't forgotten the Movement.' He let his voice drop as a waiter leaned over him with a bill of fare.

Georgia noticed a new sharp tone in his voice as he ordered his dinner, the tone of a man accustomed to paying for what he wanted and to giving good tips when he got it.

As soon as the waiter had gone again Joe leaned across the table towards her talking low and fast and spitting a little in his earnest-ness. 'I'm in trouble with the Party George. It's this Hitler business. You know, the famous pact . . . From the longterm worldwide point of view I suppose you can put up a very good case for the Soviet Union's keeping out of the fight between rival imperialisms. Litvinov certainly did his best to get the capitalist nations to go for collective security and Comrade Stalin is undoubtedly right in saying "A plague on both your houses" but damn it I'm a labor skate . . . My job is to organize American workers. It's our great opportunity to get in on the ground floor with Mr. Big backing us up and here we are throwing it away. The mineworkers, they don't dare talk back but outside of the thoroughly disciplined unions like the mineworkers and the furriers the pact spells failure. The American workingman don't like those dictators.'

'I met Greta on the street covering the White House pickets,' said Georgia. She surprised herself by the mean teasing tone in her voice.

'So what?'

His ears were red. She watched with a feeling of distaste while the waiter brought him a veal chop and a pile of spaghetti covered with tomato sauce. He began to eat in his messy hurried way.

'Not a thing since seven o'clock breakfast . . . Conferences all day,' he explained with his mouth full.

'I didn't know you had signed on the dotted line, Joe.' Georgia's voice was still icy.

'George don't be like that. Be your old sweet self . . . If you want to organize American labor you've got to work with the Communists. They are the only people who are really serious. They are a nuisance in some ways but they can be trusted to put in the work and to take the raps.'

'You don't have to hold a Party card.'

'Who said I had a Party card?' He dropped his knife and fork and held up his hands like a conjuror showing he didn't have anything up his sleeve.

'Joe it doesn't mean anything to me one way or the other. I have the greatest admiration for their zeal and efficiency. Sometimes I wish we had some party members in the Department.'

'George, you're the only person in the world I can talk to . . . You know there's so much gossip in the labor movement.'

'Give me another cigarette Joe.' She was not melting but interested, in spite of the physical repulsion, she was telling herself . . . How could she ever when there were men like Paul?. . . 'I haven't smoked in months,' she was telling him goodnaturedly, 'but your problems Joe call for tobacco.'

'Attagirl George. Have a heart.'

'Can't you just do what you think is right?'

He stared at her sullenly for a moment out of dull gray eyes. 'It ain't like back in Detroit. Here in Washington I've got a position in the labor movement, I mean nationally . . . They can make a back number out of me like so many others.'

Georgia mashed out her cigarette. It suddenly tasted sour in her mouth.

'Who can?'

'Believe you me the Party can.'

She drank up her coffee that had gotten cold, and looked around the restaurant. They were the last people left. A longfaced waiter was tidying up the next table. The red draperies in the windows had a dusty look.

'I don't think we can gain anything by going into the war either,' she said trying to think. 'Our job is at home and for the first time we've got a chance to do it.'

'Exactly,' said Joe as he spooned the last of his chocolate icecream into his mouth. 'The politburo figures the same thing . . . The pact will give them a chance to stay out and when the Nazis have worn themselves out fighting the world the revolutionary moment will come in Europe the way it did in 1918 . . . The only thing wrong with this picture is that Hitler's winning hands down and the workers are leaving the Party in droves. We sold 'em so thoroughly on antifascism that now they're oversold . . . Half the time I think I should go along with the workers and half the time I think I ought to stay with the Party.'

'If you had taken my advice you wouldn't have joined the Party in the first place.'

'I didn't for a long time.'

'Was it that Greta?'

'George it isn't like you to make catty remarks . . . It's not so easy to steer an independent course. There are plenty of guys who'd like my job . . . They can crucify me.'

Joe drank down his coffee and signalled the waiter. He paid his check with a ten dollar bill.

'We'd better move along,' said Georgia, 'before they sweep us out with the crumbs.'

'George it's done me good to see you,' Joe said as they walked towards the door. 'It hasn't been as bad as you expected, now has it?'

'But Joe I don't know how to run my own life much less to advise anybody else.'

'George would you like an organizing job? We need some bright girls.'

She surprised herself by bursting out laughing.

'I like it where I am.'

'Farm Economy?'

She nodded.

'It'll fold. Walker Watson's dreaming of higher things. All the man in the White House can think of is getting us into the war.'

They stood side by side on the empty sidewalk. Joe took a toothpick out of his breast pocket and began to pick his teeth.

'George,' he said haltingly, 'I've got to go to a little social gathering for five minutes just to stick my face in. You come too. Then I'll take you home.'

'Why Mr. Yerkes what an unexpected strain of gallantry.'

'I don't want to go either. I'd rather go home to bed. You don't have to wait for me. You can go home whenever you like. I just don't want to go alone. It's just two blocks along K Street. Sometimes you know the comrades they wonder if a guy don't turn up.'

Georgia started to say No but the thought of going home to Louise and her solitaire was so appalling that she finally said: 'All right have it your own way.'

'We'll walk,' said Joe cajolingly. 'You were always a great girl for walking.'

'It was Père's training,' said Georgia. 'Remember his peripatetic lectures?'

'My insteps ache to this day,' said Joe.

He stopped before an angular brick house behind a trodden dooryard. When a young mulatto in hornrimmed glasses wearing a light gray suit very tight at the waist opened the door Georgia thought he was the houseman but Joe introduced him as Mervyn Packett. Georgia shook a limp cold hand.

'Where's everybody Mervyn?' asked Joe.

'Out back playing poker,' said Mervyn arching his eyebrows. 'That's how they raise the cultural level of the masses.' He laughed behind his slim fingers.

He ushered them through a dark oldfashioned panelled library into a highceilinged room in the back of the house where a group of youngish men in their shirtsleeves sat with cards in their hands at a round table under an overhead light. A couple were nearly bald. Most of them wore glasses. Their faces had a pale sweaty look under the glare of the unshaded bulb. None of them looked up.

A squareish woman strode forward. She pushed a handful of short gray hair off her forehead before she stepped up to shake Georgia's hand. She wore a mannishly tailored dark green broadcloth suit. 'Of course you know Dr. Jane Sparling,' said Joe.

Dr. Sparling spoke without taking the long cigaretteholder out of the corner of her mouth. 'Georgia Washburn how do you do?' she said giving Georgia's hand a second hard squeeze. 'I heard about you out in Detroit. Weren't you on the Spanish Committee out there?'

Meanwhile two of the men at the table had grabbed Joe and pulled him down on the bench between them. 'Fresh meat . . . I know when he got paid,' somebody said. A chortle went round the table that died out as the cards were dealt.

'I hate cards,' Dr. Sparling said, 'even if they do give ten percent to Party work. Let's go into the other room and let our hair down . . . I'll get you a drink.'

'No thanks . . . I have to get to the office early.'

Georgia didn't much like the way Dr. Sparling seemed to take it for granted that they were old friends but as she was the only other woman there there was nothing to do but talk to her.

'Which is it?' asked Dr. Sparling looking up at her with a knowing fortuneteller's look. 'Labor? Agriculture? Not Commerce?'

'I'm in Farm Economy.'

Dr. Sparling grabbed her elbow and led her back into the library.

When the light was switched on Georgia found herself facing Mervyn Packett who was sitting in the windowseat beside a very younglooking white man with red hair and turnedup nose. They were talking in whispers with downcast eyes. Neither of them looked up.

'Excuse us boys,' shouted Dr. Sparling. 'They don't talk about anything but modern English poetry,' she whispered to Georgia. 'It may be revolutionary but it's certainly not for the masses. If there's anything that bores me more than cards it's modern poetry.'

She pointed to a red leather chair in front of the vacant fireplace which was littered with cigarette butts and told Georgia to sit down. Then she fetched herself a drink from a collection of bottles on the desk. 'Sure you won't have a drop?'

She squatted down in the identical chair opposite. 'This is a funny old place, superannuated I'd say . . . a friend of mine who's the daughter of a federal judge lends it to me for Party work just in summer while she's at Bar Harbor. Now let's see where were we?' Dr. Sparling set her drink on the floor beside her, brought a pencil and a little black book and a pair of tortoiseshell glasses out of her pocket and began asking Georgia questions in a routine businesslike way as if she were a patient. With a dreamlike feeling of lost willpower Georgia found herself sitting on the edge of her chair and answering.

'Now you must give me your address,' Dr. Sparling was saying, 'and phone number in case something interesting comes up. We have little meetings here, panel discussions, sometimes a stimulating speaker. I like to think of it as a public forum where questions of the day can be thrashed out.' She laughed her short brassy laugh. 'Farm Economy how interesting . . . of course you have Paul Graves there . . . What I don't know about Paul Graves. He went out to the Soviet Union,' an oily purr came into her voice as she pronounced the words, 'but since he came back he's succumbed to the social-fascist atmosphere of the New Deal. He went to the Soviet Union as a geneticist, I believe, learned everything there was to learn from the experimental stations there, was damn well paid for doing it and came back here and bit the hand that fed him. Those southerners are most of them fascists born and bred, lynchers at heart.'

Georgia was startled by the hard note of hatred that came into Dr.

Sparling's voice. She started to say something but the other woman paid no attention.

'Now what about Millard Carroll?' Dr. Sparling asked tapping her book with her pencil . . . 'Of course Walker Watson thinks he's in line for the presidential nomination but you know whos going to be President just as well as I do and his first act in his third term is going to be to involve us in the imperialist war . . . It's open and shut . . . but the vice-presidency is a different proposition. Walker Watson as Vice-President might be a useful man for the labor movement, that is if he doesn't succumb to the social-fascist atmosphere . . . Millard Carroll would be in line for the secretaryship . . . Georgia you ought to be able to tell me what kind of a man Millard Carroll is.'

Georgia felt herself getting very red. 'I only see him in the department. I never spoke to him in my life. He's very nice.'

'Nice,' said Dr. Sparling sarcastically. 'I suppose Paul Graves is nice too . . . My dear girl they are dirty fascists everyone of them. Does Paul ever take you to the Gulicks'?'

The spell suddenly broke inside Georgia's head. She got to her feet.

'I only see them at the office. I'm a very inconspicuous little researchworker,' she said. 'I'm afraid I have to go.'

Dr. Sparling jumped up and grabbed her hand. 'You mustn't mind me my dear . . . I'm just an old busybody.' She went on talking fast as she led Georgia to the front door. 'But the way people succumb to the social fascist atmosphere of this town even some of the true progressives . . .' she lowered her voice and shook her head like an old laundress gossiping over a back fence, Georgia was thinking. 'You ought to meet the Gulicks though. They have all kinds of interesting people at their house. Marice is an old crony of mine. I'll take you over some evening. Marice used to be a good radical but she's fallen for psychoanalysis, all that sort of thing, like any other silly rich woman.'

'Good night,' said Georgia breaking away from the grip of her strong hand at the door.

'We'll be seeing each other,' said Dr. Sparling laughing her brassy laugh. 'We'll meet again.'

Out on the street again she couldn't shake off the foolish feeling she had as if she'd let someone pick her pocket . . . Chattering like a jaybird, she kept telling herself. She walked out quiet familiar cosily lit Connecticut Avenue. In the apartment the lights were all out. The girls hadn't come home yet. Through the closed door she could hear Louise's light snore. She went into her tiny bedroom and without turning on the light tore off her clothes and slipped into her nightgown and into bed. 'Oh what a dreadful day,' she was saying to herself in a weak little voice. She buried her face in the pillow to keep from sobbing out loud.

The Ship of State

4

We sat round the table with the checked tablecloth in the frenchified ginmill on Third Avenue listening with chilly spines while our friend the painter from Paris
  told of the flight. It was like a Sunday in the Bois de Boulogne the day they have races at Longchamps or Enghien, he said or afterwards when the traffic's jammed on the Champs Elysées.
  All the way from Paris to the Spanish border,
  the shining great cars
  Hispanos, Dusenbergs, Isottas, Rolls Royces,
  the elegantly dressed women,
  the lunchbaskets full of truffles, pâté and cold duck cooked with oranges and champagne and armagnac,
  and the perfumes and the modish hats and the custombuilt roadsters and the limousines and here and there one of those big trucks they bring vegetables in from Normandy to the markets or wines to the warehouse and taxicabs and finally anything that had wheels. It was frightening
  the amount of money they had:
  tens of thousands of francs for a litre of gas, an omelet, a glass of

water; hundreds of thousands of francs . . .

Repairs were out of the question: a breakdown, a blowout or simply a puncture hup! you were out in the ditch.

The skies were cloudless and when they glistened with tiny specks in the blue like mica it was never our aviation. They didn't waste many bombs, a few practice runs over the target, machinegun practice, just to keep the traffic moving

all the way from Paris to the Spanish border.

Presidential Timber

THE PHLEGM RATTLED IN HERB SPOTSWOOD'S THROAT as he started to whisper into the microphone 'Though not very many people...' He honked and started afresh: 'Though not very many people speak of it openly, there is hardly a man or woman inside the Administration or out of it, on Capitol Hill or in the Executive Offices, from the Vice-President down to the lowest paid stenographer in the Bureau of Engraving and Printing, there is hardly a man or woman in Washington today who has not a certain question constantly on his mind . . . a teasing question . . . a question on which hopes fears and ambitions hang . . . a question . . .' His whisper had turned into a hiss. He was spitting all over the little bright microphone of the recording machine. He switched the thing off and jumped to his feet in a pet. 'Too singsong' he hissed to himself. 'Damn this phlegm.' He cleared his throat again and hurried into the bathroom to spray his nose with an atomizer. As he took in a deep breath of the vapor he caught a glimpse of his face in the mirror—the popeyed look of his bloodshot gray eyes behind the round glasses, the unshapely nose, the grizzly mustache, the too small chin. 'And I expect women to fall for that mug—you old fuddy duddy,' he whispered savagely at his image. The thought of age and obsolescence and death put him into a sudden panic. He could feel his heart start to pound.

To calm himself he began to walk up and down the hotel parlor with his hands thrust down into the pockets of his dressinggown. This wasn't the dressinggown he usually wore, he was thinking. Miss Albert must have sent the other one to the cleaner's. This was his black China-silk dressinggown he'd bought off an Armenian merchant in Geneva after an immense amount of haggling, an unusual extravagance for him. Of course he wouldn't have bought it at all if Jeannette hadn't been with him to tease him into it. She used to be always teasing him into spending money on himself. It was against the habit of a life-time. He was nervously clenching and unclenching his hands inside the pockets. In one pocket his fingers started playing with a little wad of something. He brought it out and dabbed at his runny nose with it. A frail ghost of the perfume she used, between lilac and lavender, brought Jeannette so close it was almost as if she were in the room. He unfolded the little handkerchief carefully and took off his glasses to bring the lace border up close to his nearsighted eyes. Of course it was Jeannette's. There was her tiny JM with a coronet over it in the corner. The perfume and the feel of the cambric and lace built up a memory of the pressure of her warm sweet woman's body through the negligée against his. 'Lonely that's what's the matter with me,' he said aloud and let himself drop so hard into the chair beside the microphone that the chair creaked, 'and old.'

He snatched up the yellow sheet and started to read again in the low urgent whisper that was his own particular invention:

'For the lack of an answer to that question false hopes are being raised in the breast of many a public servant and confusion and uncer-tainty are beginning to appear in many of the most important admin-istrative departments. Only one man in Washington or in the United States or in the entire world for that matter knows the answer to that question. That is the debonair gentleman who sits musingly smoking his cigarette out of an extralong holder in the Oval Room at the White House. He knows the answer but he sits and smokes and smiles . . .'

'Better run it off.' He got to his feet and adjusted the other arm on the record. Then he sat frowning as he listened . . . 'Though not many people speak of it openly there is hardly a man or woman inside the administration . . .' The telephone rang . . . 'or out of it, on Capitol Hill or in the executive office . . .' The telephone kept on ringing. 'Miss Albert,' he peevishly called. Of course there was no Miss Albert. She'd had to go home because her mother was sick. He switched the thing off and went to the telephone himself.

It was Ed James' velvety Louisiana voice asking him if he wouldn't come down to have a drink at the bar. No he couldn't, it was too near his broadcast time.

'I just saw Tyler,' said Ed.

'Is he with you?' A cold hand clutched at Herb's throat. He hated to have things upset him just before his broadcast.

'No Jerry Evans is with me.' Ed's voice was apologetic.

Herb remembered the big rich noisy redfaced Texan with a certain amount of pleasure and said to come up in fifteen minutes; he'd be having a cup of tea, he occasionally drank a cup of tea before the broadcast. He would order drinks. What would they like?

'We're drinking rye,' said Ed.

Herb muttered something about rye being heating but he could feel the stiffness melting out of his voice.

'It's all in the line of duty,' said Ed. 'All right Herb you polish off those few last golden words. Meanwhile we'll polish off a drink at the bar.'

Herb was in a fluster when he put the receiver down. He was telling himself his sudden streak of loneliness had made him do a foolish thing. He didn't want to talk about Tyler . . . poor Tyler, poor Tyler . . . He didn't want to listen to Jerry Evans whom he'd heard carrying on at the Gulicks'. There wouldn't be anything new. Entertaining was an effort without a woman. He'd be all in a fluster and breathless and make a mess of his broadcast. There wasn't even Miss Albert to sit there with her pretty hairdo and to put in demurely an occasional word. The parlor was full of litter. Unanswered fan mail was piled on the desk. His eyes ran over the open letters:

'Dear Mr. Spotswood: My sister and I are shutins . . .' No that was too silly. He clawed the letters all together and shoved them in the drawer. He dropped some and had to lean over to pick them up and that made his sinuses ache . . .

Dear Mr. Spotswood:

Your prowar propaganda is disgusting to any patriotic American. If you feel that way why don't you go join the British army?

With Miss Albert there with her precise humorous smile, it seemed rather fun answering and sorting the fan mail. Alone it was awful. He shut the drawer on the letters and called Room Service and ordered tea and two double ryes and gave the waiter a lecture about the importance of Apollinaris rather than club soda. He was all tidied up and fidgeting long before it was time for the men to come up. The room was stifling. He pulled up the venetian blinds in one window and leaned out over the boggy green of Rock Creek Park into the stagnant afternoon. He was trying to remember what Benjamin Franklin said about a man and a woman being like two sides of a pair of shears, one of them wasn't any good without the other. He walked over to the desk and noted down on the calendar B. Franklin: shears. He'd get Miss Albert to look it up when she came back.

'It's gracious of you to receive us Mr. Spotswood,' Jerry Evans said. 'I'm just an unsophisticated lumberjack an' Ed's been showin' me the town, so naturally we've taken the alcohol route. Ole backwoodsmen like me, we can't take civilization cold sober . . .'

As he moved talking round the room looking at the desk and the recording machine and examining the hotel pictures on the walls, his big frame and his big voice displaced so much air Herb felt pushed off into a corner.

Ed was saying in a shy sort of way that they had just come up a second to try to inveigle Herb into going to a party.

Herb said he didn't go to parties.

'Look here Herb,' said Jerry, 'you do just as you like. Ed's been roundin' up a few of the boys for me down at the Arlington. Just ask at the desk for Jerry Evans' party. Any time after seven-thirty . . . If you feel like droppin' in for a minute after you've finished your broadcast, we'll be just tickled to death. If it don't work out I'll have to have the pleasure some other time.'

The waiter came in with the tinkling tray of drinks. Herb busied himself with signing the check and seeing that the waiter poured the whiskey properly. No they didn't want Apollinaris they wanted plain water. Evans took his drink and went and stood by the window looking out over the steamy trees of the park. Herb poured himself a cup of tea. The smell of the tea filled his nostrils soothingly as he leaned over the cup. Ed was standing beside him.

'I ran into Tyler the other day on the street,' he said in his low friendly voice.

'In pretty bad shape?'

Ed nodded.

'I'm trying to get him to go to work for me. He'd be invaluable if he'd just keep away from this stuff.' Ed agitated the amber liquid in his glass. 'He said he was coming around to see you and I thought maybe you could urge him to take the job . . . He's always thought a lot of his old man.'

'I should hope he would come around to see me,' said Herb sharply.

'You know Tyler.'

'Poor boy I know him only too well.'

'He got a raw deal, a very raw deal.'

'I should think they'd aircondition these rooms,' Jerry roared from the window.

'They offered to but I've been afraid of it on account of my sinuses. I'm an old Washingtonian anyway, I'm used to this.'

'A cliffdweller eh?'

Jerry Evans turned and came towards him: 'Herb I want to put up to you the case of these poor damned oil men . . . I know from your broadcasts you are pretty much on the side of the gentleman in the White House but if you look into the facts I think you'll admit that he's made a mistake this time. Even Ed here is convinced an' he's certainly no tool of the predatory interests . . . Are you Ed?'

Herb took refuge at his desk. Jerry sat down in an easy chair facing him and threw his big leg over one of the arms and talked on and on. Herb managed to look attentive but his mind kept straying back to his broadcast. Way down inside him a complaining voice was giving him a good tongue-lashing for letting these men in. His hands began to collect the loose yellow sheets on the desk in front of him. He pulled off his glasses and peered nearsightedly for a clip to hold them together. Where the devil did Miss Albert keep the clips? He put on his glasses again and looked over towards Jerry Evans with a blankly smiling face. Suddenly he thought of the side drawers and began peeking in them furtively while his face kept its listening look. At last he found a box of clips and slipped one on to hold his sheets together.

Ed and Jerry were standing over him. 'Now we mustn't make you late for your broadcast,' Jerry was roaring with his big bull laugh. 'I'll continue the treatment later. If you don't mind we'll use your phone. Ed call up the doorman and tell him to get the car around . . . If you feel like it Herb we'll drop you at the studio . . . Now I want to say right here an' now that on your foreign policy I'm all for you. I think we've got to stop these damn dictators. On domestic issues you're all wet if you excuse my sayin' so but on foreign policy you are doin' a great job an' I think most folks down our way agree with you.'

'Thanks thanks,' said Herb and hurried into the bathroom to change into the fresh seersucker suit that was hanging on the back of the door.

Getting into the big white car beside Jerry Evans with his black briefcase under his arm he was fighting off the feeling that he'd forgotten something. He reached furtively through his pockets. He had his wallet and billfold, his fountain pen, his nose drops, his folded extra handkerchief. He had his wristwatch on. Every couple of minutes he stuck his arm out far in front of him so that he could see the time without taking off his glasses. Six-thirtyfive. Just forty minutes before broadcast time.

There was more traffic than usual. The streets smelled of scorched tires and soft tar and exhausts. He thought the car would never get around Dupont Circle. Fifteen minutes of seven. At last the car drew up to the curb. It was a relief to pull away from Jerry and Ed and their smell of cigarettes and whiskey and to step into the comparatively cool empty lobby of the office building. He was alone going up in the elevator. Thirteen minutes of seven. In the studio it was too cold. He began to think apprehensively of his sinuses. He responded to the lipstick smile that came to him from under the receptionist's pile of curled chestnut hair and hurried into the office they always kept clear for him. He spread his sheets out over the clean blue blotter. Page four was missing.

He broke out in a cold sweat under his collar. His glasses fogged so he couldn't see the time. He snatched them off and brought the wristwatch up close to his eyes. Ten minutes of seven. He shuffled tremulously to the door. 'Mr. Donnelly,' he called hoarsely down the hall.

'Don's on the air,' said a smoothvoiced young man who emerged from the next office. 'Is there anything I could do for you, Mr. Spotswood?'

'There certainly is. Page four of my broadcast has been left behind in my room at the hotel.'

'Couldn't you ad lib? You've got plenty of time to sketch it in.'

'Can't you send up a messenger?'

'Now let's just think a minute,' the young man said in a voice like the dripping of warm oil. They stood staring at each other. The young man tapped himself on his blond forehead with the flat of his hand. 'I'll call up the desk and ask them to send a bellboy down in a cab with it. Where would it be in the room?' Herb found himself stuttering that it must have fallen down behind the desk.

'A yellow sheet numbered four,' exclaimed the young man dramatically and shot back into his office. Herb could hear confidential purring of his voice over the telephone. In a moment he was back standing beside him and murmuring that they would get the lost sheet down right away. Meanwhile why didn't he sketch out a few words? The young man made writing motions with his fingers against the palm of his hand as if he were trying to communicate with a deaf person. Don would keep him covered on the time. Don was so good at that. Gently he pushed Herb back into his own office.

Herb sat down at his desk and breathlessly conned over the first three sheets. As he read the familiar sentences over he could hear his own voice whispering and hissing in his ears as he'd heard it over the recording machine.

He couldn't help looking too often at his wristwatch. One minute of seven. He tried to scribble words on a blank sheet. He couldn't think of anything. Seven-two, seven-six, seven-nine. He jumped to his feet and stood teetering over the desk.

Seven-ten. The blond young man was leading him down the hall past red and green lights over white enamelled doors. Somebody in uniform was trotting along beside him trying to press a sheet of yellow paper into his hand. It was page four. He didn't have time to thank the boy. Immediately he was sitting with ringing ears opposite Don Donnelly. Don smiled and winked at him. The 'on the air' sign lit up. Eyes stared at him through the glass pane.

Herb was breathing so hard he couldn't hear Don's suave introduction.

He was reading breathless: 'Though not very many people speak of it openly, there is hardly a man or woman inside the Administration or out of it . . .'

When he was through and they were off the air Don let his head drop back and yawned. 'Damn good Mr. Spotswood if you excuse my saying so.' He sighed at the ceiling. 'Hits 'em right where they live.'

Mr. Brackett with his hair over his ears came bustling in to meet them at the doorway. 'Masterly my dear sir masterly,' he chanted. 'Now if you have a moment there is just one thing I have been asked to take up with you.'

It was only when Herb was ready to leave the studio that he discovered he'd forgotten to wear his panama hat. Walking with a light step smiling out to the elevator in the reception hall he found himself face to face with Jean Darwin, all ivory and gold. She stretched her arms out of her fuzzy evening wrap and carefully turned her cool cheek for him to kiss.

'Herbert darling, you were wonderful.'

'Why Jean what a most pleasant surprise. What a becoming dress.'

'I've come to take you to the Arlington.'

Herb answered in a rather peevish tone that he was a little tired and planning to go home and lie down.

'Of course you must be . . . It's the best you've ever done . . . so mysterious.'

He added that he'd had an exhausting afternoon. He'd forgotten his hat.

'Herbert hat or no hat you've got to eat dinner some place.' She swept before him into the elevator. 'Jerry says you almost promised you'd come.'

He shook his head but he was smiling. He wasn't hungry he was insisting.

'We'll only stay a minute . . . Taxi!'

Before he knew it he was helping her into the cab and climbing in beside her. He began to tell her about Miss Albert's having to go home to her mother.

'Why don't I pinch hit for her?' Jean asked looking up at him sideways with her lips half parted.

'I thought you were off to Reno.'

'I've decided not to go.'

'What's Mack up to?' asked Herb, a little crudely he thought. Right away he wished he hadn't.

'He's saved me from making another terrible mistake. He's engaged to a tobacco heiress.'

'You're not going to divorce that fellow after all?' he asked in a slow fatherly tone. Since she was taking it this way he felt glad he had asked her.

'Reno's so dusty in the summer . . . It's merely a technicality. We've been divorced for years as far as anything that matters counts. They say it's lovely in the fall . . .' she said.

'Why Jean you poor child.'

She sniffed. 'There are things in this life . . .' she began but the doorman at the Arlington was already opening the taxi door.

'What time do you start work Herbert?' she asked briskly as she jumped out on the sunny pavement.

'I don't usually want Miss Albert till ten.'

'All right I'll be there. I'm prompt you know.'

She led him up the stairs to the mezzanine. They would be in one of the private ballrooms, it would be quite a party, Jerry Evans wasn't a man to do things by halves, she was explaining.

There was a crowd indeed. Herb followed Jean's white shoulder through the crush of men and women. There were bald heads, crew cuts, heads parted in the middle with patent leather hair, white heads with ducktails over the ears, curled and fluffed girls' heads blond and dark. An occasional army officer in suntans. Not many attractive women he commented to himself, never were in summer. In the middle of the long table against the wall a mound of caviar in a collossal bowl of ice stood among platters of canapés in starshapes and half-moons and hearts. Way in the back an orchestra was playing 'Begin the Beguine.' Waiters wove in and out with trays of manhattans and martinis. As Jerry Evans' red face with his big mouth opening to greet him advanced towards him other faces turned his way.

Herb couldn't help noticing the stir as people recognized him, the whispering of his name. Men and women were introduced to him on this side and that. He listened with his head on one side and a little indulgent smile playing under his mustache to compliments on his broadcasts. A woman asked him to autograph her fan.

To break it up he asked Jean to dance. She turned his way with a grateful smile. She was the prettiest girl there. After all he was the most distinguished person. Why shouldn't he be dancing with her? A little tinsel shower started swirling dizzily inside his head. He felt quite the dog. His dancing was stiff but he managed to keep his toes off her feet. She danced, so he whispered in her pretty pink ear, divinely.

Herb was breathless when the music stopped. Giggling cosily together they edged into a corner. Jo Powers, who looked New Yorky and chic in a slender black dress, brought him a plate of lobster New-burg. Jo and Jean were on either side of him eying each other with a familiar animosity that was almost friendly. The two prettiest girls at the party wanted to be seen with him and there he was standing between them. Stares and smiles converged on them. The gaspers closed in.

He listened still wearing his small tilted smile. 'Mr. Spotswood I've been wanting to ask you, where do you get so much information? . . . ' 'Your voice sounds quite different in everyday life.'. . . 'How do you get that tone Mr. Spotswood that makes it sound so interesting?' . . . 'It's funny I've never met you but I've heard your voice so much I feel as if you were an old friend of the family's' . . . 'How does it feel to be so well-known? It must be quite embarrassing . . . So many people you've never seen feel you are an intimate friend, Mr. Spotswood' . . . 'It's so hard to know what to think' . . . 'It's wonderful the feeling of confidence' . . . 'I find your broadcasts so comforting . . .'

Listening he had absentmindedly put a couple of forksful of the lobster Newburg in his mouth. No it didn't taste quite right, better not eat it, ptomaine, never safe to eat fish in these hotels, he was thinking. He bowed himself out of the circle of women and held his free hand out towards Jo Powers. 'Let's dance,' he whispered.

As they edged their way through the crowd he managed to poke his plate between the backs of talking couples onto the corner of a flable. 'I'd never thought of you as a dancing man,' Jo was saying in her friendly contralto. She danced even more lightly than Jean.

'I'm not. I haven't danced for years.' He was already out of breath. 'Not since Geneva . . . We went out to a fête champêtre and danced oldfashioned waltzes on the grass.'

Thoughts of Jeannette rose in his mind. He wished Jeannette could see him now. It would be awkward because she was always so jealous he told himself. He missed Jeannette but she was better off in Geneva. Too European ever to get used to American ways.

'Do tell me about it,' Jo Powers was dreamily murmuring.

Her head was on his shoulder. Her eyes were almost closed.

'We had to hop,' he panted. 'It was most exhausting. We got awfully hot and went and sat under the grape arbor and talked about Voltaire.'

'Sounds like fun. Isn't it awful I've never been abroad and now it's all being destroyed.'

They bumped into another couple. Herb smiled apologies. He took the opportunity to draw over to the wall. 'Switzerland will stay neutral,' he said in his severe professional tone as soon as he'd caught his breath. 'Switzerland will be the only safe place in Europe.' Then he added as an afterthought: 'I suppose it's safer to make no prognostications at this stage. You can't tell what that madman will do.'

'You've got to,' declaimed Jo Powers. 'It's your business Mr. Spotswood. The American people have got to be told what to think. If you don't tell them the isolationists will have it all their own way.'

The music had stopped. People trouped towards the drinks and the food. Herb felt shooting pains in his instep. He felt himself frowning and looked up at Jo Powers who was taller than he was and smiled into her face.

Jean was standing beside them, with her cool executive air. 'Herbert I know nobody's gotten you a drink.' A tall young man had carried off Jo Powers.

'No Jean I don't want anything,' said Herb dropping back into the cosy confidential tone. 'Maybe if there were a little white wine and soda. It's about time for me to go home . . .'

'I'll get it for you.' She gave him an intimate nudge. He followed her to the end of the long table where they found Ed James pouring himself a stiff whiskey.

'Herb you are just the man I wanted to see. A couple of us are going over to the Secretary's apartment . . . just for a minute . . . He doesn't feel like coming over but he said he'd like some company. It might be interesting.' He drank off his whiskey. 'Let's make ourselves scarce.'

Herb found his drink too cold and set it down. Jean slipped her arm in his. She had evidently decided to come along.

Down in the lobby they stood near the door waiting. Every time the revolving door turned a steamy blast of heat came in off the street. Through the glass Herb caught a glimpse of the long white Evans car coming to a stop at the curb. The doorman had the rear door open and was expectantly looking his way.

As he turned back to see if Jerry Evans were coming Herb happened to glance into the men's bar. A man sat alone at a table opposite the door with his chin sunk into his chest. The face had a sodden aging look, but it couldn't be anybody else but Tyler. The black hair was turning gray. It was Tyler of course, drunk, his son Tyler who sat there swaying with his hand round the glass. Thank God he didn't look up. Any other time, not right now, not tonight, he was too tired tonight, Herb said fast to himself. He turned his back and started for the revolving door.

'Suppose we go sit in the car,' he whispered firmly to Jean . . . 'or the doorman will send it away.'

Ed followed them, laughing. 'Not Jerry Evans' car . . . Nobody ever sends that man's car away.'

Herb was careful to sit in the back seat beside Jean. As they were settling themselves Jerry came along and handed Jo Powers in on the other side of Herb. Jerry and Ed sat on the folding seats.

Jerry was beginning to feel his drinks. 'He's a great American,' he bawled. 'I'm going to tell him he's a great American. Ed you smoke him out. Has he got the green light from Mr. Big or hasn't he?'

Ed walked over to the desk in the red and gold lobby of the apartment house to announce them. Nobody spoke going up. Jerry was breathing hard. Herb looked up at the heavy wreaths of fake gilt carving round the walls of the elevator thinking how tasteless these new Washington buildings were. Jeannette would be making one of the little funny fishfaces she made when she didn't like the looks of something.

When Ed rang Walker Watson opened the walnut door for them himself.

'Howdy folks,' he said. 'It was certainly nice of you . . . I'm all alone tonight.'

'The party's running on its own steam, Walker,' said Jerry. 'They don't need us. We've come to salute a great American.'

There was a sullen determined look on Walker Watson's long face. The heavy pouches under his eyes had a stained look as if he'd been crying. He looked hard and unsmilingly at Jerry. 'I'm afraid there's nothing in the house but cocacola,' he said.

'These boys and girls are drunk,' said Jerry. 'All I want's a glass of branch water, plain old branch water with a little ice in it . . .' They trooped through red velvet curtains into a big livingroom with brown leather chairs. There was a a moosehead over the gothic fireplace.

The telephone was ringing in a study off the big room.

'Excuse me, folks. My secretary's gone home.'

The girls dropped into the big chairs on either side and Jerry stood on the polar bear rug looking up belligerently at the moosehead. While Ed read the titles of the neatly arranged sets of books on the wall, Herb sat down by the table and started to read a volume in a black cover called *Rosicrucian Brotherhood* that lay open under a lamp with a heavily fringed salmoncolored shade. His eyes followed the lines of print but he couldn't help listening to what Walker Watson was saying over the telephone.

'But Joe,' he was arguing with somebody at the other end of the line. 'Number seven is bound to win . . . no . . . not to place to win . . . I don't care how many hot tips you've got . . . It's a mathematical certainty . . . You know that stuff don't mean anything . . . Nobody knows less than the handlers . . . If the stableboys knew anything they would all be millionaires already . . . No I want you to slap a couple of grand right on his nose for me . . . I went over the figures with our friend this afternoon . . . It's a mathematical certainty . . . Are you sure you've got the code numbers right? This time they read from the bottom up . . . I'll get a check to you about that other matter by the first of next week . . . It turned out that there was an error in the figures used to form the square . . . I discovered it myself and pointed it out to our friend and she agreed with me . . . That's why you've got to be sure to get it right this time . . . No . . . no . . . no . . . I'm interested in this as an experiment . . . all right have it your own way . . . as a psychic experiment . . . the other check'll go to you airmail the first of the week . . . No you're not getting out on any limb . . . Of course . . . You know how much I think of you . . . Well the confidence has got to be mutual . . . don't get me wrong . . . all right Joe.'

The others were chatting. In spite of himself Herb was listening so hard he thought his ears must be stretching. When he heard Walker Watson's heavy tread coming back from the telephone he felt suddenly guilty. He started to read. Walker Watson stopped behind him and looked down over his shoulder at the book.

'Do you think there's anything in it?' he asked in an eager voice.

'It's not a matter I'm really up on,' said Herb as he got to his feet.

'You read as if you were interested.'

'It's a subject . . .' started Herb slowly but Walker Watson was already across the room asking the girls to help him get some soft drinks out of the icebox. They trotted happily out after him while the men stood looking at each other in front of the fireplace without being able to think of anything to say. The big room was very quiet. It seemed an age before Jean came back with a tray of glasses. A moment later Jo Powers and Walker Watson followed. He was smiling. She held out a tray of cookies and showed all her teeth as she laughed. Walker Watson explained in his glum drawl that the young lady from New York was criticizing his cookies. Way out there in the sticks where he was raised, he added, cookies were considered a treat.

From his station by the table Herb noticed the quick look Jean shot at the two of them as they stood side by side at the end of the room. Old boy, he told himself, you can't compete with presidential timber. He was beginning to feel sleepy.

Jerry's face was crimson but he looked quite sober now, standing with his bulky shoulders squared against the mantel. He took a sip out of his glass of water and set it down behind him. 'Walker,' he asked, 'what do you think about the case of these poor damned oil men?'

Walker Watson laughed gruffly. 'I was waiting for that one Jerry . . . As I was saying the other day mistakes can happen in the best regulated families.' He paused and held up his glass against the light. 'You know just as well as I do that we have no jurisdiction. It's strictly a D. of J. matter . . .' He waited as if expecting Jerry to say something. He took a swallow and went on. 'Of course speaking as a private citizen I believe that rich and poor must find equality before the law. You big boys have had things all your own way. Government must look out for the little people too. I take my stand with the common man.'

'Down my way Walker we think we're just as common as the rest of 'em, but we like to see fair play.'

Walker didn't answer.

'What's eating Jerry up,' drawled Ed soothingly when the silence began to sag, 'is that he doesn't think they are getting equality before the law.'

The girls were quietly sipping their drinks. Walker Watson stood looking down into the artificial logs in the fireplace. Jerry was staring him in the face breathing hard. 'Democracy must establish ever broader and broader bases of equality,' Walker Watson mumbled without looking up. 'Maybe right now we need more economic equality.'

'Down my way we need a man in the White House we can trust to treat us fair an' square,' Jerry was saying slowly, trying to look him in the eyes. 'Around the seventeenth of July there's goin' to be a little gatherin' in Chicago . . .'

There was another long silence. 'Let's go ahead with the job and not worry about Chicago,' said Walker angrily swinging around and walking over to the table. He picked up the book in the black cover closed it and slipped it into a drawer.

'The collapse of the whole framework of civilization in Europe . . .' Herb began.

'We're boring these young ladies,' said Walker Watson in a different livelier tone. 'Has anybody seen any ballgames?'

'I see 'em all,' said Jo Powers. 'I'm rooting for the Cardinals.'

Walker Watson walked over towards her smiling. 'I thought you were a New Yorker,' he said and leaned on the back of her chair.

She tossed her head and showed her teeth and laughed. 'Nobody was born in New York. I'm a middlewesterner at heart.'

'Out there,' said Walker Watson languidly, 'that's where people still have hearts in their breasts.'

Nobody said anything for a long time. Herb couldn't help yawning. It was time he went to bed. He cocked an eye at his wristwatch. He could hear it ticking the room was so quiet.

'Well I better go back to my guests,' said Jerry suddenly in a brisk voice. 'They'll be gettin' off the reservation if I don't go back an' round 'em up.'

Herb hurried to fetch Jean's wrap from the hall. When he got back he found Jean and Jo chattering about the theatre. Ed stood on the hearth benevolently puffing on a cigarette. Jerry and Walker Watson had disappeared into some other room. The girls pulled themselves out of their deep chairs and started towards the hall. Ed and Herb followed them and they all four stood there fidgeting beside a marble table that had a blue Chinese bowl full of visiting cards on it. Jean was lazily moving her hand among the visiting cards looking over the names. Nobody had anything to say.

At last they heard voices coming through the livingroom: 'Well Walker,' Jerry was roaring, 'you're still the Great American for me but a man's got to make up his mind.'

'I'm not the only one,' said Watson with a new frank smile. His lopsided smile was turned to each of them in turn as if asking for their indulgence. When they said goodby his face had settled back into its expression of harrassment and loneliness.

Going down in the elevator they were all looking at Jerry but he kept his big lips tightly clamped over his teeth. The car drove up under the awning.

Herb whispered to Jean that he was going home; wouldn't she let him drop her at her hotel? 'Let's walk a block,' she whispered back. Herb was amazed at the light bounce his heart gave in his chest. They said goodnight all around. The long white car drove off.

'That's what they call a dry run,' Jean murmured yawning and gave Herb an intimate confidential small smile.

'Have you ever done any political comment Jean?'

'Do you think I should?'

'You would be good at it. You always keep track of what's going on.'

'But I can't write . . . If I had a gift like yours . . .'

They walked slowly along under the broad lightfringed leaves of the trees. 'My she sure was throwing herself at *his* head,' Jean said.

'Who at whose?'

'The Powers girl at Walker Watson's of course.'

Herb said he supposed that kind of man aroused the maternal instinct in women. Did he think so she asked giggling. At the next corner she began to whimper that her feet hurt her and she wanted a cab.

When at last a cab came by she gave him a smiling look and asked as he handed her in, 'Herbert do I arouse your paternal instinct?'

After he'd given the driver the address he deliberately turned around and kissed her on the mouth. She kissed him back. He began to feel quite giddy and breathless. She pushed him gently away. 'Herbert not in the taxi, we're not bobbysoxers,' she said breaking out into her little giggle again.

'You quite go to my head,' he said limply.

'I'm happy tonight,' she cried out recklessly. 'I'm happier than I've been in months. I so need somebody to take care of me to see that I don't do silly things . . . I almost made a terrible mistake.'

'Mack?'

'Let's not talk about that.'

Too soon the cab drove up to her hotel. She shook her finger at him smiling when he tried to kiss her again.

'You are serious about tomorrow?'

She nodded, said goodnight very gently and was gone.

When he climbed back into the cab he let himself fall limply into the seat and all the way out to the Boardman Park drifted in a revery.

Maybe he could be happy. It was so long since he'd been really happy with a home, and children. Why not, lots of people had children after they were sixty. He was well off now. At last he was making enough money to pay for it. He was young for his age, so many people told him that. When they reached the hotel he gave the taximan an extra twentyfive cent tip.

The clerk at the desk handed him a telegram with his key and a number of phone messages.

Going up in the elevator, he tore open the yellow envelope.

CHER AMI AM IN LISBON AWAITING PASSAGE VISAS FOR AMERICA EUROPE NO LONGER POSSIBLE MUCH TO TELL PLEASE CABLE TEMPORARY LOAN ONE THOUSAND DOLLARS ETERNALLY JEANNETTE VON HILDESHEIM

THE SHIP OF STATE

5

*W*e read. We listen. It's so hard to know. Going down to work
we study the faces behind their newspapers. It's so hard to
know, depends on the newspaper you read, the radio program you
listen to, what the man said you met at a bar.

All a man knows is his work and three meals a day and the faces
on the subway or bus and his family and a few friends and the parent
teachers association and a church maybe or the foursome at golf.
A man doesn't see anything for himself. He reads. He hears words.
How can he judge which words
    in the speeches the columns the captions of pictures
    are false and which are true?
    Even pictures lie.
    But dimly
    behind the turmoil of remonstrant voices, behind the columns of
admonishing print we can discern the outline of what is:
    across the ruined world the oppressor's victory; the policeman's
knock on the door after midnight, the secret agent demanding your
papers, the search, the spilt out drawers, the overturned trunks,
pathetic heirlooms mashed under the officer's boots;

—barbed wire is made to keep cattle in pasture—

the pale files of arrested persons marched to the station, the hostages clubbed into cellars, the fathers pulled away from the mothers, the tiny lost children, the bedraggled companies locked into freightcars, no food, no water, floor filthy with excrement, the sealed trains, full of dying and dead rumbling away into exile, isolators, extermination camps

—freightcars are made to carry goods to market—

the rediscovery of torture, the infliction of pain an instrument of national policy, murder become one of the industrial arts, the infliction of elaborate agonies part of the science of statecraft

—a government is made to promote the happiness of its citizens.

American History

MILLARD STOOD with his hands clenched behind his back and his shoulders to the livingroom mantel. The boys lolled on two chairs facing him. Joel's lower lip stuck out and he kept reaching down to fidget with a broken lace on his sneakers. Lucius' eyes were big and dark. He wrinkled up his nose now and then like a rabbit. Millard looked from one tanned face to the other trying to find words that would sink in.

'Lucius you don't have to make those silly faces . . . You sit up straight both of you and listen to what I've got to say. Joel you don't have to bite your nails either . . . You'd think this was a kindergarten.' His voice surprised his own ears it was so harsh. 'You boys go and pick a day when your mother's in bed with the grippe and I'm almost crazy with press of work at the office to sneak off with the car and take a bunch of toughies out riding.'

'They were all right girls, honest Dad.' Joel was talking low with his eyes fixed on his dirty sneakers.

'You know perfectly well you don't have a license. Driving without a license is a very serious offence.'

Lucius mumbled that they'd just wanted to take them to Glen

Echo, they said they'd never seen Glen Echo. Joel interrupted hoarsely he didn't know Dad wanted the car. He thought they'd be back before anybody needed the car. Millard felt the anger going to his head. He snarled at them to get up out of those chairs and added that it was lucky they didn't both get themselves killed. Lucius jumped to his feet and looked him in the eye with that straight look Millard had always liked and said honest Dad that Jo was driving awful careful.

'Then why did you have to get yourselves arrested?'

'It was a mean cop. I think he'd been drinkin'' Joel said. 'The light changed when I was in the middle of the street. He didn't like our gigglin' and carryin' on.'

Millard came back in a sarcastic tone he bet they were carrying on. He thought the boys had more sense and more consideration. They knew how hostile the press was to the Administration, always ready to make a mountain out of a molehill. Well they'd gotten themselves some nice free publicity and their father had had to waste a whole afternoon right at his busiest time getting his little pair of birdbrains out of the hoosegow.

'Dad, it was the meanest cop I ever saw,' Joel explained soberly. 'He tried to make out we'd stolen the car.'

Why did they have to sass him then? Lucius looked solemnly up into his face. Honest Dad all they'd done was ask the cop to moderate his language because there were ladies present, he explained with a righteous air that Millard couldn't help thinking he would have found funny at any other time.

'A carload of giggling bobbysoxers. I don't blame him for losing his temper . . . Well you might very well have gone to jail for six months . . . I hope you understand that.'

Joel said he'd told the cop his dad was in government and he oughtn't to treat them like that. It wouldn't have happened back home, echoed Lucius beginning to whine. Millard laid down the law: well that was the last time either of them would get to drive the car this summer.

Lucile came running downstairs in her silk dressinggown with little pink flowers all over it. 'Is the lecture over?' she asked breezily.

'Lou I thought you were going to stay in bed this morning.'

'I'm cured.' She laughed. Her voice was still hoarse. 'Now I want you two sheiks to understand I'm just as mad at you as your dad is. I could turn you both over and spank you.'

The boys moved over towards her both talking at once asking how they were going to get home if Dad wouldn't let them drive the car. Millard stood in front of the fireplace with his feet wide apart feeling for a moment that they were all against him, but he wasn't angry any more now that Lucile was there. He appealed to her: 'How am I going to make this pair of birdbrains understand they can't do things like that?'

Well it was no use letting breakfast get cold, said Lucile. She looked the boys up and down with her affectionate critical look. 'I don't believe you've even washed your faces. You boys go up and come down to breakfast looking like gentlemen.' They stamped off glumly up the stairs. 'What a pair of awful louts.' She burst out laughing. 'And Oz you looked right funny holding your kangaroo court.'

'You didn't need to come in laughing Lou,' Millard said bitterly. 'Everything I say goes in one ear and out the other as it is.'

Lucile went to him and caught him by the ears and looked him in the face with the same affectionate critical look as if he were just another of her children. Then she gave him a little kiss on the mouth and said, 'Oz you're worrying too much . . . Worry never helped. Why don't you take a week off and drive us home and come back on the plane. We'd have the trip and get the boys in hand again. They have to be trained every minute just like a couple of pups.'

He followed her glumly into the diningroom mumbling that he had to have a showdown with Walker about getting the appropriation through, if he went away now he'd lose all the work he'd put in on the agency. They sat down at opposite ends of the table. Lucile poured the coffee. She wouldn't go home this summer at all she was saying if Dad weren't so poorly. Anyway Washington wasn't any place for the boys. Millard had hardly taken a bite of hot biscuit before he heard the phone ringing. The colored girl came in to say it was Judge Oppenheim on the phone.

'Good morning Millard,' came the subtly enunciating classroom voice. 'I thought I might catch you before you left the house. How's

Mike? Entertaining the congressmen eh? So Marice says she's running a country club. I'm sure she does it very well. Our good friend Mike in spite of or perhaps because of his academic background has the faculty of making the most various kind of people feel relaxed. He even gets along with the organization men . . . Maybe it's his stutter . . . Something childlike about him. It's a gift. If only he doesn't get ambitious. This is the summer when we're going to have trouble with ambitions. I never saw so many people who wanted to be President. I'm telling them all to go fishing and forget it. You keep hold of Mike, Millard. We all want to see as much of him as we can. We don't want the Secretary to get to monopolizing him for his private purposes. Mike's really a distinguished economist. His mind has distinction. Have you noticed the great improvement in the Secretary's speeches since Mike's been polishing them? Nevertheless I doubt if any of us want Mike to hitch his wagon permanently to that star. He's too valuable as a catalyst where he is. We tend to have too many stars and too few catalysts . . . And how's Lucile? Give her a good hug for me. She's a very lovely girl. Where would any of us be without our wives? Mrs. Oppenheim and I are off to Maine in a couple of days. It's really to say goodby I called up and to wish you both a pleasant summer.'

Frowning Millard walked back to the diningroom.

'Boys not down yet,' he growled in a tone he knew was unpleasant. 'Now Lucile I don't want you to let them get around you. You can tell them from me that if this sort of thing goes on I'm going to send them to a good tough military school in the fall. If we can't give them the proper discipline we've got to find somebody who can.'

'Oz you sit down and eat your breakfast quietly.'

'No it's too late.' He drank down a cup of tepid coffee. 'I've got to go to the office . . . What are we doing about dinner tonight?'

'We were going to the Dillings but it's off . . . I'll pack up and we'll have a quiet little bite at home.'

Millard said sharply she could expect him when she saw him and without kissing her snatched up his panama hat and made for the door. Outside the sun was already hot. He was sweating by the time he picked up a cab at the corner of Pennsylvania Avenue. Driving into Washington he sat on the edge of his seat clenching and unclenching his fists. He felt aghast at himself for leaving Lucile like that. That wasn't the way he acted. Hard stereotypes of worry went round and round in his head like figures on a dial.

Walking into his office he could hardly manage to answer Louise Aldershot's possessive good morning smile. 'Louise,' he said in a tense voice, 'tell the girl to get me the house.' He snatched up the phone on his desk. 'I want to speak to Mrs. Carroll . . . Lou honey you didn't pay attention to me this morning did you? I'm kind of out of sorts . . . Don't you go do too much now packing.' Her voice sounded hoarser than ever. 'I'll be fine when I get out of this town.' Her voice croaked weakly in his ear. 'I don't think this town agrees with us so well . . . The boys came down and found me crying into my java. Wasn't that silly? Oz they may not have shown it but they feel awful . . .'

'Well I'll be in about seven . . . You make them do all the work.'

He'd hardly put his receiver down before the buzzer on his desk was sounding.

'Mr. Carroll could you speak to Mr. Graves?'

'Millard.' Paul's hardpitched tarheel voice sounded strained. 'Have you got a minute? In fact I need an hour. Things are going to hell in a hack around here.'

'All right Paul just let me straighten out my calendar a little.'

'Millard I've got things that can't wait.'

'All right Paul I'll call you back.'

Louise was standing in the usual place at the righthand corner of the desk with a stack of opened letters. He grinned up at her.

'Paul Graves is climbing up the walls,' he said. 'Try to find me a halfhour for him and call Miss Jones to see if the Secretary's got any time. I can't see that we've got anything ready for the house committee next week.'

He picked up the telephone. 'See if you can get me Mr. Gulick.'

'Mr. Gulick's not in his office sir. Shall I call you when he comes in?'

What the hell's he doing out of his office? Millard muttered to himself. He let his eyes drop to the neat stacks of letters Louise had arranged on the desk in front of him but instead of reading them he started making doodles on a pad. As the morning wore along and minor questions came up that were easy to decide, he began to feel himself drifting cosily again on the current of the familiar office routine. The harshly clicking dial of worry in his head faded away.

At lunchtime he went into the Secretary's cool office panelled in dark wood to eat a sandwich with him. In his hand he had a sheaf of papers to go over.

Walker Watson sat stooped over his desk in the blueish northern light that washed in through the high windows. On a tray in front of him was a bottle of buttermilk and a bowl of shredded wheat. 'Millard I got you a couple of ham sandwiches and a glass of buttermilk . . . you like buttermilk don't you? I hope that'll handle you. I can't seem to get anything to digest any more. This won't be a proper lunch for a big healthy farmer like you.'

Millard sat down to his tray on the opposite side of the desk. He tried to put a little cheer into his voice: 'But tell me Walker are you taking proper care of yourself? We're going to need you in good shape to dance the dance of the seven veils before Congress next week.'

Walker Watson showed his yellow teeth. 'As if I didn't have anything better to do than answer foolish questions. You'll have all the data on agricultural wages? That's where the shoe pinches.' He yawned. 'By the way, Millard, where's a good place to take a fishing trip? The doctor tells me I ought to go fishing.'

'When's that? After the convention?'

'I might even go next week.'

Millard clenched his teeth tight together as he poured the buttermilk from the bottle into the glass. 'I don't know. The only fishing I've ever done was out on the Gulf,' he said in an uninterested tone.

Walker Watson had been fumbling in the drawer of his desk. He brought out a yellow sheet typewritten in purple ink. 'Here Millard I want you to read this. You were instrumental in bringing us together. I mean in this particular capacity . . . so I thought you might be interested.'

Millard felt his brows knitting as he read. He was trying to keep from looking too impatient.

CONFIDENTIAL REPORT by *Horace Holworthy*, read the heading:
Graphology Personal Efficiency Vocational Counsel

This writer is well endowed . . . fine organic quality and brain structure . . . evidence of a well trained mind . . . flashes of intuition . . . warm personal sympathies . . . lack of restraints and inhibitions . . . make him a supremely good mixer. Mind ruled but perhaps insufficiently so . . . Clever versatile and resourceful . . .

Millard looked up. 'Who is it?' he asked.
'Guess,' said Walker. Millard read on.

May begin many diversified tasks and not have time to finish any of them properly . . . may be given too many responsibilities by those in authority . . . inattentive to detail . . . not entirely free from shallow vanity or occasional cheap showoff dramatics . . .

Millard began to laugh. 'Mike Gulick?' he asked.
'Right in the bull's eye,' said Walker. He took the yellow sheet back from Millard and put it carefully in the drawer of his desk. Then he locked the drawer with a small key and put the key in a little change purse which he slipped into his pocket. 'Proves there's something in it. I understand that many important business firms now get graphologists to read the handwriting of their employees . . . I've only tried a few but I've found them interesting. There are more things in heaven and earth . . . Millard you know my motto.'

Millard had a mind to ask if his handwriting had been sent to Horace Holworthy but he choked down the rest of his sandwich in silence. Still chewing he began to sort out his papers. 'Walker suppose we take a look at this stuff. This outlines the needs and prospects of the agency for the coming year.'

Walker wasn't listening. He was looking up with his bright sudden smile at someone who was coming in the door behind Millard's back. 'Howdy George. Howdy Mike,' he said. Telling himself not to lose his temper Millard got to his feet. George and Mike looked as if they'd had drinks with their lunch. They were all over smiles. As he walked towards the desk across the oriental carpet George Dilling was declaiming in a voice that filled the lofty office that a hundred and fifty thousand farmers were ready to back Walker Watson to the hilt. All he had to do was give the word. His locals were ready to pass resolutions, to call special meetings, to start working on the delegates. Mike could line up labor. This would be the alliance between labor and the working farmer that they had so long been dreaming of. This would be the beginning of a real progressive movement inside the Democratic Party that would capture the party and make America over.

Listening to his booming voice Millard couldn't help feeling around him the reverberating cavern of a convention hall, the blur of faces under spotlights streaked with smoke, hearing the roar of the keynoter leaning into a row of microphones. He turned to look at the Secretary.

Lips trembling a little Walker sat hunched over his desk with his eyes cast down into his halfdrunk glass of buttermilk. Mike had stepped up and put an arm round Millard's shoulder. 'Millard,' he whispered soothingly, 'it's wonderful.' His hand gently kneaded the muscle of Millard's arm. 'We'll capture the party for liberalism.'

Millard gently extricated himself from Mike's hug and leaned over to collect his papers.

'Leave those with me,' said Walker Watson. 'I'm leaving the office early. I'm taking a young lady to dinner at 1600 Pennsylvania Avenue tonight and I'll find an opportunity to put it up to him . . . Squarely, squarely. It's time for a showdown . . .' A sullen whine had come into his low voice. 'I won't be treated like this. He owes his friends a decision.'

'Well I've got to get back to my office,' said Millard. 'My wild men are climbing up the walls.'

'Millard come around to the apartment when you get through here,' Walker said. 'I'll be taking a little rest. We can go over this quietly.'

'In my opinion,' George Dilling was saying, 'this is the most crucial year in American history. The New Deal is in danger from triumphant fascism abroad and from reaction at home. We must pick new leaders and reform the liberal ranks. The New Deal Administration has given us a foundation to build on. Now is the time to pry loose from the Bourbons and to make the Democratic Party the party of the working farmer and the worker in office and factory. Sooner or later the dictators are going to attack this country because it is the last refuge of freedom. Our best defense will be a really working social democracy at home.'

'All right Walker I'll be there,' said Millard from the door. He nodded silently to Mike and George and walked back slowly to his office. There he found Paul Graves striding up and down with his elastic uneasy stride.

'I've been here waiting for thirtyfive minutes.' He gave Millard one of his black angry glares. 'Millard you know I don't mind personally, but I look at it this way. We have been hired to do a job . . .'

'Don't say it,' said Millard with a bitter laugh. 'Sometimes it looks as if we were here to provide window dressing.'

'Millard I know you're here to do a job,' interrupted Paul.

'Now Paul you just hold your horses and sit down and tell me what the trouble is.'

Paul dropped into the chair on the other side of the desk and stuck out his long legs and began fishing papers out of his briefcase. Immediately they forgot themselves in the details of the work. An hour went by. Louise started tiptoeing in to lay little notes on the corner of the desk to remind Millard of other appointments. Paul went away smiling. Another man came in. The afternoon slid along. It was five-thirty before Millard signed the last of the day's letters and pulled away from his desk.

Millard had walked over to the spot in front of the building where he usually parked his car before he remembered he'd left it home for Lucile to use. The afternoon was overcast. A bank of clouds had settled down in a soft lid over the broad green lawns and the simmering trees of the Mall and the barricade of great gray familiar façades of government buildings opposite. The top of the Monument was lost in a fringe of haze. By the time he managed to hail a cab at the corner of Constitution Avenue his shirt was clinging to his back. First he thought he'd go home to take a shower but he changed his mind and told the driver to take him straight to Walker Watson's apartment house. It didn't matter how tired he was. He was here to do a job. He felt so distraught he couldn't remember the points he wanted to impress on Walker's mind that would explain the need for a bigger appropriation to the committee. Nothing seemed to stay in his head any more. He leaned back against the seat and closed his eyes and tried to rest.

Stepping out of the elevator Millard saw that the apartment door was ajar. When he pushed on it the door opened wide and he found himself face to face with Simon, Walker's elderly Negro chauffeur. Simon blinked at him for a moment. Then he said in his undertaker's voice, 'Come right on in Mr. Carroll, you're expected. Mistah Walker's layin' down. He got de cramps.' Millard walked on into the living room. The afternoon was so dark the big lamp on the table was lit. George Dilling and Mike Gulick sat on either side of it leaning their heads together over some notes under the salmoncolored fringe. As their heads turned simultaneously towards Millard's step, they looked like conspirators in a melodrama. 'We're p-p-planning Walker's fishing trip,' Mike cheerfully stuttered.

'It occurred to me he'd better make a couple of speeches on the way out,' said George. 'He'll be out in my territory. I'll introduce him to the working farmers. They'll think he's great.'

'Where's Walker?' Millard asked coldly.

'Taking a little rest before going out to dinner,' said George. 'We'd better not disturb him.'

At that moment Jo Powers appeared in the doorway opposite the fireplace. She wore a silver lamé evening dress and had a spangled red rose in her hair. In her hands she carried a red rubber hotwater bottle wrapped in a towel.

'Come on in Mr. Carroll,' she said in her throaty whisper. 'Walker wants to see you before he gets dressed. He's lying down a minute. He said he knew you wouldn't mind.' She gave him a warm sideways confidential look out of her dark eyes as she led him down the passage. 'He's taking me to dinner at the White House for the first time and I'm scared to death he's going to get sick and we won't be able to go. We must all work to get him out of Washington and get him a good rest this summer.' There was a flash of red fingernails as she knocked on a door at the end of the hall. 'Dear may Mr. Carroll come in?' she called.

A sort of groan answered and she pushed open the door. Walker was lying dressed in a blue and whitestriped dressinggown on the bed in a big untidy bedroom. His long gnarled face looked green in the cold light that came in from the window. Outside the rain had begun. Silvery perpendicular streaks shimmered across the open window. The room was filled with the low rattle of the rain and a gurgle of full gutters. Millard glanced back from the window at Walker in time to catch the gleam of a lopsided invalid's smile.

Jo had walked over to the bed and Walker had snatched the hot-water bottle from her and pressed it against his middle. 'There there,' he panted, 'that's better.'

'It's raining,' Jo Powers whined in a voice of girlish dismay, 'and I haven't brought an umbrella or rubbers.'

'Simon'll have an umbrella,' Walker sighed between bouts of heavy breathing. 'If the rain don't stop I'll send him to your place to pick up your rubbers Jo . . . I'll be all right in a second.' He turned his smile towards Millard again. 'We'll have time to talk . . .'

'I hate myself for not bringing in an electric pad,' Jo Powers cried out.

'It's wonderful the effect of heat . . . I've been much better on this new diet,' Walker Watson sighed and let the wrinkled lids drop over his sunken eyes. The sallow skin sagged into the hollows of the cheeks.

Jo turned to Millard. 'I know the most wonderful ranch with a troutstream right on the place in Montana above Billings,' she whispered. 'I know it would do him good . . .'

Suddenly Walker was sitting up on the edge of the bed with the hotwater bottle clasped to his middle and the sallow knobs of his knees sticking out of his bathrobe. Millard noticed how hairy his legs were between the garter and the socks. 'They're trying to kill me,' Walker said in a strangling voice, 'but I'm too tough for 'em . . . Jo this damn thing isn't hot any more.'

'Mary's got some boiling water on in the kitchen,' Jo said snatching at the bag. 'I'll get some.' She ran out of the room.

'Millard put that window down, will you? I don't want to catch a chill . . . All these damn reactionaries in Congress they think they can kill me with their opposition. They think this is the opportunity to stop the New Deal from developing into a great progressive movement. They think they can put the common man back in his place. They think they can nominate that pokerplaying whiskeydrinking mean old man . . . I can beat 'em, God damn it, because I got the people with me, the underprivileged people . . . All over the country they are waiting for somebody to give 'em a rallying cry. I could do it with the help of fellers like you and Mike and George but I've got to have cooperation. I've got to have the White House. He's got to make up his mind. I won't be treated like this. He can be the great leader of the American people without being President.'

As he talked he sat hunched on the edge of the bed hugging the dressinggown round his knees.

'Andrew Jackson did it,' said Millard.

'Of course,' said Walker eagerly. 'Say Millard could you find me something about Andrew Jackson I could read up right now? There's a lot of history books in the livingroom. I never get a chance to read. There's never any time for anything in this damn town.'

'Mike would know,' said Millard. 'Mike's a walking encyclopedia.'

'Millard you've been a pillar of strength to me in the Department. I'll never forget it. I don't forget my friends like some do. A great idea . . . We'll ask Mike. I'll get all primed up about how Andrew Jackson did it . . . He likes history you know. He's crazy about American history. I'll get a chance to talk to him while the others are having their cocktails. I'm going to get tough. I did a lot for him in Chicago. In Albany he didn't know anything about the common man no more'n a rabbit . . . I got him in touch with the underprivileged . . . That's where I live that's who I come from. They know I speak their language. They know I'm just folks like they are.'

Jo Powers was standing between them nursing the hotwater bottle wrapped like a baby in its towel, staring in Walker's face with big round admiring eyes. 'Sorry to be so late. That fool woman had taken the kettle off,' she said. 'Here this is real hot.'

He took the hotwater bottle from her and held it against his stomach. 'I'm going to get dressed now. I'm feeling all right.'

'Walker,' Jo whispered after a sidelong glance at Millard, 'Madame Arno's here. I didn't know whether you wanted to see her. She says it's very urgent.'

'I'll see her . . . Jo there are some drops on the bathroom shelf they gave me at the hospital in Bethesda. Bring me five drops in a quarter of a glass of water . . . Millard I hope you don't hold it against me getting you into this ratrace.' He staggered to his feet with the hotwater bottle held tight against his middle with one hand. He put the other shakily on Millard's shoulder. 'Now you be a good feller and cook up something about Jackson with the professor . . . Good God Philadelphia is only four weeks away . . . A man's got to be able to make up his mind.'

As Millard left the room Walker Watson's tall slender figure was hunched over the glass Jo Powers had brought. She held it up to him with both hands and he was lifting it to his mouth with her hands inside his. The hotwater bottle had dropped to the floor between them.

Walking back down the hall to the livingroom he caught sight through the door of the little study of a dumpy woman with fat cheeks who stood in a wet raincoat in the middle of the rug with her mouth pursed up. She was shaking the water off a waterproof hat that looked like a fireman's helmet. Under her arms she held a long roll of something wrapped in oiled silk.

In the livingroom in front of the gothic mantel beneath the moosehead George Dilling, Mike Gulick and Bruce Slater stood in a row each puffing on a cigarette. They didn't look as if they were finding much to say to each other. Millard said Hello to Bruce.

'I just came by to bum a ride with the Secretary over to the White House,' Bruce said in his slow solemn tone. 'Are any of you men going?'

'No I'm going home,' said Millard.

Mike asked if he had his car. When Millard shook his head he suggested they catch a taxi together.

'Sure,' said Millard. He stood fidgeting in front of them until George said to Bruce he hoped they were getting this rain out in the cornbelt and Millard caught the moment to nudge Mike off into a corner and to tell him Walker wanted dope about Andrew Jackson and the third term. Mike burst out laughing. 'Good enough . . . good enough,' he said and pulled a pad out of his pocket and sat down at the table to pencil some notes on it.

'What's the funny story?' asked George.

'You are too young for this one George, it's strictly for the academic mind,' said Millard.

Bruce frowned and grinned and turned his pendulous birddog

face on their direction. 'Do you know the one about the pigeons?' he drawled. 'Well there were three pigeons who used to meet every evening up there in the architecture of the New York Public Library . . .' Millard fixed his face as if he were listening but he was too fidgety to follow the story. He kept looking at his watch. Too late now anyway.

After a while Walker came out in a dinner jacket. He had a parchment roll in his hand. His black tie was askew and Jo Powers was running after him. 'Now deary do let me straighten it,' she was saying. Walker wasn't paying any attention. He walked straight over to Millard and asked him where he would be after dinner.

'They were coming to my house but Eloise is sick again,' George said making a face.

'I'll be home,' said Millard sharply.

Bruce started to explain a second time that he'd come to bum a ride. Without listening Walker asked Millard, 'What about Jackson?' Millard pointed with his little finger at Mike Gulick scribbling on the pad at the table. Walker strode over and stood beside him with his hand on his shoulder. 'Now not too much Mike,' he was saying, 'I just need a general idea.'

'What Jackson?' asked Bruce.

Millard screwed up his face in an expression of incomprehension and walked over to the table. 'Are you about ready?' he asked Mike. 'I've got to go.'

'I'm coming.'

Still leaning on Mike's shoulder Walker looked Millard straight in the eye. 'This is the year of the common man,' he said. 'It's a scientific certainty . . . but there are things we don't know. There are factors we can't get into the picture . . .' When Mike got to his feet Walker leaned over and opened the drawer of the table and shoved the long roll into it and closed it again carefully. Straightening up slowly as if it hurt him to move he gave them all his boyish pained smile. 'You can't forecast the life of a man mathematically like you can a horserace. You've got to have the knowledge . . . knowledge.' Still smiling he looked into Millard's face. 'Don't worry about that appropriation . . . Go home and eat a nice quiet dinner,' he said in a low affectionate tone. 'I'll call you up during the evening.'

Neither Mike nor Millard said anything going down in the elevator. The rain had turned into a steamy drizzle. They had quite a walk before they picked up a cab, just in time because it started to rain hard again. As they settled back on the seat listening to the rain drumming on the roof and the sloshing of the wheels through the puddles Millard turned in an offhand way to Mike and asked him what he'd put down on the pad.

Mike Gulick grinned and said well he wasn't a specialist in the Jackson period, it was a long time since he'd read up on it but he had remembered that there was a considerable parallel between the Jacksonian revolution and the New Deal. Jackson even had a brain trust that people contemptuously called the Kitchen Cabinet. He'd solved the problem of the third term by raising up the ablest man he could find to succeed him; that was Martin Van Buren, and he'd used all his patronage to steamroller his nomination through the convention of 1836 . . .

'Mike,' Millard interrupted him, 'what do you suppose the Boss is going to do?'

'Millard I haven't the slightest idea, but I hope . . . I hope he's been reading up on Andrew Jackson.'

With his panama under his coat Millard dashed to the house through the downpour. The lights were all on in the living room. The house had a fresh tidy look. He dropped his hat on a chair and stood mopping the sweat and rain out of his eyes with his handkerchief. Lucile wearing her frilly pink dress with her hair freshcurled came running forward to meet him. 'Oz!' she was laughing. 'You poor drowned rat.'

'I feel like a drowned rat,' he said crossly. 'I'm all in . . . Did you get those little bums ready to get out of town before they get into more trouble?'

She kissed him all over his wet face and told him to go up and take a nice relaxing hot bath and change his clothes and to come down and take a good stiff drink and she'd broil him a steak for his supper. The car was all packed and ready to leave at the crack of dawn. She'd fed the boys and sent them off to the movies and had sent the maid home. This was going to be their evening together. He let her take charge of him and went stumbling off obediently upstairs.

The bath and clean clothes made him feel better but the whiskey didn't relax him as he'd expected. He didn't have any appetite. He sat there staring at Lucile at the other end of the table without seeing her and eating the good food without tasting it. The little disappointed look that came into her face when she saw he wasn't enjoying supper alone with her the way he usually did began to worry him and he kept trying to think of something to say that would make her laugh but all he could think of was Walker Watson and the program for the agency. He tried to talk about Andrew Jackson and the fun they'd had years ago at the Hermitage but it was no use. He couldn't think of anything to say. He kept his ears cocked for the telephone. Every minute he was wondering what was happening at the White House. When they'd finished their dessert he got up and kissed her awkwardly among the little curls round her forehead and shuffled off to lie down on the couch in the study for a moment with the evening paper. Almost immediately he fell asleep.

He woke up with a start. No it wasn't the phone it was the house-bell ringing. The lights were out everywhere. Switching on lights as he went he shambled sleepily out to the front door. The livingroom clock said twelve-twentyfive. They must all be in bed. Walking down the little yard he noticed that the rain had stopped and a cool wind had come up. A fresh smell came from the washed bricks and rank sweetness from the honeysuckle that grew up the wall. Still bewildered with sleep he opened the street door. It was Jo Powers in a white evening wrap, her black eyes round with excitement.

'Millard,' she cried out, 'we were afraid you'd be in bed.'

'Excuse me,' he yawned. His head was full of cotton. 'Won't you come in?'

She put her hand in its white glove gently on his shoulder. 'Millard,' she said, 'we thought maybe you wouldn't mind stepping out to the car. Walker's got to talk to you but he's all doubled up with cramps again and we thought he'd better just sit in the car . . . He's so tired.'

Millard yawned behind his hand and ran his hand up his face and through his hair. He was beginning to collect himself. 'How was the dinner?' he asked.

'Wonderful . . . Wonderful,' she kept saying. 'It was the most wonderful evening of my life . . . Nobody ever told me he was funny.'

'Who?'

'The President. He kept us in stitches . . . Millard,' she cocked her head to one side and made a baby face, 'may I go to the little girl's room?' she giggled. 'I was too bashful to go at the White House.'

'Of course of course I'll show you the way. I wish Lucile was up. She must have gone to bed,' he mumbled sleepily as he led her into the house. 'There it is . . . the door under the stairs. I'll go out and talk to Walker.'

Out in the street the leaves of the trees rustled crisply in the breeze. Millard took a deep breath and opened the door of the car. 'Good evening Walker. Good evening Simon.' For a moment Walker didn't answer. In the dim glow from the streetlight that filtered through the dancing leaves Millard could make out the long pallor of Walker Watson's face thrown back with closed eyes against the corner cushion in the back seat.

'Well?' Millard asked briskly.

After a long pause Walker started talking without opening his eyes: 'It was a great evening . . . I couldn't tell him a thing he didn't know already . . .' Millard climbed in and let himself drop on the seat beside him. 'He knows more about Andrew Jackson's second administration in his little finger than Mike Gulick will ever know. He told me things I'd never dreamed of, quoted whole passages from Senator Benton. He specially admires Jackson for not trying to serve a third term. He doesn't believe in breaking with the two-term tradition. He's got good reasons for everything he's doing and not doing. He explained the whole situation and asked me my advice and I agreed with him he was doing the right thing . . . You ought to have been there to hear him talk about Farm Economy . . . He considers it one of the keystones of his administration . . . He knows all about your work . . . he even talked about Paul Graves and the problems he was resolving in the field. Resettlement and soil conservation are his two passions. After all he's a farmer himself.'

'Did he say anything definite about the nomination?' Millard asked.

'When the time comes he'll announce his decision. He quoted the Judge about keeping our eyes on the great objectives.'

Jo Powers slid herself silkily into the seat between them. The scent of her musky perfume filled the car. 'I never saw such dedication,' she sighed. Then she started to chatter into Millard's ear that he had the cutest little house she'd ever seen. She'd always wanted a house in Georgetown herself. Yes, he liked Georgetown, Walker Watson echoed somberly. If his poor Josephine had lived he'd have bought a house in Georgetown. Millard muttered that he was sick of Georgetown or anywhere else in the District, he'd like to go home and commute from there.

'We must all help Walker take care of his health,' Jo Powers rattled on brightly. 'That was the last thing the President said. We must all do our best to keep him on his diet . . . and no speeches . . . a good rest out on a ranch in Montana . . . and particularly no speeches.'

'He wants me to take better care of myself,' said Walker with pride in his voice.

'He's got big plans for him at the convention,' said Jo Powers. 'He said he had to have Walker in good health for the convention.'

'Millard,' said Walker suddenly sitting bolt upright. 'We're keeping you up. You look all in. You go in and go to bed and don't worry about the appropriation . . . The Boss is turning on the heat. We've got his backing on every point . . . As if he didn't have enough European news to worry him.'

'Oh it was wonderful,' murmured Jo Powers cuddling back against Walker's shoulder.

'Tomorrow's another day Millard, don't forget that,' said Walker.

'Good night.' Millard closed the car door behind him. The big car began to move slowly up the hill. Millard took another long breath of the rainwashed air and went into the house. He went upstairs turning off the lights behind him as he went. In their room the reading light was on. Lucile was asleep with her glasses on her nose and a book in her hand. There was a full look of sleep about her face. Her cheeks were flushed. Poor little sweetheart, he muttered. Tears came into his eyes as he gently took the glasses off her nose and slipped them into the case on the table. She stirred and smiled but didn't wake up. He tore off his clothes, pulled on his pyjamas and slipped in under the sheet beside her. Tomorrow he'd be alone he thought with a sudden shiver. Without waking she reached out and drew him to her. With his free hand he switched off the light. He lay beside her waiting to go off to sleep but suddenly he was wide awake as if lights had gone on inside his head. He lay there rigid and still so as not to wake Lucile, staring with hot eyes up at the ceiling while the figures for the Appropriations Committee unrolled in that bright light in his head like the figures on paper tape coming out of an adding machine.

THE SHIP OF STATE

6

*O*n main street of a little cornbelt town, in the lunchroom that smells cosy of coffee and toast, we sit over fried fresh country eggs and the war-news in yesterday's Chicago papers—always the war-news, the headlines spelling death. We can't pay attention, we're producers, we're set to make crops and money, to erect new houses and build up the country—and we listen to the county agent on the phone at the end of the counter checking on acreages, soilbuilding practices, conservation, telling this one to put in hybrid seed corn. this one to fertilize, this one to try some newfangled disking

to increase the yield

per man per acre.

A lanky man in overalls whitehaired wearing glasses pulls a government check out of his pocket he got for not feeding as many hogs as he wanted to feed, passes it round the table for the other men to see leans back and scratches his head and drawls out 'I don't get it. Here's one half the government payin' us not to produce an' the other half telling us to get the hell in and root. It makes for confusion. It's like havin' a train with a locomotive at each end

pullin' in a different direction.'

THE WORKING FARMER

A S THE TRAIN LOST SPEED the smooth rumble of wheels over rails broke into a series of rattling thumps until Georgia could hear the slow clank of each individual truck across the trestle. When she looked out the window the ungainly paperbound annual in which she was reading up on farm statistics dropped into her lap. Beyond the lightgreen flicker of a thicket of sapling willows and the fringe of cattails writhing in the breeze stretched a swirl of coppery current which poured towards her patched blue and white with reflected sky and clouds out of misty distance in the silvery morning light. In the middle of the river floated an island humped with feathery trees among white gabled houses that had a New England look. The other side of it a leaden streak of still water faded into a treetangled shore. Yawning over her shoulder, Georgia asked Paul, who sat in the seat behind scowling over his notebook, what river it was.

'It's the Mississippi,' he said without looking up.

Mississippi. The word set off a little chime of bells in her head. Georgia pressed her brow against the glass. Her eyes ate up the long reaches of the river. The trestle had become a bridge. From the end of a scow with a scaly yellow house on it the hammer of a piledriver was coming down wham wham wham on one of a cluster of piles. The current rippled fast and dark round the tarry black piles. The train slowed almost to a stop. The engine hooted. Then the girderwork of the bridge started to move past again.

'This is the first time I ever crossed the Mississippi River,' Georgia said.

'Hungry, Facts and Figures?' Paul asked. He hadn't been listening. Stretching his long arms he got to his feet. 'Suppose we go eat before the diner fills up.'

Georgia still sat staring up the river at the whitish lozenge of a small towboat with two black stacks aft. She was wondering if there were any way she could tell him how happy she felt. 'Oh my,' she sighed girlishly, 'I never thought I'd live to cross the Mississippi.'

'*Oh the Mississippi river is so awful deep and wide,*' he chanted. 'I bet you read Mark Twain when you were a kid.'

He looked down into her face with his half-frowning small boy look of curiosity. Nodding happily she got to her feet. She had remembered the next verse. '*That a hound dawg's tail can't reach from side to side.*'

He swung around and already she was hurrying down the aisle of the train after his broad back in the creased mohair jacket that looked too tight for him.

Sitting in the diner, eating slowly in the leisure of an all day train trip, they talked ramblingly with many pauses about Huckleberry Finn. Georgia was saying she wished she had lived in Mark Twain's generation when there was nothing in the world but America. She'd have liked to have been a pioneer woman with a flock of children living in a sod house like Père's grandmother. She didn't have to stop to explain any more who Père was; she and Paul were getting to know about each other's people. Even Père's world had been more fun than hers she tried to tell him. People she knew of her generation were getting to lead such narrow lives. Paul scowled and asked if every generation's quandries hadn't seemed simpler looking back on them. He'd always understood Mark Twain had died a disillusioned and discouraged man. Then he tossed his head back and halflaughed and said he thought the trip they were making right now was just as much pioneering as any old drive in a rickety covered wagon. She looked up suddenly from her plate and let her eyes run up the muscles of his neck across his thin ill-shaved jaw to the sharp cheekbone and caught a greenish glint in the brown of his eyes.

'That's what I am getting around to in my clumsy way.'

For an instant she couldn't take her eyes off his. She began to feel she was going to blush. He turned his head quickly to look out the window and said well now they were in Iowa. 'I mean—' her cheeks were really burning now—'This is the first time I've done anything I really wanted to do since I used to work for Père. I certainly never expected to work for the government. In Detroit we used to think of the U. S. Government as a sort of giant strikebreaker.' He was losing interest. She could see he was already thinking of something else. 'Tell me Paul,' she asked, 'why are we going to Omaha first?'

He looked relieved to get back on firm ground and answered that it was because tomorrow was a holiday and they might as well spend the day chewing the fat with Nat Kubik. 'He's his own boss and doesn't take any man's money and I thought we'd see what he had to say before we fell into the hands of our boys who work for the agency. If there's one thing you learn in a lab it's to establish your controls.'

'May I come along?'

'Of course, Facts and Figures, we're a team on this trip.'

They paid their separate checks and started back to their seats. Running after him she started to talk recklessly loud into his lurching back saying she could hardly wait to see the real people on the real farms. 'It's the Field. It's my first sight of the Field,' she shouted shrilly to be heard above the noise of the train. Back in their own car he looked down in her face with an indulgent sort of smile, she thought, before letting himself drop into his seat. She didn't trust herself to speak. She settled back to her yearbook and her notes.

She turned to Iowa but she couldn't keep her eyes on the tables of figures. Outside the grimed double windows of the day coach the real Iowa unfolded: wide undulations of wheat beginning to go blond for the harvest, green ranks of corn that caught a little of the blue of the sky in the shimmer where the leaves curled, immense oblongs of clover, frizzly alfalfa in parallelograms that stretched to the horizon, grazing pigs black and red, whitefaced cattle kneedeep in pasture grass. It was a sunny breezy day. Under a sky piebald with small cotton clouds palegreen trees huddled in wavy bands to indicate watercourses. The roads cut straight across the hills between wire fences and looped power lines. Here and there a rattletrap farmhouse spun slowly into view dwarfed by great silver barns and silos or a truck appeared out of a cutting driven by a skinny farmboy in blue overalls or for an instant Georgia could study the figure of a woman in a gray smock who had just come out on her back steps to throw feed from a bucket into a scuttling of white fowls.

. . . 'Iowa . . . you'd ought to call it Ioway.' In the school yard after school all the big girls turned their eyes towards her their big faces twisted into scorn . . . such ignorance. She was trying to sneak away home unnoticed but she couldn't help breaking into a run and a boy yelled scaredcat . . . breathless with a stitch in her side running home down the treelined street for fear some boy might jump out at her from behind the wrinkled trunks of the elms, running along the brick side-walk mottled with sun and shade to ourhouse, but there was nobody on the porch and the shady living room yawned empty . . .'Père!' She was running upstairs and bursting into his study and there he was looking at her across his desk out of bloodshot bulging gray eyes absentmindedly tapping with his pincenez on his nose that had red marks on either side of the bridge where the glasses pinched, and Mother was snatch-ing her up from behind and saying 'Gracious child you mustn't bother your father when he's busy,' and suddenly it all had seemed so silly she couldn't tell her mother the question she wanted to ask . . .

Of course it had been Paul's idea to get up a report in the field, unheard of in the Department where they were accustomed to make up reports out of other reports. What shaking of heads. Only at the last minute Paul had managed to convince Mr. Carroll that a report of real cases, a man and his wife and the children, bank account, grocery bills, what kind of farm machinery, crops, what kind of pans they had in the kitchen, would bring it all home to the members of the Appropriations Committee. A woman along would bring home the woman's side of the story. Two weeks out of Washington. That's how she was getting the trip. Now she must plan.

Behind the clanging engine bell the train moved slowly through a town. Georgia found herself studying with meticulous care the names of the grain and feed merchants, the marble icing on the bank, the tin front of a hardware store with a tower of shiny milkpails in the window, the mudsplattered cars parked in an oblique row along the curb. A bunch of woodenfaced men in blue overalls sagged round the door of a pool parlor. A big wagon drawn by four mules with oldfashioned brass knobs on the harness waited at a crossing. Beside the tracks there rose the complicated staging of an iceplant, then the corrugated walls of a flourmill, and the soaring shape of a grain elevator.

This time she'd take the fullest kind of notes. Paul was always complaining that the reports were too vague, he could never get the relevant facts down hard and sharp so that he could really pin his statements to the ground. This time she was just going to follow him around and not miss a single word, names, acreages, figures, dates. Every night before going to bed she'd go over her notes to fill in all those little gaps. Two weeks out of Washington. Two weeks with Paul on a trip.

. . . The trip she and Père and Mother had driving that summer through the Upper Peninsula of Michigan. Mother drove because Père always said he was too absentminded to drive a car. Père sat in the back seat of the model T Ford touring car with the top down talking about the Jesuit missionaries and the Five Nations and the unhappy fate of Pontiac. Bobolinks were singing along the fences. A sweet reek of balsam came from the tall dark evergreen woods. The air was cool and the sun was hot and Georgia had the happy summer vacation feeling of all-being-together and being-on-a-trip and Père was making her note down every date and name on a little pad even if the car did jiggle, complaining with gestures like an actor declaiming Shakespeare that women didn't have any memories. And Mother laughed and laughed and said she declared he was maligning the sex and Georgia was suddenly clasping her hands deadly serious on her knees and saying that she wasn't going to be like girls she was going to be like boys she was going to remember everything . . .

Yes she said to herself looking out of the train window at the undulant carpet of crops that unravelled before her eyes, she must be wide awake every minute to help Paul, note all the relevant facts. This time she was going to prove what she could do. She was getting sleepy. She was trying to shake herself out of the drowsiness of the long train trip. The shadows of barns and houses and longlegged watertanks were lengthening over the wheat. The slanting sunlight was deepening the hollows in the marbled plain.

She'd been asleep and Paul was tapping her on the shoulder. 'Council Bluffs,' he said. 'Here we cross the broad Missouri. I don't want you to miss it.' The train was moving slowly between houses. At the end of streets full of traffic rose clay bluffs capped with green. It was evening. The train rumbled across a bridge over a pale wide puttycolored stream very glassy and smooth. Swifts circled above the water.

All at once Georgia was in a fluster collecting her pamphlets and papers and ramming them into her briefcase and reaching for her wraps and her valise because the train was pulling into the station in Omaha.

With his raincoat over his shoulder and his head tilted to one side Paul loped with long strides down the station platform. Georgia didn't dare wait for a porter for fear she'd lose sight of him. Breathlessly lugging the heavy valise that kept catching her in the shins and with the fat briefcase and the coat under the other arm, feeling that her hair was coming down and the yellow straw cloche she'd bought for the trip was slipping forward over her nose she stumbled after him. When she caught up with him he was shaking hands with a broad grinning redfaced man with a red beak shaped like a turtle's. Paul introduced Nat Kubik who was immediately all fatherly consideration. He grabbed up her bag and took her briefcase.

'I bet you're both starved,' he said. 'I got a couple of the nicest people in the state of Nebraska waiting over at the hotel to eat supper with us.'

Everything was suddenly very cheerful. Nat Kubik led the way through the station out to a big blue Buick car. He didn't need to introduce the sunburned youth in a shortsleeved shirt at the wheel as his son Nat Junior because the boy was a perfect younger replica of his father. Ushering them through the hotel lobby into the coffeeshop Nat kept having to stop to pass the time of day with other large cheerful friendly men.

'You see we're not among strangers here,' he explained as he settled them at a table beside a grayhaired birdeyed woman in a little round hat with beads on it and her husband, a silentlooking man with big soft eyes in a sallow oval face whom Nat introduced as the manager of one of the biggest cooperatives in the state. 'Of course you know the question we're going to ask,' twittered the wife. 'Is he going to run for a third term?'

Paul stared at her blankly.

Nat Kubik threw back his head and roared, 'Gladys, I'm introducing you to the only man in Washington who hasn't got a political thought in his head . . . Paul I bet you don't know who the Vice-President is.' Paul alternately scowled and grinned, but he couldn't seem to find anything to say. Nat went on talking. 'I don't give a hoot about precedent but I kinda hope he don't,' he said. 'We got plenty good men in this country. Nobody's irreplaceable except in his own eyes. Now you ask Paul about the Farm Economy Administration and you'll get an earful.'

'I'm a cooperator from the word go,' the cooperative manager said slowly, 'but what worries me about this business is that . . . when the Government steps in to put people on their feet who haven't been able to get together themselves to help each other, I don't see how it can result in anything but more politics.'

A freshfaced middleaged waitress dealt out blue plates of roast beef and vegetables. With her knife and fork poised over her plate Georgia was looking at Paul waiting for him to answer. 'I don't know anything about politics,' he said. 'I'm in this because I think there's a valuable reservoir of people in this country who haven't gotten a break, farmers who live on submarginal farms, hillbillies, migrant laborers. Prosperity is an express that goes by mighty fast and makes very few stops and a lot of good people just don't catch the train for no fault of their own. So long as this government is willing to spend a few million dollars setting these people up in new farms and houses and in machinery to work with I'm willing to string along and see how it works. I think it will pay off in better farming practices as well as in conservation of the soil and of the most valuable thing of all.

'What do you figure that is?' Nat asked smiling.

'I guess I mean manpower and womanpower and a chance for their kids to rise in the world.'

Georgia was telling herself she hadn't expected Paul to be so eloquent. She felt like applauding. You keep your mouth shut she was telling herself. She settled down to eat her supper.

'I'm for experiments all right but in my opinion,' said Nat Kubik solemnly, 'the European war has done us farmers more good than all your New Deal experiments.'

'Ain't right,' said the cooperative manager shaking his head. 'Ain't right to profit by a war any more than it is to kill little pigs when there's hungry people in the world or to burn good wheat in the stove.'

'I'm not so sure,' said Nat with his mouth full.

Young Nat gave Georgia a flash of his even white teeth in a confidential smile and whispered in a tone that made her laugh that now they'd gone over his head. She nodded. 'Mine too,' she said.

After supper young Nat brought the car around and they started off on the two hour drive to Beaver Falls. Georgia sat beside him in front hugging her briefcase, childishly happy in the deep resonance of Paul's and Nat Kubik's voices talking farm practices on the back seat and in the rank night-smell of sunseared clover and fastgrowing crops that came in from the level fields halfseen under a sky full of stars. The car skimmed the straight cement road. When they passed the yellow lights of farms there came sometimes a sweet warmth of cows from a cowbarn or the muck smell of hogs. The little towns had gone to bed. Streetlights glared on gawky storefronts. Occasionally a scattering of bulbs lit up the garish insult of the posters on the false front of a moviehouse and then darkness wiped out the lights like a sponge and there was level country again, fence posts and telegraph poles swooping past flecked with white from the headlights. 'And now we're home,' young Nat said as he turned off over a sideroad across a bridge and up a hill. 'That's Beaver Creek and there's our bluff.' He drove around the angle of a long barn between empty cattle pens that smelled of dry cornstalks and circled a piece of lawn to stop in front of a yellow frame house with a broad screened porch. When the car stopped under an overhead light they could hear the night insects and a great thumping of frogs from the creekshore below.

Georgia stood looking up at the moths and junebugs crowding round the bright globe of the overhead lamp that hung from an unpainted locust post while the Kubiks got the bags out of the car. When they ushered her in through the front door the brightly lit livingroom seemed small and low to contain so many large lolling easymannered people. Mrs. Kubik was large and dark. The twins, both boys, a year or two younger than young Nat were large and redheaded. The youngest girl was large and blonde. A large black Newfoundland dog roamed around the room and kept being put out, and two large yellow cats sat in the open doorway to the kitchen. Immediately Mrs. Kubik brought out coffee and glasses of milk and slices of blackberry pie for everyone, and made Georgia feel as if she'd lived there all her life. When Georgia went to bed tucked away in a small close bedroom under the eaves she told herself just before dropping off to sleep, the way she used sleepily to tell herself things when she was a little girl, that what she wanted was to grow up and marry a prosperous farmer and have three boys and a girl and a Newfoundland dog and yellow cats and horses and cows and pigs and lambs in the pasture, and turkeys and geese and ducks and guineas and chickens in the yard, and frogs in the creek.

She woke up stifling. A hot tongue was licking her face. The newrisen sun shone straight in her eyes through the window. It was a moment before she could remember where she was. Looking out into the dazzle she could see, beyond a shadowy fringe of small trees along the bank of the creek below, a road that stretched straight through great expanses of country broadly banded with crops lightly rolling like the ocean on a calm day to the incandescent horizon. There was no cloud in the sky. She ran into the little bathroom to wash and to do up her pale hair that she had had waved in Washington for the trip. The frizziness made it look more mousy than ever she told herself dejectedly. She got into the coolest suit she had and tiptoed downstairs. It was forty-five minutes after five by the grandfather clock in the livingroom but Paul and Nat had finished breakfast. They sat in their shirtsleeves at a square table in the kitchen while Mrs. Kubik in a big frilled yellow apron hovered over the percolator on the electric stove. 'You're early birds for city folks,' said Nat looking up at Georgia approvingly.

'Now how would you have your eggs dear?' asked Mrs. Kubik.

Paul and Nat were already in the middle of an argument. 'It just won't work,' Nat was saying. 'I can't tell you why. You can't manage a farm by committee. If I make a mistake I lose money. If I make enough mistakes I lose my shirt and somebody else takes over but if one of your bright young men fresh out of state agricultural school makes a mistake it just means more paperwork.'

'Each project is selfliquidating,' Paul insisted.

'Well let's take a look at the farm before it gets too hot,' said Nat and pulled his paunchy frame in sections out of the chair like a camel getting to its feet. From a bench beside the front door he scooped up three broadbrimmed straw hats for them. He herded them out. 'First we'll walk round the plant and then I'll drive you out to show you the crops . . . expect us when you see us Mother,' he called back over his shoulder at his wife.

Happy as she used to be as a little girl when the boys let her in on a game of three o' cat, Georgia trotted after the men past hay barns and machinery sheds and through the big cement building where they raised pigs in winter to the frame building where they shucked and graded the hybrid seed corn. Paul seemed particularly at home there and started telling Nat about how he'd worked in Connecticut on some of the early crossbreeding operations.

'Well you're probably one of the guys I owe money to,' Nat roared. 'The hybrid seed corn business is beginning to look good. It's already increased productivity by thirty percent.' They saw the silos and the choppers and the sheds where Nat kept his tractors and the long cool clean building where the Ayrshires were milked and the gleaming clean aluminum milking machinery.

The hands seemed all to be tall young men in scrubbed blue overalls. Whenever they ran into a man Nat introduced him all around and stopped to pass the time of day. They had a cheerful healthy look. Georgia caught herself wishing they were all her brothers.

At length they got back to the blue Buick.

'This is great,' Paul was saying. 'You ought to see my place in North Carolina. It's the difference between an oldfashioned oxcart and a streamliner.'

Nat grinned.

'We've been through rocky times,' he said gravely. 'It wasn't so long ago we were banding together and loading up our rifles to keep the sheriff out. We had some tough times. That's why when you try to tell the farmer that war is hell it's hard for him to believe it.'

'Nat,' Paul said suddenly, 'why don't you go to work out here for the agency for a while?'

Nat shook his head. 'I got my craw full of the blue buzzard . . . I got kids to put through college. You come out here and work for me, Paul. You are just the kind of feller we need.'

Paul laughed and laughed. 'I may take you up some day, Nat. I got kids too.'

Listening to them Georgia felt a lonesome cold chill go through her.

They looked at fields of corn and oats and clover and wheat and alfalfa and a patch of flax Nat was trying for an experiment. Then they drove across two counties to see some farms Nat managed for other people. On the way back they looked in at the fairgrounds on a cattle sale. Then Nat remembered that his three boys were playing in a Fourth of July ball game somewhere half across the state and they had to take that in sitting in the roaring sun on open bleachers eating frankfurters drippy with mustard and drinking warm soft drinks out of lily cups.

When they got back scorched and dusty to the Kubik farm they found that Nils Petersen the curlyhaired supervisor for the three-state district had been waiting for them for an hour. He got stiffly to his feet when they walked into the livingroom. Paul went straight up to him. 'What's all this trouble over at Meridian?'

Petersen stood stiffly in front of his chair in his neatly pressed light tan suit. Before he could find an answer Paul said, 'Well let's get going . . .' He turned his back on Mr. Petersen and walked over to Nat. 'Nat,' he said holding out his hand, 'this has been the best ever.'

Driving out along the highway west Paul started asking questions in the random way he had. He sat in front beside Petersen and Georgia with her briefcase had the whole back seat to herself. Kubik was a great fellow Petersen was saying, he only wished his politics weren't so reactionary. Between the Farm Bureau kind of folks like Kubik and the

Farmer's Union kind like Dodd at Meridian, he had trouble keeping the agency out of politics, particularly in a presidential year. Paul said he wished he could get Nat Kubik to work for them. He was a hell of a good farmer. Mr. Petersen was evidently a careful talker because he didn't answer, but Georgia could see his neck stiffen as he sat at the wheel.

Folks were still a little jumpy out here he explained. They'd had a bad scare. All this plowing under of crops and burning wheat in the stove had made the farmer jumpy. Talk about the land of opportunity, nobody had had much opportunity in twentynine and thirty, no matter how good farmers they were. Now Bob Brundage was an example. He wondered what Mr. Graves would think of him. He was a man who had farmed a section in the twenties and made money. He had stuck his neck out buying land and had lost everything and just about starved to death. He had made his comeback through the agency and now was all paid up and running his own farm and working for the agency on the side and one of the best all around men they had. They were going to spend the night with the Brundages.

It was a scorching afternoon. As they drove thunderheads were piling up above the horizon casting blue shadows over the ripening wheat. The level sun was shining in glaring coppery beams through the clouds when they turned through a pair of tilting gateposts into a rutted drive between a narrow unpainted house and a barn off which most of the red paint had long since scaled away. A fat popeyed man in patched blue overalls came out of the house to meet them apologizing volubly:

'I wish I had things fixed up better for you folks. We ain't got the house painted. We will though. We will. You see it's not so long since we moved in.'

He would handle all the suitcases. He had a resonant voice that came from way down inside his suety frame. Remarkably light on his feet for his size, he trotted ahead of them with the suitcases under his arm up the steps onto the porch. When they shook hands Georgia had noticed that he had lost two fingers of the right hand.

'This is Mabel,' he said, pointing out a bigbusted woman with frizzly yellow hair who was clattering the pots and pans in the kitchen.

When she saw Georgia she came forward wiping her hands on a dish towel and looked Georgia straight in the face out of sharp blue eyes. My this was a pleasure, she said, out here she didn't have no girl friends, she got so tired of nothing but men, men, men.

'You don't get tired of me, do you?' Bob Brundage stopped at the foot of the stairs and made big round eyes in their direction. Indeed she did, Mabel said. She told him to leave the bags in the upstairs hall and she'd show the folks their rooms. She looked from Georgia to Paul. 'Mr. and Mrs. Graves?' she asked.

'No, I'm Georgia Washburn.'

'Then I'll put you in the parlor and let the menfolks go upstairs.'

They ate supper in a small stuffy diningroom next the kitchen packed in among glass cabinets full of china. On top of the cabinets were teasets and coffeesets and a crowd of china figures. There were piles of plates in the corners of the room and lamps shaped like urns and vases on all the tables. We love pretty things, Mabel explained as she served them. The sweat ran down their faces as they ate in the hot breath of the oil stove from the kitchen. The air was close with the coming storm. The blueblack clouds occasionally laced with a steely flicker of lightning had settled down so tight over the plain they seemed packed against the windows. Mabel said it was the Fourth of July storm, never failed. A distant growl of thunder backed her up.

After a greasy supper of ham and eggs and turnip greens and hot biscuits Mabel beckoned Georgia into the front room just to give the men a chance to talk dirty, she explained. There they sat in overstuffed chairs between spinning wheels and two fine old carved mahogany sideboards. There were more lamps along the walls and two or three sets of andirons on the floor.

'I guess you're wondering,' Mabel said. 'This is our hobby. I buy antiques and sell 'em. I make a pretty good thing of it. But I do it mostly for the fun and now Bob's getting the bug. We love pretty things. Imagine that big old greaseball knowing the difference between Dresden and Meissner.' She brought out a box of candy, hitched her overstuffed chair up so that her knees touched Georgia's and set the box of candy between them. Outside the rain was sweeping against the house in continuous sheets drowning out the sound of the thunder. 'Take some,' she poked the candybox at Georgia. 'Now tell me,' she said. 'Are you sleepin' with him? I don't mean no offense . . . You see me an' Bob's not married an' I been afraid it would get out. Everybody knows it around here. I'm his housekeeper. Most of the folks don't care. They know about his trouble with his wife an' everythin'. I just didn't want it to get to Washington.'

Georgia's face was burning. She wasn't that kind of a person, she insisted, of course she wouldn't say anything about it . . . It wasn't any of her business.

Mabel pushed the candy in her direction again. 'Have another,' she said. 'But you didn't answer my question.'

'We're just on the same job together . . . He's happily married and has four children,' Georgia explained breathlessly. She felt she was being too insistent. Mabel's eyes were blue gimlets between narrowed lids. 'Too bad,' she said. 'You'd make a pretty couple.'

They could hear the men's voices and their feet stamping around in the diningroom. Georgia felt she couldn't face seeing Paul again tonight, not under Mabel's searching stare. She said in a weak voice that please she would like to go to bed now if Mabel wouldn't mind showing her where. Mabel led the way out into a little room right off the parlor that had been made by closing in part of the porch. The room was almost entirely filled up by a fourposter pineapple bed, made up with clean sheets and a brilliant patchwork quilt. Georgia's suitcase was standing at the foot. The rain drummed deafeningly on the tin roof overhead. Once she was closed into the room she didn't dare go to the bathroom for fear of meeting somebody, so she wiped off her face with cold cream and a tissue and slipped in between the sheets that smelled of lavender. When the rain slackened she could hear the men's voices and Mabel's in the parlor. For a long time she couldn't sleep but she lay there feeling quiet and secure as a child hidden in a hayloft.

Breakfast next morning was just the same as supper only Mabel served fried potatoes with it. After breakfast they drove into the Farm Economy office in Meridian. The office was a set of dusty rooms upstairs over the bank on Main Street presided over by a frail little man with a shock of gray hair and a youthful lined face. He was terribly thin. The skin transparent as waxed paper was drawn tight over the small bones of his face. He moved jerkily like a marionette when the wires have become tangled. His name was Warren Dodd. He explained right away that he was a spastic and that it had been only after long training and through the help of a famous New York doctor that he had gotten into shape to lead a fairly normal life. He added with his twisted laugh that they mustn't mind if he fell down rather suddenly. They could just set him up on his pins again and he would be all right. Right away Georgia decided in her own mind that he was wonderful. She could see at once that there was a situation between Dodd and Petersen. She didn't like Petersen anyway.

Although they had set out through a crisp crystal sunrise in air washed fresh by the rain, the day heated up fast. The forenoon dragged on in floods of talk. Paul had the look of not having slept well. He sat listening first to Petersen and then to Dodd with a bewildered expression on his face. Georgia wished he'd pull himself together. He didn't seem to have any control of the situation. Now and then he yawned or drummed on the corner of the desk with his two fingers. Georgia sat against the wall with a pad on her knees trying to keep track of what was going on. She kept trying to remember what they were doing out there. Of course it was to make a report. In spite of the droning electric fan the office was very hot. Except for Dodd who seemed insensible of the heat, they were all sweating. A stain of sweat began to appear under the armpits of Petersen's wellpressed tan jacket. Now and then one of them would hand Georgia a letter or a mimeographed sheet and she would stare down at it uncomprehendingly. Names, personalities, conflicts kept cropping up that she didn't know about. She let her attention drift helplessly with the eddying currents of argument just putting down words at random on her pad so that she would have the look of being busy.

At lunch with the three men it was worse. Georgia wasn't hungry and only ordered a shredded wheat biscuit. She sat in the grubby little lunchroom trying to keep her face dry with a wad of tissue while the flies stuck to her ears, listening to Dodd jerking out more and more caustic remarks about Petersen's work right to his face. Petersen wasn't answering any more. There was a flush over his high cheekbones. Paul ought to put an end to this backbiting; why doesn't he stop them she kept asking herself.

The minute they finished eating Warren Dodd struggled to his feet and said he had to go home to lie down. He would be back at the office in an hour. He was breathing hard and making such an effort to control his jumping muscles that Georgia got up and put her arm round his waist and helped him to the door. Outside a taxi was already waiting. 'Hi Warren,' the driver said cheerfully. He grinned at Georgia. 'One of us usually gets by to pick him up when he finishes his dinner,' he explained while she helped Warren into the cab. 'If you'll drive around with him, Miss, I'll have you back at the office in no time.' Warren lived in a little white frame house on a back street. Georgia helped him across the porch and onto a couch in the front room. When she tried to pay the taximan, he waved her off and said to forget it, Miss, the boys always did that for Warren.

Paul was standing in the doorway of the bank. He raised his hand and waved her towards him with a confidential mysterious sort of gesture. 'We're not getting anywhere,' he said. 'I thought we'd let the boys thrash out their paperwork this afternoon and take a look at the farms. I'm borrowing Petersen's car. I'll need you to come along. I've got a list of the places. Warren wants us to be back in time to go to his local of the Farmer's Union.

'George Dilling's going to speak,' said Georgia.

Paul made a face at that. 'I've already heard him speak.'

'But Warren wants us to come,' Georgia said pleadingly, and told Paul about the taxidriver and added that she thought Warren was a pretty wonderful fellow. 'Imagine the struggle that boy has to put up every minute,' she said. 'I find life quite hard enough as it is.'

Paul grunted absentmindedly. They were driving out of town through a patch of badlands. Small buttes and pinnacles of mustard-yellow clay stood up into the wan sky. Sagebrush grew in the gullies between, where occasionally they saw prairiedogs at the edge of their burrows sitting up on their haunches and looking at them out of tiny glass eyes as they drove past. A little puff of dust would rise when one of them took fright and dove down his hole.

At the top of a hill the country opened up into farm land again. They drove along a straight highway over a plain bounded by low eroded hills streaked with chalky pinks and whites and ochres. A couple of times they turned off at letterboxes and drove out muddy roads to the farms. Georgia would sit in the car while Paul got out to talk to the farmer. She hunched drowsily in the front seat watching Paul's tall figure all briskness and life again now, gesticulating with odd short gestures as he strode around with the tenant asking questions. At one place he was evidently getting directions because there was a great deal of pointing over towards a gap in the hills.

'This is going to be a tough one to find,' Paul said slipping in behind the wheel, 'but we'll find it.'

He drove back to the highway and followed it up to a place where the cement road made a rightangle turn. There he took one of the dirt roads branching off. For a long time he drove along it between waving tracts of wheat dappled pale yellow and palegreen. The car slewed a little in the ruts because the clay was still sticky underneath from last night's rain. The road narrowed and cut through a patch of badlands, grooved bleached skeletons of hills, and came out into another prairie brimful of wheat. They drove across it for miles without seeing a house. Georgia was beginning to mutter that they'd better turn back if they were to get to Meridian in time for Warren Dodd's meeting, but Paul drove on obstinately. At last they saw slam at the end of the road an unpainted twostory house with the door in the middle and a red tin roof and two chimneys like ears. When they came up to it the road ended in a sharp rightangle turn. Paul skidded in a deep pool of muck as he slammed on his brakes and just missed the gatepost by a hair. He turned to Georgia with a foolish grin. 'That wasn't what I'd planned,' he said.

Paul got out of the car and hopped carefully along the grassy edge of the road to keep out of the mud. When he reached the brown grassplot in front of the house he took three long strides to the front door and disappeared inside. Georgia sat looking at the unpainted weatherboarding and the broken boards of the stoop and the pile of rusty cans and bleachedout cartons out front where a few fowls picked disconsolately among the hogweed. Behind the house the windmill rattled as if every metal part were shaking itself loose. The sun was beginning to get low in the sky. When Paul came back his thick brows were knotted in a frown.

'This isn't the place but I got to stop and help the man out. His cow's having a calf and the little girl's sick.'

He climbed back in the car and managed to slew it up out of the mud onto the grass. As soon as he opened the front door for her Georgia noticed mingled with the staleness of coaloil lamps a choking sweaty smell. A tall man in overalls and a blue shirt was standing in the open back door with his arms folded and his feet apart. The skin of his face and of his hairy forearms was tanned a dark tobacco hue but his neck was red and wattled. 'This is Miss Washburn my assistant,' said Paul.

'John Hick is the name,' the man said in a hollow voice. 'You see I ain't got nobody to help me.'

'Mrs. Hick is in here,' said Paul opening one of the doors. 'We've got to see what we can do about this calf. It's a a difficult delivery.'

'I'll get a rope,' said John Hick.

Georgia went into the parlor that had heavy oldfashioned curtains of a greenish hue looped over the windows. In the middle of the floor was a cot where lay a little grayeyed girl swathed in blankets. Beside her in a rocker sat a puffy little woman with her dress all fluffed out around her like a setting hen. She was fanning the child with a palm-leaf fan. Sweat poured off the child's little sallow face all twisted up with pain. It was from her that the oppressive stuffy smell came.

Without stopping her fanning the woman started to talk in a low unaccented voice: 'It's my little girl. She's been like this for twentyone days. The doctor came an' said it was rheumatic fever but the medicine he gave us didn't help none an' now it's all gone an' the liniment too an' the doctor don't come no more. We live out of the way here an' there's just Mr. Hick an' me now the boy's joined the Navy an' she won't let me leave her a minute an' poor Mr. Hick has had to do everythin'. My poor little angel. She's so good, it breaks your heart. Her joints are all swoll up so she can't move. She's so little. It's too much for a little girl like that an' all her life she's been so good an' never any trouble to anybody.'

Georgia was thrashing around in her head for the right thing to say. At last she asked in a falsely professional tone as if she were a nurse, 'How much fever has she got?'

'I dunno. It was real bad when the doctor came.'

Suddenly Georgia thought of something and felt better: 'Have you any aspirin? I know they give that.'

Mrs. Hick shook her head uncomprehendingly.

'Here I've got some out in the car.' It was a relief to do something. Georgia ran out and found the bottle of aspirin tablets she carried in her briefcase. Mrs. Hick shook a couple of the little white tablets out in the palm of her hand and looked at them for a moment with a fixed suspicious stare and then dropped them back in the bottle.

'I'll wait till Mr. Hick comes,' she said. Then she went back to her low rapid talking not pausing between the words: 'It was real fortunate you an' your husband come along when you did because I don't know what's going to happen to us if we lose that calf. That was just goin' to be a little cash to tide us along until we sold our wheat. Well I guess we can ship the fowls, poor scrawny things they won't bring much. Your husband being from the Department in Washington he must know somethin' though he don't talk like he was no veterinarian . . .'

'Shouldn't you get the little girl to a hospital?' Georgia asked gently.

She'd hardly said it before she knew she'd said the wrong thing. The child's eyes widened with terror. She let out a little tired scream. Mrs. Hick didn't seem to notice but went on talking in her even voice. As she talked she fanned.

'There's a hospital in Meridian but how are we goin' to afford it? If we can pinch through this summer an' if we save the wheat crop it won't be so bad but if there's hail an' we lose this crop we'll lose the farm an' then what'll we do with little Margie sick an' all? Here we've been fightin' a mortgage—that's what Mr. Hick calls it—for nine years now an' it looks like everythin' we made went into it an' Jackie leavin' us and joinin' the Navy. I hope you an' your husband never get in the grip of no mortgage.'

Georgia felt her face getting red but it was too late to try to explain. She wasn't doing anything very helpful, she thought to herself as she walked out of the back door to see where Paul was. Outside the last sunset light stained the barn and the outhouses and the stanchions of the windmill and the posts of the hoglot a bright liquid red. The wind had gone down and the great expanse of wheat that stretched to the horizon was still. A few birds flew over it.

She heard voices coming from one of the stalls in the barn, and ran over and peeped in. On the threshold she stopped short. They were working over the cow. Paul had taken off his shirt. The two of them worked grunting and cursing as they tugged at something bloody that protruded from the hind quarters of the cow. Blood streamed from Paul's naked elbows. Neither of them saw her or looked up.

She felt her face go pale. She walked with tottery steps back to the house. She didn't want to go back to talk to the old woman. Maybe she could find something useful to do. She didn't want to think about the cow.

She peeped in the kitchen. A kettle of water was humming on the oil stove. In the ancient slate sink stood a great stack of dirty dishes and old dented pots and pans. She found a dishpan and some soap and began to wash the dishes. For the first time that day she felt light-hearted.

She'd almost finished the dishes when John Hick, his hands bloody, his head drooping in a discouraged way over his chest came shambling into the kitchen.

'Where's my hot water?' he asked.

'I used it to wash the dishes,' Georgia said. He didn't answer but just stood staring at her wearily shaking his head. Then he reached for the kettle, filled it up from the bucket and set it on the stove again.

Georgia went on working. It was nearly dark by the time she'd finished the pans and left them to drain in the sink. She looked around the kitchen for a match and lit a lamp and then lit another one and took it into the parlor. Mrs. Hick thanked her quite politely but when Georgia asked her if there was anything more she could do she just started her even flow of talk again. The little girl was keeping up a low continuous whimper. Georgia sat down but she got right up. She went out and began to pace restlessly up and down the hall. She didn't want to think about the cow. At last she got up her nerve to open the back door. It was thoroughly dark now, though from the back stoop she could still see a saffron glow in the west. There was a chink of light in the barn. After hesitating a long while she went towards it and pulled open the big double doors. Under a lantern that hung on a bulky piece of machinery that might have been a combine Paul and John Hick sat at a deal table. Their shirts were off and their hair was rumpled and they were covered with sweat and flecks of blood and they looked wild as Indians. Their elbows were on the table and their hands were clasped and they were looking each other in the eyes as each one tried to bend the other's hand down onto the table. A bottle stood within reach.

Georgia stood watching them with her mouth open. The men were both breathing hard. Their muscles bulged on their upper arms and stood out sharp from the shoulder to the neck. Their fingers were white with tension. The sweat glistened on them. She had opened her mouth to speak but she couldn't seem to think of what to say so she just stood silently watching them until they suddenly both relaxed and let go hands and burst out laughing.

'Paul you're all right,' said John Hick in his deep rattling tones way down his throat.

Paul caught sight of Georgia. 'Sit down Facts and Figures and have a drink of John's White Lightning.'

'But we ought to get back to town? How about Warren Dodd's meeting?'

'I'm having a meeting with John Hick that's enough for one evening . . . Sit down Facts and Figures.'

Georgia let herself drop on an upturned nailkeg just out of the circle of light. She felt frightened. She'd never seen Paul drinking before.

'What about the calf?' she asked timidly.

Neither of them answered.

John Hick took a swig out of the bottle and cleared his throat. 'Paul I've always been a gamblin' man' . . . He picked up as if continuing a narrative where he'd been interrupted. 'Always been a gamblin' man . . . Out in this country a wheat farmer's got to be a gamblin' man. We're just goddam . . .' suddenly he looked over to where Georgia sat feeling pale and mousy on her nail keg . . . 'beggin' your pardon Miss . . . Well . . . speculators. A wheat farmer's just as much a speculator as a johnny in a silk hat at his desk in the New York Stock Exchange only he works harder and he stands to lose more. But I'm no belly-acher . . . beggin' your pardon Miss . . . there ain't never been a Hick was a bellyacher. I ain't runnin' to no government with my troubles. This here wheat crops's just as much a gamble as those faro games they set up at Reno Nevada.'

Georgia got to her feet and started to tiptoe out of the barn.

'Paul take a drink,' John Hick was roaring. He'd evidently forgotten all about Georgia . . . 'the first goddam government man I ever seen do a neighborly thing. If you'd been a little better veterinary we'd a saved that calf but it looks like we saved the cow an' if you hadn't a come around we wouldn't a saved nothin' . . . Paul take your shoes off . . . You look like a barefoot kinda man to me in spite of all that college eddication . . . I like a barefoot kinda man.'

Paul threw back his head and roared and kicked off his shoes.

Georgia had been lingering just outside the barn door. She felt little and lonely and sorry for herself. She turned and walked out round the house to where the car was. For a while she sat on the front seat and tried to catnap. Then after a while she got out of the car and sat on the steps of the house looking up at the stars. The inky blue night was very clear. Overhead she could see the whole arch of the Milky Way. She picked out Cassiopeia's chair and the crowded brilliants of Job's Coffin. From out back of the house she could hear Paul's and John Hick's voices pitched high as they called to each other. What could they be doing out in the yard? Georgia was beginning to get hungry. She sat on the steps and whimpered a little to herself, she felt so lonely and abused. Then she thought of poor Mrs. Hick and her little girl and told herself to stop that foolishness. After what seemed an hour she heard rapid footsteps coming around the end of the house and made out Paul's tall figure in the starlight. He had his shoes and socks in his hand. Without a word he sat down beside her on the steps to put them on his feet.

'Will the cow be all right?' she asked. She had that tremulous feeling again of a little girl who is afraid the boys won't let her play with them.

'I had to stay to help him do his chores . . . John Hick . . . he's quite a feller. He wanted to rustle us up some supper but I wouldn't let him. Well we better push along . . . You're driving, Facts and Figures . . . Let's push along.' He sat on the step looking up at the sky with his hands clasped over his knees. 'My what a night of stars,' he said quietly.

'I've been looking at them such a long time,' Georgia said.

It was a relief Paul wasn't drunk. The liquor seemed to have just thrown him into a slow meditative way of behaving. He was drawling out his words with more of a tarheel accent than usual.

'You must have had a time with that calf Paul,' she said in her tiniest little voice.

'Too damned ignorant . . . the calf was coming out the wrong way. There's something you can do to turn it around but I didn't know what . . .' he got up stretching to his feet. 'I don't know about you Facts and Figures but I got to get some food in me. John Hick says to take the dirt road to the left and that'll bring us out on the highway.'

Nervously Georgia got into the driver's seat.

She managed to get the car through the mudhole all right and found the turning but there must have been some mistake because she drove on endlessly along a muddy straight road. She had to drive very slowly to avoid sliding off into the ditch. At last they picked up a row of telephone poles and after another halfhour came out on macadam. There were no signs so there was no way of telling which way they ought to turn towards Meridian. She was going to ask Paul but when she turned to him she saw he was asleep. At random she turned to the left and drove and drove. The road didn't seem to be much of a highway. It turned and twisted through a country of nibbled hills and gullies that rose up to take jagged bites out of the starry sky first on one side and then on the other. At last she caught a glimpse of a little string of electric lights flickering far away across the badlands. Several times she lost them behind small corrugated hills with crazy pinnacles but at last she saw them dead ahead and drove up to a small fillingstation and restaurant ornamented with a sign made out of rustic logs on a white ground: PHEASANT HILLS CABINS.

Paul woke up with a start when the car stopped. 'I smell steak,' he said. He strode ahead of her into the little whitepainted restaurant. The squarefaced man in a white jacket behind the counter had just finished wiping off the oilcloth with a rag. 'Pardner I'm closin' up,' he said in a drowsy voice.

'Oh come now brother, it won't take you a minute to fix us a T-bone steak for two,' Paul plead. 'And a glass of milk . . . two glasses of milk.'

Georgia could see that the man was weakening. 'How about some French fries?' he asked in a friendly brisker tone.

'Brother,' Paul said in a way that made them all laugh, 'We'll eat anything you've got and more.'

'How far is it to Meridian?' Georgia asked when they were settled at a table and she was sipping a glass of milk.

'Meridian? Why that's in another part of the state altogether. I'll have to look at a highway map,' the man said.

'You look at that steak first,' roared Paul laughing. 'Well Facts and Figures we lost our way.'

'What a day,' sighed Georgia.

'Never felt more discouraged in my life . . . except for old John Hick. I kinda liked my bout with old John Hick.'

'You sure were going native Paul,' said Georgia beginning to laugh again. 'I can laugh about it now,' she said cosily, 'but you scared me.'

'First thing tomorrow we got to do something about getting that little girl in the hospital.'

Smiling broadly the man brought a big untidily cut T-bone on a sizzling metal platter and set it before them.

'My this is good,' said Paul with his mouth full. 'A good meal's a mighty good cure for discouragement sometimes. There are times,' he added forking fried potatoes into his mouth, 'when I just feel like a phony, a miserable chair-warmer. I can talk about it now that I don't feel so bad . . . My you're a help Facts and Figures . . . you and this steak . . . when it seems absolutely impossible to arrange all these divergent human relations in any kind of way that makes sense. I told you how I felt about it that night at Meridian Park. Funny Meridian seems to be our key word. Your relationship with people changes when you try to organize them into doing things. You have to kind of lower their consequence. First thing you know it's your career instead of the work gets to be the important thing. I suppose that's how politicians are made. Oh God don't let me turn into a politician . . . What's the use of talking about it?'

'Talk about it Paul.'

'I get to wondering if all this social service work . . . that's what it is . . . is just dogooding . . . isn't just putting up a front for the politicians even if you don't get to be one yourself . . . I'm out of my depth. I want to be home on a nice experimental farm with a laboratory. Let somebody else save the country . . . I get so horribly depressed . . . I wish I could go back fifteen years and start over . . .'

'Maybe,' said Georgia, 'the country can't be saved unless it's born again.'

They'd finished eating. They sat in silence for a long time looking at each other. The man in the white coat was beginning to put out the lights. 'If you folks don't mind,' he said in a cozening voice, 'I have to open up early, for the truckdrivers.'

Paul was yawning. 'I'm all in,' he said. 'Brother have you got any cabins?'

'I got right nice cabins all fresh done over last winter.'

'Suppose we take a look at one.'

Georgia started to tremble. She let the men walk ahead. Her hands were icy. She was trembling. The stars were so bright the liquid darkness was all aflame with them.

Paul met her at the door of a glowing yellow varnished box. The man had gone.

'I took it,' Paul said in a gentle apologetic tone. He took her hand and looked down at it meditatively. Then he drew her gently towards him into the cabin, closed the door behind her and kissed her. She felt herself falling. The hard knots of muscle of his arms held her from falling. The ten fingers of his hands were holding up her back. 'I guess this just had to be,' he said breathless when he took his lips away from hers. 'I guess it just had to be.' They sat down side by side on the edge of the double bed. She let her head drop against his shoulder.

'Do you want anything particular out of the car?' She'd never heard his voice so gently concerned with her. She shook her head. 'I'll lock it up and fetch our bags.'

She grabbed his arm tight. 'Let's go together. You mustn't leave me alone. I'd get to thinking. Oh Paul we shouldn't . . .'

'Too late now,' said Paul gruffly and strode off to the car. She watched him helplessly while he hauled the two bags out of the trunk.

'Oh God Petersen's bag's in there. Poor devil I forgot about him,' said Paul.

'Paul,' she grabbed his hands. 'Hadn't we better drive right back to Meridian?'

'Can't be helped now,' Paul said again. He picked up the bags and strode back fast with them to the cabin. By the time she caught up with him he was coming out the door again.

'But Paul,' she started.

He reached over and caught her by the shoulder and drew her roughly to him. 'Hush,' he whispered. 'I thought I heard something . . . Listen.' They stared out over the windworn dark shapes of the badlands. The night was growing cold. She gave a little shiver and snuggled closer to him. Then she heard away far off a thin wailing dog-like sound that rose and trailed off into the starpacked sky. 'Facts and Figures I think that's a coyote,' whispered Paul.

'It's the West,' Georgia whispered back. 'Oh Paul we've rolled off the edge of the cornbelt into the West.'

'You funny romantic little kid,' he said kissing her all over her face. Their ankles touching, their thighs touching, their arms interlocked, they squeezed together back into the cabin. She was melting inside. She was going to faint. She clung to him. The cheap bedsprings clanked as she let him stretch her out gently on the bed. 'No no no, Paul, no . . .' she kept saying in a tiny voice until his lips clamped down on hers again.

THE SHIP OF STATE

7

W'*e're funny in this country,*' *said the man who sat next to us at the ballgame . . . *'*Every four years, the year when February has an extra day, we knock off work to listen to the oratorical efforts of the gentlemen who have somehow decided that the thing they want most in the world*
    is to be President.
    We sit round the radio after supper to hear them, we even leave home and crowd into ballparks and convention halls and granges and theatres to hear them
    promise high wages and low prices and high prices and low wages and economy in the administration and plenty of public money to spend in everybody's home state
    and to keep us out of war.'

THE THIRD TERM

IT WAS A BREEZY SUNDAY MORNING. Herbert Spotswood had just finished dictating his last letter. While Jean typed it off, her white slim fingers skipping fast over the keys, her lips compressed to give her face a little absorbed professional air that pleased him, he got to his feet and walked with his hands clasped behind his back to and fro in front of the open windows watching the wind ruffle splotches of dull silver into the treetops below . . . Could I? he was thinking, a man of sixty, could I? He was drawing her gently to him, feeling her mouth under his, her little breasts against his. He had kissed her quite often, very gently, very fatherlyfriendly but further he hadn't dared . . . Could I? could I? he was thinking . . . There were nights with Jeannette when he'd done quite well after a good meal and some wine, but Jeannette was so experienced. Frenchwomen understood those things . . . Could I? Now? Here? Jean had gotten to her feet and was walking towards him with her stiff serious smile. 'Well that's that,' she said briskly. 'Now if you sign them, Herbert, we'll clear away and I'll fix the flowers.'

He sat at his desk glancing thoughtfully at a phrase or two of each letter he signed it. She came back and stood beside him at the telephone on the corner of the desk to call room service for some vases.

She was so close that the light perfume of her clothes rose to his head and her warmth and slenderness made his arms tingle. She looked down into his face.

'Hurry up Herbert . . . we've got the cocktails to make,' she said briskly as if to a child who was slow dressing.

Her voice brought him up sharp out of a trance. He had been dreaming of a big old New England farmhouse and dogs and children on the lawn and Jean running the household for him so capably, a whole other life to be lived before he died. He was sitting with his fountainpen poised over the end of a letter. He finished quickly and meticulously feeling like a little boy trying to make haste under his mother's eye. Then he sat a moment watching Jean bustle about the room, bringing roses out of the bathroom, telling the waiter where to set the table, sending away some knives and forks that hadn't been properly washed. When the waiter had gone out he said, 'My Jean it's fun to have you here,' and looked up at her out of moist eyes.

'I told you I was a good secretary Herbert.' She laughed her brisk laugh that always had little sound of metal in it. He got to his feet and walked towards her with his arms outstretched. 'Jeany do you suppose you could'. . . He managed to plant a glancing kiss on her cheekbone.

'Could I what?' She pushed him away. 'You've got to get ready for this luncheon. And I said not to call me Jeany . . . My name's Jean.'

'Suppose you mix the martinis, Jean. I don't mix a very good cocktail. I've never been a drinking man.'

She seemed delighted. He followed her around while she bustled about, bringing out the cocktail glasses, mixing the gin and vermouth in the shaker. She kept talking about Philadelphia. Jean was saying, as she deftly cut a zest of lemonpeel for each glass, that she'd never had such an exciting time in her life as at that convention, she thought the Republican candidate was the greatest man since Lincoln, she was so sold on him she had taken a job, a paid job for a change with Women for Willkie. A good thing Miss Albert was coming back, Herb grumbled and added half in fun that he hadn't quite made up his mind about the Republican candidate, maybe he was jealous of him. They both got to laughing over that. The smell of the roses began to spread through the morning air of the room mixed with a festive fragrance of gin and vermouth and lemonpeel. He was going to be the next President, Jean insisted with a toss of her head, so Herbert would have to get used to all the girls falling in love with him.

'It's going to be dull having just Miss Albert in the morning,' said Herb. 'Jean you must have lunch with me every day.'

The phone rang. She answered and then handed Herb the receiver. 'It's a Mr. Spotswood, Herbert. I didn't know you had any brothers.'

Herb felt the color leave his face.

'Tyler is that you?' he asked in a hollow voice.

'Sure Dad I thought it was about time I came around.'

The voice sounded a little thick but Herb couldn't tell whether he had been drinking or not.

'Come up for a minute. I'm having some people in to lunch . . . It's my son Tyler.' He turned to Jean forcing a smile. 'He's coming up for a minute.'

He caught the quick searching glance she gave him as he picked up the shaker and hurried with it into the bathroom. He just had time to pop the gin and vermouth in the clothes closet before he heard a knock on the door and there was Tyler tall and gaunt standing stiff as a ramrod in the threshold.

'Come in,' Herb said trying to put some warmth into his voice. 'Tyler how many years it's been.'

Tyler came forward impulsively as if he were going to kiss his father on the cheek. Then he stopped and grabbed his left hand and shook it awkwardly.

'Dad you don't look a day older,' he said.

Herb right away knew from his breath that he'd been drinking.

'This is Mrs. Darwin,' said Herb. 'She's been helping me with my correspondence.' The words sounded tinnily in his ears as he said them. Tyler stepped forward ceremoniously and made a little bow when he shook her hand. There was a feeling of ice in Herb's breast when he noticed how much younger she looked than Tyler. Why she was young enough to be his granddaughter.

'Sit down Tyler.'

The moment they sat down constraint seized them all. Tyler's thin lined face had a bruised look. As he sat there fiddling with a straw hat that had several nicks out of the rim his face began to redden as if the skin had been flayed off it. Herb was remembering the handsome blackhaired boy with the lively blue eyes. Now Tyler's eyes bulged out of his head and the blue was washed out as if it had run into the white. And this is my son, Herb seemed to see the words written out in front of him like a caption on a picture.

He glanced at Jean. She sat there with a bored expression on her face. Suddenly he pulled himself together and cleared his throat.

'Tyler when could you come in to have a real talk?'

Tyler's shaking hands were kneading the straw hat. The rim cracked. He gave a start and looked down at it in a dazed way as if a bee had stung him.

'Dad could I speak to you alone for a second right now?'

Herb got to his feet and saying to Jean in a weak explanatory voice that if she'd excuse them they'd talk while he dressed, led the way into the bedroom.

Tyler let himself drop into an armchair and drew his fingers up over his face.

'Dad I got the shakes so bad I can't think. This has all gotten me down a little . . . My digestion is upset. I wonder if you've got a drink around the house. I find it's the best thing for indigestion.' He looked up suddenly at his father with a ghost of his appealing boyish grin.

Herb frowned. He didn't want to go back into the parlor where Jean would see him fetch the gin bottle from the closet. 'The only thing I have is some cocktails Mrs. Darwin has prepared for my guests. Perhaps one drink won't hurt you.'

Tyler had jumped to his feet. 'Come on, Dad. Let's talk afterwards,' he said hoarsely.

Shaking his head Herb went into the bathroom and poured a little of the cocktail out into a tumbler.

'That won't do me any good Dad. Fill it up,' came Tyler's tremulous insistent voice over his shoulder.

Herb poured out some more in the glass. 'It hasn't any ice in it yet,' he said. Tyler had already drunk it down. 'Now Tyler you must go. I've got to get ready for my guests. I see Ed James quite often and he's spoken to me quite frankly. In Ed you've got one of the best friends ever a man had.'

Tyler pushed out his wet lips. 'That's a matter of opinion,' he said.

'He's been hoping you would work with him on his column.'

'I don't propose to be Ed's errandboy.'

'Tyler you have got to pull yourself together somehow. I'd be perfectly delighted to set you up to several months in a good sanitorium. When you were a boy I was never well enough off to do much for you . . . for either one of you . . . but now . . .'

Tyler's face wrinkled slowly into a frown. He already seemed a little unsteady on his feet. 'I have no intention of being set up to a Keeley cure by anybody. If people didn't nag at me this would all straighten out . . . It's just a nervous reaction. What you can do Dad if you want to be helpful is lend me fifteen dollars right now. It's Sunday and I happen to find myself out of cash. No place to cash a check . . . Banks closed, you understand,' he added hoarsely.

Herb groped for his wallet in the pocket of his white linen suit that was hanging in the closet and took out three fives.

'Call me tomorrow morning Tyler and let's have a long talk. Better come to lunch.'

Tyler took the bills roughly and shoved them in his trousers pocket and snatched his hat off the bed. Suddenly he seemed in a great hurry to be gone.

Herb escorted Tyler through the parlor where Jean with an air of elaborate unconcern was sitting in the window reading a magazine. When the door closed behind him Jean looked up. Sweat was pouring off Herb's face.

'I must hurry and change my clothes,' he said. 'Jean you'd better make some more cocktails. I had to give Tyler a little.'

'How I hate relations,' blurted out Jean in a harsh tone. 'My God I bet my relations are stinkinger man for man than yours Herbert.' Herb gave her a mild hurt look. 'I know,' Jean went on. 'You're not supposed to say those things . . . just think them . . . Bring that bucket of ice out of the bathroom and let's you and me have a stiff drink Herbert to forget our stinking relations.'

'Just a moment I'll change into my white suit first,' Herb said and closed himself into the bedroom. He took off all his clothes and stepped into a cold shower. Then dressing slowly so as not to get hot again he put on clean things. When he came back out into the parlor ice was clinking and Jean was pouring cocktails for Ed James and the Gulicks. She looked handsome in her pale yellow embroidered dress with one wave of her pale blond hair over her narrow forehead. The roses looked pretty. The sun was bright in the windows. It was going to be a nice luncheon.

Ed was saying he'd put up twenty-five bucks against a row of rubber dummies that the Skipper would make up his mind this week. Marice was showing all her pearly teeth she was laughing so. Mike stood with his feet apart looking down into his glass with the expression of a man who knew more than he was willing to tell. The bright sunlight from the windows shone through a crinkle of cigarette smoke.

'Mike, are you going to Chicago?' Ed asked suddenly.

Mike nodded. 'Yes Walker suggested I make the trip with him.'

Mike was taking his cocktail in little sips and giving himself a long time to think before he spoke. It wasn't like him, thought Herb. He had been left so nervous by Tyler's visit he'd drunk down two martinis before he knew it and felt a little giddy.

'What ever happened to Jerry Evans and his oil men?' he asked.

'Jerry is out having lunch with the Boss on the Williamsburg right at this minute,' said Mike Gulick letting out his words in an oracular tone.

'I saw Jerry this morning before he went,' Ed rattled on. 'He was riding high wide and handsome. He seemed to think the Skipper was passing the word to the D of J to go easy on his oil men . . . A consent decree or something like that. I wouldn't be surprised if Jerry headed the delegation from his home state to the Democratic Convention. At least that's what I'm saying in my column tomorrow morning. I may be sticking my neck out.'

'That might very well be,' Mike started to stutter a little. Everybody waited for him to go on but he stopped short.

Eloise Dilling came in wearing a pink dress with candy stripes and too many ruffles. The color didn't go too well with her red hair. There was a look of pain on her face and she was limping more than usual.

A few steps after her came George. The frown left his face as he came through the door and he squared his shoulders and advanced into the room with the bonny look of a tenor in a musical show. He shook Herb formally by the hand.

The waiters started bringing in the lunch. Herb was so busy getting people seated, ordering red pepper to go on the mayonnaise that went with the crab salad, making sure that the Johannisberger which had been cooling in a white metal bucket in the corner of the room was properly cold before it was poured, that for a while he lost track of the conversation.

George Dilling was talking addressing everything he said to Jean who was quite the stately hostess at the end of the table. George was saying he had just come back from a tour of the Farmers' Association locals in the West. He'd found the working farmers all for Mr. Big, he said. Some of the large operators might fall for the Republican candidate but not the working farmer.

'Wait till they hear him speak,' said Jean with flashing eyes.

'They like their little checks from the three A's too well,' Ed interrupted.

'By the way Mike,' asked George, 'is Walker still in town?'

'The doctor finally insisted he get away for a rest,' Mike said ponderously. 'He's not a well man.'

'Who insisted? Dr. Powers?' asked Jean.

'He's gone out to a Montana ranch for a little troutfishing.'

'She fancies herself in a riding habit,' said Jean.

'Well she has got a very pretty figure,' piped up Eloise Dilling.

Ed was talking. There was a funny story going around about Walker, he said slowly. There was a sort of crystal gazer in this town named Madame Arno, a woman who got up horoscopes. She had quite a large clientele. In fact he'd almost fallen dead when he'd heard some of the names. He laughed. The present company needn't worry he hadn't found any of their names on the list, not yet. Well evidently the horoscope business wasn't so flourishing as it might be because the story was that Madame Arno had approached someone on the Republican National Committee with a packet of letters purported to be written by Walker Watson. Ed had seen copies of some of them.

They were the darnedest farrago about telepathy and clairvoyance and Rosicrucianism and tips on the races. In fact if they ever saw the light of day they would do the Administration a great deal of harm. He looked directly across the table at Mike Gulick. 'Come clean Mike is there anything in it?'

Mike kept his face stiff but he reddened. 'Of course there's nothing in it . . . Did your reactionary friends take the bait?'

'No. I understand the letters were shown to the Republican candidate and he decided in view of the dangerous world situation they just would give too much aid and comfort to the enemy.'

'Of course he wouldn't do anything like that,' said Jean. 'He wouldn't do anything underhanded not if it meant the presidency.'

'Silliest bunk I ever heard,' said Mike.

Silence settled down on the table. Mike was staring at Ed James as if he wanted to strangle him.

Herb felt it was up to him. The Republican candidate, he said, was perfectly sound on foreign policy and on the continuance of aid to Europe. He had been very much impressed with him at Philadelphia. Of course he hadn't quite made up his mind yet. Nobody was listening to him, so he suggested they get up and drink their coffee near the window where it was cooler.

Jean led the way with George Dilling keeping close to her ear. Marice and Eloise sat on the sofa keeping up a cheerful chatter and Mike and Ed James sat stiffly opposite them. Neither one addressed a word to the other. Herb took the opportunity to slip off into the bedroom. He was beginning to get a headache. Cocktails never agreed with him. He looked at himself in the mirror of the dressing table. Tired, seeing Tyler had made him look tired and old. He brushed his hair and ran a little comb through his mustache. Then he shook a couple of tablets out of a medicine bottle and went into the bathroom after a glass of water. There he noticed Jeannette's last letter with its Portuguese stamp lying unopened on the glass shelf. He'd taken it in there to read when he got through shaving that morning but he'd been thinking so much about Jean he forgot it. He'd had it for several days in his pocket unopened. He knew all too well what it would say. It would be asking him why he hadn't managed to get her a plane reservation. He tore open the flimsy envelope and took in the letter at a glance.

Cher ami I write to practice the English but I cannot understand why you who are so powerful in your country now have been not able to get me plane reservation, but I know you do your best. Thank you. Thank you. What courage I have taken in your assistance. It is very complicated and dishonest here about reservations on the plane. Je cherche des tuyaux. But I have no hope for a month. If only the madman does not decide to enter Spain where he has many sympathies and even in this charming country. I shall not rest until I tread the sacred soil of America. Ta pauvre Jeannette.

The letter threw him into a swirl of indecision. Suddenly he remembered his guests, dropped the letter in his pocket and hurried back into the parlor. They were much too quiet. Ed James sat looking through a League of Nations publication at the desk. The Gulicks were sitting blankly by the window. Eloise with a bleak look of unhappiness on her face was studying her husband's back as he laughed and chatted with Jean.

Herb had twisted his mouth into a genial host expression and had his lips parted to speak when he heard somebody fumbling against the outside door. As he stepped towards it the door swung open. Tyler with his hair over his eyes stood in the doorway swaying slightly on the balls of his feet. He was squinting so hard to see who was in the room his face was knotted into an exaggerated scowl.

'Why Tyler Spotswood,' Mike cried out in a tone of real friendship and strode forward with his hand outstretched. Tyler made swimming motions with his arms. He was trying to speak, but his slobbered lips only made a bubbling sound. Before anybody could reach him he pitched forward flat on his face on the carpet. Everybody stood around while Herb tugged at him. At last with the other men's help, Herb lifting his legs and Ed and Mike hauling on his arms they managed to drag him into the bedroom and to roll him on the bed. They left him there and Herb carefully closed the bedroom door. All the while George and Jean stood merrily talking in the window as if nothing had happened.

'Think nothing of it,' Herb said, tittering nervously. 'But now that we've laid out the corpse hadn't we better have a drink ourselves. I'll order up some Scotch.'

The Gulicks excused themselves hurriedly and then Ed James went. There was nobody left but the Dillings. Herb got the fidgets trying to talk to Eloise while George went on chattering to Jean.

At last Eloise got up and hobbled to the window to remind George that they had promised to drive out to see some people in Arlington and they said goodby. Jean and Herb were left standing in the middle of the floor looking at each other. They each took a long deep breath.

'My that was a turkey,' said Jean.

'I thought we were having a rather interesting time until Tyler appeared,' Herb mildly expostulated.

'Interesting!' said Jean. 'Nobody ever opened his mouth except to put his foot in it what with Ed James putting the Gulicks through a kind of inquisition and I didn't help much by coming out for the Republican candidate. People are beginning to take their politics hard in this town.'

'Let's get a car and take a ride in the country,' said Herb. 'I don't want to stay here.'

'He'll come to and drink up what's left of the gin and vermouth. I know those rummies,' said Jean. 'I had a father and a husband who were rummies.'

Herb took a step towards her and grabbed both her hands in his. 'You poor child,' he said. 'You haven't had it too easy.'

'For God's sake let's not talk about that.' The sound of metal came back into her voice.

He tried to draw her to him. She tood stiffly leaning away. He gave up trying to put his arms around her and patted the hand he still held.

'You've been an awful cute little girl today,' he said feeling tears come to his eyes. 'There are things I could do for you. I'd like to help . . . Why don't you let me? How about just going out to Reno and getting that divorce? I could find a place somewhere near and keep you from getting too blue. I'm so afraid that if we wait too long something will come up.'

'Or somebody?' she looked him teasingly in the eye.

'George Dilling was certainly handing you a red hot line as the young people put it.'

'He's attractive . . . but he doesn't make any sense, not in my life,' she said musingly.

'Sit down beside me here Jeany, just for a second.' She let him place her primly beside him on the sofa. 'For the first time in my life I would be in a position to offer something rather pleasant to the girl I married. A nice house in the country, interesting friends . . . There might even be children . . .' He choked on the last word. 'They say a man's as young as he feels,' he blurted out. His heart was thumping so he couldn't go on.

She got to her feet. 'Do you remember the number of that garage? Let's drive over the back road to Baltimore and eat dinner. I feel like getting out of Washington.'

He couldn't remember the number. The sense of failure began to creep through him. He took off his fogged glasses and wiped them on his handkerchief.

'I have it,' she said in her cool businesslike voice.

When she was through phoning she came back and sat down a little away from him on the sofa. She began picking at a loose thread on her dress.

'I'll tell you what I'll do,' she said in the same precise tones she'd used to order a car and driver from the garage. 'I think it's our duty to do everything we can against the third term . . . it's against the whole spirit of American institutions . . . I have a duty there and I hope you'll feel you have too. But after election . . . we'll see. After all a divorce only takes six weeks. Meanwhile . . .' She gave him a little quick encouraging smile, 'let's be friends.'

He picked up her hand and kissed it. 'The best of friends,' he said.

She got briskly to her feet.

'Let's get out of here before the boyfriend wakes up . . . I'm going down to the ladies' room downstairs. I'll meet you in the lobby.' She snatched up her bag and gloves and her broadbrimmed black straw hat and was gone.

Herbert Spotswood sat in the emptiness of the hotel parlor looking at the crumbs on the table and the dropped napkins and the ashtrays full of cigarette butts and the empty glasses with lipstick on the rims. The roses had started to wilt. 'Lonely,' he said aloud as he got slowly to his feet. He shuddered and without going back into the bedroom to fetch his hat or his key went out into the hall and shut the door behind him.

THE SHIP OF STATE

8

O utside it was raining. *The barroom smelled sharp of lemon of vermouth and of gin.*

'We all got to work to do in this country but when we get into a political campaign we like to take a vacation from the ordinary meanings of words and watch the candidates for public office turn themselves inside out with doubletalk

so that no one of any color creed race or profession

shall be in the least offended,' says the man who has ordered a beer.

'They want us voters all to be happy the way the Declaration of Independence said,' the barkeep puts his word in while he rinses a glass.

'After baseball and football and basketball and possibly hockey the great national game,' says the small hoarse man who's ordered a stinger,

'is politics . . .'

'. . . played according to the oldtime rules, interrupts the refugee professor, the one with a gray goatee who teaches at the University in Exile. 'The trouble is that we live in a world where they've changed all the rules

—seizure of power—

the way the moneymasters changed the rules of business through interlocking directorates. In the modern state

power is total . . .'

'. . . You form a party of disciplined members with power as the single objective. You espouse the cause of the outofwork, the underpaid, the incompetent, the outcast; they are the wedge that splits society. You talk whatever language suits the moment, no matter what, so long as you get a disciplined member into the driver's seat of the tradeunion, the professional association, the chamber of commerce, the corporation, the political party . . .'

'You vilify every independent man, the rule of the lie, the lie a thousand times proved false eventually takes root and grows with a life of its own. You carefully list your opponents waiting the day when you have won the police or the army and can rub them out or work them faceless in a slave gang . . .'

'Power is the total control of the means of coercion and of the network of communications, the power to withhold, to seize, to march a man out of his door into the faceless mass.'

'The driving force is man's hatred for man, the hatred of the poor for the rich, of the Jew for the Gentile or the Gentile for the Jew, of the downandout for the welltodo, of the cripple for the runner of the hundred yard dash.'

'The eventual aim of course they'll tell you is peace on earth goodwill to men but the means are war and pillage and starvation and death;

the total exercise of power.'

'Now tell me one thing' asks the little man at the end of the bar 'Why do they want to do it?'

VACATION

GEORGIA MOVED SLOWLY ABOUT THE KITCHEN cluttered with still unfamiliar pots and pans. The late afternoon heat held everything tight in its vice. Her steps dragged as if she were making her way through a tank of warm water. Out of the open window she could see in the wilted garden a patch of blue delphinium shimmering in yellow sunlight and the great dusty heartshaped leaves of the catalpa near the fence and beyond through the tremulous haze the arbors and dense crepe myrtle bushes of other Alexandria back yards. A rooster crowing suddenly and insistently near by startled her. For the fiftieth time she looked at the loudticking clock on the shelf. It was not quite six. Paul wouldn't come till seven, even if he weren't late. It would be cooler then she was hoping. This afternoon the heavy heat seemed even to have slowed the progress of the minutes round the clock. The ticks seemed to come slower and slower as she listened to them.

Thinking about Ann Arbor and the musty freshness of Père's old house there, she let herself drop into the kitchen chair. She could hear above the ticking clock the purr of Negro voices from the street outside, and a low clucking of hens from the next yard. Sitting there with her legs stuck out in front of her she let herself dream of taking Paul to Ann Arbor, showing him Père's house and the University, and the streets she'd walked home through and the soda fountain she used to go to with Joe and the hilly walks through the apple orchards above the town. In her memories she found herself dubbing in Paul's long black head with its black hair and small neatly formed ears instead of Joe's squat blond bateared countenance. She began to try to imagine what Paul had looked like in college, about the same as now only smoother-faced and even worse dressed probably. She felt the muscles of her arms grow tense and her breasts tighten under her brassière as she thought of him grabbing her close, kissing her on the mouth.

The front door bell was ringing. She jumped to her feet breathless. At first she told herself it was Paul. No it wouldn't be Paul because he would have walked right in. Maybe the latch had snapped. He'd be impatiently stamping up and down outside. Walking briskly across the little parlor shuttered tight against the heat she felt herself wearing in spite of the flutter in the pit of her stomach her everyday grave face.

She opened the door.

Outside in the sun stood Joe Yerkes with his red ears sticking out like the handles of a sugarbowl under his straw hat, and of all people Dr. Jane Sparling. 'Why come in,' Georgia said in a voice that sounded cordial to her own ears. Joe had that familiar look that suddenly made her feel warm and soft towards him. Jane looked unusually feminine today in a white piquet dress with a straw hat shaped a little like an oldfashioned sailor on her head. As she walked in she gave Georgia that hard inquisitive look Georgia always felt got somehow under her clothes. Jane plunked herself down on the horsehair sofa and complained that the room was so dark she couldn't see to talk.

'So this is Bertha Manning's little hideout, an old southern mansion in miniature eh?' she said looking scornfully around at the black walnut furniture and the jam of porcelain and silver knickknacks on the table and the Wedgwood in the corner cabinet. 'If I had this place I'd get an antique dealer to back up his truck and clean it out for me. So you're quite the southern belle Georgia dear. Alexandria makes my flesh creep.'

'It was George Washington's home town, wasn't it?' Joe asked vaguely.

'George Washington was the first American Fascist,' Jane came back at him in her most scornful tone.

'Well,' said Georgia. 'It was awfully nice of Bertha to lend me the place.'

'She can afford it. She's filthy rich. It does give you privacy,' said Jane pausing a little over the word in a way that made Georgia uncomfortable. Then she rattled on that she herself couldn't imagine living in an apartment packed with another woman's things, she couldn't imagine living with a lot of possessions, not even her own. Georgia brought out some cigarettes but she decided against bringing out a drink. She had to get them out of there before Paul came. Dr. Sparling already had her hat off and was putting a cigarette in her long cigaretteholder in a leisurely way and settling down to smoke.

'We see quite a lot of your old roommate, Georgia,' she said.

'Who?'

'Louise Aldershot. That ancient virgin from the cowcountry. She comes around to the forum regularly,' said Jane with some complacence. 'After all we mustn't forget that the Negro isn't the only proletariat in the South.'

Georgia burst out laughing.

'Well what's so funny about it?' asked Jane.

'I just can't imagine Louise Aldershot a proletarian, that's all . . . Where are you people off to? I have to go out directly. I have an engagement,' Georgia added, feeling her face get red. She never was any good as a liar, she thought.

Jane answered right away that she was going around the corner to dine with Bertha's brother Chad. They'd invited some Negro intellectuals. She bet George didn't know where the boyfriend was going, she prattled on and poked Joe, who had been sitting on the sofa beside her without saying a word, in the ribs with her elbow. He was going to an important political conference with the big boy who lived up the street.

Joe frowned. 'It's all right to tell George,' he said, 'but the whole thing is strictly under the hat. It looks like the big boy was eventually going to come out for the Republican candidate.'

A Republican victory Jane Sparling announced echoing Joe, was the only way of keeping us out of the imperialist war which would bring fascism to this country and the loss of all the gains the working class had made in the last eight years.

'But it'll split the trade union movement wide open,' said Georgia.

'Anything's better than war and fascism,' Joe insisted doggedly.

'Of course your big boy's always been a Republican anyway,' Georgia said. Time had suddenly speeded up. It must be seven o'clock. Her fingers began to fidget. Oh lord she didn't want them to be there when Paul came. Jane Sparling talked and talked. Georgia lost track of what she was saying. Georgia had left the front door open and sat looking out apprehensively along the stretch of uneven brick sidewalk she could see from her chair. At last she couldn't stand the strain any longer. She got to her feet in a panic. 'Have you got the time Joe?'

Joe looked at his wrist watch which was a new one mounted on a silver bracelet she'd never seen before. The boy's stepping out, she told herself.

Her voice was more apologetic than she intended. 'I've got an engagement . . .'

Joe stared at his watch for a long time. 'It's five minutes of seven,' he said. He got up out of his chair and took hold of her elbow. 'George may I take you out to lunch some day? I miss you if I don't see you . . . Just for old times' sake.'

'Coeds,' snorted Jane Sparling. 'Well I'll be going along. I hoped I could take you with me, Georgia. It's going to be ideologically an interesting evening. One of the Negro comrades is a Party member but the others are political illiterates.'

Georgia was at the door, stammering that they must forgive her, that she was late, that she had to wash up and change her clothes. Jane started to talk again. She seemed hours putting away her cigarette-holder in her bag and putting on her hat. To hurry them along Georgia found herself telling Joe yes to be sure to call her at the office and making a date to go by Dr. Sparling's forum one evening. Jane held Georgia's hand a little longer than usual and gave it a significant squeeze before she let it go while her hard insolent stare seemed to travel up Georgia's arm under her blouse.

When they finally left Georgia's knees felt weak and she had to sit down. Paul walked in so fast with his long silent stride that before she knew it he was there beside her. She got up and leaned against him and suddenly started to cry. 'Some people came and I was so afraid they wouldn't go away,' she blubbered. Paul laughed and kissed her, tenderly for him, through her tears.

'I'm all a muck of sweat,' he said. 'I think I'll try that shower.'

As Georgia walked to the street door and locked it the thought flitted across her mind that now she knew how a streetwalker felt when she'd brought in her man off the street. She brushed the thought away. It was Paul and she loved him. She walked back into the parlor and stood awkwardly beside him.

'I mixed up some spoonbread for you. I hope it comes out right . . .' I am talking like a wife, she thought. She rattled on . . . 'I've got cold chicken and a bottle of wine on ice.'

He'd thrown his coat and tie on the sofa. Already he was pulling off his damp shirt. 'Hello, Facts and Figures,' he said looking down into her face with knitted brows. He kissed her. His knotty brown arms tightened round her shoulders pressing her breasts against his bony trunk. 'You feel sweet tonight,' he said as he drew her with him into the bedroom. The shutters were still closed. The bedroom was very dim. Only a few bars of ruddy sunlight made rays through the broken places on the shutters onto the wall above the bureau. Standing by the bed his hands were very deftly undressing her. His hands were everywhere. He had hold of her breasts. She couldn't help it was her last thought before she let herself go in his arms.

She made him wait while she went into the bathroom and took a douche and a shower. Then suddenly feeling very light and cool in her dressinggown she went into the kitchen and lit the gasoven. By the time he came out of the bathroom barefooted and wearing only his shirt and pants, she had the table all set in the parlor. She poured him out a glass of white wine and they sat opposite each other, silently sipping it while they waited for the spoonbread to cook. He sat scowling and silent. He lifted up his wineglass and looked at it inquisitively against the light.

Georgia was just getting ready to ask him whether he wanted his salad with his chicken or afterwards when suddenly he came out with what was on his mind.

'Millard's gone to Chicago.'

'What on earth for?'

'To hold Walker Watson's hand I guess. That buzzard still thinks he's got a chance . . . I'm about ready to pull out of the agency.'

Georgia was afraid she was going to cry again. She ran off into the kitchen to look at the spoonbread. It had risen high. A smell of burning cornmeal came from where some of it had spilled on the floor of the oven. Getting the hot pan out onto a plate she gave her hand a nasty burn against the oven shelf. She hid the searing red bar on her hand under the table and sat watching him ladling out the spoonbread. He speared himself a leg of cold chicken without looking at it and sat there eating hungrily.

'I'm going on my vacation. There's no hope of getting anything done in this damn town till they get over this convention mania,' he went on, talking with his mouth full. 'I reckon I'll hop me a train and go on down to Hawk's Nest tomorrow. I got to see what the kids are up to.'

Georgia sat surreptitiously rubbing butter on her burn with the tip of one finger looking at him across the table out of stinging eyes.

'This is a good supper Facts and Figures,' he said. 'You'd better eat some of it.'

'I can't.' Tears spurted from her eyes like from a little child's. He was looking at her with one of his sharp black searching looks. She held her burnt hand up to him. 'I burned myself,' she snivelled.

'Why all the waterworks?' he asked coolly. 'Have you got any bicarbonate of soda?'

He jumped up and padded out of the room in his bare feet. She heard him slamming around in the kitchen. She dried her eyes as fast as she could. 'It's in the bathroom Paul,' she called after him.

He came back with the yellow can, quickly mixed some soda up into a paste with a few drops of water and put a thick layer of it over the burn. 'Let it dry on there,' he said. 'That won't hurt long.'

He stood a moment looking down at her, then he tapped her

peremptorily on the shoulder. 'Facts and Figures, you must hold onto your nerves better . . . We've all got things to cry about.'

She sat dryeyed and crumpled in the chair, hanging her head like a little child that's been scolded. She wanted him to know how apologetic she felt. She wanted to throw herself down on the floor beside him. 'Paul don't pay any attention . . . I'm tired out . . . It's the heat . . . I'll be all right . . . Now I've spoiled your supper.'

'Don't be silly. You made it. It was a darn good supper.' He held out his hand to her and pulled her to her feet. 'Let's go out and walk around. I've never had a chance to take a look at Alexandria. Here where did I leave my shoes?'

'All right Paul,' she said obediently. 'Let me wash my face. I'll be ready in a jiffy.'

When she came out from the bathroom, he was already dressed except for his necktie that hung out of the pocket of his jacket, and pacing impatiently about the parlor.

He shot ahead of her out the front door. When she caught up with him she put her hand through his arm for fear she might trip on the uneven bricks of the pavement. The sun had set. Great arched streaks of orange and carmine were fading fast out of the sky leaving a dense cloudy lavender. The shadows were growing hazily blue under the dense trees that lined the street as green in the stifling twilight as spinach boiled with a pinch of soda in the water. Behind the trees the brickwork of the small eighteenth century houses shone dull red under a coating of soot. The panelled doors and the shutters and the window frames on the little pointed dormers stood out a faint blue white. The slate roofs matched the plumcolored haze that thickened in the gardens. Here and there an electric light already glowed orange behind a delicate fanlight. Dragging her after him Paul walked down the street towards the river. She clung to his arm in a modest oldfashioned way. He stopped at a slip between sagging ancient wharf buildings to look out at the puttycolored river where lingered a smooth silvery sheen brighter than the sky. The hills opposite were a very light rosy green. The colors in everything seemed to run as if melting from the heat.

Before Georgia had really caught her breath Paul started off over the cobbled pavement of the road parallel to the river. At the corner of the high wire fence of the torpedo factory a sentry in khaki stopped them and mumbled gruffly that they couldn't walk that way. They turned up the hill again instead.

'That shows how near we are to it,' Paul said in a low voice.

'What, Paul?'

'War,' he said savagely as if it were her fault. 'War. Well I missed the last one. Might as well go that way as any other. But it's going to interrupt everything anybody's trying to do.'

'I'm a regular blockhead tonight,' whispered Georgia. Stop apologizing, she was telling herself.

At the next corner Paul turned abruptly. They zigzagged back and forth block by block for some time. At the parish church he stopped to read all the inscriptions carefully by the light of the streetlight. Then he looked up frowning at the steeple still bright against the sky which had darkened to a rosy slate color.

'You really can get an idea of what this place was like a hundred and fifty years ago,' he said.

She wanted to talk about George Washington, but everything she could think of seemed so silly to her she didn't dare answer. Her shoes weren't comfortable. She was beginning to feel a blister coming on one of her toes.

'Georgia you look pale,' he said. It startled her to have him call her Georgia. She'd never heard him call her Georgia before. 'You mustn't get too tired. I'll take the Washington bus. You go home and get a good night's rest. I've left a raft of work for you at the office.'

Walking over to the bus station she was hoping hoping in spite of herself the bus wouldn't be there. The bus was waiting. People were getting aboard.

'Well I'll see you in a month,' he said cheerfully. With one foot on the step he turned back. 'Georgia,' he whispered in a low intent voice. 'We mustn't get too emotional about all this. It's a mean nervous bronco we're trying to ride. If we let him shy at trifles he'll run away with us.' With a wave of a long hand he was gone.

Walking home along the broad thoroughfare against the moving headlights of the cars she felt dead tired. All the strength had suddenly drained out of her. Under the streetlights she walked fast with her eyes downcast for fear somebody would see on her face a tinge of the bitter misery that was spreading through her mind and body the way ink spreads through water. When she turned into her dark back street it was already night.

THE SHIP OF STATE

9

*W*e *went down to meet the boat the European refugees were coming in on. Not so many people on the dock, interpreters, girls with armbands from relief committees, a stout woman at an oilcloth table setting out hot coffee and sugarbuns. There still was the old close smell of the steerage about them as they walked heavily up the gangplank looking up into our faces out of eyes as monkeys' anxious. Men had beaver hats, old shaped caps, women were hunched in worn capes and military coats of a foreign cut. The hair of the youths was much too long. Faces were the color of roots that have sprouted in the cellar.*

There were not many of them. They had very few possessions, ropedup suitcases, a tin trunk or two some canvas bags. Waiting for the customsofficer we talked to the aged revolutionary, an old woman with thin gray hair and a lined gray face and gray agate eyes without luster: 'Watch for the day,' she said toilsomely twisting the language on her tongue. 'When you see hope liquidated and every truth become a lie, and they tell you it doesn't matter because people go on believing just the same . . . Watch for the day when all the words turn traitor.'

A GREAT AMERICAN

A s MILLARD WALKED DOWN THE LONG HOTEL CORRIDOR
he took off the alternate delegate's badge he found still hanging
from his lapel and poked it in his pocket. He knocked on the door of
Walker Watson's suite. There was no answer so he went on down the
hall to his own room. He let himself drop into the chair at the desk and
took out his fountainpen to write a letter to Lucile. Dear Lou, he started
but he couldn't phrase an opening sentence. His head was hollow. His
head reverberated hollowly like the great cave of the ZStadium with
words bawled over the public address system with bands playing Hail
to the Chief and Happy Days Are Here Again and For He's a Jolly
Good Fellow and the jazzing organ coming in to top the cheers and
the bellow of applause. His hand was sore from handshaking. He'd had
too many drinks. His nose reeked of cigarsmoke and cigarettesmoke
and of the sweat of packedin delegates. There were motes before his
eyes from the dazzle of spots and Kleig lights and the flashlight bulbs
of photographers. He could still feel the nudging of elbows in his ribs
and the slap of broad hands on his back. He sat nodding over the piece
of hotel writing paper. Dear Lou he wrote again. Dear Lou was all he
could write. He needed Lou's sharp neat little phrases to cut the fog in

his head. He'd call her long distance. He gave the operator the number and went into the bathroom to take a shower.

He'd barely slipped out of his clothes and stepped under the cold water before the call came through. With a towel round him he ran dripping across the room. Lucile's voice was precise but far away at the end of a humming tunnel. 'Hello Oz. Holding up?' 'Oh Lou I wish you were here. No it's not much fun. I never have a minute to myself but I'm damn lonely, never felt lonelier in my life. I guess it's all the doubletalk that gets me down . . . You probably know more about what's happened than I do just from listening to the radio. Mr. Big was renominated sometime in the small hours. You know he released all his delegates. So far as I could make out it was a real draft. A great spontaneous demonstration. That was a moment I wouldn't have missed. And now if they can settle up the vice-presidency we can all go home and start acting like grownup people again . . . Maybe we can use all this war production to accomplish something useful . . . Boys all right? That's good . . '

All at once the connection cleared and it was almost as if she were in the room with him . . . 'Oz come on down for a weekend before going back to Washington. You can do it if you try. We'll go take the boys fishing at Port Isabel.'

'It would have to be nearer than that. I can't tell yet. I'll call up when this madhouse is over. It'll take me a month to get the agency running again. They're all loco with the big balloons now . . . Lou I wish you were here . . . Goodnight honeybug sleep tight. I'll be thinking of you.'

After he'd hung up he sat there at the desk looking tenderly down on the piece of writing paper with a picture of the hotel on it where he'd written Dear Lou Dear Lou Dear Lou.

'Mugs Allen's the name.' Millard started at the big sidewalk voice behind him that bit off each word and spat it out. He got to his feet with the towel held tight round his middle. 'Mugs for Mulligan.'

A squarish young man with a crew cut and a pinkstriped silk shirt over which gushed a blue necktie ornamented with the signs of the zodiak, was standing in the middle of the room. He wore a big red badge. He grinned confidentially into Millard's face and, talking strictly out of the corner of his mouth, repeated his name. 'Mugs Allen

of the James P. Toohey Democratic Club on the Sout' Side . . . Put it
dere Mr. Carroll.'

Millard shook a beefy hand. 'Excuse me a second. I was in the middle of taking a shower when I was called to the phone.'

'Take yer time. I got all night. Chimmy sent some o' de boys over
to help you gents out.'

Millard went back into the bathroom to finish up his shower.
Then he slipped on a bathrobe to go to his suitcase to fetch a clean
shirt. Mugs was all primed for him. 'How did yer like de spontaneous
demonstration Mr. Carroll?' he started as soon as Millard stuck his
head out of the bathroom door. 'Chimmy, he calls de boys together
an' he says boys de mayor says dis gotto be de biggest spontaneous
demonstration ever was. Chi's de convention city an' we gotto make it
stick . . . It was Chimmy's idear. Boys he says if you don't lift dat Stadium roof ten feet off its hinges it's no dice' . . . Millard slipped on the
clean shirt and went to the mirror to tie his necktie . . . 'So dey rigged
up some highpowered mikes for de guys down in de basement. Dey
had claxons an' cowbells an' every goddam ting. De girlfrien' she told
me it sounded real natural. She was tuned in all night.'

'What can I do for you Mr. Allen?' Millard asked coldly as he
straightened his necktie.

'De Honorable Walker Watson wants you to step over to his suite.
Dere's sumpen he don't dare discuss over de phone.'

'Thanks. I'll be right over.'

'Got any hot tips on de VP Mr. Carroll?'

'Not the least idea,' Millard said. 'Don't look like I knew anything
about what was going on around here,' he added inaudibly to himself
as he pulled on his jacket.

'De gang's gettin' up a pool . . . I got my idears but I ain't tellin'.'

'Well good night Mr. Allen.' Millard rattled his key nervously.

'Mugs' de name.' The sidewalk voice trailed off as Millard hurried
down the corridor.

The parlor door of Walker Watson's suite was open this time.
Inside the rooms were full of bustle as a railroadstation. A secretary
sat typing something at a desk. Two large rednecked men in pongee
suits stood whispering together in a corner. In the center of the parlor

waiters were setting a round table for dinner. Jo Powers in a long black and gold evening dress was trailing back and forth in front of the windows taking quick anxious puffs on a cigarette while she listened to Marice Gulick who was expanding in an overstuffed chair over a cocktail. Beyond them through the windows stretched the hazy expanse of the lake blue as a robin's egg. Mike Gulick, pale, his face beaded with sweat in spite of the air conditioning, sat hunched at the phone near the door: 'In a rapid poll of a number of delegations during the recess we find Walker Watson sentiment definitely growing . . . He's a Westerner, at least a middle Westerner. He comes of sturdy farming and missionary stock, born in a log cabin and educated in the little red schoolhouse, you know what I mean? He's a staunch New Dealer and a true liberal but he has not been associated with the lunatic fringe of radical experimentation. He has the confidence of all groups of organized labor. He appeals to small business. He's a man of the people who can talk to the common man in his own language. He's very much the cracker barrel philosopher . . . his brilliant personality will add earthiness and color to the ticket . . . He's a great American.'

Jo Powers caught Millard's eye while he was still standing just inside the door without knowing exactly what to do with himself and hurried over to him. She stared solemnly into his face.

'Millard we're expecting you to dine with us,' she said in her throaty voice . . . 'This is a very wonderful experience . . . The great spontaneous demonstration when the President was nominated. It was the most wonderful moment of my life.'

'Where is Walker?'

She tilted her head gravely. 'In through that door,' she whispered in a voice droning with portent.

'How is he?'

'Millard, he's not a well man . . . Please go to him.'

As Millard went through the door that led into the other rooms of the suite he caught sight of Mugs Allen sidling into the parlor behind him with the reverential look on his face of a man about to take communion. It was quiet between the double doors after the hubbub of the parlor. He had no sooner closed one door behind him that Mugs opened it to follow him. He walked faster.

He found Walker sitting in his underclothes on one of the beds in a large double bedroom. An electric pad lay on the counterpane beside him. With an air of great concentration he was dropping some yellow liquid with a medicine dropper into a glass on the bedside table. His long face was yellow and bloodless but his eyes swam feverishly bright under his pale brows. Immediately he started talking low and fast. 'Millard I've got a favor to ask you. I want to use your room for a few minutes while I interview a certain person . . . I want you to be present at the interview if you don't mind . . . I know I don't have to explain myself to you and I know that you are not a man who goes blabbing around . . . This is a personal matter between ourselves. There are things going on, dirty sinister things that might do us all a great deal of harm, might even harm the President. The people have spoken. We must all stand behind the President.'

'Sure Walker,' said Millard. 'You can count on me. What's the trouble?'

First tell me the number of your room . . . No you better . . . Please call the desk and tell them to send Madame Arno up to your room. She is waiting in the lobby. We'll go and meet her there. You'll be interested . . . You are interested in human psychology.'

While Millard was at the phone Walker got slowly into his clothes. 'Want a drink?' he asked reaching for a flask in the bureau drawer. Millard shook his head. 'You know I'm not a drinking man. In fact I hate the taste of the stuff . . . But tonight I'm taking a good stiff one, the doctor recommends it in a glass of milk.' He showed Millard the silver flask. 'Jo gave me this. Wasn't it sweet of her? You see, it's got my initials on it, W.W.'

When they went out the side door into the hall they found Mugs Allen waiting for them still wearing his churchgoing expression. 'You know Mugs,' said Walker cheerfully. 'He's going to see that no one interrupts our little conference.'

'Yessir,' said Mugs with a confidential grin and doubled up his left fist.

Back in Millard's room Walker sat down glumly to wait, Millard hurried the soiled clothes trailing on the bed out of sight.

The door opened and a stumpy woman in a dull maroon cape

walked in without a word. Her black hair was slicked back off a bulbous forehead. Her face was red and her breath came very short. Her eyes looked as if she had been crying. The heavy lids trembled as if she were still holding back the tears. All of a sudden she plunked down on her knees on the carpet in front of Walker. He gave an astonished start but sat with his face to the window without looking at her.

'Master,' she said, 'it was a terrible misunderstanding. Forgive the mistake of a lonely woman ignorant of the world or the evil motives of men. How could I imagine that the publication of those beautiful letters could do you harm?' She spoke with a slight European accent, pronouncing her words with drama school unction. 'Oh my injured friend, they are full of truth and inner wisdom. How could I know that our researches into the sublime mathematics of the universe could bring you anything but credit in the world of men. We learn from suffering . . . Here they are every one. They have been safe in my bosom. I swear to you I have allowed no copies to be taken . . . Forgive me, Master. I allowed myself to be deceived.' Still on her knees she reached down between her broad breasts encased in black silk and produced a packet tied with red ribbon.

Walker snatched at it. After he had counted over the letters, he gave a deep sigh. 'Well that's that,' he said and walked over to the window. Madame Arno started to follow him across the room on her knees. He stood without looking at her studying the bright triangles of the sailboats on the lake all lit up with the sunset. A tanker left a long chocolate smudge of smoke along the horizon. Millard walked over to her.

'You'll tear your stockings that way,' he said. He gave her a hand to help her to her feet.

She stood beside him short broad and panting.

'Before I go I must speak two words to my injured friend. What I have to say is for his ears alone.'

'I haven't time tonight,' said Walker without turning around.

'It is about tonight. There has been no change in the stars . . . I swear it to you.'

Walker turned and made a gesture with his hand towards the door. Flushing with vexation Millard went out and stood in the hall outside. Mugs Allen greeted him like an old friend.

'Some dame,' he said making a clucking noise with his tongue. 'Where did he dream her up? Now if any of you gents want to meet real classy dames, you know entertainers, after de convention recesses tonight just say de woid. Chimmy he says, "Boys de best ain't none too good for dem delegates. You watch over 'em boys like dey was your own daddies, an' see dey don't get no bum steer . . . Don't you go wid no dames widout clearin' 'em wid Mugs."'

Millard didn't answer. He felt the blood rising to his head. In another minute he was going to sock somebody in the jaw. The door opened and Madame Arno, her face set in a look of exultation, the corner of her cape pulled tight across her bulging chins, stalked out into the hall. 'Peace,' she whispered and moved slowly towards the elevators. A moment later Walker Watson followed. His face wore the same set look. His chin was thrust out. 'It's time we were back,' he muttered fretfully to Millard as if it had been Millard who had kept them waiting. Millard found himself keeping step with Mugs forming a sort of bodyguard after Walker Watson down the corridor.

At the door of the suite Mike Gulick met them with two big red-necked delegates in pongee suits. Mugs stayed outside to hold back a camera man and some skinny young reporters.

'Walker, meet Alderman Pasternak and Alderman Sullivan,' said Mike.

'We just came in to greet . . .' began Alderman Pasternak . . . 'A great big man,' took up Alderman Sullivan.

Walker held out both hands to them. While they were pumping each of his hands holding them encased in their great paws, Walker Watson looked back over his shoulder at the reporters' faces peering across Mugs' thick arm. 'Come in, gentlemen, come in,' he called.

'How does it feel,' asked Alderman Sullivan who seemed to have had a couple of drinks, 'to be in line for the greatest office . . .'

'. . . within the gift of the 'merican people,' took up Alderman Pasternak . . . 'Or any other people,' said Alderman Sullivan in his deep whiskey baritone.

The bulb on the photographer's camera flashed.

'Boys,' Mike cried nervously, 'this is strictly off the record.'

Walker cleared his throat. 'If, I say, if the party should honor me with the nomination . . . my fervent prayer . . . my dearest hope . . . would be . . . that I should never be called . . . to exercise that office.'

'You know just as well as I do,' said Alderman Sullivan, 'that the Boss'll never live through another term.'

'B-boys I don't n-n-need to remind you,' Mike stuttered shrilly, 'that every bit of this is off the record.'

'We are one big happy family,' said Alderman Pasternak and turned towards the reporters a jowly smile.

Walker Watson bowed his head. 'The Lord giveth and the Lord taketh away. Blessed be the name of the Lord,' he said.

'If we are going to get a bite to eat, we had better eat,' Mike rattled excitedly. 'Boys you'll excuse us, won't you? We've none of us had a bite all day.' He started crowding the reporters towards the door. Mugs took up the position of a professional bouncer beside him.

'Just one more shot as he sits down to eat,' plead a second photographer who had just come in.

Walker had hurried over to the window and was whispering into Jo Powers' pink ear. As Walker talked, though Millard couldn't hear what he was saying, he could see Jo Powers drawing herself up to her full height and filling her lungs like a contralto about to launch into an aria.

Both cameras pointed towards the window.

'No, no . . . At the table,' Mike shouted. 'You boys are covering the convention not the society column . . . At the table . . . that's it.' Mugs balancing on his toes stepped in front of the cameras. Marice was bustling about with her competent laughing hostess manner getting people seated. The waiters were advancing from the serving table with their bright-covered dishes. Walker strode over from the window rubbing his hands together gently with an abstracted look on his face as if he were alone in the room. As he sat down the waiter snatched the whitemetal covers off his plate to disclose two pieces of buttered toast. Walker sat stooping over the plate with his eyes halfclosed. Then he solemnly poured a little hot milk out of a pitcher over his toast and started to eat. The flashlight bulbs flickered. 'All right boys, that's enough . . . Thank you very much,' said Walker gently and yawned. Mugs skillfully herded the newspaper men out into the hall and closed the door behind them.

As Millard slipped into a chair beside Marice a string of sentences was running through his head like the illuminated letters spelling out the news in front of a newspaper office: Millard O. Carroll Secretary . . . The Carroll Plan Adopted to Save the Familysized Farm . . . The Carroll Plan for Migratory Labor . . . the Carroll Plan for Industrial Peace . . .'

Marice was talking to him . . . 'I wonder how many years it's been since we've had a First Lady who was really young and pretty,' she was saying.

Jo Powers had been sitting next to Walker with her eyes fixed on his face while he ate his milk toast. All at once she turned towards Marice and Millard a smile so radiant her gums showed. 'How do you address the Vice-President's wife?' she asked. 'I never met her.'

Marice threw back her head and laughed until tears came to her eyes. 'My dear like anybody else.'

'My poor little mother,' Walker's voice had started its deep drawn . . . 'My poor little mother used to say . . .' As people stopped talking and turned towards him Walker looked around the table with his slow lopsided smile. Millard looked up from his broiled chicken and watched Alderman Pasternak's suety countenance crinkle into grins as Walker looked at him. Next him Mike's worried frown had turned into a showman's possessive proud smile. 'My poor little old mother out in Nebraska had a saying,' Walker went on, 'that a cat may look at a king.'

The phone rang. Frowning again Mike jumped up. In a second he tapped Millard on the shoulder.

'It's Judge Oppenheim, Millard. He wants to talk to you.'

Millard excused himself and wiping his mouth with the napkin went to the phone at the desk. 'Millard how are you? Is Chicago pretty hot? I thought . . .' The meticulous voice was quietly sarcastic . . . 'I thought I'd tantalize you a little by describing the fresh Atlantic breezes. I never saw Penobscot Bay more beautiful than it is tonight. It's been a warm day. Nell and I both wish we had you and Lucile here to eat some lobster with us. Is she with you in Chicago?'

'No Lou went home with the boys for the summer.'

'Well how are things? Are you pretty much worn out?'

'I've never been so confused in my life. I guess conventions aren't my dish. Lord Judge I'll be glad to get back to work I understand.'

The Judge's laugh came softly over the wire. 'How's Walker holding out?'

'Very well I'd say. Do you want to speak to him? He's right here. We're all of us eating a bite of supper before going back for the rest of the show.'

'No no I don't want to bother him now. I just wanted you and Mike to know I was thinking about you and commiserating with you. Of course you know the European news couldn't possibly be worse. Massacre and dictatorship advancing unchecked . . . Britain knocked out, kept alive only by the mighty spirit of one man . . . I just want you to remind our friend a little of this situation. No matter how the events of this evening come out the man in the White House has got to have an administration that works together like a welltrained team. Whether a man is in one position or another doesn't really matter so long as he gives his best. I'm telling you this Millard because I know that you aren't subject to the frenzies that seize some of us when we are confronted with the possibility of high office. Your influence can be very stabilizing . . .'

'I get your drift Judge, but I'm sure enough in a daze.'

'Well I wouldn't worry Millard. You have nothing at stake in this situation personally. Your good honest spadework is very highly appreciated . . . where it needs to be appreciated . . . you know that. Well I shan't keep you. Give our love to Lucile when you see her and goodnight. Get a nice long rest when this is over.'

Millard hated to have the Judge hang up. The distant amused dispassionate voice gave him back the feeling of aloof selfconfidence he had been losing all afternoon. He was still smiling when he went back to the table. Nobody was talking. Everybody had stopped eating. 'Where's Walker?' he asked.

Mike looked up at him, his face worried as a monkey's.

'He's on the phone. It's the White House. He's taking it in the bedroom . . . This is it.' His voice came in a breathless rasp.

Marice was making up her lips looking intently down into the little mirror in her handbag and now and then giving Mike an anxious protective glance across the table. Alderman Pasternak was eating peach melba and seemed sunk in his own thoughts. With a silent and catlike tread Jo Powers walked up and down in front of the window where the dusk over the lake had deepened to violet.

Millard started to hack at the broiled chicken that had grown cold on his plate. He put a piece in his mouth but it had a rubbery taste. Everybody was smoking with fury. Alderman Sullivan handed him a cigar and, although he didn't usually smoke cigars, he accepted it. He heard a step behind him and found himself looking up into Bruce Slater's black eyes. He got to his feet.

'Why Bruce,' he said. 'Where on earth have you been?'

Bruce didn't answer but gave him a slow ponderous wink. Then he pulled a small pad out of his pocket and wrote a name on it and showed it to Millard.

'Well I'll be God damned . . . begging your pardon, Marice.'

Marice was on her feet. Her handbag closed with a sharp click. 'It's time we left you gentlemen to your smokefilled room,' she was saying. She walked over to Jo Powers and put her arm around her waist. 'Well dear let's go to my room and tidy up and then we'll take a cab to the Stadium.'

Mike's hand was shaking when he stepped over to take the piece of paper out of Millard's hand. He gave it a glance and handed it to Alderman Sullivan.

The alderman let out a loud whistle. 'Well gentlemen,' he said, 'we live and learn.' He walked around and whispered a name loudly in Alderman Pasternak's ear.

'Well thank God it ain't the incumbent,' said Alderman Pasternak.

Mugs had come forward from his place by the door. 'Well there goes my twentyfive bucks,' he said.

Jo Powers face had knitted up like the face of a little girl who'd been scolded. 'I must go to him,' she almost sobbed. She pulled away from Marice and with her eyes on the floor made for the door into the bedroom. As she brushed past Millard he heard her muttering low to herself, 'I'll marry him anyway . . . I'll marry him anyway.'

Bruce walked up to Millard with that solemn birddog look of a man who knows much more than he's able to tell, opened his mouth as if to say something but changed his mind and merely shrugged his shoulders heavily. Alderman Sullivan and Alderman Pasternak were already out the door. 'See you over to the Stadium,' they called back as they left. Bruce slipped away after them. Mike had dropped into the chair at the desk and sat with his head bowed making doodles on the blotter. Marice stood beside him stroking the sparse hair off his forehead with little pats of her hand.

When Walker Watson came back into the parlor he was breathing heavily as if winded from a long climb. Jo Powers had hold of him under the arms and seemed to be propping him up on his feet.

His voice had a weak spiteful sound.

'Mike,' he said, 'you'd better get busy while there's still time . . . I shall not allow my name to be put before the convention. It is my irrevocable decision.'

PART III

THE POWER
AND THE GLORY

. . . And when the sky begins to roar
It's like a lion at the door
And when the door begins to crack
It's like a stick across your back
And when your back begins to smart
It's like a penknife in your heart
And when your heart begins to bleed
You're dead and dead and dead indeed.
(Anonymous jingle out of old editions of *Mother Goose*)

THE POWER AND THE GLORY

1

*W*hen the President assembles his press conference he sits
at his desk with a great globe the world in the window
behind his head. In his topsecret staffroom the walls are brightly
lit maps where attachés mark out the positions of the armies . . .

here ten thousand men have died on the steppe, this river is
swollen with the rotting dead . . . the position of convoys, packs of
submarines, magnetic mines: here a hundred drowned last night.

The President knows geography; he is interested in history.

Fourmotor planes arrive secretly at dusk, depart at dawn, Very
Important Personages are hurried in long limousines to the White House.

(Like as not it's only a light thud amidships instead of the explo-
sion you expected. Sometimes you don't know when the torpedo
strikes. The blackedout ship, shambling easily through the slow swells
on the zigzag course in a sighing surge of broken water through the
night of faint moonlight smudged with soft low clouds, begins all
of a sudden to lose steerageway, to wallow gently in the trough, the
wind is silent in the rigging. Abandon ship. The tilting deck is quiet.
Nobody loses his head. It's so like lifeboat drill

except that there's something jammed in the davits and the lifeboat hangs white in the pale night nosedown in the water. Skillfully we cut the lashings of the liferaft. Where it smashes the surface a fringe of phosphorescent flecks lightens the black swell. We go through the motions of abandon ship so like lifeboat drill . . .

but then it's a man alone thrashing in wreckage, hands failing to tear loose, legs kicking into vacant cold that drags him down into black oil, swallowing, strangling . . .)

In Argentia Bay under the chill slate sky the British sailors in their funny caps

piped the presidential party

up the gangway of the doomed ship:

gold braid, aiguillettes, ribbons on the breast, all the old pomp of empire. The Heads of States attended services on the battleship's quarterdeck according to the rites of the Church of England and sang Onward Christian Soldiers; at lunch they toasted Gentlemen the King and the old scepter of the waves slipped from the hand of the Prime Minister even as he was proclaiming that it was not his intention to preside over the liquidation of an empire.

'After the war one of the preconditions of a lasting peace will be the greatest possible freedom of trade,' said our President. It was a time of Caesars: the Heads of States declared a few new freedoms to order the tortured world;

the battlefield was the whole blue globe.

LEND LEASE

YAWNING AND DIGGING HIS FISTS INTO HIS EYES Winthrop rolled off the bed and walked over to the window. When he gave the shade a yank it flew up and spun round the roller. The sunlight outside stung. Green flames flickered painfully brilliant off the ragged patch of grass in the middle of the trampled yard below. A starling flew up with a flap of shiny black wings. The bird's bright eye seemed to give Winthrop a sharp look as it passed the window. Blinking he turned his back on the summer morning that glared like the open door of a furnace. In his undershirt on the edge of the bed Mervyn Packett sat with his lips in a pout. There were violet circles under his eyes and his skin had a dead green tinge.

'Merv,' stuttered Winthrop, 'you look absolutely g-g-god-awful.'

'No worse'n you do Winthrop.' Mervyn Packett pronounced his words carefully. His voice was keyed high. 'What you can see in that old black faggot is beyond me. He isn't even educated.'

Winthrop folded his arms defiantly over his narrow chest. 'Everything I've done has been for the s-s-sake of the Negro p-p-people.' He felt himself letting go. The words started to flow of their own accord. 'I did get Mother to loan him the money to start the Cabin an' that's all. Well it's a great success. I guess that's what burns you up. You don't want me to be successful . . . You want me to be a failure all my life . . . *The Daily Worker's* given it wonderful writeups.'

'You had a time getting that loan back,' said Mervyn spitefully.

'Rutherford has paid it back, with interest too. That's why I think I can get Mother to put up for this memorial meeting. It's the first time she's gotten a loan back since she came into the estate . . . Of course it's not as much as people think it is.'

'She had to sick her lawyer on him first.'

'You're just jealous that's all.' Winthrop's voice broke. 'I should think you'd want to help me help the Negro people instead of nagging and criticising all the time.'

'I don't like to see you getting in with a low element that's all.'

'The Party thinks it's all right.' Winthrop felt his voice rise to a high falsetto but it was too late to try to hold it down. 'I don't care what any bourgeois intellectual thinks . . . no matter who they are . . . and that's all.' He stalked into the bathroom and slammed the door after him.

'I wouldn't care about myself,' he muttered as he turned the key in the lock. 'It's the Party I'm thinking of . . .' He turned on the hot water in the tub. The sound of the water drowned out his voice. 'Talking to yourself again,' he said to the faucet. 'Talk to yourself, talk to the devil Miss Drake used to say when I was a little shaver . . . Blackmail . . . No Merv wouldn't but the other boys at that party . . . Oh Lord.' While the tub filled he looked at himself in the mirror over the washbasin. His eyes were bloodshot and his skin did have a puffy look. He'd shave after his bath when his hands didn't shake so. He squeezed out a black-head on his nose. 'Oh you . . .' He caught himself making a kissing motion with his lips towards his face in the mirror. After stirring the water around carefully with his hands to make sure it wasn't too hot he stepped into the tub.

He sat there soaking a long time with his eyes closed and his head dropped back against the hard rim, halfenjoying the idea that he was keeping Merv waiting. Merv had been awful last night chattering about books with his voice in his palate like a schoolgirl through all the boogeywoogey. He'd never been able to get away from Merv's prim face watching him through the white roll of eyeballs and white teeth laughing against dark tense motion of jaw muscles and the striped silk shirts and astronomical neckties and signet rings on big fingers and the shoulders beating time and the jiving hips and the whiskey gushing into thick glasses . . . they were always filling his up they liked him so . . . 'Hot Lips. Lord what a sax, but I mean on the ivories . . .' Rutherford was in the groove. No wonder he'd made a success of the Cabin . . . tops . . . tall lithe terrific and then Merv had to make them go home. Merv was right. He'd never forgive himself if he got in a scandal . . . blackmail . . . My, Mother would squall. He didn't care about Mother, it was all her fault anyway for starting his Oedipus complex, she was so selfish . . . But oh God jail. They sent people to jail. It was the horrible decadent society he was brought up in. Won't be long before the comrades make a clean sweep of it . . . A boy could go to work then with the other young workers in the harvestfields, in an automobile plant, go to sea on a freighter and come back tough as any of them muscled and regular . . . a Party Member . . . then a guy would belong.

His fingers were crinkling like prunes. The water was beginning to get cool in the tub. He stepped out and dried himself. Then he shaved hurriedly and opened the door into the bedroom. Merv had gone. The big pig, thought Winthrop, he didn't even wash his face. But he missed him. He was over being sore. He felt all friendly now. It took him a long time to get dressed. He couldn't find his socks and none of the shirts in the bureau drawer had their buttons on them. 'It's mean of Mother not to take care of my clothes for me,' he muttered. 'She's always neglected me shamefully . . . Career woman.'

He couldn't decide what necktie to put on. First he put on a red one but he took it off, made him look like a fairy, he told himself. The green one was too green. Merv oughtn't to have walked out on him like this. The knot stuck when he tried to undo it he was so nervous. He pulled and yanked at it with both bands and finally pulled it off over his head mussing his wiry red hair that he'd just managed to brush into place. At last he picked a tie at random and tied it without looking in the glass and tiptoed shakily downstairs.

In the little hall back of the pantry he smelled coffee. He pushed open the diningroom door. Dr. Sparling sat at the round table set with breakfast dishes in the full glare of the sunlight with a grizzled man with bushy eyebrows and a bulbous nose that drooped over a curved briar pipe. Every inch of the tablecloth was covered with last week's New York and Washington papers. HITLER JUMPS REDS, REICH ATTACKS RUSSIA, the headlines shouted.

'We'll hold on the Volga; that I can absolutely guarantee but nothing before.' The man was talking tensely through his briar.

When she caught sight of Winthrop Dr. Sparling jumped to her feet and stumped up to him with an angry sharp look in her eyes.

'How about knocking before you come into a room?' she said between clenched teeth. Winthrop stammered that he hadn't meant to intrude, he'd just smelled the coffee. 'I thought Anna had brought you up better than that,' Dr. Sparling went on in her sarcastic tone. 'All right since you're here I'm going to introduce you to somebody but if anybody asks you this isn't where you met him.'

She pushed Winthrop forward into the room with the short hard fingers of her hand pressing into the small of his back. As she did so she cleared her throat to attract the attention of the man at the table who between little squeaking puffs on his pipe was making marks on a map cut out of a newspaper.

'Comrade Weeks, this is Winthrop Strang. He's the son of my friend Anna Winthrop and is a staunch friend of the Negro people in his own right . . . Winnie shake hands with Elmer Weeks.'

Winthrop who had been holding out his hand wincing a little in expectation of having it wrung in a calloused fist, was surprised by the chilly limpness of the four fingers that were placed for a second in his.

'Oh yes . . . Rutherford, the Cabin, the Hungry Baby Blues . . .' mumbled Comrade Weeks along the stem of his pipe without looking up from his map. 'Yes we watch the awakening of the Negro people with sincere approval. Keep up the good work . . . thataboy . . . Jane,' he went on as if he'd forgotten Winthrop's existence. 'We've got to have help . . . We've got to get in under Lend Lease. Time is of the essence. All true liberals will be on our side now. They will throw off the shackles of fascist propaganda . . .'

Winthrop's lips were moving as he spelled out the headlines. He was trying to say something.

'Winnie,' interrupted Dr. Sparling severely. 'Go in the pantry and get yourself a cup of coffee and come back and sit here quietly. There's some toast and bacon keeping hot in the oven.'

As Winthrop went about obediently doing as he was told he heard her saying, 'I can vouch for him Comrade Weeks. Let him eat his break-fast. There's something he can do for us right this morning . . . Com-rade Weeks I'm just a professional woman, and in the movement I've always been one of those who were willing rather to take direction than trying to give it but I've got to tell you this morning that I think the analysis of the situation that has come from Thirteenth Street is highly incorrect. Hitler's attack on the Soviet Union is the best thing that ever happened to the movement in this country. For the first time we are marching shoulder to shoulder with the great masses of the American people. In the common war against the Nazi aggressor we will have direct access to Congress and the Administration.'

'We must not let ourselves forget that from their point of view it's still an imperialist war.'

'Of course Comrade Weeks the average American is completely incapable of understanding that the capitalist democracy which he things he's fighting this war to save is through whatever happens.'

'Whoever wins, capitalism, sucking the blood of the workers behind its false front of liberal democracy, is dead,' Elmer Weeks answered in an absentminded ritual tone, his eyes still on the map.

Dr. Sparling turned to Winthrop with one finger lifted like a schoolteacher: 'Winnie I thought you were going over to see your mother this morning about that memorial meeting.'

'I am. I'm going right over now,' Winthrop stammered with his mouth full.

'That's a meeting, Comrade Weeks, we're planning for Madison Square Garden in honor of the American antifascist fighters for free-dom on the soil of Spain. Anna Winthrop Strang is very much inter-ested. Herbert Spotswood has consented to speak . . . It's almost twelve Winnie, are you sure you won't miss her? You ask her to call me will you?' Winthrop felt his face getting red under the commanding stare of her hard eyes. Reluctantly he got to his feet.

'She's just at the Tarleton.' He got up choking down a last piece of toast and a scrap of bacon. The breakfast had done him good though his head still had a ragged iron band around it and what he'd eaten lay a little uneasy in his stomach. If he could only keep it down, he was telling himself, he'd be all right. He lingered by the table waiting for Elmer Weeks to speak again.

Dr. Sparling grabbed him by the arm and hustled him out the door into the narrow corridor. 'Glad to have met you Comrade Weeks,' he tried to say over his shoulder as he left but she was already shushing him. 'Nobody knows he's here silly,' she spat in his ear. 'Don't tell your mother. Just ask her to call me understand?'

The door to the library was open. The click of keys from two type-writers came from the long table in the center. Dr. Sparling twisted Winthrop's elbow as she pushed him impatiently ahead of her into the room.

'Louise Aldershot meet Winnie Strang.' A longfaced woman with thin irregular features looked up from her typewriter and smiled. 'She gives her Sundays to the Anti-Fascist League,' Dr. Sparling whispered reverently in Winthrop's ear.

'There are two letters from Mr. Spotswood's secretary asking about the date of the meeting. What can I tell him?' asked the longfaced woman. 'He's got a very tight schedule,' she added severely.

'You see Winnie,' Dr. Sparling gave Winthrop's arm a shake, 'you ought to have been over there two hours ago. We can't set the date because they won't hold the hall till they have the check. Everybody's losing time because you overslept.'

'Don't mind her, Winthrop,' said a pleasantfaced woman with fluffy white hair from the typewriter at the other end of the table. 'I bet you don't remember me . . . Elizabeth Trumbull. Give your mother my love. She's an old friend. I haven't seen you since you were a little red-headed toddler.'

'You'll have plenty of time to see Elizabeth when you come back. She's our hostess,' said Dr. Sparling. 'She just blew in last night . . . As soon as she got in I put her to work writing letters.'

At the door they met Joe Yerkes. With him was a pale blond buxom girl in a blue print dress who seemed to Winthrop to give him a friendly look. Joe Yerkes didn't notice him. He was all excited. 'Jane have you got any news? What's the reaction? I was so wrought up I couldn't sleep. I wanted somebody sensible to talk to. At the crack of dawn I woke George up and induced her to come over. A guy can't find anybody to talk to in this town.'

'It's certainly a great historical moment,' said the blond girl.

'Gosh isn't it?' Winthrop spluttered eagerly. 'I've been so excited ever since it happened I can't see straight.'

'Joe,' said Dr. Sparling without paying attention to Winthrop, 'there's a friend of yours come to town . . . I think Georgia ought to meet him. I don't think she ever has.'

Winthrop lingered with his hand on the knob of the front door. He wanted to hear what Joe Yerkes had to say. He wanted to talk about the war news. Dr. Sparling noticed him and gave him one of her disapproving looks. 'Well so long,' he said and hurried off along the hot sidewalk under the wilted trees feeling like a scolded schoolboy.

Everybody ordered him around he complained to himself peevishly as he walked. He hoped Mother would be out just to show them. He didn't care if they never did have their memorial meeting. All they cared about was getting money out of him. He'd show them. Mother would be mad anyway because he was late. She'd told him to come to breakfast. He started to walk past the hotel but he couldn't think of what to do if he didn't go up to see Mother. He was already sweating and his clean shirt clung to his wet back. At least her suite would be airconditioned. It was already cooler in the lobby. Going up in the elevator the goodlooking elevator boy gave him a nice smile. Winthrop knew all too well where her suite was. She always had the same suite when she came to Washington. The door was ajar. He felt the usual sinking sensation at the bottom of his stomach which was still a little jumpy from last night. He hesitated for a moment. Then he took the plunge. 'Hello Mother,' he called in a cracked voice as he pushed open the door.

Immediately he heard Mother's voice dictating, 'Whatever may have been the reason for this cowardly and unexpected attack upon the soviet ally . . .' Yes there she was sitting in the window in a green dressing gown with red poppies on it . . . 'we in the western democracies . . .' A man in a white coat was curling her hair. It looked redder than ever, too red Winthrop thought. A blond manicure girl had just finished her nails and was packing up her kit . . . 'may take a deep breath in the realization that taking the long term view we may be sure that the Naxi régime in repeating Napoleon's mistake has signed its own death warrant . . . Elsie, dear,' she added to her secretary, 'I'll have to run over that this afternoon. I won't have time now. Type it out for me like a good girl and leave it on the desk. Be back at four-thirty for the corrections.'

Without turning her head because the hairdresser was holding her tight with his curling iron, she continued, 'Well Winnie this is a nice time to come to breakfast. I suppose you were out on the town again last night. I don't know when you are going to grow up.' The warm light from outside shone along the profile of her big forehead and long straight nose and sharp chin. The rest of her face was in shadow. She had the handsome haggard look that had been so much admired, and that always made Winthrop feel all melted up inside. 'Well,' she was saying pettishly, 'I know you want to see me about this check for the memorial meeting but I don't know when we're going to get time to talk about it because I'm going over to the White House and I've got to leave here in twenty minutes. Though she happens to be an old friend, when the first lady of the land asks you over to an informal Sunday dinner it just isn't the thing to be late, now is it?'

Winthrop bit his trembling lip. 'Mother I was detained by meeting Elmer Weeks,' he said.

'Well . . .' her voice took on a fresh bell-like tone of interest. 'What did he say? What's their line going to be?' The hairdresser had given the red curls on the back of her head a last admiring pat. He pulled the towel off her shoulders with a flourish. She rose to her feet letting the dressinggown slip off as she did so and revealing a black and green lace blouse and a black skirt with some sort of green bow on the side. When she strode over to give Winthrop a little pecking kiss on the forehead she was so much taller than he was she had to lean over him. The light scent of heliotrope mixed with the warmth of a big vigorous woman's body that came from the hurried rustle of her clothes was unbearably familiar. 'What did he say?' Her gray eyes were searching his impatiently. 'I can't wait to hear. Mark . . .' She addressed a pair of wellshined yellow oxfords that stuck out from legs covered by sheets of the Sunday papers piled on the chaise longue in the corner of the room. The pages of the *New York Times* held out by two hirsute hands emerging from stiff cuffs dropped and Mark Burgess' square face appeared as heavily shadowed as a reproduction of his own photograph . . . 'Mark, this is interesting. Winthrop's just come from talking to Elmer Weeks.'

'You don't say.' Mark Burgess shook the papers off him and got to his feet.

'I was asked to keep this confidential,' said Winthrop in a firmer voice, 'so Mother don't you tell Doc Sparling that I told you . . . She asked me to tell you to call her up. She has something most important to talk to you about. She wants you to call her right away. She must have guessed where you were going for lunch.'

'But Winthrop what did Elmer Weeks say?'

'He said . . . Oh gee I forget.' Winthrop started to stutter. 'He s-s-said the way things were going was the greatest thing had ever happened to the working class movement in this country.'

'It's the end of isolationism,' his mother said emphatically. 'That's what I'm going to say in my tomorrow's column.'

The hairdresser and the manicure girl were sidling out of the room. That hairdresser must be a queer, Winthrop was thinking, the look he gave me.

'Mother d-d-don't you th-th-think you could write that check now? If we wait we won't be able to get Herbert Spotswood.'

She threw back her head when she laughed. 'I can take Herb or I can leave him alone . . . Now Mark what do you think? You know five thousand dollars isn't hay as they say on Broadway, even for the Strang Estate it's not hay. It is for a memorial meeting for the American boys who fell fighting for the Spanish Republic. Of course Winthrop . . . you know what a pushover he is . . . he's told them he'd get it out of me.'

'Right at this moment it might be a useful gesture.'

'All right Elsie,' she called after her secretary who had gone into the other room. 'Write up a check on the Strang Foundation for five thou'. Mr. Burgess and I will sign it . . . And get Dr. Jane Sparling for me on the phone.'

Suddenly they none of them had anything more to say to each

other. Mark Burgess sat down on the chaise longue again and picked up a section of the paper. Winthrop stood fidgeting in the middle of the floor like a messengerboy waiting for a telegram while his mother, humming tunelessly in a way that always got on his nerves walked back and forth between the desk and the window. Winthrop was wondering what he was going to do with himself all day now that Mervyn had gone off in a pet. Once he'd delivered that check nobody over at Dr. Sparling's would care whether he had a good time or not.

Elsie came out solemnly with the check. Mother and Mark Burgess signed it. Mother looked at him disapprovingly when she came over to hand it to him. 'Oh Winthrop I wish you'd find something to do . . .' she almost screamed at him. 'It makes me so nervous the way you idle around fiddling with this and that . . . If I only had some of the time you waste.'

'You . . . you don't know what all I do,' Winthrop started: and you don't care either, he was planning to say but Elsie had called from the other room, 'I've got that phone call for you Mrs. Strang.'

'Coming,' his mother answered happily and strode off. Already she'd forgotten all about him. He waited for a second to see if Mark Burgess would look up from his paper to say goodby. He ought to. Mark was his lawyer just as much as he was Mother's. He didn't look up. Winthrop opened the door quietly and tiptoed out into the hall. After he'd rung for the elevator he began to wonder if that nicelooking elevatorboy would smile at him again, but it turned out to be another one all broken out with acne whose looks Winthrop didn't care for at all.

The Power and the Glory

2

*T*his was something we knew how to do: appropriations
mount, defense loans, the banks multiply credit. Under
neon tubes in the long drafting rooms engineers pore over their
tables. Every toolmaker in the country is busy; tool and dyeshops
work round the clock. Additions are building on all the airplane
plants. Amid a proliferation of railroad tracks factories spread out
over acres where in a niagara of electric power nitrogen is fixed from
the air, magnesium from seawater, aluminum from clay; ingots of
rare metals mount in the freightcars. Measuring the tolerances with
micrometers electrical workers furnish the parts for new generators.
Trucks, halftracks, tractors are driven endlessly off the assembly line.

There is no surplus of anything:

a job for every man, for many women. High wages. Time and a half
for overtime, bonuses. Break the production records. In the shipyards
they rig races to see which gang can build a Victory Ship the fastest.

Men go jaunting all about the country with the wife and kids in
a trailer

shopping for a better job.

Production is something America knows how to do.

Economic Warfare

THE SEPTEMBER AFTERNOON THROBBED SHRILLY with dry-flies and katydids. Wearing sneakers and an old pair of khaki pants, Millard was pushing the lawnmower over the stubbly grass. Lucile, muffled in a faded lilac smock with her hair tied up in a bandana, was pulling weeds out of the dahlias in the bed along the driveway. Near her the terrier with one eye half open was stretched out flat as a mat under a bush. Every time Millard reached the flowerbed at the end of one of his cuts across the lawn he would stop for breath and they would both gaze at the long white frame house that needed painting and the brokendown pergola covered with grapevines and the silver trunks of the clustering beeches under their dark thatch of latesummer green.

'Do you wish we hadn't, Oz?' Lucile would ask.

'Uhum,' he would say. 'It's a good buy.'

The sweat was trickling down his back under the soaked undershirt. He stopped to wipe his face with a wet handkerchief. 'First thing to do is fix that tennis court. Out here the boys really will have space to thrash around.'

Lucile got to her feet. Her face was suddenly pale. She walked over to him and put her hand in its gardening glove on his arm as he leaned on the handlebar of the lawnmower.

'Oz I'm so scared. Make me be brave like other women are. Joel's too young to be flying. He's just a little boy.'

'Lou . . .' He found himself talking fast, more roughly than he intended. 'They've got to take their chances with the rest. You heard the President's speech. "Shoot first," he said. That's going to mean war. I'm mighty proud of Joel for the way he jumped right in and when the time comes I'm going to be mighty proud of Lucius.'

She stared up at him with a look almost of hatred in her face. 'No, Oz, no . . . I pray to God it'll be over by that time.'

Kerry was barking and wagging his tail.

'Look who's here,' said Millard. 'Quiet Kerry.'

Mike Gulick was sitting in an open convertible in the driveway grinning his bony grin at them from under the shade of a broad-brimmed panama.

'Well well, isn't this nice?' he was saying. 'Want a hired hand?'

'Drive on up to the porch Mike. What do you think of our Maryland estate?' Millard followed the car to the house while Lucile ran in the side door to tidy herself up.

'Why Millard,' said Mike as they shook hands on the nagged terrace. 'I never thought of you as a gardening man.'

'Just an old farmer at heart,' said Millard grinning. 'Shall we go inside? I think it's cooler inside.'

'This really is nice,' said Mike looking around at the panelled living room and the long french-windows opening on another lawn and a tennis court bowered in shrubbery in back.

'It'll mean a lot of work . . . Kinder keep Lucile busy fixing it up . . . You know what I mean.' Millard felt his voice getting too serious. 'Joel has started his training down at Randolph Field . . .' Joel wasn't what he wanted to talk about. He shook his head frowning. 'What's new around the east wing of the White House?' he asked.

'I suppose you've seen Walker.'

'No I haven't,' Millard said still in the same heavy tone. 'Say Mike if you'd excuse me for a second . . .'

But Mike had already started talking: 'Walker came in from Moscow fit as a fiddle. His health seems really improved. M-m-matrimo-ny's a great thing . . . What I really came by for was to see if I couldn't pick you and Lucile up. I thought we'd go by and collect Marice and go over to the Arlington together. There'll be a terrible crush there and I thought we'd have more fun if we made a phalanx of it.'

'Just excuse me for a sec while I get these wet things off Mike . . . I don't want to catch cold.'

'Sure sure go ahead . . . Say Millard what on earth are you doing with that newspaper? I wouldn't have it in the house.' Making half-comic clucking noises with his tongue Mike settled down in a chair to read it.

Millard ran upstairs. Lou was in their bathroom in a hot tub. He went into Joel's room and stepped for a second under the cold shower. By the time he'd dried himself and had gotten into his underdrawers and was hunting for a clean seersucker suit in the closet Lucile had come out of their bathroom in her slip and stood in front of the pier-glass powdering her arms and neck with a big powderpuff.

'Lou I don't want to go to that thing.'

'Mr. Evans' party for the Watsons? Well then let's not,' Lucile mut-tered absentmindedly. She went over to the dressingtable to fix her hair that looked very blond as it always did when she'd been out in the sun.

He would explain to Mike, Mike would understand, he was saying to himself as he went down the stairs.

He went in through the pantry. 'Mike have a glass of cold beer?' he called.

'Sure it's just the afternoon for it,' came Mike's cordial voice in return.

By the time Millard walked into the livingroom with a tray of glasses and beerbottles opaque with moisture he was ready with what he wanted to say:

'Mike, Lucile and I thought we'd skip the Watsons' party I'm sure Walker and Jo will understand. Lucile's tired out from moving and with all these war preparations I just don't feel like parties.'

'Millard I feel the same way you do. After all I've got the twins in college . . . You know this party was originally to be a sort of wedding breakfast but it had to be postponed on account of Walker's having to fly to Moscow. Harry said he wouldn't go without him. Now Jerry insists on pushing it through. His heart was set on it.'

'Well that's another reason. Since I was put in charge of this Economic Scarcities Commission I particularly don't want to be beholden to Jerry Evans for anything. He's making things as hard as he can for us all down the line. In my opinion he's decided there's going to be no war profiteering except by Jerry Evans. Well we've decided there's going to be no war profiteering, period.'

Mike strode up to him dramatically and handed him the evening paper folded down to a column. 'Well that's just what this miserable scurrilous isolationist paper has to say. You just read Ed James' column. I thought Ed James was a friend of ours but he's sold out to the interests. He says Jerry's got Walker in his pocket. The only way of countering that kind of talk is for the old guard to rally round Walker. We know him and believe in him. This is just a friendly gesture on Jerry's part. It has nothing to do with politics or contracts or anything. It's a large gesture but you know Jerry. He doesn't know any other way of doing things.'

'You don't know Mr. Evans as well as I do,' muttered Millard with his eyes on the column of print. 'Well Ed's not far wrong . . . but putting it baldly like that at this time does look like giving aid and comfort to the enemy . . . If that's the way things are I guess we'd better go.'

With a grim frowning face he walked to the foot of the stairs. 'Lou,' he called, 'you'd better put on your glad rags. I guess we're going to that party after all.'

While they were talking the phone started to ring. The ringing stopped so Millard knew that Lucile had taken the call upstairs. After a while he heard her voice calling 'Oz.' Snapping his fingers to ease his jumpy nerves he walked out into the hall. She was looking down over the bannisters, still in her slip, but her hair was done. She looked rested and pretty. She was making jabbing gestures with her forefinger towards the phone on the little marble table in the hall. The happy outdoor feeling Millard had felt all afternoon had drained out of him. His mouth was twitching as he picked up the receiver. His hello had a snarl to it.

'Why Judge Oppenheim,' he heard the oil welling up in his own voice in a way he didn't much like. 'How are you? I didn't know you were back in town. What kind of a summer did you have?'

'Good enough, Millard, good enough . . . I hear you and Lucile are now old Maryland landowners. What a sweet child she is. Talking to her for a minute has been the only pleasant moment since we got back to take up the burden of Nineveh . . . tell her I said so.' Millard found himself smiling as he listened attentively to the carefully pronounced sentences. 'But Millard what strange transmogrification has taken place in our friend the columnist? Has he had some kind of personal falling out with the great big rough diamond who is giving a party for the Watsons this evening? It is most embarrassing because the President is about to announce an important appointment which concerns him. I mean our rough southeastern diamond . . . Walker stays where he is . . . I suppose you have already been informed. After all he's a man of great energy and ability whose cooperation is absolutely necessary to the Administration in the present emergency. It results that Nell and I after considerable urging from the very highest quarters have rather reluctantly consented to attend for a few moments, though it's the last thing on earth we want to do. The Chief Justice has refused. His rule about large parties is unshakable for reasons of health. Well that's his prerogative. But I think a couple of the Associate Justices will be there. If we can have the support of you and your sweet Lucile it will make the adventure less painful. We rather dread the performances of a somewhat raffish element that seems to come in the train of the new Mrs. Watson.'

'We just decided we had better go . . . for the same reasons.'

'Good enough . . . The British and French ambassadors and the members of the Russian purchasing commission and hordes of lesser embassy folk and most of the Hill will be present. As you know there will be no lack of malicious tongues from the fourth estate. We'll be making the best of a rather bad business but I don't see quite what else there is to do. Well we'll look out for each other. By the way is Mike still with you? May I speak to him for a second?'

While Mike was talking to the Judge Millard walked heavily upstairs and started to change into his dinnerclothes. 'Oh, we're in for it now,' he groaned.

Lucile looked fresh as a daisy he thought in her plain dark blue taffeta dress with its little lace collar. 'Anyway I love champagne,' was all she would say. They took the Carrolls' Buick instead of Mike's convertible because Lucile didn't want to have her hair blown. When they got to the Gulicks' house in Georgetown they found Marice very much dressed up in red with black sequins. Her necklaces and bracelets jingled as she bustled about giving little pigtailed Pamela her supper at the marble table in the garden. Marice looked from one of the men's faces to the other and then turned to Lucile and said with one of her little quick grins, 'What a pair of thunderclouds. Lucile can't you cheer up the boyfriends?'

'I can't do anything with 'em.'

'You'd think we were going to a funeral instead of a wedding party . . . Lucile let's just shake this pair of undertakers and have ourselves a time. A party's a party that's how I look at it . . . Mike you hurry up and get dressed . . . Pam run into the pantry and fetch the cocktail tray. Careful now . . . Here I am the darling of the society columns and not a servant in the house.'

Little Pamela came back walking very carefully on the tips of her toes with the tinkling tray of glasses. With her lips pursed and a tiny tip of a red tongue sticking out on one side of her mouth she dropped the ice in the shaker, solemnly shook up the cocktail and poured it into the glasses.

'There's Mummie's own daughter.' Marice let out one of her shrieks. 'Now you run over to the Swansons and call me up when you get there.'

'No thanks,' said Millard grimly. 'I'm not drinking tonight.'

'Then us girls'll get cockeyed . . . Come on Lucile, lap it up.'

They were late getting off. The traffic was slow on Connecticut Avenue. Millard had to drive round a block to fall into the line of cars waiting to reach the front door of the hotel. Uniformed attendants were ready to park the cars, that was a relief. The sidewalk was crowded. There were extra police on hand. As they filed into the lobby of the hotel Lucile whispered in his ear that it looked like opening night at the Metropolitan Opera House with a mixture from the football crowd at the Sugar Bowl.

The first man Millard saw he knew was George Dilling. George was wearing striped pants and a cutaway and was carrying a homburg hat. He had a white carnation in his buttonhole. Eloise in green was stumping along behind him. The Dillings were on their way out. They made a little group behind the newsstand and chatted a moment. 'Too rich for my blood,' George said. Eloise added excitedly that she hadn't seen anything like it since they opened up the Russian Embassy. Millard asked if George had read Ed James' column. George wrinkled up his nose and said that wasn't half of it. He happened to know the worst was yet to come.

When Lucile and Marice went off to leave their wraps Millard found himself standing in line at the hat check room. He'd lost Mike somehow threading his way through the jam in the lobby. As he reached the counter he met Judge Oppenheim coming away with his hat in his hand and a light topcoat over his arm. The Judge pressed Millard's hand solemnly, whispered something about their worst fears being justified and was gone. Millard followed with his eyes the slender black figure under the frizzle of curly gray musician's hair moving through the particolored crowd. Mrs. Oppenheim looking very Bostonian with her pink face and porkpie hat was already waiting for him by the elevator. They lost no time in leaving the hotel. What teamwork, Millard thought.

The parlor that led into the large ballroom was decorated with immense plumes of gladiolus arranged in sunbursts in vases hung from the wall. 'My aren't they handsome,' said Lucile who had caught up with him. It was reassuring to feel her hand tucked into the crook of his elbow. 'No they really are too big,' she whispered on second thought. 'Let's go say hello to the Watsons and get the hell out of here,' Millard whispered back.

The receiving line was up at the end of the large ballroom which had been decorated with strings of signal flags and with red white and blue streamers draped from replicas of the great seal of the United States set high up along the wall under clusters of French, British and Russian flags. Dressed up men and women waiting to say how do you do to their hosts stretched in a straggling crowd halfway round the room. 'It's like the crowd at the Congressional waiting for the gate to open,' whispered Lucile. Against the wall opposite tables were set out under an enormous redstriped awning like at a sidewalk café and past crowding figures and clustered heads they could catch glimpses of long white tables garlanded with green set with a row of silver bowls and gleaming platters and stacks of plates against another bank of giant gladiolus. In the smaller ballroom beyond a band was already playing a Strauss waltz. Through the hedge of onlookers in the doorway they could see the flicker of dancing figures.

'Oh Lord we'll never get out of here,' groaned Millard.

'Let's just take our weight off our feet at one of these little tables,' said Lucile suddenly very bright and cheerful, 'and pretend we've bought our tickets and come to see the show.'

'All in the worst possible taste,' said a familiar voice. Behind a bay-tree in a green tub they found Mack McConnell sitting all alone at a marbletop table. He had a plate in front of him piled high with caviar and a glass of champagne in his hand. It evidently was not the first. 'Sit down my friends and enjoy the hospitality of the grand Mogul.'

'We might as well,' whispered Lucile, 'till they thin out a little.'

'Genuine beluga,' went on Mack squeezing a little lemon on his caviar. Then he sprinkled chopped egg and chopped onion on it with exaggerated care and looked up with a smile full of drunken blarney. His face was plumper and sleeker than it used to be. Little silvery duck-tails curled out over his ears. 'In view of the emergency it's in the worst possible taste . . .' Mac was expanding as he got his listeners' attention. 'But so delicious . . . Do you suppose Walker brought it back from Moscow with him? I'd never thought of Walker as a gourmet not with all those duodenal ulcers, begging your pardon ma'am. What a scene for a philosopher . . . And among all these gaily bedecked throngs I am the only happy man. "There was a sound of revelry by night. And Belgium's fairest . . ." It is what I imagined the nation's capital would be like when I first came to Washington an impecunious attorney from a little Jersey town and used to flatten my nose against the glass of the jewelers' shops on Connecticut Avenue on misty fall nights. Washington seemed a dream of beauty then but it proved to be all hard work and more kick than ha'pence as our British cousins put it. What the columnists won't do to this . . . God's gift to the isolationist senator from Montana. You ought to see the New Dealers, my old comrades in arms scuttling out as if the hotel were on fire. They give one look at the baked meats and the flowers and flags and out they go. Dragons guard this caviar . . . the gorgons of the press. If they relax for a moment under the influence of this first rate Moët and Chandon they'll be pilloried in some isolationist column. With what apprehension do they see the treacherous reporters jotting down their names on their cuffs. Don't say I have given up the fight. Even Achilles retired to his tent . . . The day may come when we can reform our ranks and give the country a new New Deal a real one this time. Meanwhile in my humble opinion I pulled out of government just in time. I tried to get old Mick to come along but he hesitated too long and now it's too late. Can't quit during an emergency. Millard shake the hand of a private citizen. I say what I please. I eat what I please. I drink what I please. I go to the office when I please . . . McConnell and Gleason at your service. I work half as hard and I make twice as much money and I love it and I'm planning to make a million dollars . . . and I love it.'

Millard got to his feet. 'I think we can get past them now,' he whispered to Lucile.

'Millard, my dear fellow, you look hungry and worried. Come back and have something to eat and drink and I'll introduce you to my wife, one of the sweetest little women in the world, and one of the richest.'

When they finally did reach Walker and Jo and big rawboned Mrs. Evans all upholstered in salmoncolored silk, Millard couldn't find anything to say to them. Fortunately the women kept up a chatter. Walker's hair and shirtfront were rumpled and he kept looking round the room from out of the deep sockets of his eyes with a suspicious glowering glance until, when his eye caught some friend's, his mouth would relax into a deprecating cornered smile. He looked in pretty good health; Millard couldn't tell whether he was enjoying himself or not. Jo looked very handsome in gleaming white with a little ermine cape. Walker seemed really pleased to see Lucile. As the group started to move towards the dancefloor Walker said with a giggle that he'd promised himself two dances, one with Jo and one with Lucile. A short man with a beard from one of the Balkan embassies had carried off Mrs. Evans. Immediately Jo became the center of a group of glossy young men who had a Wall Street look about them and Millard found himself alone in the doorway. 'Oh Lord we'll never get out of here now,' he was saying to himself.

An Englishman from some wartime mission or other whom he'd met at dinner someplace was talking to him in an immensely exaggerated Oxford accent. 'Fluid, my dear Carroll,' he was saying. 'That's what I keep telling myself, your country is so fluid . . .' Millard turned to him smiling politely. The Englishman had a beaked wooden face with uneven blotches of red on the cheeks like a hastily painted doll. 'Of course you have all the advahntages and disadvahntages of fluidity . . . improvisation . . . impermanence. Your cities my dear fellow, are carelessly erected bivouacs, even New York . . . and Washington's an architect's model . . . It wouldn't matter a bit if you were getting bombed instead of us; you'd never know the difference because you are so very fluid.'

'Capitalist society is not fluid. It is rigid,' said a flatfaced Russian officer with a shaven skull who looked remarkably like the doorman of a nightclub in his heavy gray uniform all strung with medals. 'How shall I say? Crystallization of monopoly causes American capitalism to break in pieces.'

'We don't know yet my dear Boris,' said the Englishman in an indulgent tone as if talking to a child, 'whether the fluidity of America is the fluidity of growth or the fluidity of decay.'

'Capitalism cannot grow. It is impossible. But meanwhile Meester Carroll . . .' The Russian bowed stiffly from the waist. 'I toast American capitalism arsenal of democracy against fascist mad dogs.'

Millard smiled again and edged away. The music had stopped but he couldn't see Lucile anywhere. He slipped into the larger ballroom where another orchestra was starting up on 'You're the Tops.' He had for an instant the strained lost feeling he sometimes had in dreams of looking for somebody he'd forgotten whom trying to find his way to some place he had forgotten where, the feeling of trying to walk through deep water through the pull of waterweeds. Inside his head a band was tightening. A man and woman were smiling at him. At first he didn't recognize Paul and Peggy Graves in evening dress. The tight feeling melted out of his head as he shook hands with them laughing. 'For gosh sakes, you are the last people I expected to find here,' he said.

'I reckoned we might as well come. Peggy had never been to a Washington party.'

'We're going to live here this winter so Paul thought he better kinder break me in.' Peggy had an independent angular country look Millard always liked. Her voice had a country twang.

'We dreaded it but I've been having the time of my life talking to the Russians,' drawled Paul . . . 'And my what ikrá!'

'The best caviar we've had since Moscow,' shouted Peggy.

'A foretaste of reverse Lend Lease,' Millard answered laughing. Then he asked seriously, 'What are the Russians saying?'

Paul had his mouth open to answer when a low insistent woman's voice interrupted. Jean Darwin in a very lowcut strawcolored evening dress that matched her hair had appeared at Millard's elbow. 'Millard,' she was whispering severely in a tone weighted with hidden meanings. 'Our friends are looking everywhere for you.'

He broke reluctantly away from Paul and Peggy and followed her sleek head of hair, combed straight tonight to a curl on her shoulders and impossibly blond, along the edges of the throng past the long tables where the buffet supper was laid out. Here and there in a sort of niche of dahlias and gladiolas stood a big silver bowl on a base wreathed in asparagus fern. Each silver bowl contained a glass bowl full of gray caviar set in cracked ice. Between there were hams and roast turkey and smoked turkeys and smoked salmon and lake whitefish and cold sirloins wreathed in parsley. Waiters behind the tables were deferentially carving with their thin sharp knives. Other waiters passed along the edges of the crowd with trays full of glasses of freshpoured champagne.

All along the line jaws moved, hands lifted glasses. There were naval officers in whites and army officers and marines in dress uniforms and a great many more pretty girls than usual. A waiter could hardly take a step out into the crowd with a tray of drinks before they were gone and he had to go back for more. Voices were loud, laughs and giggles were getting high and shrill. Couples were jiving among the tables. At the edge of the floor a group of young people had cleared a space and were dancing the Big Apple.

Millard had to stop to say good evening to Milt Rafaelson and his wife who both looked broader and better fed than ever and seemed to ooze selfconfidence from every pore. They were with a party of people whose faces were all turned expectantly towards a silvery hot chafingdish from which a waiter was ladling lobster Newburgh. They all had glasses in their hands, their faces had an odd identical look as if all their mouths were watering. Milt introduced a crosslooking grayhaired woman as Dr. Jane Sparling and a whitehaired Mrs. Trumbull, Justice Henderson's daughter, and a stocky young man from the Steelworkers' Washington Bureau named Yerkes.

'Can't compare with the Soviet Embassy,' Dr. Sparling was saying, as she forked a piece of lobster into her mouth. 'Capitalism can't even stage a decent party any more . . . When decay sets in in one place it goes through the entire bloodstream like a streptococcic infection.'

'Oh Jane how you do talk,' giggled Mrs. Trumbull.

Young Yerkes stood with his feet well apart as if he expected somebody to jump on him from behind. 'I could feed a lot of hungry people with all this grub,' he was saying.

'I more or less agree with you. It's not the moment for this sort of thing,' Millard said looking at him with interest. He smiled. 'But our host comes from a part of the country where if we do something we like to do it with a bang.'

A gray man from the edge of the group spoke up in a quiet voice. 'The watchword is every support to the American manufacturer until fascism is defeated . . . It will be the last fling of American capitalism . . . If they can only hold together long enough to furnish the Red Army the arms to defeat Hitler with we'll be satisfied.'

'We hope it's not as bad as that,' Millard started to say, but he noticed that Jean Darwin was making little tilting gestures with her head at him. He smiled absentmindedly and moved on after her.

'Thirteenth Street come to Washington . . . Jerry sure didn't leave anybody out, not Jerry,' she said in her sullen mutter as he walked along beside her.

Near the door they bogged down again in a group of embassy people speaking French around Herbert Spotswood. Herb looked pudgy and compact as a woodchuck staring uneasily out through his pincenez with his small chin tucked into his wing collar. 'Millard,' he cried

hastily as if he were talking fast to keep ahead of some embarrassment that was catching up on him. 'Allow me to present you to an old
friend of mine from Geneva . . . Jeannette this is Millard Carroll who
is rapidly becoming one of the most important—efficient and public
spirited he always was . . . er . . . activators of the preparedness program
in Washington . . . Millard this is the Baroness von Hildesheim . . . She
is staunchly French in spite of her German name. Without her wit and
spirit Geneva would have been barren indeed . . . Jean meet Jeannette.
I trust you will find you have much more in common than your
Christian names.'

The baroness was a small decisivelooking woman in black lace with
fine dark eyes and brows and somewhat too auburn hair. She spoke
with a sharp French accent. Immediately Millard was aware that she
was looking past him at Jean Darwin with an unpleasantly cold smile.

'Oh you must have been through so much,' Jean was chanting. 'Life
in Europe must be so wearing on a woman . . . Well Herb,' she went
on in a matter of fact tone. 'It's about time you took me to the airport.' Millard noticed how Herb winced and blinked. Millard teetered
uneasily on the balls of his feet at the edge of the group and began to
back away to escape any more introductions. Jean remembered his
existence. 'Millard dear,' she said putting her hand on his arm, 'I'd forgotten that it was so late. I'm catching an eleven-forty plane and I'm
just going to have time to make it if Herb's kind enough to take me
in his car. Dear Lucile is waiting for you with our friends in private
diningroom D just off the mezzanine.'

'Why that's too bad,' said Millard. 'Are you going far?'

'I'm going to Reno to get my silly little old divorce,' said Jean in a
cold clear voice looking straight into the baroness' face.

What the devil's biting them all? Millard asked himself vaguely as
he made his way out into the hotel lobby. He would never get Lucile
out now. Should have made a getaway first thing. His feet felt very
heavy as he climbed a short flight of thickly carpeted stairs. He was
tired and hungry and he wanted a drink. He felt older than he'd ever
felt in his life. Oh Lord he wished he could go home and go to bed, he
kept saying to himself.

At the head of the stairs he met Marice.

'Millard we've been looking for you everywhere . . . Out skylarking with the Powers models eh? Will Winship's latest story is that Jo is really a Powers model and Jerry has brought the whole troupe down from New York to liven up the party. Isn't that a scream? Now really . . . Came over the air at nine o'clock. We've been having a cosy bite in here waiting for Jerry to come back from the White House. He's been over there for two hours now.'

They were all sitting round a table under a cutglass chandelier in a private diningroom with heavy red draperies. Walker and Jo sat very close together at the end of the table. Bruce Slater and Mike had pushed back their chairs and had their heads together over their cigars. Lucile looked sleepy. She was yawning and making up her lips into the little mirror in her handbag. 'Do you know what I thought Oz,' she said. 'I thought you had stood us all up and gone home.'

'No I've been roaming around like a highschool kid at his first prom who can't get any of the pretty girls to dance with him.'

Marice pulled out a chair for him. 'What you need is a good stiff drink of bourbon and a piece of steak.' She pulled the oval whitemetal cover off the remains of a porterhouse steak in a platter in the center of the table and served him several slices with a pleasant motherly look of concern on her face.

'Marice you always were my friend,' said Millard.

'Now you listen to Mike,' said Marice severely. 'Mike's got something to say tonight even if he is my husband.'

'Millard,' said Mike and hitched his chair away from Bruce Slater's, 'what I've been saying all evening is this. You are setting up your Economic Scarcities Commission and Walker as we all know will be the President's deputy as coordinator of the War Procurement Board. Between the two of you you have an unexampled opportunity to influence the way American power is used in the whole armament effort all over the world. It will be up to you two men, and if you take the lead others will follow in your footsteps . . . to see that this great worldwide effort to block the advance of tyranny and barbarism is conducted in such a way that it leaves us a better world when the war is won. Otherwise the war for civilization will have been fought in vain. The mobilization of wealth at your command will be so overwhelming that it will make it possible for you to impose American standards of wages, working conditions, labor relations, etc., all over the world . . . The sort of thing we managed to do on a national basis under the NRA codes . . . I know we haven't won a perfect score but we have raised the status of the working people of this country.'

'The common man,' said Walker dreamily. Jo looked up in his face with an adoring smile.

Millard listened as he ate. He felt his heart beginning to beat. This was something he believed in.

Mike got to his feet and leaned over the back of his chair making gestures with his cigar. 'And we know very well that in the postwar world we shan't be able to protect the American standard of living at home if we don't establish a comparable standard abroad.'

Nobody spoke. The room was completely still. Millard set his knife and fork down in his plate and looked up into Mike's set face.

'Go on Mike, this is great,' he said.

'We must so set up our war effort . . . because it is a war effort . . . let's not kid ourselves. We hope and pray that we may accomplish our aims without a shooting war but we all know in our hearts we must be ready for it any day . . . We must so use our financial power that when we buy commodities abroad we raise the standard of living of the common man in South America, in Africa.'

'New frontiers beckon in all the nations of the world,' interrupted Walker Watson, the muscles of his sallow face suddenly tight with excitement. 'We must set the common man on his way to a more abundant life . . . Here's an example. We have managed to give the little people in this country a decent amount of milk for their children . . . The standard of living of the little people of the United States is fairly safe but it won't be really safe until every gaucho in the Argentine, every Negro in Africa can step out of his hut in the morning and find a bottle of milk on his doorstep. That's what I'm going to say in my radio address tomorrow night.' He turned to Jo. 'You see dear you have to be graphic in these things . . . Keep it simple.'

'In my opinion,' said Millard, speaking slowly and seriously, 'it is the only way we are going to be able to justify to the American people or to ourselves the sacrifices we are going to have to demand. As I understand it, Bruce,' he looked straight at him across the table trying to see his eyes under their heavy lids, 'the President sees eye to eye with us.'

'Of course, of course,' said Bruce drowsily. He smiled his heavy smile. 'After all it was the President who first gave these ideas circulation.'

Mike started to talk again excitedly. 'The postwar world must be a better world, a world where little people everywhere have the right to form unions for their economic betterment, to be free from the terror of unemployment and the fear of poverty in their old age. The only way the common man can protect his gains at home is to make them worldwide.'

'In Lincoln's great words which I'm using tomorrow night,' intoned Walker Watson, 'the world cannot subsist half slave and half free.'

Jo was dabbing at her eyes with her handkerchief screwed up into a ball. 'Dearest it's so beautiful, it's so terrible, it's so true,' she whimpered and snuggled her head into her husband's shoulder.

Millard caught a wary startled look on Walker Watson's face. Walker extricated himself tenderly and got to his feet and said with his wry smile: 'My little old mother used to say that if she didn't have her convictions she couldn't live a week . . . Life would be too horrible.' Walker let his chin drop on his chest and let his eyes run from one face to another round the table. 'Well,' he drawled, 'if we didn't have our convictions that behind the changing karma of life in this world there were divine powers and laws as certain as mathematics . . . What do you say Jerry?'

'I say amen,' came Jerry's deep rattling voice from the end of the room. The boards of the floor creaked as he came towards the table.

'Sit down Jerry and tell us all about it,' said Walker with a wave of a long arm.

'Have they been taking care of you all right?'

'Wonderful, Jerry . . . loveliest party I ever saw . . . Charming . . . Magnificent.' The women's voices chimed in. They turned their chairs towards him.

Jerry Evans let himself drop heavily into a seat at the end of the table. 'I do hope so . . . Mrs. Evans and I think the world of Jo and

Walker and I only regret I had to be called away.' Every man and woman at the table was looking into the big face above the big frame squeezed into the white messjacket with the gold buttons. He looked pale for him and seemed to have lost his bluster.

'Well friends,' he began slowly with his eyes fixed on the table-cloth before him. 'After fifty odd years of running free on the range old Tom Evans' son has been corralled and bridled and probably had the blinders put on him . . . The old man sure would cuss if he knew it. What do you think of that? It took the emergency to do it . . . You know the President has been laid up with grippe . . . I believe he still has a little fever, but he asked me . . . It's no use telling you this Bruce because you were there. With your passion for anonymity you carried me upstairs . . . Well there he was lying in bed in that great old mansion where Jefferson and Madison and Andrew Jackson entertained, where Lincoln worried through the Civil War. There he was smoking a cigarette in his long holder although the doctor had told him not to . . . by God I'd smoke hashish if my head was on that man's pillow . . . and sipping on a highball, and on little tables around the bed there were piles of papers and documents high as the ceiling . . . just to make him sleep better . . . "Now Jerry," he said to me, after Bruce had gone . . . "I'm going to talk to you like a Dutch uncle . . . It takes a Dutchman to make a proper Dutch uncle." Then he laughed and laughed. "There comes a time in every man's life when he has to choose between serving himself and serving his country. We've come to a point in this nation's history where a great many of us are going to be called to give our lives. Look at those poor boys who are being killed in training to be flyers or the merchant seamen risking their lives with the submarines . . . I'm not asking for your life, Jerry, though I know you'd give it. I'm just asking for your brains, for a loan of your brains . . ." Of course I just stood there saying Yes Mr. President, No Mr. President . . .'

Millard felt all his body go tense. There was not a sound in the room. Walker cracked a joint in one of his fingers.

'. . . And tomorrow morning the papers will say that Jerry Evans has accepted the post of coordinator of the new War Procurement Board.'

Jerry's cordial confident voice went on: 'Friends, I feel limp as a dishrag. After two hours with that man in the White House I feel limp as a dishrag . . . We have a very great President.' Jerry got slowly to his feet. 'If you'll excuse me I've got to go and see after my other guests a little . . . Now if there's anything in the world you want . . . All you have to do is ask for it.' He walked out of the room and Bruce Slater flitted after him like a long shadow.

Nobody said anything for what seemed several minutes. Millard pulled out his watch and stared glumly at its familiar dial. A quarter to twelve. Walker had slumped back into his chair with his eyes half-closed. The skin sagged in green wrinkles off his face. All at once he brought his fist down with a bang on the table.

'By damn I won't stand for it.' He began to talk in a shrill quavering voice. 'It isn't the first time. He told me he'd put Jerry in Commerce. He talked for a whole hour about how I was the right man for Procurement because it would tie up with my work in the Department and because I had freedomloving forwardlooking clearthinking men around me.' He jumped to his feet and waved a tremulous finger over the table. 'Only a worldwide New Deal can stop the advance of tyranny and dictatorship . . . And now this . . . By God I've had enough.' He started to walk up and down wagging his head as if he were going to bang it against the wall. 'This time I'm not going to take it. I've taken enough crap. Where's Slater, that sly bastard? Mike you've got to fix up an appointment for me with the President. Tomorrow. I've got to see him tomorrow. I don't care what his goddam schedule is . . . I'll stump the country . . . I'll expose him . . . I'll go back home and buy me a newspaper.'

Jo sat looking around the room with a little frightened face. Suddenly she brightened and jumped to her feet and threw an arm round Walker's shoulder. It's really a blessing in disguise . . . Now you'll be able to take that month off you promised. Walker I know the President was thinking of your health.'

Lucile had slipped her hand under Millard's arm. They stepped over to Walker with their arms linked and Millard patted him on the shoulder with his free hand. 'We all got tough sledding ahead,' he said hoarsely. 'Can't do anything about it tonight. We better go to bed . . . Walker and Jo I wish you every happiness.'

When he and Lucile were on their way down the stairs from the mezzanine he turned to her in a fit of nerves and asked peevishly, 'Now Lou what did I do with my hat check?... You must have seen me put it somewhere.' His hands clenched and unclenched in his empty pockets. 'Oh God did I have a hat? You oughtn't to let me come without a hat.'

THE POWER AND THE GLORY

3

*W*e were of various minds in this country but we all backed the President and believed in the draft and preparedness and in kids training for the airforce and we were in one accord in hating

the enemies of the human race.

We read our favorite papers and listened to admonishing voices on the radio and waited for the President to tell us

exactly who they were.

'The trouble with the 'Merican People,' said the old miner sitting in his backyard among dahlias, 'is they read the newspapers but they don't read careful . . . They read headlines. They read funnies. They don't read careful.

'What this country needs is leadership.' The bookreviewer jumped up from his desk with a ferocious scowl and walked up and down his office with clenched fists. 'I'm throwing up my job and going to work to teach the American People to kill Germans. I'm going to kill a million Germans.'

'The people of this country know how to do some things but they are not good haters,' said the country doctor in khaki who had just pinned a pair of silver bars on each shoulder. 'They don't know history.'

'A lot of these boys are America Firsters,' said the advertising man miraculously become an army major. 'They are the ones we must indoctrinate. We got to teach 'em to hate.'

In the motion picture theatres whenever we saw a Russian partisan (the marxist mechanicians of the Kremlin had hold of the handle of the old handpress of dialectical materialism and by a rapid machine computation were able to discover who exactly at any historical moment

were the enemies of the human race.

They said hate the Nazi, but they weren't telling us, nor even their catechumens between Twelfth and Thirteenth Streets in lower New York—they needed American planes and Lend Lease and the ships loaded to fall in line into that deadly convoy course to Murmansk—that we were the ones who they had discovered to be the enemies of the human race.)

Whenever we saw a Russian partisan in a fur cap shooting Nazis off the screen

we always cheered,
like at the sight of the President's cigaretteholder
or the flag.

THE LIBERAL FRONT

HERB SHAVED THAT MORNING walking back and forth with a springy step from the bathroom to the long mirror in the bedroom. The chirrup of Miss Albert's typewriter from the parlor gave him a cheerful feeling of business going forward. His face stinging from the listerine he had dabbed on it, he looked out at the reds and yellows and russets of the trees under his window. The sky was a deep slaty October blue. A good flying day. He slipped off his dressinggown, put on his collar, carefully tied his dark satin tie with little blue commas on it and fastened the small gold stickpin with a safety clasp, smiling as he thought to himself that the wearers of stickpins were a vanishing race. He had slept well. The speech he was going to deliver in New York that night was ready—Miss Albert was typing it now—and the notes for his evening broadcast were all neatly pencilled out. He ran the little comb through his mustache and, squaring his shoulders, gave himself a last look in the mirror. He looked rested, vigorous for a man of his age, he decided. He put his arms into the jacket of his gray suit and shaking out the folds of a clean handkerchief walked into the parlor.

'Good morning Mr. Spotswood,' Miss Albert said briskly looking up at him with a tight carefully rouged smile. Her fingers twinkled uninterruptedly over the keys. 'There is a Miss Greenberg downstairs.' Her face didn't look any too approving. 'She said she'd wait.'

He guessed he had better see her mumbled Herb. It was about the memorial meeting. Miss Albert stopped typing just long enough to reach for the telephone. Some chrysanthemums she had brought that had all the colors of the October foliage stood in a vase on the table. 'Thank you, that was very thoughtful, Miss Albert,' he said sniffing them absentmindedly. She was almost ready to smile again when there came a knock on the door.

Miss Greenberg was very dark and neat. She wore a little pointed red hat with two black feathers shaped like question marks. Her black eyes flashed understandingly and admiringly into Herb's. There was a warm undertone in her voice like the cooing of pigeons. He must forgive her for intruding, she knew what a busy man he was but she was doing publicity for the memorial meeting. She wanted a copy of his speech to release. Of course anything Mr. Spotswood said or did was news but she did want a human interest story.

Herb looked at Miss Albert . . . 'Two pages to do,' she whispered shaping the words with her mouth while her fingers went on trotting along the keys. Something bleak had come into the set of her jaw at the sight of Miss Greenberg.

By the time they had finished their little talk, Herb said giving them each a paternal smile, Miss Albert would have a clean copy typed off . . . How jealous the girls are he was thinking. Even at my age . . . and now Jeannette here in Washington coming to lunch and Jean in Reno getting her divorce . . . at that party they looked as if they could tear each other's eyes out . . . *How happy I could be with either, were' tother dear charmer away* . . . He found himself smiling down on his secretary's neatly pinnedup head.

'Oh Miss Albert please put in a call to Mrs. Darwin Bar Double T Ranch, Silverfield Nevada,' he said, 'not now but just when you finish copying the speech . . . Well suppose we sit over here in the window Miss . . .' Her black eyes looked up at him with a melting smile. 'Greta, everybody calls me Greta.'

She pulled off her red gloves with black stitching and brought a little pad out of her handbag and murmured that she understood he was an old Washingtonian. Oh yes, he said, a cliffdweller. Was it in Washington that his son Glenn had gone to school, she asked. What were the early experiences that had made him a . . . a liberal?

Well said Herb stammering a little, he'd brought up both boys to be independent. They were an independent family. Glenn had gone to Washington public schools and worked his way through college. He started at a middlewestern school and took his degree at Columbia. After that he'd hoboed around, worked in a bank, in the harvest fields, on small town newspapers, as a labor organizer, he had done most of the things American boys did when they were trying to find themselves.

The other son's name was Tyler? Wasn't that the Tyler Spotswood of the Spotswood case? Herb felt the blood going out of his cheeks. Her smiling questions were deft as the quick fingerwork of a surgeon taking out stitches in a wound. There had been several Spotswood cases, he answered belligerently. A family of prominent people she cooed. And what was Tyler doing now? Tyler had been betrayed by his political associates, he had taken the rap as the saying was. Now that he was a free man, Herb's voice faltered a little, he believed Tyler was preparing to take up journalism.

He'd been in hot water himself in his time, he added, feeling himself soften again under the sympathetic warmth of her smile. Perhaps there was a family propensity for getting into hot water. 'Hew to the line and let the chips fall where they may' might be taken for the family motto. He himself had been brought up for the ministry and though he had found his life's mission in other fields than preaching he still felt the tough old evangelical roots at the bottom of everything he thought and did.

'A family of American rebels,' declaimed Greta. She looked up into his face. For a moment it seemed as if there were tears in her black eyes but in the bright light from the window he could see it was the tiny blobs of mascara on her lashes.

'We have fought the good fight,' said Herb squaring his shoulders.

She looked up at him with an appreciative batting of eyelashes. So Mr. Spotswood himself had suffered in the cause? she whispered breathless. Oh that was ancient history. At the time of the first war he had been forced out of a teaching job at Columbia on account of his unpopular pacifist opinions. Well he still thought that at that time he had been right but since then he had learned to his pain that some evils could only be fought with high explosives.

Oh yes, she agreed we liberals had learned that we must be militant and disciplined. Lack of discipline had been the historic weakness of American bourgeois rebels. Lack of discipline as some of her friends in the labor movement had told her had been Glenn Spotswood's weakness but in the end he had recognized his error and set himself at the forefront of the fight against the bloody fascist reactionaries in Spain. He had died a hero. In her opinion Glenn Spotswood stood beside John Reed as a class war martyr.

'My they were a cute couple of kids when they were little,' Herb said after a long pause remembering the sandy head and the black head and the cosy evening feeling of coming home to the old walkup apartment and their sleepy babble after Ada had given them their baths and was getting them their supper . . . No she didn't want to reopen old wounds, Greta's voice was hurriedly soothing. She could get the fill-in on the Spanish war from the records of the Brigade in New York . . . 'Thank you, thank you.' She got to her feet looking up in Herb's face through brimming eyes. 'I can't tell you how much this has meant to me and with what real emotion I look forward to hearing you . . .'

'Telephone, Mr. Spotswood,' interrupted Miss Albert dryly. For some time her typewriter had been silent. It was Jeannette: 'Cheri, you must take me for a walk in the park. We must have the walk for our health cher ami. Then we shall return to your suite for lunch. No . . . no . . . you must. Quelle belle journée d'automne . . .'

While he was talking Greta was taking a copy of the speech from Miss Albert and slipping it with a deferential expression on her face into a manila envelope. When she had pulled on her gloves she stood in the door batting her dense eyelashes at him for a moment and said, 'At a quarter to eight at your suite at the Biltmore . . . you won't forget?' and was gone.

After he had assured Jeannette he would be down in the lobby in fifteen minutes he looked at his watch. It was only eleven so there really would be time for a walk. Jeannette was always right about things like that. When he'd fetched a light buff overcoat and his gray hat out of the closet he admonished Miss Albert to check over any news stories off the teletype the boy brought up from the office. Miss Albert tossed her head and said she always did, and what about his call to Reno? She must try to get Mrs. Darwin on the phone at one precisely. Miss Albert looked doubtful but Herb hurried out before she could say anything more.

Jeannette certainly did have that European refugee air when he found her in the lobby. She had on a tweed cape and a tweed hat with a pheasant feather in it that made her face look broad and rather illtempered. She took both his hands in hers and began talking right away about the beautiful autumn season. Why hadn't Herb told her the American autumn was such a beautiful season. As they walked slowly down the street she wanted to stop and exclaim over every tree they passed. Along the winding cement path in the park the sunlight filtered down out of the intense blue sky through a dazzle of pointed crimsons and yellows. Here and there a maple loomed like a bonfire. 'Que c'est beau,' she kept exclaiming in her murky precise voice. She walked well. It was pleasant to feel her beside him. He was breathing deep of the smell of dry leaves. His shoes were comfortable. He didn't have that feeling of too much fat compressed into tight clothes he sometimes had. He felt he could walk all day. He straightened his shoulders and pulled in his belly when she tucked her hand in his arm.

'Cher ami il faut parler affaires,' she was saying. The time had come for both of them she felt when it would be more convenient to be married . . . more convenable. 'Un petit marriage de convenance, qu'en dis-tu?' For her it was necessary . . . Her German name, Madame la baronne . . . Ça c'est fini, c'est trop bête en pleine démocratic . . . And for him too she felt it would be convenable. He needed her. A man in his position, of a certain age, should be protected by a loving and intelligent wife who understood his best interests . . . Now he was surrounded, no he needn't try to deny it, by un tas d'intriguantes . . . In Geneva for both of them it had been the love, the romanticism of the lake. Now they needed marriage, un ménage sérieux, something calm and gracious for the autumn of their lives, the beautiful American autumn.

'But Jeannette,' he stammered. 'We must be sure we are doing the right thing.'

She stopped to look at a squirrel that crossed the path with a greencased nut in his mouth. The bushy gray tail flowed in waves as he ran. He stopped, ran again, sat up with his tail erect to look brightly at them and then was gone in a rapid upward scuttle straddling the mottled trunk of a sycamore.

She tugged at Herb's arm. 'Oh qu'il est joli.' She looked up in Herb's face with eyes as bright as the squirrel's. 'Oh le mechant, il ne m'aime plus.' Her face turned up towards his was suddenly freshcolored and tender the way it had been afternoons on the iron bench by the lake or walking home through the palegray rainwet stone streets of Geneva. Quickly glancing back and forth up the path to see if anybody were coming he leaned over to kiss her. Immediately her little tongue was busy between his lips.

She pushed him away and laughed. 'Zat is besser,' she said exaggerating her accent. His arm was round her waist as they walked on. But cher ami she must explain. All those months alone in Lisbon . . . 'Tu m'a laissé poirotter au Portugal, le salaud . . .' while he was making the flirt with the little intriguing blondes . . . But that girl was impossible. So cold. She was not for him. He must remember what the oracle told Panurge. She let out a cackling laugh. All those months he had let his poor little Jeannette cool—what do you say?—her poor little heels in Lisbon. But all the time she had made the business. She had a little capital in Swiss francs and there were unfortunate refugiés from all over Europe who in panic expedited to Portugal their furniture, laces, bric-à-brac, porcelain, paintings, statuary, antique furniture . . . de très belles choses . . . 'I bought very cheap many things because I did not have confidence even the Swiss franc would survive the fury of that madman.' And everything she expedited to America. So now they were arriving in New York at Staten Island en dépôt. All at once she had discovered in herself a flair for the affairs. Drôle n'est-ce pas? It was necessary for her to form a company. She needed an American citizenship. As soon as possible of course she would take out first papers. Europe was finished. Always she had been citoyenne du monde now she wanted to be citoyenne of America . . . She would speak in perfect frankness . . . as Mrs. Herbert Spotswood, the wife of the great commentator, it would all be so easy . . . in Geneva they had been church mice the pair of them little employees of the Secretariat but now . . . 'Mon petit je t'apporte un dot.'

She stopped and made him sit beside her on a bench while she dug in her handbag for her bankbook. With the red enamelled nail of her little finger she pointed to a balance in five figures.

Herb gave a gulp but he continued to insist he wasn't a business man, he had no experience in the import business.

'Moi je me charge de tout . . .' They weren't so young as they used to be, neither of them. The time had come for them to make themselves une petite situation. There might be sickness, political overturns. He might be unable to broadcast. These days nobody could know what would happen. A nice little antiquarian's establishment, perhaps in Washington, perhaps in New York, would be a protection against the reverses of fortune . . . 'Cher ami j'en ai vu les revers de la fortune.'

She snuggled her face against his vest and started to sob.

'There, there, Jeannette,' he stammered in a flustered voice. 'I didn't know you cared so much.'

They had come out on a grassy green meadow flecked with russet and yellow of fallen leaves. Beyond was the glitter of the amber water of Rock Creek speeding over the stones and cars glinting in the sun beyond the boles of trees as they hissed past along the drive. Round the edge of the thicket where the mower had not reached grew a tangle of milkweed pods and yarrow and late goldenrod still in bloom and purple asters backed by a few last tall rose heads of Joe Pye weed. A flock of little gray and yellow warblers were perched at all angles on the fluffy seedheads pecking and gobbling with bustle and flutter of wings. As Herb and Jeannette walked across the grass the warblers flew up chirruping past them in a wavily skimming crowd.

'C'est beau, c'est beau ton Amerique. C'est sauvage,' she whispered throatily. 'Cher ami we can be happy . . .' Her eyes twinkled with a little joke: 'Paul et Virginie mais d'un certain age . . . Now take me to the hotel. I'm hungry and tired.'

As they waited laughing for a chance to cross the highway through the dense traffic, Herb noticed a little stone sentrybox with a pay telephone in it. He patted Jeannette encouragingly on the back and went in and called the hotel.

'Miss Albert,' he said, 'I'll be back in a short time with the baroness for lunch. Mr. James and possibly Tyler are coming . . . No cocktails but please call up for a bottle of nice dry sherry and see if you can get me another seat on the plane to New York. You have the car ordered for three-fifteen haven't you? And by the way cancel that call to Reno.'

In the taxi driving back to the hotel Herb sitting with Jeannette's firm hand in his hand, with her plump knee against his knee, felt buoyed along on through the sunlight under the deep blue October sky . . . today he kept saying to himself . . . in the growl and rattle and glitter of traffic through the treebordered streets . . . today, he kept saying to himself . . . across the great bridge with the lions on it, buoyed on a rising tide. Today he kept saying to himself. He had laid hold on life. He was fighting the good fight, hewing to the line, today he kept saying to himself, letting the chips fall.

In his parlor at the hotel he found Ed James looking very large and round and prosperous in an outrageous hennacolored houndtooth tweed suit talking cheerfully with Tyler and Tyler was sober thank God for once and not quarreling. Miss Albert started to collect her gloves and handbag to depart but Herb insisted, today he said meaningfully, that she stay to eat lunch with them. Jeannette was attentive to everybody, but particularly to Tyler. She cut him a slice of lemon for his cocacola when she deftly stripped lemon rind for each of their sherry glasses. The smell of the lemon peel mingled with the warmth of the sherry and the tang of dry leaves under the sun that came in through the open window. It was a smell Herb loved. The hotel's mixed grill was dry but it might have been worse. At least, Herb found the voice in his head saying, with Jeannette we'll eat well. Everybody seemed to enjoy the lunch.

Ed did most of the talking. Had Herb seen Millard recently? Well if he had the time he'd write a play about Millard and call it the Last of the Mohicans. But what about Walker, wasn't Walker still a New Dealer? asked Herb to lead him on. Well Walker was like the soul of man in the old mystery plays, between the bright angel and the dark. What about Mike? Wasn't he a real progressive? Mike, said Ed laughing his soft laugh, was by nature a sucker.

Herb turned to Tyler, who had been sitting silent and seedy with that knownothing blank look on his face.

'You know Jerry, Tyler, what do you think of him?'

'Jerry's strictly an operator,' said Tyler without interest.

Nobody was astute enough to take on the Skipper, Ed went on expansively to explain. He asked for some more sherry. He smacked his thick lips over it. 'The Presidency, Herb,' he went on, 'is a mighty institution. The White House makes its own rules . . . a few days ago I was up on the Hill listenin' to some damn ole cornfed senator or other battin' the breeze an' when I came out it was rainin' an' there was Walker Watson climbin' into that long black hearse he rides around in. I thought, bein' a modest kind of guy, I might still be ratpoison to him since I razzed him an' Jerry about that three ring circus they conducted over at the Arlington . . . to my surprise an' I must admit delight the old boy offered me a lift an' then as if nothin' had happened he began to light out at the Skipper. Didn't even tell me to keep it off the record. I suppose he knows I can be discreet when I want to but I don't always want to.' He laughed creakily. Herb felt his flesh puckering with dislike. He tried to keep his hospitable smile. Ed was a wellinformed fellow, he told himself, useful to know.

'He was considerably set up'—Ed seemed to be maliciously enjoying the story as he told it—'by a luncheon he'd been having with some congressional cronies an' he just carried on about how he'd taken all he was goin' to take from the Skipper. He was either goin' to resign or the Skipper would order Jerry off Millard's reservation. Of course I was interested because they are both boys from our ole sandlot teams back home . . . That's the Economic Scarcities Commission where we all know Millard is doin' a highly original job, but it don't suit Jerry because it's not business as usual. All Jerry can think of in the emergency is to use it to turn things back into the business as usual channels an' we all know that in the southeast at least business as usual means Jerry Evans' business. Of course he has cleared his skirts technically by resignin' from the directorates of most of his corporations . . . But they are still his corporations.'

'You leave Jerry alone Ed,' Tyler suddenly blurted out. 'Jerry's one of the whitest men I ever associated with.'

They all looked up at Tyler in surprise. After pausing to see if he had anything more to say Ed went on with his story: 'Well Walker drops me at the corner of Fifteenth Street an' I run up to my office an' start sketchin' out a red hot piece about Walker's resignation an' the New Deal's last stand in foreign buying for defense production . . . and that bein' the basis of a real new uptodate democratic foreign policy. Why Millard's even tryin' to put clauses in the contracts of those bastardly tin barons in Bolivia that they've got to allow collective bargainin' an' pay a livin' wage to the indios . . . Well I couldn't release this story till I checked on it so I barged around to see our friend Mike that evenin' an' there was Walker large as life an' Marice tuckin' a rug round his knees an' Jo pretty as a picture bringin' him a little bicarbonate of soda an' Walker tellin' all and sundry what a great job the Skipper thought Jerry was doin' an' how in the interests of coordination an' economy Economic Scarcities was goin' to be moved over to his department where Jerry could keep his eye on it. Walker said it had been his idea all along. Jerry and Millard, the realist an' the idealist, that's the kind of team that will make rearmament hum Walker kept sayin' . . . Now wouldn't that stop a clock? He'd been to the White House an' he'd had his treatment an' there he was the Administration zombie all over again. I tell you the Presidency is a mighty institution.'

Herb found Jeannette's dark eyes exploring his face to see how he was taking it. He let an expression of distaste wipe out his quiet host's smile as he looked across the table into Ed's fat face round with amusement at his own story.

'That's undoubtedly the position the isolationists are taking,' he said coldly. 'In my opinion the President has determined to let nothing stand in the way of defense production and immediate assistance to Russia.'

'Nothing except politics,' Tyler said.

Herb felt himself just beginning to lose his temper when Miss Albert said in her cool voice she was sorry to interrupt but that Mr.

Spotswood would have to hurry if he was going to catch that plane. For an embarrassed moment Herb and Tyler and Ed stood around the table looking at each other unhappily with their napkins in their hands, then Ed, suddenly the oily old southern gentleman again, paid his respects to the baroness with a little bow and left. Miss Albert already had sent Herb's valise down to the car. He went through his briefcase to make sure that he had the right copies of his speech and his broadcast and Miss Albert went through her briefcase to make sure she had the carbons in case of accidents. She would meet him at the Biltmore after his broadcast in case he needed her. Since she was letting the baroness have her seat on the plane she was off to catch the Congressional.

'May I go with you?' asked Tyler. 'I'd like to see what kind of a show they put on for ole Glenn.'

Miss Albert looked up at Herb in a flustered questioning way. He clenched his hands over his briefcase. 'Of course, why not?' he stammered.

Now he was in a rush. The one thing he had wanted to avoid was getting into a rush. If he waited around making any more arrangements he would miss the plane. He felt the nervous sweat breaking out under his collar. Taking a firm grip on Jeannette's elbow he started to push her towards the door. Tyler took a few steps along with them down the corridor.

'Dad,' he was saying. 'I wanted you to know. The confusion's over, no more bottlework. I'm enlisting in the Navy.'

'Will they give you a commission?' Herb asked sharply.

'I said enlisting.' Tyler's voice rasped. 'It'll take more than an act of Congress to make me a gentleman.'

'That's your business.' Herb felt the red blinding anger boil through his head. 'No time to talk about it now.'

The elevator came just in time.

Herb's breath was short when he let himself sink down beside Jeannette in the back seat of the car. She gave his arm a couple of little familiar pats. 'Oh la politique . . . Je n'y comprends rien,' she said making helpless circular motions with her hands. 'J'en suis toute étourdie.'

'You'd think your own kith and kin would have better sense . . . It's bad for my blood pressure to get into a rush like this.'

He couldn't help looking at his wristwatch every minute and keeping up a nervous drumming with his fingers on the briefcase. Particularly while he sat waiting in the car at her hotel for Jeannette to fetch her overnight bag he was all of a twitch. Driving through the traffic and across the bridge to the airport he was so nervous he couldn't trust himself to speak. When at last they stumbled up the gangway into the plane his shirt was soaked with sweat. Now he would probably catch cold, he was telling himself peevishly. After the tension of the take-off, once the plane was droning evenly under big white cotton clouds through the sunny afternoon sky he felt the pull on his nerves slacken like a loosened rope.

Jeannette had slipped her hand in his. 'Mon dieu quelle vie mouve-mentée,' she whispered happily and let her head droop against his shoulder. Jeannette was always good for him, he was thinking. It was better this way. It would have been too difficult with Jean at his age. There wouldn't be children but they could have dogs and cats. If there were ever peace in the world, after the enemies of the human race had been overthrown, they could make a happy autumn for their lives. She could be a help to him. The secret of managing a busy life, he started to explain to Jeannette, lay in always keeping a little ahead of schedule. She had drowsed off. He let his lids droop and tried to go to sleep himself.

When he opened his eyes the stewardess was tapping him on the shoulder and telling him to fasten his seat belt. The plane was circling for La Guardia Field.

Jeannette sat bolt upright looking out the window at the bright glitter of the East River curved like a boomerang, and the swooping bridges, and the umber blocks of apartment houses studded with windows that caught the sun as they swung past, and the tall violet mass of Manhattan piled against the flaring west. 'Que c'est laid,' she was muttering. 'Que c'est beau.'

When they filed out of the cabin into the cold gusts out of the northwest, Herb caught sight first thing among the windbuffeted people behind the barrier of Greta Greenberg holding onto her red hat with its two twitching black feathers. She introduced Mark Burgess massive in gray with his bulldog jowl set in a smile and a plump olive-skinned young man in some kind of a uniform whom she addressed as Colonel Farrington. They ushered him out to Mr. Burgess' car. On the way Farrington tapped Herb on the shoulder and told him in a hoarse peremptory voice that he and Glenn had been friends in Horton way back in the days of the pecanshellers' strike. Weren't they in Spain together, Herb asked eagerly. 'Different sectors, different sectors,' said Farrington.

They placed Herb on the back seat between Greta and Jeannette. Greta started talking fast into Herb's ear, now and then leaning forward to say something past his nose to the baroness. Jeannette's being a baroness seemed to excite her. She never addressed her without the title. It was baroness this and baroness that. She said she hoped they didn't mind that a little dinner had been arranged for the speakers before the meeting, just a snack in a private room in a restaurant next door to Madison Square Garden. Of course the baroness would come. After all they had to eat somewhere.

'Quite impossible,' Herb answered tartly. 'I shall eat nothing. Please drive me directly to the studio. I lie down for half an hour before my broadcast.'

Greta batted her eyelashes in disappointment. The feathers shook on her little hat. It was too bad because at the dinner they were forming a committee for a bazaar for the relief of the innocent people made homeless by the unprovoked attack on the Soviet Union. Perhaps, she smiled brightly through her almost tears, Herb would allow his name to be used as chairman. Anna Winthrop Strang was organizing the drive. Might they have the Baroness von Hildesheim's name too? They hoped to get some Washington people. Especially they need Mr. and Mrs. Walker Watson because he had just returned from Moscow. Surely Mr. Spotswood could help them get the Watsons. Anna Winthrop Strang had promised to bring in the First Lady. Greta's eyes gave an upward roll. As she talked she kept consulting a little notebook. Oh yes there was one other thing. A group of libertyloving Americans were cabling a protest to the British Prime Minister urging him immediately to open a second front in Europe. She read off a list of names. Then, she whispered confidentially, if Mr. Spotswood could find time to do an article for a magazine of national circulation on the partisans behind the German lines Colonel Farrington, who had been a leader of the International Brigade would be delighted to furnish Mr. Spotswood the material. He had organized the partisans in Spain and now he had just returned from Moscow where he had put himself at the disposition of the Soviet Government, possibly to organize a brigade of Spanish Republicans to fight the Fascists. She could outline the story for Mr. Spotswood herself if he didn't have the time. The Spotswood name would sell anything. This was the Spotswood year. Farrington had turned around in the front seat when he heard his name mentioned. 'Moscow,' he said in his husky tense voice, 'will hold. You must tell the American people that. The panzer divisions are bogging down in snow and mud and the partisans are cutting their communications. My God what men!'

After the meeting, went on Greta in an even voice, there would be a reception at a private home. She had started checking off the items in her notebook with a pencil. Seats in a box would be arranged for the baroness and for Mr. Spotswood's secretary. Tyler Spotswood had been invited to sit on the stage with the families of the antifascist martyrs. They would all be called for at their hotels by volunteers from the Junior League. Arrangements again, thought Herb peevishly. His head began to swim with all these arrangements. After this he must never go anywhere without Miss Albert to handle the arrangements. He found himself saying yes to all sorts of things, even saying he'd think about the possibilities of an article. He was groggy with arrangements when the car drew up at the building of the broadcasting concern. 'Moscow will never surrender, the partisans will cut the Nazi communications,' said Farrington and Greta Greenberg in unison as he was getting out of the car. He didn't even have a chance to say a word to Jeannette.

It was a relief to go up in the empty elevator. The receptionist said good evening in a quiet impersonal voice. In the corridor a bland soft-footed young man whose name he had forgotten met him and escorted him to the little office with a couch in it where he was accustomed to stretch out for a moment before his broadcasts. He sat down at the desk before a clean unmarked blotter and read through his broadcast in a low voice, marking the pauses and stresses in pencil. He added a word or two about the activities of the partisans behind the German lines on the Russian front and made his forecast that Moscow would never surrender a little more positive and then lay down on the couch and closed his eyes. He was too excited to rest. Slogans calling for a holy war against the enemies of the human race kept crowding into his head. He was pacing back and forth the length of the couch when the bland young man opened the door and whispered in his soothing voice that it was time for Mr. Spotswood to go on the air.

After he had finished Herb walked back with a confident tread. He had to admit, even to himself he was thinking, that this had been a remarkably successful broadcast. On his way back along the corridor a door opened and Mr. Brackett with his hair as usual over his ears stuck his head out and chanted, 'Masterly, my dear sir, masterly.' The bland young man was in his office to say that there was a call waiting for him on the phone. He sat down at the desk and still smiling picked up the receiver.

It was Tyler talking from the Pennsylvania Station. He was drunk. He was launching into some kind of a rigamarole about not letting somebody take somebody for a ride. His voice was so blurry Herb couldn't make head or tail of what he was saying. 'No more a memorial meeting than a rabbit, Dad, it's a party rally.'

'Tyler,' he said severely, 'I haven't time to enter into a discussion of this sort now. I am preparing to deliver an important address. Call me tomorrow morning at the hotel.' He hung up.

Immediately the phone rang again. 'But Dad, it's not a memorial meeting,' started Tyler's drunken voice. Herb blew up the way he used to years ago when Tyler was a little boy trying to talk himself out of some scrape or another. 'Tyler,' he shouted, 'I refuse to discuss anything with you when you are in that condition.' He hung up again. Then he called the operator to ask her to put through no more calls as he was leaving the building.

Highly agitated he snatched his hat and coat and strode down the corridor. He forgot his briefcase and had to go back for it. Alcoholism, he was thinking, what a horrible thing. He was so preoccupied he almost walked past Greta Greenberg who was waiting for him in the reception hall with a stocky woman in tweeds whom she introduced as Dr. Jane Sparling. Herb frowned at them questioningly. Greta hastened to explain that they had come to escort him to Madison Square Garden. It had gotten so late she didn't feel he had time to go back to the hotel, she thought they had better go straight to the meeting. There was a sort of religious unction in the way she pronounced the word 'meeting.' Anyway he looked very handsome in that light gray suit, she said looking up at him through her dense lashes, it would be a shame to change. Dr. Sparling was waiting to exclaim that the broadcast had been magnificent, the deft strokes about the partisans disrupting the German lines, and the mud and the snow and Comrade Winter, what a happy thought. She clasped her hands together and shook them approvingly under his chin.

Just one thing before they left, she added in a small unexpectedly wheedling voice. Would he mind putting his name to a petition? Only the choicest, most influential names would do. It was a petition to the President to pardon the classwar prisoners who had been convicted under various pretexts while the country was still under the influence of fascistminded isolationists. 'And I've been asked,' added Greta with her tearful smile, 'to get a small contribution for the Mullins Defense Committee . . . You know that was the young Negro liberal who was arrested for distributing handbills in Atlanta . . .'

Herb felt his nerves beginning to jump. 'My dear young ladies,' he said, 'If I am to deliver an address this evening I must have a few moments of perfect quiet.' He snatched his glasses off and pressed the tips of his fingers against his smarting eyeballs. His temples had started to throb. None of them said anything while they waited for the elevator.

The night was clear and cold. The streets were full of sharp moving glints of light. Faces, the bright work of cars, the curve of mudguards gleamed with reflected light. While Herb helped the women into the cab he looked up past tapering planes of buildings dimly glowing with light into the flawed violet crystal of the sky. As the cab made its way with many waits towards Eighth Avenue a drift in one direction began to appear among the faces on the pavements. It was the crowd heading towards Madison Square Garden. Above the slow flow of wraps and overcoats faces looked fresh and youthful in the slapping wind. The Spotswood year, Greta had said. It was to hear him talk about Glenn they were all pouring out of subways and buses. Years ago, thirty years ago when Glenn and Tyler were babies, he saw himself a young man walking home with Ada after preaching stiffly on the Dedicated Life to empty benches in the old clapboard church on Myrtle Drive, walking home with Ada to Mrs. Appleton's—whenever he heard the word sleazy it made him think of Mrs. Appleton's three rooms—in a hurry for fear something might be wrong with the children and dear Ada was chattering on about how well he talked and how the time would come when he would pack the halls. Poor Ada, if only she had lived to see this day. He squinted out of the window of the cab at the crowds hurrying to hear him. This was the willing crowd, the great cause, the opportunity. He felt very humble he told himself before this great opportunity. At the end of the dark tunnel of the years he could dimly see sweet Ada's face full of trust and belief in him urging him on. He was so wrapped up in his thoughts that Greta had to say several times, 'Here we are Mr. Spotswood,' before he roused himself enough to get out of the cab.

He walked in a daze up crowded cement ramps and through corridors echoing with footsteps. Dr. Sparling led the way with her short determined stride. Greta had him by the arm. Before he was ready they came out into the immense cave of the auditorium, where lights glowered through a blue haze and distant faces flowed slowly down aisles and gangways, crowded as apples he'd seen as a boy flowing down a chute into a cidermill. Red flags hung from the ceiling and round the galleries. Here and there the stars and stripes hung limp between slogans lettered white on red bunting.

ALL AID TO THE SOVIET UNION
Defend the Besieged Workers of Moscow and Leningrad
ANTIFASCIST FIGHTERS NEED
FOOD CLOTHING GUNS

Immediately there were introductions among the ranked chairs on the platform. A man with a long black beard pressed Herb's hand encouragingly and showed him the speakers' table with its gleaming bank of microphones and introduced a redhaired woman in purple with the face and figure of a haggard Gibson girl as Anna Winthrop Strang, and Elmer Weeks a gray man with a bulbous nose with an unlit pipe perpetually in his mouth and several Spanish Republican diplomats in evening dress and a row of flatfaced refugees from Balkan countries buttoned into Russian tunics. Along the line of chairs he caught sight of a few Washington faces, the Rafaelsons and Mick Goldfarb. A nervous hand was on his shoulder. He turned round and found Mike Gulick's face grinning into his. Mike slipped into the seat next him.

'Is Walker here?' asked Herb in a whisper.

'I'm kind of representing him,' Mike said with a low giggle. 'He was detained by the President who is trying to get him to take on a new job, Herb, a job of really epochmaking importance. If only his health holds out. He's doing enough work now to kill an ox. I'm here to give the assurances of the Administration on Russian aid . . . everything we say here will be fully reported in Moscow.'

The orchestra had started to play the 'Marche Slave.' Herb leaned back in his chair with his eyes halfclosed to shield them from the glare of the spotlights and looked out past the heads and shoulders of the people on the seats in front of him at the hazy distant faces banked round the huge oval hall. He opened the notebook into which Miss Albert had clamped the pages of his speech and let his eye run along the lines. He wanted to be able to speak it without reading it. As always when he was going to speak his heart was pounding and he had a funny empty feeling in his head.

The man with the beard was chairman. The first speaker he introduced was a young man in a sort of uniform who had lost a leg and who stood up on his crutches making the clenched fist salute while the galleries roared with applause.

'We of the Brigade did our best,' he shouted, 'to stop the fascist butchers outside of the fortress Madrid . . .' He had to stop for the cheers . . . 'They had the help of the Munich appeasers in England and in our own State Department . . .' 'Boo . . . boo,' came a long drone of scorn from the hall . . . 'There were too few of us . . . Now again comrades the defenders of the working class are giving their lives to stop the fascist hordes. They are not too few ... In front of Moscow, in front of Leningrad they will stop them ...' The hall bellowed like one throat. The young man raised his spread hand for silence. 'I talked today to my old commanding officer from the Spanish front. He had just come back from the Moscow front. Comrades he is unable to greet you today because he has been called to Washington to confer with the President ...' Cheers and handclapping beat like surf against the speakers' platform. He raised his spread hand again. As the shouts died down a little triumphant curl appeared at the corners of his mouth. 'This is the message he told me to deliver. The Red Army needs everything, guns tanks food ammunitions everything but guts ... If we don't fail them they won't fail us ... Where can we help? We can help them right here in New York and in Washington. Write your senators. Write to your congressmen. Keep those damn politicians hopping. Worry them to death. Demand arms for the Red Army ...' The roar rose in a wave to swamp his voice. Rhythmic cheers echoed from gallery to gallery. He was waving his crutches at them. His youthful face pale, a set look of exultation stiffening the corners of his mouth, he was being helped back to his seat.

Herb looked down at the staid lines of his reasoned account of the importance of the Spanish war: the sacrifices of these young men: Americans, Frenchmen, antifascist Germans had been, he was going to say, the first reaction of decency and civilization against the enemies of the human race. It all seemed too tame. While Mrs. Strang was bewailing in the voice of a prophetess on the tripod the fact that nobody in America had heeded the warnings of wellinformed people that if fascism were not stopped in Spain it would bring war and ruin to the world, Herb tried to recast some of his sentences to get a little more passion into them. This was an audience he told himself that wanted passion.

Too soon Herb's turn to speak came around. The man in the black beard gave him quite a buildup in his introduction. After saying that his young friend who had spoken first represented the brave antifascist fighters who however maimed and mutilated had survived the Spanish war, he said that the man he was now introducing spoke for

the heroic dead . . . other claims to fame as a staunch battler through
many years for liberal causes . . . the voice they were about to hear
was as familiar to every man and woman in that hall as the voice of a
member of their own family . . . the father of a young man who after
giving his life to the cause of the workers of America . . . had laid down
that life on the stony soil of Spain . . . for the freedom from oppression
of the working class of the world . . . Herbert Spotswood.

This time the roaring voices and the rattle of beaten palms were
for him. Herb stood behind the speakers' table carefully adjusting
his glasses and waiting with a little modest smile on his face for
the noise to die down. When he first started to speak his voice was
husky. He stopped to clear his throat several times. He stumbled over
words, cut corners, plunged on into extemporized phrases. He felt
too keenly to be at ease the ears waiting impatiently for the phrase
to cheer for, the linked breathing of lungs ready to roar in unison.
The glare of the spotlights made him blink. There was the distracting
flicker of the flashlight bulbs. At last he managed to fix his attention
on the familiar microphone before him and started to talk evenly
and smoothly.

He skipped lightly over the attempts of men of good will in the
years between the wars at Geneva and elsewhere to build some structure of peace. He spoke about the good work for collective security of
Tchitcherin and Litvinov and got a few scattered cheers. Mention of
the failure of the League of Nations brought boos. Then he went on
to the attack on the Spanish Republic by the enemies of the human
race and spoke modestly of the young men like his son Glenn who
had thrown their lives into the breach. A few cheers. The boos were
on his side when he spoke sarcastically of Chamberlain opening the
umbrella of appeasement, but when he spoke of the rape of Poland and
the disastrous consequence of the Hitler-Stalin pact he began to notice
that the boos were right in his face. 'Can that talk,' a voice shouted.
Ranks of mouths booed in unison roaring him down. Sweat broke out
on Herb's forehead. His collar felt cold and wet. He stumbled over the
word Finland and hurried on, first skipping sentences and then whole
paragraphs, to the part about how the souls of those young antifascist
fighters were marching on to defend the holy soil of Russia. The boos

had settled down into a regular snarling rhythm. At the word Russia they stopped.

Herb's throat was dry but he didn't dare pause for a drink of water. He decided right there to drop the text of his prepared address. 'The peoples of the world's great democracies,' he yelled into the mikes, forgetting his carefully pitched radio whisper, 'are uniting in a war for civilization. Their victory will be slow but sure. Their alliance will endure until the last of the enemies of the human race has been shot down like a dog.' Gradually applause began to crackle in the corners of the hall, cheers rose to meet him, voices merged in a roar. They were on his side now. He took a swallow of water. He drank down half the glass. 'Nothing,' he went on, 'said the timid men in chancelleries and bureaus, nothing can stop the Nazi advance. Nothing, said the wise men in the staff colleges can stop the panzer divisions, but tonight while we are gathered in this hall they are being stopped and they are being stopped forever by the two great heroes of the Soviet Union Comrade Winter and Comrade Stalin.'

The man with the black beard was shaking his hand. His glasses were misted. The loud applause followed him as he started back to his seat. 'Comrade Stalin and Comrade Winter that was good,' he heard Milt Rafaelson saying to Mrs. Rafaelson as he stumbled past them.

Mike put his arm around his shoulders and whispered in his ear: 'Easier in the studio, isn't it, Herb? Here they can talk back.' He giggled creakily. 'It's a great force . . . It's the force that will overthrow reaction everywhere.' His voice trailed off. The orchestra had started to play the '1812 Overture.'

When the music stopped Elmer Weeks appeared behind the microphones. With a sound like coal being dumped into a cellar feet scraped as people rose all through the hall. When the racket subsided he shouted, 'The invincible Red Army.' Volley after volley of hand-clapping and cheers answered his words. Herb watched the smile that was almost a sneer that flickered under his grizzled mustache as he made quieting movements with his hands like the movements of an orchestra leader. 'The Red Army has done what the broken remnants of the forces of the decadent capitalist democracies of Western Europe were not able to do. It has stopped the Wehrmacht dead in its tracks.'

He paused for more applause. In the corner of a gallery a group had started to sing the 'Internationale.' Herb sat mopping his forehead with his handkerchief while the noisy response to Elmer Weeks' speech beat about his head and ears. His hands were trembling. He was dead tired.

After the speech there was a confused stirring about as ushers with red armbands moved through the crowd with collection boxes. Herb got to his feet and distributing nods and smiles right and left to people he knew tiptoed out. Finding an empty corridor in back of the platform he hurried down it fast. He didn't want to be intercepted by Greta Greenberg. He didn't even want to see Jeannette. It had been a tough day. He oughtn't to let himself get so tired. The cold clear air out in the street was delicious. A taxi was passing. He jumped in. When he reached the hotel he hurried up to the room Miss Albert had reserved for him, found to his relief that his bag was there with his night things, called the desk to say he had retired, hung a Do Not Disturb sign on the door knob and went to bed. He couldn't get to sleep but he lay secure in the darkness listening to the distant drone of traffic in the streets. He was helplessly wakeful. After a while he got up and went to the phone in the dark and asked the girl to give him the Baroness von Hildesheim's apartment. 'Quelle eloquence,' her nasal French twanged in his ear. 'Viens cher ami, viens.'

THE POWER AND THE GLORY

4

*W*e read the newspapers. We went to the movies. We had no other way of knowing. We listened to the commentators over the radio. Security: everything that happened in Washington was topsecret but we had a dim notion that the Atlantic sea frontier was dented and that there were shortages on the production line, and that the President was babying along the two Japanese ambassadors in a play for time
> while the ships were launched
>> and the cannon forged
>>> and the planes assembled.

We couldn't believe our ears that dull Sunday afternoon when the radio programs broke off for the announcement of the attack on Pearl Harbor.

We couldn't believe our eyes when we read of Nichols Field and Bataan,
> Corregidor.

The President was calm. We saw his picture sitting at his desk. We heard his voice when he asked Congress for a Declaration of

War. It was the Secretary of State who blew his top and cussed out the minute Nipponese ambassadors in old mountain muledriver style. At the White House the President's aides whispered 'I told you so.' Official persons generally agreed,—

> *and the War and Navy Departments*
> *and the members of commissions appointed by the President*
> *who flew to Hawaii*
> *to view the ruin and the sunken ships and the newdug graves;—*

they laid the blame, a little of it, on a brace of admirals and a general; but official persons generally agreed that the responsibility for sending bombing planes off without machineguns or ammo and for the lack of an air sea patrol and for the neglect of radar,

> *and for the huddling of battleships like ducks in a yard,*
> *and for the fact that Sunday morning follows Saturday night,*
> *lay with the American people.*

It was all the fault of the American people who wouldn't learn history and were negligent of geography.

The Japs taught us geography.

CIVIC COURAGE

GEORGIA WOKE UP SWEETLY but immediately she remembered and the pain closed down over her like the lid of a box. Looking out of her misery as if through a peephole into a faraway room she could see over the bureau her mirror with a bunch of fusty cloth roses in the upper corner and a pair of stockings draped over them and the shuttered window with its white muslin curtain and a rosy streak of sunlight along the edge of one shutter which had swung open a little. Beyond was a haze of delicately unfolding spring leaves. The rain had stopped but drops still dripped from the eaves. Birds chirped and rustled in the bushes outside the window. She started drowsily to stretch. When her hand touched his shoulder she jerked it back . . . No I can't go on living, no, no . . . She began to shiver. Her feet were icy cold. She crept carefully out from under the covers so as not to waken him. His breathing was heavy with a slight wheeze at the end of each breath. She walked on tiptoe. She tried not to look at him but from the door she couldn't help glancing back. In the slaty gloom of the room Jed Farrington's pallid sleeping face with its small sharpcut features and domed forehead had a chalky look that made her remember the smudged plaster bust of Napoleon she used to play with as a child up in the attic back home in Ann Arbor. She slipped out into the livingroom and began to walk up and down to try to warm her clammy feet.

. . . This can't be me. It can't be me this is happening to . . . She was taken with a fit of shivering again. So as not to have to go back into the bedroom for her dressinggown she went to a hall closet and hauled out the worn old rabbitfur coat she'd had since the university. She felt more like herself in it.

She began to tidy up the living room. When she pulled up the shades the pale greens of the early spring morning filtered into the room. The black pain had closed again like a mask tight over her skull. Through eyeholes she looked out at the bright world. She dusted the cherry desk.

Where the glasses had stood last night, there were white rings on the mahogany table. She popped into the kitchen after the rag she used to polish with. The furniture wax had a homey smell. It was Paul she bought the table for, it was Paul she bought the old Virginia desk for. There had been no sense to it but when she took over the ground floor apartment in the old white Alexandria frame house and Bertha Manning moved her Victorian walnut furniture away, she had run around the antique shops buying furniture and thinking continually of Paul, Paul sitting writing at the desk with his angry scowl, Paul eating cornbread and fried oysters at the table with that absentminded look he had at meals.

Georgia was beginning to forget herself in her housework. Outside the mockingbird nesting in the paulonia tree had started to sing pouring out grace notes and long fluent trills. The mockingbird's song made her remember again and she burst out crying. She felt better crying. She found herself sitting in a chair dabbing her eyes with the waxy rag.

God she'd been silly to think that Paul could ever leave his children and break off a whole life built up over years on account of a passing weakness for old Facts and Figures. It would have been wrong too. God she'd been silly. But now it was worse than silly. This creature she was inside of just wasn't her at all, this aching automaton with painfully hinged motions that had let Jed Farrington drive her home in a cab that snowy night from Jane Sparling's Forum. He hadn't even asked if he could come in but just pushed right along beside her and slammed up and down the room talking class war strategy and class war logistics. She had let him take command of her as if she were a squad of wretched farmboys he was lashing into shape for partisans . . . This isn't me, she muttered aloud . . . No, no, this can't be me.

She jumped to her feet and went into the bathroom through the door that led from the kitchen to wash her streaky face. She took a shower and dressed in what clothes she could find in the bathroom closet so as not to have to go into the bedroom. Oh if he would just never wake up. Oh if he just weren't in the world . . . or if I weren't . . . To be doing something she lit the gas oven and put on the coffee percolator and started to squeeze some oranges for breakfast.

'My George, you look desirable,' his voice drawled heavily behind her. He stood in his underdrawers in the bedroom door pudgy and oliveskinned smiling sleepily with the black hair ruffled round the bald dome of his head. She turned away to finish the oranges. As she leaned over the reamer his lips were greedily kissing the back of her neck. His fingers were feeling for the nipples of her breasts. 'Jed you're mussing my clean blouse,' she heard her voice whining helplessly as he pulled her backwards into the bedroom. She couldn't help herself. His impatient fingers were fumbling with the hooks on her skirt.

While he was bathing and shaving she lit the oven and mixed up a pan of cornbread. Breakfast was ready by the time he came out of the bathroom showing his even white teeth in a small smile that gave a cruel curve to the contour of his lips.

'It's an elegant mornin',' he was saying, 'even if those old churchbells are ringin' . . . Reminds me of down home. The most hypocritical damn sound in the world . . . Cornbread an' scrapple! My . . . my . . .' He reached for her hand but she drew it away. She was bustling round the room as she brought him butter and preserves and salt and pepper like a waitress in a restaurant. His black eyes caught hers and held her still. 'George,' he said looking up at her with his mouth full, thoughtfully chewing, 'You're mighty good lovin' do you know it?'

She dropped in the chair opposite him. 'Jed I can't . . .' she started.

She had to explain. She had to defend herself. The words would not form in her mind.

'Better eat some breakfast,' he said. He was patting his jaw gently with his short hand. 'I got a toothache do you know it? I had it all day yesterday.' When he spoke of his toothache his face grew small and peevish and withered, so that she began to feel sorry for him.

'Now Jed, you must go to the dentist first thing tomorrow,' she said gently.

'I will, honest I will, George. Doc Sparling knows a dentist who's a Party member . . . George,' he added suddenly as if her interest in his tooth had touched him, 'suppose I make an honest woman of you. This is Sunday but we could take out a license tomorrow. I don't know how long it takes to go through a form of marriage in the District of Columbia.'

Georgia jumped out of the chair and started to walk up and down the room. 'Jed you make me feel like a prostitute,' she whispered through clenched teeth.

'Ain't my fault if in a capitalist society every woman has to act the whore . . . You're a damn good girl George . . . I want to make a good soldier out of you. In the Soviet Union in the partisans the women take rifles an' go right out with the men . . . I know a cute little girl named Dasha who's shot seven boches already . . . Whether we like it or not the law of the world is war for years an' years to come . . . We've got to be soldiers, soldiers of our side. Over in Spain it took me a long time to get used to it. At first I tried to kid myself along with the notion that it was all a game of chess . . . the dead were just pawns taken off the board . . . but then I learned that you had to hate the fascists so bad you enjoyed killing 'em. I was a staff officer over there but in my spare time I used to go out huntin' fascists like shootin' birds down home, except that I hated the fascists an' enjoyed seein' 'em die. It was damn funny the way some of those fascists died. There was a fat old banker in a white vest we shot through the belly . . .'

Georgia felt her face stiffening. There was too much saliva in her mouth. She started to walk stiffly towards the bathroom. She had to get to the bathroom before she threw up. Jed got to his feet and poured her a cup of black coffee.

'Don't be like that,' he shouted. 'You sit down there and drink that coffee.' She sat down humbly and began to sip the coffee. The nausea began to pass. 'It's this damn soft bourgeois bringin' up we've all had,' he grumbled. 'Thatagirl . . . You're the only thing makes this Washington assignment tolerable . . . What I am is a professional killer. I ought to be at some damn front or other.'

'Would you fight in the U.S. army?' she asked with her hands limp on the table before her.

Sure, he said suddenly looking up at her with an innocent schoolboyish look he occasionally had, he'd fight in any army that was out to kill fascists, he didn't care whether they were Jap fascists or Nazi fascists. He only wished the U.S. army would start doing something more active than surrendering Bataan. The Russians meanwhile went to work and recaptured Rostov. That was exactly the difference between the two nations.

He pushed back his chair.

That was a dandy breakfast, thanks. Now they must get down to business. He guessed Georgia was wondering what he was doing in Washington. A soldier had to go where he was sent, didn't he? Well he been fixed with a civilian war job over at the Pentagon so they couldn't draft him right now, but his real job was seeing that these damn socialfascists in Washington didn't sell out to the real fascists. Tough assignment, eh?

His black eyes bored into hers. 'George you can be damn useful to us . . . Even though you're not a Partymember maybe you agree with me that the Party is the only force that can bring peace an' order to the world . . . We're seein' capitalism's death agony. It ain't pretty. It's tough but that's the way it is. They didn't consult us when they made the world . . . Now George you're a mighty bright girl and you're right up in Millard Carroll's office in this War Procurement Board. Millard Carroll today is next to the President about the most powerful man in Washington. He's able, I wish he was on our side but he ain't. Now we're allied for duration with this damn socialfascist government of ours but we can only trust 'em as far as we can see 'em, so we've got to be informed . . . so we can plan our strategy . . . global strategy. How thick are you with Paul Graves?'

'Jed,' she cried out. She wanted to get up from the table and go away. She wanted to hit him in the face, but all she could do was mumble, 'you oughtn't to talk like that.'

'I'll talk any way I damn please. You keep him stringin' along, see? He'll come in handy one of these days but what I want right now . . . Doc Sparling's been pumpin' Carroll's secretary but she's too dumb to be any use. Doc Sparling herself don't know what it's all about if you ask me. With all her connections she hasn't been able to get a copy of WPB order 56 or a list of the names of the WPB agents in South America. That lists' probably on Paul Graves' desk. I don't believe it's even classified.'

'Jed I can't.'

'Which side are you on anyway, George?' He got to his feet and talked down at her with his hands on the back of his chair. 'We're fightin' two wars in this town. In the shortterm war we're allied to the Squire of the White House and his big business friends but in the longterm war they are our most dangerous enemies.' He went over to the couch to pick up his buff stetson. '. . . You think it over, see? I got to go over to Washington to see Elmer for a few minutes. He's in town today. Then I thought I'd come back an' take you for a little airin' in the *Niñã*. It sure turned out a bright notion of mine anchorin' the lil' ole tub off Alexandria.'

'Have you got your harbor permit?' She looked defiantly up in his face. At last she felt herself stiffening. She was questioning him like a police captain.

'Sure I'm cleared with the Coast Guard all down the line.'

'How do you get gas?'

'You never mind how I get gas.' He waved his stetson in front of her face. A light whiff of hair oil and leather came from it. 'I've got enough to run down to Indian Head and back up to the yacht club basin in the mornin'. A little sniff at the river'll do us good and we'll have time to talk this out.' He put his hat on his head and suddenly sat down on the couch holding his jaw with both hands. 'Gosh I sure won't be able to go if this toothache gets worse.' His face was taking on a pale greenish look. 'Say George have you got any aspirin?'

'I've got some codeine the nurse gave me at the hospital.'

'You don't dope, do you?' His cold black stare was searching her face. She didn't understand.

She stared back at him.

'Skip it, Georgia, skip it . . . Lemme have a couple. I got to make sense when I talk to Elmer. He sends in reports.'

She hurried into the bathroom to find the tiny envelope of codeine tablets.

'You really ought to lie down for a minute to let it take effect,' she said forgetting herself for a moment in her concern over his toothache.

'I'll be sittin' still goin' over on the bus.'

He shook three pills out in his hand, gave the stetson a flip onto the back of his head and walked off with his little strutting walk that had a trace of a limp, so Georgia found herself remembering tenderly, from the time a machinegun bullet had shattered his hip in Madrid.

When the door had closed behind him all her feelings came back with a rush. She tore the sheets off the bed and stuffed them into the laundrybasket. The light acrid hairoily smell of him was still in her nostrils. She went into the bathroom and washed her hands and face with lavender toilet soap. She scrubbed her face with the washcloth till it stung. 'I want to die, I want to die,' she whimpered.

It was ten-thirty by the kitchen clock. She lit the gas oven and started hurriedly mixing up the stuffing for the chicken. She'd asked her old roommates Louise and Elsie and Phyllis over to Sunday dinner. How could she have thought of such a thing? And now they would be here in two hours and the breakfast dishes weren't washed and the place wasn't swept and nothing was ready. While she was hurriedly skewering up the chicken the telephone rang. She ran to it her fingers dripping butter and breadcrumbs. It was Joe Yerkes.

Why what on earth was the matter George, he asked after she had answered his first few questions. Nothing she answered breathless. But her voice sounded upset Joe said in a tone of concern. It was just that she was in a rush because she'd asked a lot of people for dinner and nothing was ready. Couldn't he come, he asked. No he couldn't, she said, it was a hen party and he'd be bored to death. Well next Sunday wouldn't she save the day to go out with him some place? Joe's stuffy staid voice rumbled on. He wanted a whole day to try to convince her about she knew what.

'Joe,' she found herself shouting into the telephone, 'I'd rather die than marry you . . . or anybody . . . I'd rather die.' She jammed the receiver back on its hook and hurried back into the kitchen. She slammed the chicken down in the roasting pan and shot it into the oven. It would never be ready by one. How could she ever get anything done if people wouldn't leave her alone? She felt the hysteria mounting in her as she piled the breakfast dishes in the sink. Rinsing them she broke one of her favorite coffee cups, a white cup with little moss roses, the last of a set that Père had bought in England. She threw the pieces down on the floor and ground them under her slipper. What did that matter now? What did anything like that matter? 'I'm the one who ought to take codeine,' she said aloud as she swept the broken pieces into a sheet of newspaper.

In the bathroom medicine closet she found a smudged glass cylinder half full of triple bromides. She dropped a couple of the flat tablets into a glass of water and watched the stream of bubbles rise from them. She started to sip the fizzy liquid. If I stay on here I must get myself a maid, she was telling herself in a matter of fact way, I can afford one now. She pulled the vacuum cleaner out of its shelf and went deliberately to work with it.

When she finally heard the girls' voices giggling and chattering at the front door the table was set and she was ready for them. She was quite calm outside but inside she could feel herself continually atremble like a chinese doll mounted on thin coiled wire. She set her face in a quiet smile as she opened the door. Elsie and Phyllis looked very pretty in their wash dresses and spring hats. Louise's long upper lip had very much its old suspicious cast. 'Now you really are expecting us?' she was asking. 'Of course she is.' 'I can smell the chicken.' 'My it smells good.' The others drowned her out with their cheeping chorus.

It was like the iron maiden. Outside there was a metallic shell that went on with automaton gestures pouring sherry into little glasses for her guests, putting rolls in the oven to heat, dishing up the chicken, browning the gravy, smiling and making little cracks, while inside the crushed ruins of herself screamed out in agony. When she sat down to eat they all talked at once telling her she must get in on Civil Service. No matter how good a job she had they all insisted, she'd never have security until she had her Civil Service classification. They all had theirs said Elsie and Phyllis and Louise, and Georgia must get hers. But her present job was under wartime emergency powers, it depended from the President. It didn't matter they almost shouted, she'd worked long enough in the Department before that, it was the time you worked and your record, not what you did that counted. The war wouldn't last forever and after that all she'd have to fall back on would be her Civil Service rating. At last Louise lost her temper and said drat it she'd get the forms and fill them out for Georgia and all she'd have to do was sign them. Georgia gave in. All right, she said she'd look into it. She couldn't very well explain to them, she was telling herself almost with amusement, that the Civil Service wouldn't do her any good if she just decided one of these days not to go on living. Security, they kept saying, the Civil Service would give her security.

They had gotten through as far as their chocolate cake and coffee when the knocker went wham on the front door and there was Jane Sparling come to call. She took Georgia's hand in her cold possessive grip. She looked her up and down in that searching way she had and said quietly, 'You're upset about something, Georgia . . . probably trying to live without sex life.' She laughed her harsh laugh and her eyes tried to hold Georgia's eyes with her probing glance. 'At your age dear it can't be done. Maybe it can't be done at any age.'

Georgia pulled her eyes away and tilted her head back towards the diningroom. Jane stood listening appraisingly to the chatter of voices.

'Humph, you've got company,' she whispered, lingering over the word as if it had some sinister implication. 'I'll just stop for a second. I'm on my way to a meeting at the Mannings. We are getting up a letter to be sent to a few key congressmen urging them to put their weight behind a tough policy towards Vichy and the establishment of a second front.'

'It's just the girls I used to have that apartment with,' said Georgia in an apologetic tone.

'You're a kind good girl Georgia . . . Position hasn't gone to your head,' Jane stated in her sarcastic tone. As she pulled off her tan coat and headed for the diningroom door she gave Georgia another long look. Georgia found herself giving her something back in the expression of her eyes as if there were a kind of understanding between them. She felt herself blushing.

It was relief that she remembered, as she followed Jane Sparling's square back and the firm tread of her lowheeled walking shoes into the diningroom, that nothing mattered now. Nothing need matter any more.

She found her a chair and insisted on bustling round the kitchen finding her a plate of icecream and cake. Whenever somebody addressed a remark to her she managed to dart off to the kitchen again, to put on some more coffee or to stack the dishes or to sweep up the crumbs off the breadboard. She was hardly back to her place at the table when the phone began to ring.

'A rich social life,' said Jane making a sour face.

Georgia closed the door behind her before she answered. Why don't they let me alone? she was asking herself in a flustered crybaby voice, why won't they let me be miserable alone? It was Paul. Oh no it couldn't be. Her ears started to throb so she could hardly listen. It was Paul. His voice sounded full of business and faraway.

'Georgia there's something I want to talk to you about I don't feel like talking about in the office. I'm over in Alexandria.'

'No no,' she interrupted hurriedly. 'Please don't come here.'

'It'll only take five minutes.'

'Paul let's make it the hotel. We can meet in the lobby and have a cup of coffee in the coffeeshop.'

'That's where I am now.'

'Wait,' she plead. 'I'll be right around.'

Still breathless, she put her head in the diningroom door and said to the girls please to make themselves at home, she'd be back in ten minutes.

'Mysterious appointments,' jeered Jane with a roll of her eyes.

'It's just somebody from the office. Something I forgot about yesterday.'

'Well if the bureaucrats start working Sundays, maybe we'll start winning the war.'

'Toodleloo,' chanted Georgia in a tone of voice that went on chiming like a silly bell in her ears.

She couldn't find her light coat in the hall closet. She'd forgotten where her hat was. She pulled out her old rabbitfur that would look thoroughly out of place on a warm spring afternoon and ran into the bedroom to try to do something about her hair. Lord it was hopeless. She had better get a permanent. Permanent. Permanent, no, this misery couldn't be permanent thank God. You could only stand a certain amount of misery and then the cord would snap. As she started down the narrow hall for the door she noticed that she still had her slippers on. She had to go back to the bedroom to change into some street shoes. She didn't dare go out past the livingroom again for fear those women would hear her, so she slipped out through the kitchen and the back door. She caught her coat on the latch of the screen door and it tore. Blinking in the brilliant afternoon sunlight she stood on the uneven bricks of the little yard looking down at the rent in the dyed rabbitfur. Didn't matter now, it was her old coat, ready to be thrown out; me too, she thought almost happily.

Over her head the paulonia raised its elaborate purple clusters against the blue. The appletree in the next yard was dense with pink and white bloom . . . Oh Lord Père's apples in Ann Arbor . . . Along the wall of the house the wisteria was out. The musky flowers were full of bees. A hummingbird poised over a bunch of raw red columbines along the privet hedge. The warm air resounded with spring's low soft bustle. It was much too warm for a fur coat.

She must hurry. She began to run down the street. At the corner she half turned her ankle on a loose brick. She caught herself up short. She stood a while panting staring without seeing it at a clump of rosy bleeding heart that grew amid the rank grass of an untidy dooryard on the main street. She was holding on to the iron fence with both hands. A string of army trucks rumblerattled behind her. She began to feel the tumult inside her dying down. Then she took a deep breath and biting her lips walked very slowly to the traffic light. She waited carefully for the light to change and then crossed the street.

The hotel lobby was full of girls and young men in uniform. Right away she saw him. He stood taller than the people round him. He stood by the window looking away from her down into the street. He was thinner than she'd ever seen him. His face under his dark brows had a sallow puckered look. She doesn't feed him properly Georgia caught herself thinking. The thought amused her so that she was able to walk up to him with a little abstracted smile on her face.

He started to put out his hand but she didn't dare touch him. If she touched him the blinding spark would strike them all dead.

'The coffeeshop's closed,' he said in a quick practical voice. 'There's an empty table in the corner of the drugstore downstairs . . . or would you rather walk around?'

She felt her lips getting cold. 'I don't want to walk,' she said.

Without touching each other they went side by side down the grimy marble steps. In the drugstore she had to wait without fidgeting while he pushed his way through the crowd of highschool kids at the counter. The smell of sodas and drugs and growing kids brought back the college drugstore back home, the banana splits and the fudge sundaes, the chatter, the busy gossip about dates, the arguments about economics with Joe, the cosy certainty of finding Père at home ready to cock his beard with an amused pontifical sardonic answer to each question. Paul was making his way towards her looking down with severe attention at a glass in each hand so as not to spill them.

'It's a security problem,' he said talking in the same low quick voice as if he wanted to get through with this painful interview as soon as possible. Her cold hands kneaded the little handkerchief in her lap. Opposite her Paul wound his long legs around the legs of the chair and teetered back and forth on it as he talked. 'I want to consult you about it, Georgia, because I trust your judgment and because you see a good deal of the communistic element . . . through old associations and so forth.'

'Yes?' She couldn't keep a little sarcastic note out of her voice.

'It concerns Millard. In my opinion and I think in yours Millard is doing the outstanding wartime job. That's why I hang on in his outfit though God knows I'm out of my depth in international industrial politics . . . I came to Washington because I thought I knew something about hybridizing corn . . . Anyway we've got a war to fight. But it turns out we've got two wars to fight . . .' Funny, a little voice whispered inside her head, Jed said the same thing. My wasn't Paul being prosy, the little voice jeered . . . 'One war against all our various and assorted enemies and one against Jerry Evans and his allies in the State

Department. Jerry Evans was mortally offended when the President took Millard's agency out of his department and so were the pantywaists . . . And although it's his baby—after all Walker is chairman—and he himself has reached the stratospheric heights of the Allocations Board where the President talks only to Stalin and Churchill talks only to God, they tell me Walker Watson's a little jealous of his protegé's success . . . This is just to fill you in . . . As you know just as well as I do we're not doing any cloak and dagger business in our outfit . . . At the same time we do a lot of things that don't need to be in the public prints. Millard's absolutely determined that this money we're spending on war contracts all over the world is going to be spent in such a way as to encourage a decent wage level, collective bargaining and all the basic New Deal objectives. It was all in that speech about a bottle of milk for every headhunter that Walker got Mike to write for him.'

'It sounds wonderful on the air,' said Georgia with the same little cold sting in her voice. She couldn't follow what Paul was saying. She didn't care. Why wouldn't he shut up and let her go home?

'It is wonderful,' Paul went on patiently and severely. 'It's the only thing that can implement all this blather about the century of the common man the speeches of Walker Watson and the rest of them are so full of. Anyway, to make a long story short, what I want to ask you about it this: We've been having leaks in the office. The investigators have pretty well caught up with the Nazis but they are babes in arms when it comes to Reds. The leaks can in my opinion only come from the communistic brethren . . . You know that horsefaced girl, Millard's secretary he brought up from the southeast with him, well they are givng her a tremendous ride.'

'You are not suggesting that I . . .' she began angrily. Her voice was shrill. She felt her face reddening. 'She's over at my house right now. We used to live together.'

'Now Georgia just hold your horses.' His troubled eyes looked full in hers. 'I'm asking your advice. I think you sympathize with them in a certain way like many generousminded people but I don't think you would help them to make a nuisance of themselves . . . I know a good deal about the Russkis but I don't know much about the brethren in this country at least not since way way back when one of my best friends went that way. But from what I do know about the Russkis I know they can no more get out of the conspiratorial habit than fly to the moon. Wherever you have a Russian purchasing commission or a Russian controlled political party you'll have espionage and counter-espionage and countercounter espionage ad infinitum till they get so tangled up all they know how to do is shoot everybody they can lay their hands on . . . Ever read about Azev?'

Her nerves were beginning to jump. It took all her strength to keep her mouth from twitching. 'But Paul where do I come into all this?' she asked in a trembling voice.

'Forgive me Georgia,' he said gently, looking her over in a kind and sorrowful way. 'I'll lecture about Azev some other time. I wanted to ask you, because I admire your judgment and honesty and everything like that whether you think there's anything in my suspicions.'

She stared at him with round eyes. She couldn't answer because she couldn't catch her breath. She wanted to let herself pitch forward sobbing into his arms.

'Actually these leaks aren't of any great importance in the real war,' his drawling gentle voice went on. 'After all we are allies . . . But they can be used with real effect in the Battle of Washington. Jerry's got plenty of good friends in the investigation bureau who would be ready enough to believe as Jerry would tell 'em that Millard's a dangerous visionary who has let himself be taken for a ride by the comrades . . . and after all some of our commie operatives were all too chummy with the Nazis a year or so ago . . . A very nasty little report could be placed on the President's desk and that would be the end of the New Deal in global strategy and the end of all our efforts to make sense out of our war aims.'

Georgia couldn't speak. She was trying to keep her face stiff to keep the tears from spurting out. She got to her feet hastily dabbing at her eyes with the little ball of a handkerchief.

'Appointment waiting . . . Got to go,' she managed to blurt out.

'Forgive me for the long lecture Georgia,' she heard his kind concerned voice rumbling behind her as he followed her up onto the sidewalk. 'Suppose you think the problem over and give Carroll the value of your advice about this.' She started to nod. 'I'll tell him to expect a call from you.' She stood there looking back at him in the stinging sunlight nodding and blinking at everything he said.

She had turned her back and left him. As she walked home elbowing her way through the spring afternoon full of flowers and sunlight on green leaves and the chatter of robins and singing mockingbirds and people sauntering about in Sunday clothes the familiar roaring corridor of pain closed in about her.

The house was quiet. There was only Louise left. She had set up the card table in front of the livingroom sofa and sat there tranquilly playing solitaire.

'Dr. Sparling had to run,' she explained, 'and some boys came by for the girlfriends. How do you suppose they get the gas? In wartime like this I just think it's outrageous.'

'Headache. I'll be right out . . .' Georgia put her hand to her forehead as she ran through the livingroom and kitchen into the bedroom. When she had closed the bedroom door behind her she lay down and burrowed her face in the pillow and started to sob. After she had quieted down she lay there a while looking up at the blank ceiling. When she moved her head she found that Louise was sitting in the chair beside the bed.

'Nervous exhaustion,' Louise announced flatly when Georgia stirred. 'My dear the thing for you is to stay right in bed the rest of the afternoon. I'll get you a hotwaterbottle and I think you ought to take a little spring tonic.'

'Thanks, Louise, thanks. I'll be all right.' She yawned. 'If you'll forgive me I'll take a little nap right here and now.'

Louise moved about the house muttering, 'The poor child's tuckered out, cooking that big dinner and all.'

Louise deftly slid the pillow out from under her head and puffed it up. Then she brought a blanket and spread it over her and tucked a hotwaterbottle in at her feet. Georgia could hear a soft clinking and splashing as Louise washed the dishes in the kitchen. She let her eyes close and for a second forgot herself. She dozed off.

She woke with a start. Instantly every nerve was screwed up tight with pain. Louise stood over her dressed in her hat and coat. 'Well I said I'd go around and type some letters for the Russian War Relief,' she was saying. 'I like it,' she went on in her dry singsong. 'I meet new folks . . . interesting people . . . It gives me something to do evenings.'

After Louise had gone the house was quiet except for the distant traffic sounds of the main street and the crazy ceaseless singing of the mockingbirds in the yard. For an hour Georgia lay there looking up with dry eyes at the ceiling. It was worse when she was alone. With relief she heard the front door pushed open and Jed's sharp irregular tread in the livingroom.

'George,' he called. 'Where are you? That comrade dentist was a butcher. He musta come in through the Boilermakers' Union.'

She put her shoes on and brushed the wrinkles out of her dress and washed her face and walked deliberately and slowly into the livingroom. Her hands and feet were cold but she was quite calm.

'I was just taking a nap,' she said.

'Girlfriends wore you out eh? Well let's get going . . .' Jed's face was greenish pale. He was shakily smoking a cigarette as he walked up and down.

'The comrade dentist filled me up with novocaine an' pulled the tooth out then an' there. I can still hear the jawbone crunch. He's a direct actionist.'

She could see that he was all shaken up. It made her feel stronger to see him so shaky: 'Do you think you'd better go Jed?' she asked coolly. 'Wouldn't it be better for you to stretch out here a while?'

'An' miss the most beautiful afternoon of the year? Not on your life. You know George everybody but you thinks I'm crazy for holdin' on to that little ole motor boat but it's the only thing that keeps me from goin' nuts in this man's town . . . You're not goin' in those clothes?'

Obediently she went into the bedroom and changed into khaki jodhpurs and a woollen shirt. Rather than do her mussedup hair she pulled a beret on over it.

'Shall I take along any food?' she asked in a dead voice.

'No, galley's all stocked up . . . Better bring a sweater . . . It'll be cool when the sun goes down.'

Like two people in a picture on a magazine cover she saw Jed and herself walking through the streets of little old brick houses set in yards full of flowering shrubs that filled the air with varied streaks of spice and sweetness in the mellowing sunlight of the late afternoon. From some screaming hell outside of herself she saw herself walk out on the dock and climb into the ricketylooking cruiser that needed a coat of paint, and help Jed open up the cabin and spread the kapok cushions in the cockpit. She was arguing with him about whether they ought to take the tender or not. Times he didn't take it he always needed it Jed insisted. She agreed and stepped back on the landing to loosen the rope while he fiddled with the starter and managed to get the motor to turn over. She took the wheel and steered down river while the wind through the open forward window fluttered against her forehead the little wisps of hair that had gotten out from under her beret.

Like something she had read in a book she began to remember an evening when she was a little girl the summer Père and Mother had hired a cruiser on the lake and Cousin Washburn Smith, Père's eighteenyearold nephew had come along to run it because Père never could understand motors. She used to admire Washburn's serious navigator's look as he stood hawkeyed and sunburned at the wheel. Père got to reading them passages from the Odyssey translating them right out of the original Greek. It was a special evening she was remembering, passing along a beach towards a sandspit and a red sunset behind a bunch of pines at the end and the boat cutting through the clear gray water, so clear she could look over the side and see rocks and green green weeds and the dark shapes and vanishing flash of a school of fish. She had had that sensation of being all transparent, the itchy thwarting of clothes and commands and hurt feelings melting away till she was clear as the lake, slicing through the bright world cool and clear as the lake water, swelling with the sunset to the immense stillness of the lake and the sky.

'Hey for cryin' out loud the buoy's over there,' Jed's gruff voice rasped as he pushed her away from the wheel.

'Sorry Jed,' she said humbly. She went back and sat in the stern. The motor made too much noise for them to talk so she sat looking out unthinkingly across the still brown river at the various greens of the trees along the parkway that melted into dim peacock colors where the low sun combed through the hills beyond. There were a few sailboats out. They passed a government tug. Several formations of planes flew over. After a while they had the river to themselves. Jed kept as near as he could to the Virginia shore cutting off the windings of the channel until they passed Mount Vernon that looked like a postcard picture of itself against the hill with the sun setting behind it. Then he crossed towards Maryland and steered into the mouth of a creek he knew and gave her the wheel again while he unsnarled the anchor and dropped it over. 'Astern, astern,' he shouted while she fumbled with the brass lever. 'Now cut her off.'

As the motor stopped the stillness rose about her like a wave. She could hear some crows sleepily cawing among the cedars along the shore and the glassy chiming of the spring peepers from the reedy flats up the creek.

'I thought this was far enough,' Jed said as he came back and sat down scowling beside her. 'As the novocaine wears off this damn thing hurts like hell. I think that comrade dentist splintered the bone on my jaw. The bastard's probably a Trotskyite . . . I think I'll take another of those tablets you gave me and turn in. How many of those damn things do you suppose a man can take safely?'

'I don't know not too many,' she said without interest. 'I brought the rest along just in case. You ought to keep your jaw warm.'

He ducked into the cabin and lit the gasoline stove. Then he wrapped his head in a blanket and lay down on the bunk.

'George suppose you heat us up a little soup. That's all I want.'

His words started some sort of little motor inside her. She went to work. Without thinking of what she was doing she straightened out the canned goods, opened a couple of cans of soup and started them heating, searched around for the salt and pepper, sliced some bread, unwrapped the margarine. While she went dully through the motions of getting supper he lay on his back and talked in a muffled voice.

'Do you know George I always dreamed of findin' a girl . . . God knows I've had a stack of women in my time . . . But never a one that was good lovin' an' . . . an' somethin' more . . . a companion intelligence, let's call it that. First thing you know I'll be gettin' jealous . . . You got to string that Paul Graves along, but don't you do sleepin' with him now . . . Do you suppose I ought to take that codeine before eatin' or after?'

'I suppose it would have more effect on an empty stomach,' she said. Her hands had begun to tremble. She couldn't keep the loathing out of her voice. 'Take it now while I heat up the soup. It takes some time to work.'

He swallowed the tablet with an obedient trusting look on his face. 'Don't be sore at me George,' he whined in the voice of a little boy who's been scolded. 'I know I'm not housebroken. I guess I'm strictly the outdoor type. That's why I couldn't stick with the law. Some people are strictly outdoor types. Coop me up in an office an' I just try to find out how much whiskey there is in the world by drinkin' it up . . . Listen those are ducks flyin' overhead . . . flyin' north . . . Gosh they're late. I guess they might be coots . . . I love huntin'. George I could take you out an' make a good shot out of you. You've got a clear eye . . . That's why I think I make a pretty good field commander. You got to have a feel for country . . . topography . . . the hunter's feel . . . Say I better take another. This hurts like hell.'

She brought him another tablet. She deftly lifted up his head and held the chipped enamel cup for him while he washed the pill down with little sips. Watching his lips sucking babyishly at the water she couldn't hate him. She didn't hate him any more. She didn't hate anybody any more.

'You'd make a good nurse do you know it George? You don't baby the patient but you do all the necessary . . .' He closed his eyes. 'Kinda watch the anchor will you George,' he went on in a slow drowsy drawl. 'And Jesus, light up the anchor lights. The tide'll be runnin' out pretty strong in a little while. Don't want to drag. It's the beginnin' of the ebb now . . .' He took several deep breaths. For a long time she sat watching the hissing blue flame on the stove. The soup was taking an endless time to heat. By the time she brought him the cup of hot soup the taut look was out of his face and he'd gone to sleep.

Georgia didn't want to eat. She turned off the stove and stowed the food away carefully in the little icebox that didn't have any ice in it. It had grown dark in the cabin. She went out and sat in the cockpit. The breeze had dropped. With the blue dusk, mist had risen out of all the hollows of the hills. Occasional lights along the shore had a ruddy look. The headlights of cars flashed out hazily from a road that skirted a hill back from the shore. Everything was quiet now except for the sound of the peepers coming across the still water and the little lapping of the tide round the boat's bow. She took the paper of codeine tablets out from her handbag and put one on her tongue. There were only four left. She couldn't swallow it dry and she couldn't go back in the cabin where Jed was so she leaned over the side and scooped up a little water with her hand. The water was cold. She got just enough into her mouth to wash the pill down. The water had a grimy fueloil taste. Hurriedly she took another tablet.

'I can't stay, I can't stay,' she whispered.

She hauled the tender up to the side and stepped carefully in the center so as not to tip it over. She found the oars and the oarlocks and rowed very gently out into the river. She was used to rowing. Père always praised her rowing. Once she was far enough away from Jed's cruiser she spoke out loud. 'Oh Lord what a silly thing to do,' she said. 'But I can't stay. I can't stay,' she explained tearfully as if to somebody else.

She rowed downstream. She rowed gently, half the time with her eyes closed but she didn't feel the sleepiness coming on. The mist was settling down on the river with darkness. Behind the vague reclining shapes of the Maryland hills there was a faint luminous blur where the moon was going to rise. She wasn't sleepy enough. In a panic she swallowed the tablets she had left drinking little gulps of river water out of a tin baling can she found in the bottom of the boat. At times she stopped rowing and let the current carry her along. She passed close to a black spar buoy tilted sharply downstream. The moon was up now but she could only see a vague silvery blur through the mist. The mist was chilly but the rowing had kept her warm. She began to feel drowsy. She began to feel she was melting into the luminous mist all about her.

A rushing noise startled her. She was frightened. The river was full of beating wings and the sound of broken water. Dimly around her she could see dark shapes skimming away from her over the water . . . Oh the coots, she thought, I scared them . . . She must keep in the channel. She couldn't see the shore. All round her was a dazzle of mist. She rowed desperately hard in what she guessed was the direction of the channel. The water must be deep. Her rowing was getting clumsy. She had dropped an oar. She reached for it but it was gone. She couldn't feel her hands. Her tongue was numb. Now. She floundered heavily to her feet and pitched over the side of the boat. The cold water slapped her awake. Her hands made a last effort to grasp the gunnel as the boat drifted out of sight into the mist.

The Power and the Glory

5

We learned. There were things we learned to do.
We learned to redesign war's equipment; to the air-
craft carrier, the battleship, the cruiser, the troop transport we added
the duck, the weasel, the landing ship tanks, the host of motor-
boats and flats and barges in ingenious shapes and the floating piers
that carried the amphibious landings.

We learned to roll out an airfield in a week, to push the jungle
aside with bulldozers, to keep our rifles dry wading at night through
surf over the shoals of pitted slippery coral.

We learned to lie on the beach beyond the surge of the breakers
and there in complete silence
to bite the marl and die.

We learned to palletize supplies, to keep the tankers moving
in a steady flow; officers in control rooms plotted the position of
freighters, refrigerator ships, floating drydocks, repairships; on
squaredoff maps they played a grim parchesi with the rule of the geo-
metrical rise in the difficulty of supply in proportion to the distance.

We learned to refuel at sea, in the air for that matter, to transfer

*anything from one moving ship to another from a sixteeninch shell
to an icecream freezer.*

We invented the floating base.

*By reorganizing the notion of the bridge of ships;—keep the
supplyline dense; an army travels on its transports;—we changed
the rules of war.*

*Sea war was the engagement of carrierbased planes. Capital
ships hid behind the bulge of the globe. In the Coral Sea the issue
was doubtful but by the time of the great threeday battle off Midway
Island our torpedo planes and divebombers were ready*

to inflict on the Japs a decisive defeat.

*At home we organized bloodbanks and civilian defense and imi-
tated the rest of the world by setting up concentration camps (only
we called them relocation centers) and stuffing into them*

*American citizens of Japanese ancestry (Pearl Harbor the date
that will live in infamy) without benefit of habeas corpus:*

I swear loyalty to the United States and enlist in the War Relocation Work Corps for the duration of the war and 14 days there-
after . . . I accept whatever pay, unspecified at the present time,
the War Relocation Authority determines . . . I shall be financially
responsible for any government property I use while in the work
corps: and that infraction of any regulations of the War Relocation
Authority will render me liable to trial and suitable punishment.
So help me God.

*The President of the United States
talked the sincere democrat and so did the members of Congress.
In the Administration there were devout believers in civil liberty.
'Now we're busy fighting a war; we'll deploy all four freedoms later
on,' they said.*

*At the desk in the White House in front of the brightlit globe
sat an aging man, an ill man, a cripple who had no time to
ponder history or to find the Danube or the Baltic or Vienna on*

the map: so many documents to sign, so many interviews with Very Important Personages, such gloss on the young men: 'Yes Mr. President,' 'No Mr. President.' The decisions were his. He could play on a man like on a violin. Virtuoso. By the modulations of his voice into the microphone he played on the American People. We danced to his tune. Third Term. Fourth Term. Indispensable.

War is a time of Caesars.

The President of the United States
was a man of great personal courage and supreme confidence in his powers of persuasion. He never spared himself a moment, flew to Brazil and Casablanca Cairo
to negotiate at the level of the leaders;
at Teheran the triumvirate
without asking anybody's leave got to meddling with history;
without consulting their constituents, revamped geography,
divided up the bloody globe and left the freedoms out.
And the American People were supposed to say thank you for the century of the Common Man turned over for relocation behind barbed wire so help him God.

We learned. There were things we learned to do
but we have not learned, in spite of the Constitution and the Declaration of Independence and the great debates at Richmond and Philadelphia
how to put power over the lives of men into the hands of one man and to make him use it wisely.

THE LEVEL OF THE LEADERS

PAUL SAT FROWNING at his broad mahogany desk in his panelled office in the new building. He felt shivery. He hadn't slept well the night before. His head was stopped up with a cold. The new office was large and bare and airconditioned and had two windows that looked out through trees on the flashing sunlit traffic of Constitution Avenue. The airconditioning seemed unusually cold that day. On the new blue blotter lay spreadout letters, a thick bundle of reports and a pile of contracts awaiting approval that half hid the list of appointments for the day . . . Dupee, Wilks, Hutchinson, lunch with M.C.. . . written out in Miss Stevens' neat hand which was propped against the big brass inkwell. Pencil in hand Paul was checking over the provisions of a contract for peanut oil with the firm of Gadsby Smith Ltd in the Congo . . . party of the first part does hereby grant bargain, sell and convey . . . time being of the essence . . . of such agreement . . . He came to a snap. Brazzaville, where the hell was Brazzaville? He reached for the phone. His lips were ready to form the words 'Miss Washburn please' when he remembered she was dead.

Immediately grief gripped and spun him like a fit of dizziness. Wouldn't he ever get over reaching for the telephone to call Miss

Washburn? Old Facts and Figures . . . It was weeks now and still time and again he had to catch himself reaching for the telephone to call her. Grief and a feeling of guilt rose up in him bitter as the bile from a sour stomach . . . It was my fault. Poor little thing. I should have done something to save her . . . His thoughts began to pace the old heavy treadmill of remorse. God he couldn't go on forever picking over these recollections. He should have been kinder, he should have walked home with her and tried to get her to talk. He should have seen she was terribly overwrought. If he could have gotten her to talk about it he might have saved her . . . If . . . If . . . He sat for a long time with his elbows on his desk combing his fingers through his hair.

Miss Stevens was standing in front of the desk. He looked up with a guilty start into her cool doll's face. Mr. Graves, she was explaining, she had thought she had better come in because Mr. Dupee had been waiting ten minutes and the schedule was tight today.

'Show him in, he's just the man I want to see,' Paul said in a steady voice. He felt better now that the routine had started again. 'Good morning Gibbs, how's your health? Say Gibbs,' he was scowling and tapping pettishly on the papers with his pencil, 'I can't see there are any labor standard provisions in these contracts at all.'

'The understandin' seems to be that they are to be dropped.' Gibbs spoke in a vaguely soothing tone. 'There's no way of checkin' an' it would just cause trouble . . . Those Congo nigras, good Lord . . . they have the contract labor system . . . work six months for a pair of shorts . . . Things are very different from what they are over here.'

'I bet they are . . . But has Millard approved them?'

'I'm not sure about that but Fred came back with the notation after a conversation with Walker.'

Paul got angrily to his feet: 'Walker Watson doesn't know anything about the detail work of this agency. How can he? His hands are full with allocation . . . You know just as well as I do that Millard has the word. I'm lunching with him today . . . Meanwhile I'll send these back to the legal department.'

'All I wanted to do was speed things up . . . after all there's a war on,' muttered Gibbs.

The buzzer on Paul's desk burred. He turned the switch on the interoffice dictaphone and Miss Stevens' voice came out from back of the piled papers: 'Mr. Wilks is here. He's the gentleman they called up about from the Investigating Bureau.'

'Send him in.' Paul settled back at his desk. He tried to force a smile onto his face. 'Gibbs I'll give you a ring after lunch. We'll know what the score is then.'

He looked down at his papers again . . . Lord he missed her, he was thinking, so much had died with her, that funny little accurate mind, the way she flared up to defend anybody in trouble or hurt or held in contempt . . . that feeling of warmth and freshness that came from her. Old Facts and Figures.

Suddenly there was a great racket in the office.

'Why Joe Wilks.'

'Well if it ain't Gibbs Dupee? Can't tell who you'll find in Washington these days.'

'Scrapin' the bottom of the barrel eh?'

Paul got to his feet trying to smooth the scowl out of his aching forehead. A big redheaded man had hold of Gibbs' hand and was advancing towards the desk dragging him back with him. 'My ole partner from Bedbug Inn . . .' With his free hand he reached for Paul's. 'You remember in Masonboro?'

Gibbs pulled himself free and went out the door, calling back to Wilks to drop by his office before he left the building.

Paul began to laugh: 'Sure and the sour waitress who ran us out of the diningroom . . . But you were with the A. F. of L. then.'

'It's all in the same alphabet.'

'Manna from Heaven!' Paul threw back his head and laughed.

'Exactly,' said Wilks. 'Well times change. They seemed to think my experience rootin' the comrats out of the unions might be useful in Washington so Joe I says to myself there's goin' to be a war on an' you're too infirm an' aged to be any good at the front so you go up to Washington an' do what they tell you, so I kissed the Bible an' here I am.'

He pulled a bundle of newspaper clippings fastened to a typewritten sheet out of his pocket and waved them under Paul's nose

WAR DEPARTMENT EMPLOYEE HELD
Mystery Girl's Body Found Near Marshall Hall
GOVERNMENT WORKER A SUICIDE

Paul didn't need to read them. He knew them by heart already. He felt every muscle stiffen. He brought his eyes down to the contract on his desk and read a line with exaggerated care.

'Do you think it was suicide?' he asked in a numb voice.

'That's what I'm here to ask you.' Wilks dropped sprawling into the chair beside the desk.

'I think it was,' Paul answered. 'Of course we all feel terribly about it around here. She was a very valuable person. She was one of the most brilliant people I ever worked with . . .'

'Paul did you ever try writin' any of these detective stories?' Wilks bellowed out the question with his eyes on the ceiling. 'I sometimes think that's a field might appeal to me . . . Ought to have some good plots when I get through with this job.' He let out a guffaw: 'I've made a flop at about everythin' else . . .' Paul was staring at the red hairs on the back of the thickfingered hand Wilks was stroking his chin with. 'Anybody round the office layin' this dame?' he was asking in a dreamy voice.

'If I tried to keep track of the private lives of everybody who works in this building'—Paul was surprised at the steady tone of his answer—'I'd be a candidate for your organization.'

'Nice work if you can get it,' Wilks said, laughing again. 'It's one of the most interestin' jobs I've ever had, to tell the truth. An' the material, Jeesus boy when the war's over I'll make me a mint of money writin' detective stories. If I can't write 'em myself I'll hire me a ghost . . . You know: 'as told to . . .' Tell me there's real money in them things.'

'She was worried,' Paul heard himself saying. 'She was a very high-strung girl. She hadn't had at all a happy life. What makes me feel bad is I helped worry her. The day she disappeared I went over to see her in Alexandria to ask her if she knew anything about Communists.'

'That's our angle,' Wilks interrupted. He had jumped to his feet and was charging excitedly up and down the room. 'That's our angle. There' some very funny angles to his story.'

'Mr. Carroll and I had been worried over some leaks,' Paul went on. He was sure of himself now, though he still felt the blood throbbing in his ears. 'Of course we haven't anything really top secret around here . . . but . . .'

'Pravda knows more about what you're doin' than you do yourself I can swear to that,' interrupted Wilks from the window. 'But hell they're our goddamned allies . . . In the Bureau they won't believe me. Hell no. They think I'm spinnin' a damn detective story . . . You know what they're like because you've worked in the Soviet Union . . . I know what they're like because I've worked twentyfive years in the labor movement. That's why I want to crack this case wide open. Of course it won't get any publicity . . . As far as this administration is concerned the commies are all gentlemen and scholars . . . Can't offend our damn allies. But just for the record . . .'

Paul wasn't listening. His head ached from his cold . . . Dead, he was thinking. When you died it wasn't just yourself that died . . . all her memories, the little mythology she spun out of her old life at Ann Arbor and the University. Now he'd never hear about Père any more . . .

Wilks brought down his fist on the corner of the desk. 'My angle on this business is that she was murdered.'

'I don't hardly think so,' Paul drawled. 'I don't think any of these leaks were important enough for that.' His voice drawled on cool and judicious. 'I don't see how it would have been to anybody's interest.'

'That's what we got to find out . . . She sure did run with the reds . . . Maybe she knew more than we think. Maybe she was plannin' to come clean to Poppa . . . She thought a lot of you Paul we know that.'

Paul got stiffly to his feet. 'Now Joe,' he said severely. 'I've got a very full schedule today but tonight I can find time to jot down everything I know . . . everything that could be cogent, and I'll ask Mr. Carroll to do the same. Then we can get together some evening later in the week.'

'Great . . . Put it there Paul . . . I knowed you'd be a great help . . . We'll keep in touch.'

. . . What a waste, Paul was thinking, what a waste to have her poor life shattered so soon. So gentle, so good. Old Facts and Figures. She ought to have had a proper husband and children. When a good woman died it was worse than a man dying, so much hope died with her . . .

His hands were shaking. He shoved them in his pockets. Instead of Wilks a grayhaired man with pincenez was sitting in the chair by Paul's desk talking about manganese. Paul pulled his mind out of that grieving groove with a wrench the way he would pull a plow out of the furrow and settled down to listening to the man talk about manganese. Halfway through a call came from Commander Peterson of Naval Personnel.

'Hullo Paul this is Nils Peterson . . . Say Paul you let drop something at dinner at your house the other night that interested us. The navy's heading up a new organization to raise food. Don't laugh it makes perfectly good sense . . . This project is to go in for intensive cultivation on some of our new Pacific bases to take a little of the strain off supply. I mentioned your name to Admiral Standish and he was very much interested. You would have sufficient rank to put a program across. Of course I told him it all depended . . .'

'Nils,' Paul interrupted, 'I've promised to stick here for the present. I'm certainly obliged to you for calling . . . It all depends . . . as I said . . . give me a little time to think it over, will you?'

He'd hardly gotten back to his manganese when another call came through. It was Millard. 'Hello Paul.' Millard's voice sounded dead.

'Millard I just heard,' Paul hastened to say, 'when I came into the office this morning. Miss Aldershot was crying going up in the elevator. Gosh it's tough. Tell Lucile how much I feel . . .'

'That's not what I was calling up about,' interrupted Millard in a harsh peremptory voice. 'We can't have lunch. I managed to get an appointment with Walker. Call me around two-thirty will you?'

To explain his strained face Paul said to the manganese expert, 'That was Millard Carroll. He just had news yesterday his boy Joel was killed on his first solo flight . . . It's tough . . . He and Lucile are the finest people in the world.'

The manganese expert sighed and wiped his glasses on a piece of clean tissue he pulled carefully out of his pocket. 'What times,' he said softly.

They went back to the problems of scarce metals. When the manganese expert got to his feet to leave Paul followed him out into the hall, telling Miss Stevens as he passed her he would be back at one. 'But Mr. Graves,' she began. Behind her he could see the expectant faces of men waiting to see him. Already he was striding towards the elevator. The manganese expert looked up at Paul blinking through his glasses in a puzzled way as if surprised to find him in there beside him.

'Got to see a man on the ground floor,' Paul explained, he hardly knew why. 'Goodby sir.'

It was a relief to duck out of the dead atmosphere of the airconditioned building into the rank steamy summertime. Paul felt too agitated to wait at the corner for the lights. He crossed the avenue through the traffic blindly, getting a sharp yell from a taxidriver who just missed him 'Wassamatter buddy, suicide pact?' Paul clenched his teeth and struck out across the Mall. The sun beat hot on his bare head. He was sweating already. He walked through a brick street of grimy stores and little oldfashioned houses with swings in their weedy dooryards towards the waterfront.

The sweat running down his face, the breath pumping sorely through his lungs with a bronchial wheeze, he strode down the waterfront street. Smells of frying fat came from the doors of fish restaurants as he passed. From a garbage can he got a sweetish reek of stale shrimps. Hardly looking where he was going he hurried round the edge of the yachtbasin. His legs stopped walking. He stood still. His eyes were on the brass letters on the sterns of a shabby white cruiser anchored out from the end of the wharf. The letters spelled NIÑA.

God that was the boat. Astern between a grapefruit rind and the drenched front sheet of a tabloid a tiny plyboard tender hung poised in the glaze of noonday heat on the still water. He looked beyond the boats across the blazing film of puttycolored river at the too green willows along the opposite shore. A crow flew lazily up into the white sky. Georgia's Potomac. She loved rivers. The Mississippi, the Missouri that night getting into Omaha. Paul had a strangling feeling in his throat. He was shaking all over. The sun was beating like a baseball bat on his feverish head.

'Let's get outa here,' he said aloud.

He walked on past the steamboat wharves until he came to a patch of green on the waterfront. His head ached. Still shaking he sat down in the shade of a willow. Two young sailors in whites were skimming pebbles out across the water. A brown girl in green with big breasts lay sprawled on newspapers beside an angular black man in a straw hat. With a faint tingle of lechery Paul studied absentmindedly the contours of her body under the cheap dress. He turned his head. Narrowing his eyes for the glare he looked out over the river still and bulging full of oily colors like an opal. Poor old Potomac River, that dead girl's river. He started for the hundredth time to tell over for himself what it must feel like to drown. Or was she so unhappy she didn't care? He could imagine that.

Before he knew it his eyes had gone back to the mound between the brown girl's legs that showed in the fierce sun through her green dress, and his mind had switched to things Glenn had told him about Washington when he was a small boy: the Potomac River boats and the oyster wharves and poolrooms and whores in gaslit bars on Four and a Half Street. Glenn was dead, like old Facts and Figures, so long dead. There was alive only somewhere in Paul that memory of him, not much older than Paulino was now, so many dim years distant. Their common boys' adventures still showed up bright as a showcase of cheap candies at the end of a subway corridor. The world must look like that to Paulino right now, full of mysteries, enticing girls' thighs, beckoning alleys. Poor kid. He sure had a right. Too soon the war would reach out after him. He wondered if he'd lost his cherry, that's what we used to call it . . . I ought to think more about those kids and snap out of this, he told himself soberly, and Peggy, good Lord, Peggy . . . Oh Lord if this business all comes out, poor Peggy.

Paul got to his feet and keeping on the shady side of the street walked quietly back towards the Mall. Waiting for a traffic light he caught sight of the blue bell in the window of a drugstore. Without thinking he went in and called up the house. Peggy sounded quite flustered at getting a call at such an unexpected time. Paul, she kept asking was anything the matter? No, his cold was making him miserable, he drawled cheerfully into the mouthpiece. As far as the office was concerned things couldn't be worse. He would tell her about it this evening. Then just to say something he asked what she would think if he joined the navy?

Her voice was suddenly all choked up.

'But honey nothing definite's happened yet . . . to either of us . . . Paulino or me.'

'I'm just a little hoarse,' Peggy explained quickly. 'I must be catching your cold.'

'I may be a little late to supper. I've got to have a long talk with Millard.'

'Do give them both my love. Tell him he's my favorite man. If it had only happened to somebody else except to them. You come home as soon as you can and we'll put that cold to bed, Paul.'

Thinking wryly that now he had to pull himself together and keep Peggy up, he walked at his usual brisk pace across the Mall. He'd no sooner sat down at his desk feeling the wet shirt chilling under the air-conditioning than Miss Stevens was standing over him with two slips of paper in her hand.

He blew his nose hard. 'Something very important came up,' he explained. 'I hope you told everybody I'd been called away.'

'I fitted as many as I could in this afternoon. We'll be in a snarl all day,' Miss Stevens said letting a touch of exasperation get into her quiet voice. 'Mr. Carroll and Judge Oppenheim both wanted you to call back as soon as you came in.'

Paul reached for the phone. 'I'll get Mr. Carroll first.' Miss Stevens disappeared. Millard's voice had an angry crackle to it: 'I tried to get you but you'd gone off someplace. Well Paul, Walker's stood me up again. You never can get to him when you need to see him. I'm fed up and I'm through. I'm writing out my resignation right this minute but I want to give him one more chance. He'll see you because he still thinks there's something can be gotten out of you. He wants you to stay on to keep Jerry's boys from overrunning the place the way they will when I get out. Tell him if I don't hear from him this afternoon my resignation goes in to the President. If he wants me out he can have me out. I'll go but I'll spill the whole story. Ed James'll print it and Herb Spotswood'll carry it on the air. I'll give 'em chapter and verse. All right, I'll be here till four o'clock and then I'm going home. If I don't see you come on out home. Be sure and come Paul. It'll do poor Lou good to see you.'

Millard had no sooner hung up when the Judge's soft dry voice was in Paul's ears, concernedly enquiring after Peggy and the children. Paul's voice sounded hoarse, he said. Summer colds were always long drawn out affairs. Nell had had a touch of bronchitis. Michael was none too well, growing too fast. Neither of them would really be fit until they were taken off into the balsam-laden air of the Maine woods . . . a period of strain and ill health, the strain of this war, relaxing a little now maybe. The President's cold was better, the resilience of the man. The Judge had just come from lunch at the White House. Both our friends had been there but amid all the hurlyburly and the coming and going of naval aids and military aids, he hadn't had a chance to exchange more than a word with either one of them. They seemed unusually friendly. The rumor of disagreements between them must have been spread by malicious persons. The President had talked for a moment about the need of gearing every part of industry and every department of the government into the war effort. Production was not reaching a high enough level. Demands on American production due to commitments entered into at Casablanca and the exigencies of the policy of unconditional surrender were increasing daily. We must raise our sights. It was the time for every man to sacrifice his private ambitions and convictions and plans. Unless the war were won there would be no postwar world for us to plan for. Planning now was putting the cart before the horse. The President spoke with understandable bitterness of those in private life and in public office who were unwilling to sacrifice pet theories to the winning of the war. With some amusement it had occurred to the Judge that this little lecture was addressed to both the gentlemen he had mentioned, of course in the pleasantest tone imaginable. Walker had certainly grown with the times. There had been every reason to fear that he would be more wedded than most to humanitarian schemes and commitments but since he had been in contact with the higher echelons, with the best military and strategic brains of Europe and Asia and America, he had made frequent sacrifices of his private views. It was impossible not to admire him for it. Jerry he had to admit was far from being the financial buccaneer he'd seemed at first. Under a rough exterior he had vision.

The Judge's voice became very warm and intimate, as if he were sitting right there in the room with Paul. 'You know Walker's a very shy man. It's hard for him to make the first move. Why don't you give him a ring, Paul? I think he'd like to see you . . . Why don't you give him a ring right away before he is engulfed for the rest of the day by the four o'clock meeting of the Allocations Board? You'll probably find him in his little temporary office in the East Wing . . .'

After the Judge had hung up Paul obediently told Miss Stevens to call the Allocations Board. Mr. Watson could see Mr. Graves immediately came the answer back. Any excuse to leave the office, Paul thought and started right out.

Paul felt leisurely all at once as if none of this concerned him. He took his time along Pennsylvania Avenue, stopping to squint at war headlines on the piles of newspapers on the corners, glancing in a friendly inquisitive way into the doors of lunchrooms and at the people seated along the counters of drugstores. The asphalt was soft underfoot from the heat when he crossed the Avenue. Yellow cabs were unloading women in summer dresses at the Willard. The hot sidewalk was crowded outside Keiths, young men and women meeting to go to the show together. Most of the young men were in uniform and some of the women. Paul suddenly wished he went to the movies sometimes; he'd get her to take him. Instantly he remembered and the grief spun a stinging veil between him and the bright afternoon. He made his way slowly through the bustling thronged sidewalk. The public thought Paul wearily, the multifarious public. There was a group of Filipinos in front of the Treasury. An elderly Negro in a white suit wearing a panama hat was walking in under the dark portal. Military Police in white gaiters lounged at the White House gate. The ruddy young soldier smiled when he took Paul's identification card from him. He went to a desk and immediately came back with a pass and ushered Paul down a short corridor.

Right away Walker Watson himself was opening the white colonial door to a very small office. Paul couldn't help feeling flattered.

'Come in Paul,' he said as if Paul were the one man he'd been waiting to see. Walker Watson still looked gaunt with tired bags under his eyes, the look of not having slept the night before, but his hair was well cut. His white tennis shirt had a fresh well laundered look. He wore a neatly pressed pinstriped blue suit with a gardenia in the buttonhole. He saw Paul look at the gardenia and smiled disarmingly. 'Jo gave me that . . . some kind of anniversary,' he drawled.

They stood on each side of the desk grinning awkwardly.

Paul found himself looking beyond him out the french-windows at the brilliant green grass and the tall trees towards the curved white south portico of the White House. They settled themselves in their chairs and right away came a heavy moment of silence.

'Millard,' Paul said with an effort, 'asked me to come over to see you.'

Walker's eyes gave him a sudden darting snakelike look and then went back to a spot on the plaster above his head. Paul sat looking straight ahead of him out over the green lawn.

'We all got to sacrifice in wartime,' Walker began to mumble. He couldn't seem to sit still in his chair. 'You know what the Boss said about Dr. Win the War taking the place of Dr. New Deal? We've all got to make sacrifices.' He talked faster and faster in a low mumbling voice. 'Those Russians they've made sacrifices . . . You ought to go to Russia, Paul. I think the President has something in mind for you in that connection, not now but later . . . Are they fighting this war to spread communism?' He waited breathing hard for Paul to answer, then he shuffled his feet and went on emphatically: 'They are not. They are fighting to repel a barbarous invasion. They have sacrificed their private notions of what sort of world they want to build to the common business of killing Germans . . . Talk about Millard . . . Millard ought to understand we must sacrifice some of our notions of standards and procedures to furnish them the munitions to kill the greatest number of Germans in the shortest possible time. Since they are doing more of that than anybody they must have the lion's share . . . I wanted you to come over Paul because I felt you would understand. You have a scientific mind. You're detached. There's something in the divine machinery of the universe that picks man for a destiny . . . You understand how things look from the level of the leaders.'

'Millard,' said Paul. His head was spinning. He couldn't think of the right thing to say. He had to say something. 'Millard wants to fight a New Deal war . . . install the Four Freedoms as we go along, you said it yourself . . . a bottle of milk for every headhunter. Well Millard thinks that's the way to civilize the world, get the headhunters away from headhunting, make decent citizens of them before they brutalize us. I think the people of this country . . .'

'The people of this country have got to learn to make sacrifices.' Walker pounded with his fist on the corner of the desk. His eyes glared out from redrimmed lids. 'Paul, only a few days ago I was in Moscow at one of those big official banquets where Harry and I don't eat anything because that rich food don't agree with us . . . We didn't have food like that out where I was raised . . . I learned of some of the sacrifices the Russians were making. In Leningrad they're starving to death by the tens of thousands but they won't give in. They build the frozen corpses of their friends into the redoubts. They don't bellyache about hours and wages. We Americans have gotten soft. The American public thinks we can fight a war without getting hurt . . . That banquet . . . Stalin that little square man with a big moustache jumps up and proposes a toast: "Here's to killing a million Germans this year" . . . That's the fighting spirit . . . Things look different Paul from the level of the leaders . . . To win this war people have got to make sacrifices. Millions have sacrificed their lives. Some of us have got to sacrifice a few little private notions about procedure. The trouble with Millard is he can't see the wood for the trees. He's got to make sacrifices. That's what the people of this country won't understand. That's what Congress won't understand.'

'Millard . . .' began Paul again.

'Tell Millard . . .' Walker interrupted himself. 'Paul you must excuse me I've got to go to this meeting with a VIP who's just arrived.' He got to his feet turning his lopsided smile right into Paul's face. 'Tell ole Millard . . . It's just a funny little personal quirk. It don't mean anything to anybody else but he'll get it because he used to kid me about playing the ponies. I used to find it gave me needed relaxation . . . Well tell him I've given up betting for duration . . . That'll amuse him. Millard's a great feller. Tell him to look at this thing from the level of the leaders.'

Paul had risen to his feet. They stood looking at each other across the desk. Walker's face twisted up as if he were trying to find something more to say but couldn't find the words. Paul stood looking past him over the green lawns. Then Paul had to blow his nose and Walker made a kind of beseeching gesture with his hands turned up in front of him and swung around with one shoulder low and his narrow head a little on one side and went out the french-window. Paul stood watching him tall and stooped and lanky as he walked with his uneven gait along the curving path towards the central building of the White House.

When Paul turned in his pass he was surprised to find he'd only been in Walker's office seven minutes. He felt as if he'd been there all afternoon.

Instead of going back to the agency he jumped into a waiting cab and gave the driver Millard's home address out in Bethesda. It was a surprise to find himself sitting back in the cab; he wasn't much of a one for extravagances like cabs. The level of the leaders, he told himself. It was catching. No he didn't belong there. He belonged in his lab, or with the public on the hot sidewalks. A man of the multifarious public. He was making excuses to himself, the kind of excuses he used to make when Dad scolded him when he was a kid. This damn cold did make him feel horrible. He didn't feel like himself at all. He hadn't felt like himself since that morning he'd read in the paper that poor girl was dead.

Zinnias with brilliant scalloped blooms filled the flowerbeds in front of the Carrolls' long vinecovered frame house. The dog started to bark out back before Paul reached the front door. Lucile came to the door herself. She had a small withered look. He'd never noticed before that her hair had a streak of gray in it. She looked up at him out of frightened blue eyes as if she had trouble recognizing him. Then she smiled quickly as if it hurt her.

'Paul,' she said. 'Come in.'

'Millard back?'

She nodded. 'He's out working in the victory garden. He'd have lost his mind I declare if it hadn't been for that victory garden. You're early.'

'We're all playing hookey today. May I see him?'
She was fumbling with a telegram she held in fluttery hands.

CONGRATULATE ME MA THE FAMILY STILL GOT A REPRESENTATIVE IN THE
AIRFORCE DON'T WORRY LOVE LUCIUS

'Accepted for training,' she said in a tiny explaining voice while Paul read it.

He took hold of one of her hands and patted it when he handed her back the telegram. She pulled it away shyly but looked up at him in a timid grateful way. 'We're in this together Lucile,' Paul said. 'Paulino's turn'll come mighty soon now.'

Something of the old spirited springy note came back into her voice: 'Since Oz has resigned we'll be able to go down and help them bury Joel. We're leaving tonight.'

Millard had come around the corner of the house with a hoe in his hand. He looked smaller than Paul remembered him but somehow younger. Must have lost weight thought Paul. His eyes looked very dark in a lined face white as the face of a man working in a flour mill. The corners of his mouth trembled before he spoke:

'Well this is it.'

Paul had an impulse to put his arm round Millard's shoulder but Millard stood there leaning on the hoe on the gravel path without coming towards him. They all three stood looking at each other until Lucile said briskly to come on in she had some cold lemonade on ice. The men stumbled into the house after her awkward as schoolboys. Millard sat down in a straight chair with the hoe on his knees.

'Resignation accepted to take effect at once . . . like firing a janitor,' Mallard whispered to Paul when Lucile went off into the kitchen. 'Some day we may know whether it was worth it . . . Maybe we'll never know.'

When Lucile came back with a pitcher and glasses on a glass tray he stopped talking suddenly and gave Paul a little beaten guilty look and started quietly sipping the lemonade.

They sat there a long time on the white chairs in the shaded living-room drinking the lemonade without saying anything until they heard the dog bark and the sound of wheels on the gravel. Peggy walked in looking tall and brown and flushed from the heat. She talked fast and loud: 'I called the office. Miss Stevens was in a terrible stew. She said you all were out here having a conference but I decided just to come on over with the station wagon and crash it.'

'I'm glad you did.' Lucile ran up to her and turned her face up to be kissed like a little girl back from school.

'No more conferences,' said Millard sitting still in the chair. He sat with the long handle of the hoe on his knees and the empty glass in his hand looking down at the carpet. The two women stood in the middle of the floor with their arms round each other. Paul had gotten to his feet but he didn't know what to do next.

Peggy was very businesslike and noisy: 'What time's your plane, Lucile?'

'Ten-thirty.'

'War time?'

Lucile nodded. 'Sure is,' she said.

'Well,' Peggy went on in her twangiest country voice, 'I'm going to take this man home and put him to bed.' She bustled over to Paul and picked up his hand and dropped it. 'Yes he's got a fever. I thought so. And then I'll come back and help you finish packing and drive you over to the airport. I may have to bring a couple of the kids to keep them out of Paul's hair.'

'Peggy that's sweet,' said Lucile with a tiny tired smile.

Millard was still staring down at the carpet when Paul and Peggy left.

'He's like a man who has had all the blood drained out of him. I never expected to see Millard so sunk,' Paul said when he climbed into the battered stationwagon beside Peggy. He was glad to let her drive. The flowers, the green lawns, the trees, streets flamed unbearably bright in the heat.

'Commander Petersen's been after you all afternoon,' Peggy was rattling on. 'That's how I knew you weren't in the office. He left a number to call. Paul I been thinking that navy proposition might not be so bad. You would have a change. I can make out on the pay, don't worry about that. I might take a job myself. The kids are big enough now. He told me all about it probably from the mistaken notion that I might have some influence on you.'

'It'll mean the end of a career in government.'

'Paul you are sick right now.'

"That's no lie. I been to see Walker Watson this afternoon. All he could talk about was the level of the leaders. I guess that's not for me. I guess we're the crowds along the sidewalk. It would be a relief in the navy . . . just lay back and take orders.'

Peggy wasn't listening. 'I'm going to put you to bed,' she was telling him severely, the way she'd talk to Paulino or Georgy.

Paul sat beside her with his eyes closed as she drove. His lids felt red and feverish. When the car stopped along the curb he opened them on dazzle. Already the Spanish style stucco bungalow in the block of identical bungalows that he'd had to buy to find a home in Washington at all looked alien and longago like a picture of a house in an album of old snapshots. The kids' racket inside the house even, Bettina practicing on the piano, Paulino picking out a letter on the typewriter, Oliver rattling a pair of rollerskates, Georgy's strident voice yelling from out back somewhere seemed to come to him through curtains of distance. Already he was imagining himself sitting up on a tractor in a tenacre field fringed with palms. The phone was ringing. Paul went to a stand in the hall and plugged his ear with a finger while Peggy rushed around smothering the noise.

It was Joe Wilks. 'Are you all right Paul?' The boisterous voice jarred the receiver. 'They said at the office you had gone home sick.'

'Just a touch of flu,' said Paul.

'Well I'm calling to tell you not to worry yourself further about what we were talkin' about . . . Do you get me?. . . We've been called off . . . orders from the very highest quarters. I've been put on somepun else. I jess wanted to give you the word . . . Well Paul see you in church.'

'So long Joe.'

Paul hung up. Without meeting the enquiry in Peggy's face he hurried with downcast eyes into their bedroom and pulled off his clothes and got into bed. Lying flat between the cool sheets looking up at the ceiling he let himself think for the first time that day that all the time he'd been scared to death, scared of inquests, reporters, enquiries, columnists, broadcasters, scandal and its miseries: a career in government . . . You ignoble bastard, he told himself. Well that's over . . . He was so ashamed he was blushing. The blush faded on his cheeks as he lay picturing himself sitting up on that tractor turning over new soil for crops he didn't even know the name of, different plants, odd birds and insects. When Peggy came in with her experienced trainednurse's manner bringing him a thermometer and cold tablets and a mug of hot lemonade on a glass tray he smiled up at her happily and said, 'Thanks Peggy you're curative do you know it? I feel better already.' She smiled down at him in that amused investigating half abstracted way she sometimes smiled at the children and he looked up and mumbled timidly with the thermometer between his teeth, the way Georgy or Oliver might ask whether they could go to a baseball game, 'That navy deal, Peggy? What do you think? You wouldn't mind?'

She shook her head. 'Paul . . . in uniform,' she said. 'You'll look a sight.'

We learned; but not enough; there is more to learn.

        The American People
entered our years of defeat with so little preparation
we have not learned how deep the disaster. We had leaders but
like Moses they led us into the wilderness and like Moses
    died;
    and I am left leaderless
    in wild darkness and the terror of death. (Death is not terrible;
    but the misgiving of our light, the little light that gave hope's
inkling flicker to the toilsome piecing of torn deceits into a fresh,
hazardous, already perhaps threadbare, so sought for
    phrase that may perhaps with luck hold true;
    the fear
    that our drudgery, the urging of mind and muscle to hard work,
laughter and the sick surprise of pain, our common comfort
    in the sayings our fathers said,
    in the grimy comicalness of everyday,
    might not,

as I believed,
be the beating out of a link, however flawed, however badly made,
in the chain of lives, linked by danger and miseries and splendor and
crime through suffering generations, proceeding, blunderingly and
illadvised, to some better, though hardly explainable, destination;

that fear is very terrible.)

As an American I believe:

always in the beginning long ago way down, beneath my father's
doubts and the fears his father felt,
there was belief that stood them in good stead:
in the anguish of departure and the queasy ships,
in the quick heartbeat of arrival in sight of the low gray land
afloat on bays and inlets, the lowering forests inland, (everpresent
the threat of fires, the smokepall over the jerrybuilt settlement);
there was belief that flared against fear under the bright sky,
the newworld wind northwest;
in the sight of fish in unimaginable millions churning the
estuaries in their spring rush upriver to spawn, in the green corn's
quick sprouting, and the abundance of peaches; and in the pack of
furs the trapper brings in on his back
promise of independences:—the hut of sods
will next year be a cabin, the muddaubed log house will next
year be tight clapboard or a mansion of brick; exultation
in the windy freedom of a continent, the singing birds, plentiful
shots along the woods' edge at game for the pot:
in the jostle of immigrants in the seaport slums,
busy to forget the old world, to learn the new, to make
money make money, to turn an honest dollar, busy to cheat,
to be cheated, to invest, to get plenty for nothing, busy to
enjoy opportunity, to exercise independence,
always in the beginning long ago,
way down, there was belief that next year:

'Me I'm not much but my boy:
he'll go to school and learn American.'

In our years of defeat
in our century of power we have forgotten
our American:
the harangue delivered from a stump at the edge of town, the
affirmation penned by candlelight in a Spencerian hand, the pro-
tests of delegates in convention assembled, the congregations sitting
silent with furrowed brows searching for the light within, the blank-
faced obstinacy of townmeeting, the brawling, hot with torchlight
and whiskey, of mobs for independence, the battering down of
obstacles, the opening of waggonroads, canals along the rivers;
the fury of secession; the Union made irrevocable
in massacre and in sorrow and in murder
and by the sacrifice of righteous men; the founding of states out
among the sagehens on the prairie, railroads advancing rail by rail
with clamor of hammers through the West. My father knew
that language; those things his father learned; but there is more
to learn. Shall I sicken for the lack of will
to blazen in words my belief
against the driving sky that rains disaster? Our century of
power to ruin has wrought no answering power to build,
to establish, to plant securely on foundations.

Do we lack the penmanship to declare again the indepen-
dence that lived in the flourish of my father's signature, in Mother's
homilies:—'An American is as good as any man, he must behave
better,' to a naughty small boy made to stand in the corner; in the
needlepoint (the careful jams and jellies, the meticulous rinsing of
china, the affirmation of old prints, The Peaceable Kingdom stored
in dust in the attic, pride of ancestry in the notes in the family bible,
shade trees planted with posterity in the mind), of Grandmother's
domestic economy?
It was how they behaved: my father's goodhumor with dark-

*skinned diggers of ditches, the enquiry after the health of the waiter,
his daily joshing with the officer fresh from County Cork full of
sweat under his high blue helmet at the Avenue crossing, the way
his deference brings out the innate gentle manners of the bushy old
barefoot man*

   who shows us the spring on the mountainside

   *who can't read and write but no matter in a land where there
is plenty*

      of freedom

   *a man's worth his weight; a man free from hate or suspicion or
envy will recognize kinship in other men for no other reason than
that they are men; a free man has a splendor about him,*

      *moving easily joshingly courteously among a variety of equal
citizens, varying in antecedents, in ancestry, in honesty, in schooling,
in attainments, each smirched with the common (in which I share
by inheritance, by education, by preference) degradation of the
shoddy mean,*

      *but sharing an infinitesimal, always near extinction but never
extinguishable, inkling of splendor.*

*My father, my grandfathers living out their lives, in some things
fortunate, in some things unfortunate, Americans varying in antecedents,*

      *assumed without thinking, taking it for granted, often denying it,
      their belief in the precarious splendor*
      a man's life assumes when he is for a moment free
      *from tyranny and taskmasters and the cramping cage of
enslaving institutions. The words*
      *are tired and old: 'democratic,' 'republican,' a coinage worn
senseless in the market's transactions, the birthright's daily sale,
but they ring. (There is so much evil in the life of man that a tiny
good, a moment's opportunity, a breath of independence, produces
us immediately abundance of lesser goods so readily mortgaged and
sold that we forget*
      *the price our fathers paid. That is why God's temple is always
full of moneychangers, because of the riches it offers.) The words are*

slurred with too much saying but they ring
as loud as the meanings we endow them with.

The republic's foundations are not in the sound of words,
they are in the shape of our lives, fellowcitizens.
They trace the outlines of a grand design. To achieve
greatness a people must have a design before them
too great for accomplishment. Some things we have learned, but
not enough; there is more to learn. Today
we must learn
to found again
in freedom
our republic.

THE END